CATALYST
DOWNWARD CYCLE

by JK Franks

Book One of the Catalyst Series

Published by Red Leaf Press
Made in USA
2016

Cover art: Grady Frederick

Back cover design: JK Franks

Editor: Kate Juniper

ISBN-978-0-9977289-1-0

Visit JKFranks.com

to sign up for the authors newsletter

and learn more about the Catalyst books

www.jkfranks.com

Twitter: jkfranks

v2.0711

To my wife Christy,

thank you for believing.

Introduction

For many years, I have become interested in how prepared we are as a nation for a large scale crisis. We have handed over responsibility to our government to provide for us in emergencies, yet we have seen how poorly they function in that role. Often politicians and bureaucracy seem better suited to creating problems than solving them. In many dystopian novels, individuals take the lead and look after themselves. These Preppers or Survivalist seem to always have the right tools and skills to survive. What would an average person do if faced with a similar scenario? This was my initial question as this novel took shape on a long bike ride along the Gulf Coast of Florida.

The research that went into this manuscript was extensive and, on the issues of EMP/CME and Power Grid Damage, is based largely in fact. The projected casualties and secondary issues caused are also based on numerous studies. While this is a work of fiction wherever possible, I have used factual data to help develop the story.

I am not a prepper, but I appreciate those that are; I respect the dedication and their focus on personal responsibility. I am also not a conspiracy theorist but confess to having a healthy skepticism for much of what I hear, particularly from politicians and the media. In the modern connected world relying on the "facts" from a single source, or the Internet is rarely sufficient.

I have attempted in the Catalyst series to present a more realistic "End of the World" scenario. While it does present numerous conspiracy ideas and various social and economic commentaries; I have tried to be realistic in the portrayal of reactions to such a widespread catastrophe. I do believe many people would simply try to ignore the seriousness of such an event, while a very few would take steps to ensure their survivability. The ultimate debate the Catalyst stories raise is, which is more important, Our Survival or Our Humanity. I offer no commentary on that, as it is a personal question for each reader to determine for them self.

legraph station would also feel the continuing wrath of the solar
. On the morning of September 2, 1859, in Boston, the American
ompany was to bear more witness to the phenomena. One of the
ators, David Selfor, had been unable to send or receive any messages
g on shift. With telegraphs being a common modern convenience,
businesses depended on their reliability. Here in the Boston office,
ked at one of the most updated of all facilities. Like most operators,
at unusually strong occurrences of the Northern Lights and other
s in the ether could cause occasional problems on the lines. The
s the last few nights had been so bright that he had gone outside and
o read a pamphlet with no other illumination. Mr. Selfor had feared
nenon would likely give him headaches at work today, and indeed, that
g to be prophetic.

had a queue full of outgoing messages, but he was having trouble
to any other stations reliably. Occasionally it seemed to help to
the batteries, so he managed to get a garbled message through to the
aine station to do the same. David was surprised to hear a message
ck in from the other station: "Will do so, it is now disconnected."
transmission lines between Boston and Portland were still connected,
ust dead wires; no power should be flowing through them now. David
that he was disconnected as well, and they must be using only the
rrent. Indeed, the air itself was electric and powering the telegraph
ter than even the batteries had! For the next several hours, this was the
ey used to send and receive messages. Eventually, the electrical discharge
to a point where they could resume somewhat normal operations.

ver the course of the bizarre week many were convinced that the end
rld was at hand, but what Carrington had spotted was the true cause
ange happenings: the two white plumes on the sun were massive solar
y contained the estimated energy of ten billion atomic bombs. The
s flung electrified gas and various subatomic particles toward Earth,
n a geomagnetic storm that was later called the "Carrington Event".
er massive solar flares happen on a regular basis, thankfully most go
out into space: The Earth is a rather small target to hit. The 1859

PROLOGUE

This late summer evening of 1859 was not much different from countless others for Mr. Curtis Smythe. He had intended to leave his office near the railway station earlier than this, but it was not a problem. His father had been a very strict man, and punctuality his primary tool to gauge a person's character. Curtis reached his delicate hand into his waistcoat and removed the fine American Waltham pocket watch to check the time. Being a bachelor, his housekeeper Martha would hold dinner for him.

He stopped in the adjacent office to speak with his neighbor Frederick. His friend ran the local telegraph office. He always had the latest news and was good for a laugh. As usual, he found Frederick leaning back in his chair with his head resting near the sounder, waiting for the next message to come in. The embroidered sampler hanging on the wall said: "*What hath God Wrought.*" Curtis knew from earlier conversations that this was the first telegraph message sent between Samuel Morse and Alfred Vail less than fifteen years earlier.

Fredrick looked up with a smile, "Fine day, Mr. Smythe."

"Excellent one at that, Mr. Royce. Tell me, any more news about that damn fool Blondin? Is he going to have the knackers to walk over the falls again this year?"

Fredrick looked conspiratorially over and said, "Not if our boys here in DC have anything to say about it. Those chaps are furious about the last stunt. Damn little Frenchie."

The two gentlemen chatted for several more minutes until a cable came in and Fredrick had to copy down the message. Curtis heard a faint buzzing. The humming sound grew in intensity until eventually it seemed to emanate from everywhere.

Curtis was about to ask his friend about the noise, but Fredrick raised his hand. "One moment, this is urgent, have to get it sent over to Richmond." Looking out the window, Curtis noticed something peculiar. The telegraph wires seemed to be glowing, and the buzzing noise intensified. He was becoming quite alarmed now. Curtis could see what looked to be sparks of fire arcing off many of the wires coming into the little office. The sound grew increasingly louder.

Curtis looked over with concern at his friend who was preparing to initiate the next call. Fredrick's hand was resting on a metal plate, ready to begin tapping out the Morse Code for the next station. His finger was just about to touch the sender key when a bright flash jumped from the key to his finger. Recoiling from the shock, his head neared a cable, and another giant blue spark of fire struck Fredrick's head and ran down his shoulder. He slumped into the wooden chair with a groan.

The normally implacable Curtis was mortified; he had understood that the telegraph lines were not powered at all until the signal was sent, and even then it was not considered a dangerous current. Admittedly, he was not well-versed in electricity, but if it was this dangerous, he hoped they never tried to do anything more than send messages. He went over to check on his friend who was clearly in pain. He thought briefly of fetching the doctor but after several minutes, Frederick roused and came to and for none the worse it would seem. "The good Lord was merciful to you my friend," Curtis said looking down with concern.

"Merciful? Huh, not to seem too disrespectful brother, but that didn't feel like mercy." Frederick said as he took in his smoking and ruined sending station.

Neither of the baffled men could guess that what had caused the electrical discharge had nothing to do with the telegraph, wires or attached batteries. In fact, the cause was not even something limited to Washington D.C where they

were. Many other people had noticed similar eve days. Across North America, telegraph lines faile snuffed out by a strong breeze. For days after ac sky erupting with brilliant colors. These auroras turn the night into day. Many on the southern Ea described the color of the eastern sky as blood red became blood. The brilliant colors were so intens to be on fire. The Aurora, or so-called "Northern as Cuba.

. . .

Nineteen hours earlier, just outside London, a Carrington climbed the steps up to his estate's pri respected amateur astronomer, he felt a thrill eac sky. While many of his associates spent their night stars, and planets, Richard had a fascination with t ways of observing the sun and in doing so discove was very active. Today he was enjoying an almost p sketching what he saw reflected on the paper bene day, he found he was drawing a series of enormou the face of the sun. This in itself was not strange a spots many times, just not in this number. Sudder called "two patches of intensely bright, white light" from the sunspots. After several minutes, the white of star matter, he saw, had burst away from the Sun was heading directly toward Earth at almost 1,000 m

The impact was felt across the planet w incredible Auroras the most benign aspect of the ev

. . .

Another t super-stor Telegraph young ope since com people and David wor he knew t disturbanc aurora lig been able the pheno was provi

H connectin disconnec Portland coming b While the they were keyed bac auroral c system be process th dissipated

(of the w for the st flares. Th solar flar resulting While ot harmless.

PROLOGUE

This late summer evening of 1859 was not much different from countless others for Mr. Curtis Smythe. He had intended to leave his office near the railway station earlier than this, but it was not a problem. His father had been a very strict man, and punctuality his primary tool to gauge a person's character. Curtis reached his delicate hand into his waistcoat and removed the fine American Waltham pocket watch to check the time. Being a bachelor, his housekeeper Martha would hold dinner for him.

He stopped in the adjacent office to speak with his neighbor Frederick. His friend ran the local telegraph office. He always had the latest news and was good for a laugh. As usual, he found Frederick leaning back in his chair with his head resting near the sounder, waiting for the next message to come in. The embroidered sampler hanging on the wall said: "*What hath God Wrought.*" Curtis knew from earlier conversations that this was the first telegraph message sent between Samuel Morse and Alfred Vail less than fifteen years earlier.

Fredrick looked up with a smile, "Fine day, Mr. Smythe."

"Excellent one at that, Mr. Royce. Tell me, any more news about that damn fool Blondin? Is he going to have the knackers to walk over the falls again this year?"

Fredrick looked conspiratorially over and said, "Not if our boys here in DC have anything to say about it. Those chaps are furious about the last stunt. Damn little Frenchie."

The two gentlemen chatted for several more minutes until a cable came in and Fredrick had to copy down the message. Curtis heard a faint buzzing. The humming sound grew in intensity until eventually it seemed to emanate from everywhere.

Curtis was about to ask his friend about the noise, but Fredrick raised his hand. "One moment, this is urgent, have to get it sent over to Richmond." Looking out the window, Curtis noticed something peculiar. The telegraph wires seemed to be glowing, and the buzzing noise intensified. He was becoming quite alarmed now. Curtis could see what looked to be sparks of fire arcing off many of the wires coming into the little office. The sound grew increasingly louder.

Curtis looked over with concern at his friend who was preparing to initiate the next call. Fredrick's hand was resting on a metal plate, ready to begin tapping out the Morse Code for the next station. His finger was just about to touch the sender key when a bright flash jumped from the key to his finger. Recoiling from the shock, his head neared a cable, and another giant blue spark of fire struck Fredrick's head and ran down his shoulder. He slumped into the wooden chair with a groan.

The normally implacable Curtis was mortified; he had understood that the telegraph lines were not powered at all until the signal was sent, and even then it was not considered a dangerous current. Admittedly, he was not well-versed in electricity, but if it was this dangerous, he hoped they never tried to do anything more than send messages. He went over to check on his friend who was clearly in pain. He thought briefly of fetching the doctor but after several minutes, Frederick roused and came to and for none the worse it would seem. "The good Lord was merciful to you my friend," Curtis said looking down with concern.

"Merciful? Huh, not to seem too disrespectful brother, but that didn't feel like mercy." Frederick said as he took in his smoking and ruined sending station.

Neither of the baffled men could guess that what had caused the electrical discharge had nothing to do with the telegraph, wires or attached batteries. In fact, the cause was not even something limited to Washington D.C where they were. Many other people had noticed similar events and would for several more days. Across North America, telegraph lines failed as though they were candles snuffed out by a strong breeze. For days after accounts poured in of the night sky erupting with brilliant colors. These auroras were so bright they seemed to turn the night into day. Many on the southern Eastern Seaboard of the country described the color of the eastern sky as blood red. The ocean, reflecting the sky, became blood. The brilliant colors were so intense that adjacent towns seemed to be on fire. The Aurora, or so-called "Northern Lights", appeared as far south as Cuba.

• • •

Nineteen hours earlier, just outside London, a young man named Richard Carrington climbed the steps up to his estate's private observatory. As a much-respected amateur astronomer, he felt a thrill each time he got to examine the sky. While many of his associates spent their nights watching the moon, comets, stars, and planets, Richard had a fascination with the sun. He had designed new ways of observing the sun and in doing so discovered that the Earth's local star was very active. Today he was enjoying an almost perfect blue sky and had been sketching what he saw reflected on the paper beneath the brass telescope. This day, he found he was drawing a series of enormous dark spots scattered across the face of the sun. This in itself was not strange as he had seen the mysterious spots many times, just not in this number. Suddenly he noticed what he later called "two patches of intensely bright, white light" seemingly coming up directly from the sunspots. After several minutes, the white lights vanished. This plume of star matter, he saw, had burst away from the Sun with unimaginable force and was heading directly toward Earth at almost 1,000 miles per second.

The impact was felt across the planet within just a few hours, the incredible Auroras the most benign aspect of the event.

• • •

Another telegraph station would also feel the continuing wrath of the solar super-storm. On the morning of September 2, 1859, in Boston, the American Telegraph Company was to bear more witness to the phenomena. One of the young operators, David Selfor, had been unable to send or receive any messages since coming on shift. With telegraphs being a common modern convenience, people and businesses depended on their reliability. Here in the Boston office, David worked at one of the most updated of all facilities. Like most operators, he knew that unusually strong occurrences of the Northern Lights and other disturbances in the ether could cause occasional problems on the lines. The aurora lights the last few nights had been so bright that he had gone outside and been able to read a pamphlet with no other illumination. Mr. Selfor had feared the phenomenon would likely give him headaches at work today, and indeed, that was proving to be prophetic.

He had a queue full of outgoing messages, but he was having trouble connecting to any other stations reliably. Occasionally it seemed to help to disconnect the batteries, so he managed to get a garbled message through to the Portland Maine station to do the same. David was surprised to hear a message coming back in from the other station: "Will do so, it is now disconnected." While the transmission lines between Boston and Portland were still connected, they were just dead wires; no power should be flowing through them now. David keyed back that he was disconnected as well, and they must be using only the auroral current. Indeed, the air itself was electric and powering the telegraph system better than even the batteries had! For the next several hours, this was the process they used to send and receive messages. Eventually, the electrical discharge dissipated to a point where they could resume somewhat normal operations.

Over the course of the bizarre week many were convinced that the end of the world was at hand, but what Carrington had spotted was the true cause for the strange happenings: the two white plumes on the sun were massive solar flares. They contained the estimated energy of ten billion atomic bombs. The solar flares flung electrified gas and various subatomic particles toward Earth, resulting in a geomagnetic storm that was later called the "Carrington Event". While other massive solar flares happen on a regular basis, thankfully most go harmlessly out into space: The Earth is a rather small target to hit. The 1859 super solar storm is the largest on record to have actually struck the planet. The fact that this solar super-storm struck repeatedly over multiple days is even more unusual.

On the 10th of September that same year, not far away from the nation's capital in a particularly desirous neighborhood on the Eastern Shore of Maryland, a small group of gentlemen was gathered at an exclusive country estate. Several stood around one of the three snooker tables located in the luxurious billiards parlor. Spread out over the table was a large map of the Eastern portion of the United States. Some of the lower states were colored green, while most of the northern ones were shaded red. A number of territories and states in the middle and off to the west were a muted gray.

Since no actual names were ever used at these gatherings, the participants had taken to referring to each other by pseudonyms of their own choosing. The man calling himself Mr. Levi stuck a pushpin in the large map rather near Charleston, S.C.

Looking up at his longtime friend he asked, "Mr. Church, have our friends in the RAS given us an estimate yet?"

The other man, a rather nondescript fellow, looked up as the valet refilled his glass with more of the marvelous Bordeaux. "Yes, the observer's assistant in Surrey was very helpful." The valet handed Mr. Church the leather-bound ledger. Selecting the correct page, he removed the ornate bookmark with the symbol of a Scorpion wrapping around an ancient sword. On the page was recorded the exact time, date and relative magnitude of the past few weeks' solar disturbances.

"Was it as large as we thought?"

Mr. Church nodded, "Even more. It was twice as large as any others we have in our records." Inscribed on the page were dates going back hundreds of years.

Mr. Levi nodded appreciatively, "Still on the same eleven-year cycle, I see. I assume a donation has been made?"

"Of course," another man nearby said, "It was discreet, but rest assured our enlightened English friend will never get an official scientific post. Mr. Joshua will see to that."

"Very Good," replied Levi. He was not sure how this would help the group, but he felt sure in time that it would. Motioning to the well-dressed black man stationed by the door, he called, "Harland, show our new friend in, I believe it's time we had a word with the esteemed Senator Davis of Mississippi." He turned to Mr. Church. "You know him and that Lincoln fellow that ran for Senate are from the same part of Illinois?"

Mr. Church looked over at his friend with a wry grin. "Even though this chap was not part of the guard unit, you still think it will work?"

"I do… I do, my friend. He will do what we ask."

Harland reentered the wood paneled room followed by a tall, gaunt man.

"Jeff, so very good to finally meet you. Please do come in."

ONE

Day 1 - August: Mississippi Gulf Coast

The barely perceptible click of the shifters and the whispering of the wind sweeping past were the only sounds Scott Montgomery could hear. His head was lowered, his eyes constantly scanning the road ahead. Time on his Trek racing bike had been hard to come by lately, and he was committed to doing another metric century by November. People were often amazed at the distance and the speed that even amateurs like him could attain on a bike. A short ride for him was usually thirty-five miles and rides of seventy, or even a hundred miles were routine to him now. His American-made bike was not something most kids had in their garage. While not truly classified as an exotic machine, the pricey ultra-lightweight carbon fiber frame, with its high-end SRAM components, was a beast. It was his one real indulgence; a thoroughbred horse made by craftsmen and designed to be ridden fast. Today it was fulfilling that mission.

His bike-mounted Garmin GPS showed the miles, speed, and pedal cadence, which were all near the top in what he considered one of his best efforts. Here, so close to the Gulf of Mexico, the roads were flat and the hills were mostly low rollers, so his riding was steady and most days not overly taxing. Frequently, the wind off the ocean would make it this far inland but today, for now at least, it was calm. Like most riders he detested the wind; it could make an ordinary ride into a grueling fight for survival—something akin to jogging in mud. Cold and rain he could deal with, but the wind was torment.

The temperature was already climbing into the low nineties. The sky was a beautiful azure blue, and there had been only a little traffic since he left his cottage mid-morning. In short, a perfect day for riding.

Rounding the sharp corner at a severe lean onto Highway 50, he knew it was about fourteen miles before the next turn. Scott's eyes swept the road ahead, constantly watching for potential problems: deer jumping in the road, loose gravel, potholes, dogs, cars pulling out from a hidden drive. Situational awareness is what the military called it; to always be on guard. For a cyclist, every danger was real and potentially catastrophic. Getting hit by a car could be deadly but just as dangerous were the little miniature terriers with attitude. Hitting one at high speed could launch a cyclist over the handlebars with potentially fatal results, for the rider and the dog.

Comfortable that the road was clear, he fell into his familiar rhythm. Scott's body and pedal strokes entered into autopilot, and he let his mind drift a little. Whatever occasional illusions he may have harbored, Scott knew he was no serious cyclist—he wasn't even overly athletic—but he did love to ride. It had started about eleven years earlier on a doctor's recommendation. His high-pressure job and a strained marriage had led him into the ER convinced he was having a heart attack. Indeed, his cholesterol and blood pressure were elevated, especially for a person in his early thirties, but not alarmingly so. Thankfully for Scott it had been diagnosed as stress.

Later that week his general physician had suggested he may want to consider taking a break from climbing the corporate ladder, maybe even take an occasional vacation and step up the aerobic exercise.

"Try working out at a gym or start jogging," the doctor suggested.

Scott couldn't believe he had let himself go. While never a jock, he had been firmly committed to never looking like a computer nerd, although that was an accurate description of what he was. Soon after he'd joined a gym. It was too cold in Chicago to start jogging that time of year. And like a lot of computer guys he was not very comfortable around strangers, especially people who looked better, obviously didn't need to be in a gym, and seemed to look down on him in his baggy sweats. The often unpleasant sounds he made as he worked his way around the weights and resistance machines probably didn't endear him to any of the other members either. After three months, he found himself going only occasionally and decided to abandon this avenue. After that, he did try jogging, albeit briefly. He enjoyed the solitude but could never really get motivated to do it on a regular basis.

While scanning Craigslist for a suitable alternative his eye had fallen on a sleek looking road bike for sale nearby. He could ride a bike, he thought. "You never forget right?" He had biked all through college, as most of the students did. He and a friend had biked nearly everywhere back then.

He made the call and went to take a look. It had been a mid-grade Italian racing bike; not great when compared to the Trek he had now, nor even as good as his backup Cervelo training bike, but it had been far better than anything he had ever ridden at that time. The guy who listed it had upgraded to a new triathlon bike, and he let Scott take the older bike out for a test ride. Scott was shocked at how easy it was to maneuver and how fast the damn thing was. It was super-light and seemed to just leap up hills. He'd gone nearly five miles before he pulled back into the guys' garage. Scott paid the guy the $900, got a helmet tossed in as well, and picked up a few basics in maintenance. He also learned about a small group who rode together over by the lake each Saturday. If he was ever interested, he should let the guy know.

No real surprise, Scott's wife had hit the roof when she found out what he'd paid for it, despite the fact that it was his money, and they weren't exactly on a tight budget. From that day on, Scott was on the bike every moment he could get. It was transportation. It was therapy. And it got him away from the day-to-day problems. If he had a challenging issue at work or, more likely, he and his wife, Angela got into it, he would take off on his bike. Never big on confronting problems, he was much better at dodging them.

Over the months, the rides got longer, and his health steadily improved. The club rides with the small group taught him much about being safe and improving his riding skills. A job change helped as well. After getting his government security clearance, he moved from the corporate rat race to IT consulting, which paid better and offered more freedom. Now he could choose to work from home and even the hours he wanted to work each day. For some reason, this more flexible schedule infuriated Angela but it allowed him to ride anytime weather would permit.

Turning off of Highway 50 onto the nearly hidden road that wound around the reservoir lake, this beautiful little park was a nearly forgotten relic of another time. It was a familiar ride to Scott, and he knew this stretch of road was often tricky, as deer and squirrels would dart out and in front of the bike. As he reached speeds of over thirty-five miles an hour in many areas, hitting nearly anything with the lightweight but somewhat fragile wheels would be unpleasant.

Coming out of the wooded section, he approached the familiar stained and pitted concrete structure up ahead. He dropped into a full tuck position as he descended the slightly sloping road down to the top of the dam. The road here skirted the top part of the dam. It was barely large enough for two lanes with side rails on both sides. The lake stretched out to the right for several miles and to the left was the sheer drop of the backside of the dam. Nearing the center of the structure, Scott heard a small pop followed by a rapid hissing sound that he knew all too well. "Shit," he thought. Twisting his right foot quickly in an unnatural motion he unclipped his Italian cycling shoe from the pedal and slowed to a stop.

The rear tire was flat. Most likely he had caught a stone. Luckily he always carried spares as this was about a once a month occurrence, sometimes more. He paused the ride button on the GPS at 42.67 miles. He moved the bike aside and into some welcome shade to change the tire. His gloved hands levered the brake caliper to the open position, then flipped the quick release. Using the small hard plastic tire levers, he quickly had the flattened inner tube out. He checked the inside of the tire meticulously to make sure nothing was sticking through it. Satisfied that all was well, he began tucking the new tube into the tire. Focused on the task at hand, he jumped at the noise that suddenly sounded from below him. Looking over, he saw a large metal structure with winches that raised and lowered the water gates. Someone was slowly coming up a nearly hidden set of steps on the far side.

"Howdy," the man said, "Looks like you got a damn flat," he said, amusing only himself. The large man, who was probably in his late fifties, came over to the rail that separated the roadway from the electrical equipment. "Need any help?"

Since he already had the replacement tube in and was about to attach the compact Co2 inflator to pump it up, Scott replied, "No, but thanks, I just about have it." He thought he had seen this man in the park before. His green trousers and light khaki work shirt looked somewhat official.

"I've seen you come through a lot this summer," the man said. "Not too many people come out this way anymore."

"You must keep an eye on everything to notice one bike rider," Scott said a little surprised. Taking off his fingerless riding gloves he walked over and extended his hand, "Hi, I'm Scott."

The old man snorted, grinned, and took his hand in a firm grip. "Name's Pete and what the hell else do I have to do out here babysittin' this abandoned old park? Everyone goes over to the beach at Grand Isle to swim, and there are lots better places to fish."

"What about the dam?" Scott asked. "Surely it needs attention."

"Used to," he said. "Before they decommissioned it."

Scott now recalled an old plaque on the road stating that the lake and dam were built in the early 40's, making it most likely a remnant of Roosevelt's Public Works projects—the controversial Social Welfare project that many say helped pull the US out of the depression. Love it or hate it, everything from the Golden Gate Bridge and the Hoover Dam to countless small parks and flood control dams had been built across the country as a result.

"Why was it decommissioned?" Scott asked.

Pete frowned, "Its old and tired ....like me," he snorted, and quickly recounted how the dam had been on limited duty when the last of the larger generators, housed in the bowels of the structure, had started having control issues. It wasn't even needed anymore since they put the nuclear plant over in Port Gibson in the 80's.

"That would have been ....hmmm, I suppose back around '97. They said it would cost more to repair than it was worth. Now all the power stations are on the "Smart Grid" so they can control the distribution from the capital or wherever, but not this old girl. Now she's only used for flood control and honestly there's rarely even a need for that. The park service keeps cutting the budget and well…" Pete looked away, and Scott could tell he was somewhere else for a second. "They're planning on closing off the park and probably shutting down this access road around Labor Day."

"Crap," Scott said, thinking selfishly that this would eliminate one of his favorite rides.

Nodding but misreading Scott's reaction Pete said, "Yep… crap, thirty-five years working here and I don't even know if I'll have a job after that. I got some health issues, need the insurance from the state. You know, time was we had a team of twelve people or more doing maintenance and routine patrols 'round here. We were with the COE then—the Army Corps of Engineers—then they handed us off to the Park Service, then over to the state, who eventually just contracted us out to a facility management company. Now…well, now it's just me. All the grass cuttin', paintin', and of course inspections of the dam itself."

Pete was bitter, and Scott could see why. He felt bad for the guy but he wasn't exactly a people person and by now he was getting anxious to get back on the bike. Knowing he still has almost eighteen miles to go, he wanted to get moving before the build-up of lactic acid in his legs made them stiff or they began cramping. Curiosity did begin to get the better of him, though. Looking over at the man, he said, "I always assumed when I came over the dam, and the water was flowing through the gates that it was generating electricity."

"Nah, mostly just lettin' enough water flow to keep wildlife alive downstream. Sometimes we open it for flood control as well… we can let out excess water to keep the lake level from getting too high."

Pete unlatched a gate and said, "Come and take a look at this."

Scott followed him through the warren of fencing and superstructure at the top of the dam over to the backside to look where Pete was pointing. The backside of the structure was an impressive 200-foot drop to a small black river below. At first, he saw nothing, then he noticed the small rectangle at the base of the nearly invisible steps. The door and steps were the same shade of beige as the dam.

"Once a day I have to go down those steps, unlock that door and go inside to check out the leaks."

"That looks dangerous," Scott said. "You mean you look for leaks?" he suggested, offering a correction.

"No, no, no… all dams leak, they're designed that way. Concrete is porous, you know. I just measure the rate as it collects and flows down the interior walls each day and then send my reports over to the office. Occasionally the engineers will come out and do a bit of maintenance, but that's pretty rare these days."

Scott shook his head, not wanting to admit that he always thought the dam was solid and …leak-proof. He looked back over his shoulder at the deep lake piled up on the backside and began to rethink the wisdom of standing here. "Pete, I appreciate the tour, and I hope I get to see you again. Hopefully, things will work out."

"Sure thing Scott, ya never know… they may find a use for me yet," Pete gave a hearty laugh. "By the way, young feller, where d'you go to church?" It was the question that seemed to come up whenever Scott met a local for the first time.

Scott grinned and shook his head, not wanting to get into that conversation. The tired-looking maintenance man laughed and said, "Had to ask, you know." Pete began re-latching the gates and waved goodbye as Scott clipped back on the bike and pedaled hard, now slightly more anxious to get to the far side of the lake.

TWO

As the miles quickly rolled by, Scott found his rhythm again. He felt a car coming up behind him, close. It was another one of those senses that seem to sharpen for cyclists: the feel of danger before you hear or see it. Although no one else was even on the road, the large cream colored luxury SUV passed within inches of Scott. The asshole blew his horn just as he got beside him. *So much for the three feet of clearance required by law*, thought Scott. He could also see the top of the guy's outstretched hand flipping him the bird as he passed. Some drivers did not like sharing the road, especially with bikes. Scott could never understand why. *Just another asshole rushing to be somewhere.* That was one more reason he loved it down here at the beach; life was slower, less rushed than the city-life he had escaped. He pumped his legs furiously to get exactly nowhere just as fast as he could. Scott always felt invincible out on the bike, much less so when he was off.

Getting close to the beach but still about ten miles from home, he noticed the bike's GPS was giving an odd reading. He honestly wasn't sure he'd even restarted it after changing the tire, though he felt pretty confident he had. For whatever reason, though, it was now giving the wrong information. Instead of the total miles, which should have been about fifty by this point, it was reading a hundred-and-twenty-six, then five, then it switched to kilometers. Then the numbers went away, and the screen remained blank for a few seconds, the 'Acquiring Signal' error flashing. *Probably just a dead battery.* What had begun as a great ride on a beautiful day was starting to get rather tedious.

He topped a small hill revealing a great view of the wetlands that stretched several miles over to the Gulf of Mexico. This was one of his favorite sections of the ride. Coming down the other side of the hill was another speed stretch where he would be in a full tuck position to minimize wind resistance. Some moments on the ride seemed more like flying than riding.

As he moved to readjust his hand positions on the bars, he caught sight of a jet's telltale contrail in the distance and could just make out the passenger jet, probably heading to South Florida or maybe even somewhere tropical with its load of late summer vacationers. The normally arrow straight vapor trail emitted by the engines seemed unusually erratic. The closer he looked the more it seemed like the profile of the jet was…well, wrong. Although far away it seemed like he could see more of the jet than was normal… maybe it was just a different angle. As he slowed to watch it also seemed to be descending too quickly toward the horizon. For a second Scott would have sworn it was dropping toward the sea as the contrail suddenly ceased, but the jet appeared to continue on. He assumed it was normal, probably altitude change or something similar. Still he watched with an uneasy feeling as it faded from sight over the sliver of ocean that was visible from here. Immediately dismissing the scene, he dropped back down into the tuck position and began the exhilarating descent.

The last half hour of his ride was uneventful and thankfully involved virtually no traffic. Correction: there was *actually* no traffic. This was odd; his cottage was not on any of the main roads and this area consisted mainly of weekend cottages and vacation homes, but even now during the late beach season, rentals were high and there should be at least some cars on the road. The few he did see were all parked in the bike lane.

"More fucking rude-ass idiots," he mumbled. In his opinion, a lot of car drivers, like the guy a few miles back, felt they owned the road and had zero consideration for cyclists.

Getting closer to his home, he heard an unusual siren coming from the direction of town, which then abruptly stopped. Closer to his cottage, Scott's face broke into a grin as he saw the same cream-colored SUV on the side of the road with the hood up. A red-faced man in a suit was yelling and gesturing into a cell phone as if to somehow get a signal from an only slightly higher position. Scott now recognized the guy as one of the locals, a developer or maybe a politician. He was not sure he had ever actually known his name. As Scott got close, the guy noticed him and stepped out directly in the path of the bike. "Hey! You got a phone?" the guy yelled angrily.

Scott answered, "Yep...asshole." With a smile, he returned the bird salute to the shocked looking guy and rode past without slowing down.

Getting home, he slipped in the side door to his garage, took a minute to wipe the grime from his beloved bike, and applied a quick mist of oil to the mechanical parts. The salt air in this area could wreak havoc on anything metal, and Scott was a bit obsessive with his bikes. He lifted the Trek onto its stand above his older and noticeably more weathered training bike. He was tired but buoyant from the endorphins the vigorous workout had pumped into his body.

Putting his cycling shoes on the shelf, he climbed the few steps and entered the cottage. Odd, he noticed, there were no sounds—no stereo playing or AC running. *Well, shit ...the power is out. This day is just getting better and better*, he thought.

It didn't make any sense to him... there were no storms such as the area frequently had, and that knocked the power off particularly during the hurricane season. *Probably some drunken tourist hit a power pole over near town.* Although he had no idea how long it had been off, it was already beginning to warm up inside. He stripped off the sweaty Cinelli padded riding shorts and jersey and slipped into some shorts and flip-flops. Scott headed back to the garage, grabbed an icy cold Red Stripe out of the old refrigerator, and went to relax on the back deck. Opening the beer and taking a long and wonderfully satisfying pull, he enjoyed the cooler air in the shade of the oaks as he looked out over the black water canal meandering behind the house. Cypress trees also lined much of the view, each draped with a cloak of Spanish moss. He sat back on the deep padded chaise, which felt good on his tired, over-worked muscles. Scott finished off the beer and closed his eyes.

THREE

The sun was in full force, beating down on the Mississippi Gulf Coast with fury. The county equipment shop manager known only as Bartos had come back to the shop to escape the heat and to weld bracing supports on one of the roadway trimmers. The over-sized tractor had an articulated cutting deck that could reach out nearly twenty feet to clear trees on the side of the road. The arm and cutting deck took lots of abuse in their never-ending mission and seemed to need constant maintenance.

The man's ever-present teammate Solo lay in the shadows nearby as Bartos' welding suddenly stopped halfway down the seam he was reinforcing. "Shit," Bartos said to the empty shop. The small, wiry man checked the welding unit, then went to the breaker box. Looking at the dog, he said, "Fuck Solo, looks like we're knocking off early today. The power's out."

Bartos had started his career with the county working as a lineman, back when the county owned and maintained the local electrical grid. Now they contracted all that to a massive power company conglomerate out of Jackson, and this was their problem. Bartos smiled as he wiped his filthy hands on the shop rag. "Thank God I'm not the one they call anymore when shit goes dark." Solo looked at him quizzically.

As the shop foreman, Bartos had nearly a dozen men scattered around the county on various assignments. He hoped none of them had clipped a power pole or dug into a junction box and been the cause of this. Picking up one of the handsets he began recalling the crews. Only a few of them responded, but they would get word to the others as they made their way back in. He began putting the tools he'd been using away.

It took most of an hour to clean up and close the large bay doors. The heat inside the enclosed space was already becoming unbearable. Solo's ears perked up as Bartos heard someone yelling from outside. He glanced briefly at his go-bag on the workbench, knowing there was a pistol inside, but then thought better of it. *Well fuck*, he thought, *who's making that Goddamn racket? Not like we get many visitors out here.*

Walking out of the shop door Bartos recognized the man in the dusty suit coming up the gravel turnaround. "Mr. Hansbrough?" he said with as much respect as he could force into his voice.

"What the fuck is going on?" the man said. "My new car dies, cell phones are out, there's nobody on the road. I had to walk miles. I need something to drink."

"We got water," Bartos said. "Come on in." Grabbing a coffee-stained cup from a peg, Bartos filled it with water from the dented old-style aluminum water cooler.

"Don't you have bottled water?" the man asked as he looked around the dark and grimy shop. Laughing, Bartos replied, "Nope, that didn't make it in the county budget this year…along with our long-overdue raises."

In fairness, Ronald Hansbrough was a city councilman, and this was a county shop, but Bartos put all politicians into the same group. Uneasily, Ronald raised the cup of water to his mouth, tasting it tentatively, then drinking deeply. He refilled it twice more before his thirst was satisfied. "Thanks, Bartos, you got a phone I can use?"

Bartos pointed to the office and said, "Yea it's on the desk, help yourself." Solo silently watched the bedraggled man head off in that direction.

Bartos did not care for this man, mostly because of his arrogance and the numerous run-ins they had had over the years. Hansbrough's family had money, but Ronald had seemed intent on burning through it quickly after his father's death several years earlier. As far as Bartos knew, Ronald had never actually had a job. He owned a questionable real estate development company, but no one had ever heard of anything actually being developed by the company.

Bartos heard the receiver of the old phone being slammed back into the cradle with a small ding. Sweating heavily and visibly angry Ronald returned. "That phone is dead too and why don't you have any lights in this goddamn place?"

"Power is out," Bartos said, "Someone must have clipped a pole carrying a phone line as well."

"Well, what about my car and my iPhone not working?" Ronald asked as if that was Bartos' fault. Bartos just shrugged, "Got me."

"Well, what the fuck *do* you know Bartos?" Ronald asked indignantly. Solo eased up onto his front legs, generating an almost inaudible growl. Bartos silenced the dog with a gesture.

"Give me a ride to town," the angry man said, not even remotely like a question. "I have an important meeting this afternoon, and it's too far to walk."

Bartos shrugged and got the keys to his county truck. He could have refused, could have told the guy to fuck off; he wasn't his boss or his problem. Bartos preferred to pick his battles. People like Ronald Hansbrough were not to be trusted. They could make life difficult for him. While Bartos didn't care if the man liked him or not, he wasn't going to go out of his way to make him an enemy. They had gotten into it once before when Hansbrough tried to get a county work crew to pave a road into some property he owned. When Bartos got the call from his work crew that some rich dude was threatening them to do the work, he'd gone down there to put an end to it. Hansbrough had never brought it up again, but Bartos was pretty sure he remembered.

To his credit, Ronald climbed into the seat of the pickup without wincing at the litter of coffee cups, work orders, gloves, and spare parts littered throughout the interior. Bartos caught a dark glimpse of Solo leaping quietly into the bed of the truck in the rearview mirror. He felt sure that Ronald had barely known the dog was there, much less the fact that he was always ready to attack at the wave of Bartos' finger.

The county shop was only a few miles outside of Harris Springs, and Bartos headed into the main street assuming the City Councilman wanted to be dropped off at the government building. He was surprised when Ronald instead motioned him down a side street to a much less traveled area of town. He pulled to a stop in front of a generic looking community center that Ronald indicated was his destination.

Stepping out of the truck and slamming the door hard, Hansbrough walked away without a word. Smiling slightly, Bartos pulled away from the curb. He had noticed that all the traffic lights in town were out. Not a big problem since traffic was always light, but he knew the electrical grid loop for the downtown area was not the same as the one the county shop was on. This area had its own separate substation over past the marina. It'd take more than just a traffic accident to cause a blackout over that much area.

He radioed his crew leader Scoots telling him to lock up the shop before he left for the day. He was going to the bar for a cold beer, then maybe to the river to do a little fishing. Seeing his friend about to enter the sports bar he yelled, "Padre, wait up," and swung the truck into a spot near the door. The preacher smiled and held the door for him.

"Knocking off early?" the robust man said.

"Can't do much without electricity," Bartos answered with a smile. "Hopefully, the beer tap works ok without it," he continued.

FOUR

Scott woke up several hours later to the sound of insects buzzing and the daylight fading. Checking inside the house, he confirmed that the power was still out.

"What in the hell?....seriously!" he said aloud. He picked up his cell phone, intending to call the Gulf Power office and, finally finding a bill, punched the number in. But nothing happened. No ringing, no busy signal, no generic greeting telling him they valued his business but to call back later… nothing. Whatever had happened could have taken out a cell tower as well, he guessed. He tried the call once more with the same result. Then he tried his brother's number; maybe he knew something. Still, it would not go through. The phone showed a few bars of signal but every number he tried failed to produce anything. Giving up, he dropped the phone back to the table.

The move from the big city of Chicago to the coastal region of Southern Mississippi had been a way to escape after the divorce. Scott's family had owned the fishing cottage since he was a teen. Mercifully, Scott had the place to himself these days. His only relatives were his older brother Bobby and his wife and daughter who lived up in Little Rock, too far to travel for casual weekends.

The Montgomery boys had grown up on a farm in the Piedmont region of the state. Somehow his dad had managed to buy the land and build the cottage, mostly as a fishing camp. As their dad's health deteriorated and the boys concentrated on family and careers, they came down less and less. Over the years, the lack of attention and frequent storms had not been kind to the place.

After their father's death, he and Bobby had decided to fix it up. Partially in memory of how much the place had meant to their dad, but also so that it would be more acceptable to their wives whom they'd hoped might approve and maybe even occasionally accompany them on a visit. Bobby's wife did so enthusiastically. Scott's wife Angela, on the other hand, never had.

To be honest, in Chicago, Scott had mostly just supplied money and moral support for the renovation. Bobby and his buddies had done the real work. Over several years and countless weekends and vacations they had turned the place into a true showpiece. The craftsman style bungalow was simple looking from the outside, but it was beautiful inside and out. You could see the quality and care in every beam and joint. It had been a labor of love and the handful of times Scott did get to come down and help with the work had been some of the best times he'd had in his adult years. Although a firmly avowed geek, growing up on a farm had taught him how to work hard, and building things was something he and Bobby had always had to know how to do.

Twilight settled in, casting the house in a lonely darkness. He went in search of illumination and managed to find two old hurricane lamps with some fuel and a few candles. The heat trapped inside the house was oppressive. Scott knew he could open the doors to the cooler gulf breeze, but he would also have to deal with swarms of mosquitoes if he did that. Instead, he went back outside and closed the hurricane shutters on several windows front and back. He and Bobby had made these shutters with screen mesh inserts behind the slats to help keep the bugs out. Going back inside and opening those same windows offered a very nice breeze and within an hour it was bearable at least.

Not being able to reach anyone by phone was making Scott anxious. He knew he was probably being ridiculous. He had done so much the last few years to distance himself from stress that now he could spot it coming from a distance. *Worry and stress are a misuse of the power of creativity*, he reminded himself. *Focus on the things you have some control over not those you can't.* This was one of his daily mantras. At that thought, his stomach rumbled. He decided it might be good to focus on dinner. He could control that.

Although the power was out, he had a gas range and the food in the fridge would be fine for now. He did need to be quick about whatever he pulled out of it, though, if he was to preserve the cold air inside. Thinking it through, he decided to make a simple blackened chicken breast dish with asparagus and rice. He opened the door, grabbed the ingredients and had the refrigerator closed again within fifteen seconds. Everything in there still seemed nice and cold. He measured out enough rice for one and added it to a saucepan of water with a little chicken base for flavor. Placing his favorite cast iron skillet on the large burner, he began pounding out the chicken to an even thickness. As the pan began to smoke, Scott rubbed some olive oil, blackening seasonings and lemon pepper into the chicken. Placing it gently into the hot pan, his stomach rumbled as he began to smell the aromas.

Once again he realized he had forgotten to eat all day. He'd had nothing other than a couple of energy bars while he was riding. Odd that as much as he loved to cook, eating was not as important to him as one might expect. After a few minutes, he flipped the chicken and prepped the asparagus, breaking the most tender stems away from the woody base. Pulling the chicken out, he de-glazed the pan with some white wine, scraping all the good bits from the bottom of the pan. As the simple sauce began to reduce, he dropped in a little butter and then the asparagus. Within a few minutes, all was done, and he sat down at the empty candlelit table to eat. He had to admit the food was excellent, even if his own company was a bit dull.

While it might seem strange to some, he never minded eating alone and was pretty comfortable living with only his own company. To be honest, in the two years he'd lived here he had made no new friends. Not that he had really tried. Scott Montgomery was always something of an introvert. Undoubtedly the way his marriage had ended probably contributed to his general distrust—even dislike—of most people. It all contributed to his tendency to isolation. And combined with the often sensitive or classified contracting work he received from the government, he was wary of even casual relationships. In Scott's mind, everyone he met was automatically classed into one of two groups: those who added to his life and those who took away. There were few that ever made it into the first group. As for the second, it stayed over-populated. It amazed him how much some people seemed to expect others to freely give… time, money, even just attention… some people—*most* people—were just takers.

While he would never consider himself selfish in any way, he did not suffer fools easily, nor tolerate a weak work ethic or lack of drive. In his computer security job, he saw all manner of scams and hacks designed by people to exploit loopholes or take that which simply was not theirs to take. Unlike many, he was more distrustful of the general population than he was the government. Sure, the government had its issues and way too many people trying to solve every possible problem that garnered a headline... He believed the vast majority of people in government wanted to do good, but they were often hamstrung by ridiculous bureaucracy. His benevolence did not, however, extend to the politicians; they were a waste of perfectly good oxygen in his opinion.

The majority of humans on this planet baffled him, though. Was he the only person alive without a Facebook page? Why would you reveal every possible aspect of your life? And to complete strangers. Did none of these people realize the risks? He had seen lives wrecked, even lost over people trusting others with mere scraps of private information. Scott was not paranoid; he simply preferred a more prudent level of exposure. He had been betrayed and blindsided by his divorce and was determined to never be that oblivious or trusting again.

He cleared the few dishes from the table and washed up by the flickering light of the smelly hurricane lamp. He wondered how much lamp fuel he had. He was pretty sure it was just kerosene but knew he'd better make sure. He tried the phone again but still nothing. Scott was beginning to get concerned—the power had been off pretty much all day now. He briefly thought about driving the few miles into Harris Springs but wasn't sure what good that would do, other than let him know he wasn't the only one in the dark. Ultimately he decided to get another beer, and headed out to the garage fridge where he kept them. Grabbing another Red Stripe, he was pleased to find that it, too, was still cold. As always, he began mentally calculating the extra miles he would need to ride tomorrow to work off the extra calories.

He enjoyed the cold beer as he walked toward the short driveway. He thought he could see from the road if any other street lights or houses were lit up. Although the closest house was at least a half-mile away, he thought he should be able to see it or the glow of any light from town. Scott had only made it a few steps into his yard when he began to realize it wasn't that dark out. At first, he thought his eyes were playing tricks on him. He noticed a flickering of color in the bayou and the trees surrounding the small yard and everything seemed to be ....well, glowing green...no, it was bluish violet. "What in the fuck is going on?" he expelled.

Walking toward the road he was finally out from under the canopy of trees that covered much of the property and had obscured this odd light from the kitchen. He looked up to see a sky that seemed to be on fire. He was stunned. It was the Northern Lights: Aurora Borealis. Scott was immediately shaken to his core. He had seen them once before when he was up north on a trip to Wisconsin— apparently it had been a pretty rare sight even there. It was completely unheard of down here on the southern coast of the country.

The lights he had seen up north were pale compared to what he saw now. The brilliant ribbons of color shimmered and danced with highlights of bright pinks, reds, and vivid blues, before settling into a green which paraded out over the Gulf of Mexico like a ballet of light. It seemed just as bright to the south as it was to the north, spread out from horizon to horizon. It was an amazing sight.

Taking a sip of the almost forgotten beer, alarm bells began to ring in his head. What did this mean? He'd began racking his brain for something...some small thought that was nibbling away in his memory. As an avid reader and science TV fan, he knew that the Northern Lights were the result of solar winds: charged particles from the sun interacting with electrons in the earth's atmosphere. The excited electrons fluoresced different colors as the sun's particles struck them. It was a sign that the planet's magnetic field was doing its job, protecting the Earth from the potentially deadly solar wind. Nothing alarming there. So why on this balmy southern night was a chill slowly climbing his spine? He was transfixed, mesmerized by the spectral show, then all at once...it hit him. *Oh shit! A CME would cause this.*

"Oh my God," he said aloud.

Thinking feverishly, he considered that the sun itself had weather, caused by the variances of its magnetic fields. Solar flares: giant loops of the sun's energy blasting out into space. These solar flares, also known as Coronal Mass Ejections or CME's, could mean relatively nothing as most went harmlessly in other directions. In the very rare case that they did head straight at our planet, however, they could potentially cause localized issues such as cell phone outages or unusually bright northern lights. Some years ago he remembered reports of a large part of the Canadian power grid being taken down by a particularly large CME event.

For the lights in the sky to be seen this far south, though, it had to be an enormous one. Probably meaning that Earth had taken a direct hit. He hoped this was not the cause of the power failing, but then he recalled his GPS error, the jet that looked to be in distress, and even the empty cars on the side of the road… dead cell phones, the power outage… he had a sinking realization that this was exactly what it was. For some reason, he remembered back to his high school lit class and one of his favorite poems by Dylan Thomas:

Good men, the last wave by, crying how bright
Their frail deeds might have danced in a green bay,
Rage, rage against the dying of the light.

"The dying of the light," he repeated. Scott dropped the now warm beer into the garbage as he headed back inside.

FIVE

Scott's mind began to race; the power was probably out due to a massive solar flare. *Wasn't that one of the doomsday scenarios?* He remembered reading several novels about a terrorist EMP blast leaving the world in perpetual darkness. *We're so dependent on electricity for everything,* he worried. *Not just for light but to get our information and interact with others… to pump and refine the gas to fuel our cars… our healthcare, grocery stores…*

What in our modern world did not depend on a consistent power supply? Ironic that he had been happily pedaling away on a mechanical marvel as the rest of the world had probably been going to hell. From ninety-six million miles away, a nearly insignificant burp from a minor star on the fading edge of its galaxy had possibly just caused unimaginable chaos for the human race.

Scott immediately went into analysis mode. *Work the problem.* What did he know? What could he assume and, most important, what could he do right now to improve his situation and his future? He thought about his brother who was an active "prepper", always planning for worst-case scenarios. He was always riding Scott to get a gun, have some survival rations put away, and most of all have a plan. Scott always joked that he didn't need to "All I need to know is where Bobby has his hidden," he had joked.

"Bro," he said out loud, "I think I was wrong."

In his defense, Scott *was* a realist and being a cyclist had made him acutely aware of needing contingency plans. Nothing like being alone fifty miles from home on a crippled bike to teach you to carry what you might need with you. Bobby had even helped him put together a small "EDC" bag; EDC stood for Every Day Carry. It was a medium Maxpedition pack that he kept in the Jeep along with a first-aid kit. Thinking about that he decided to grab it. He was going to need to inventory everything he had. While he was not a survivalist, but he wasn't stupid either. He knew that if this *was* what was going on, the steps he took now would be critical to his well-being.

Grabbing the keys to his Jeep Wrangler, he headed back out to the garage. He began to open the tailgate, then decided to see if the Jeep would even start. It was a top of the line model, only two years old, but it had a lot of electronics which could be damaged. Scott prayed that it had been spared from the full blast of the CME. He knew it would take a powerful burst to fry the electronics on a car, but he thought about the jet he had seen and the cars on the side of the road earlier.

Opening the door, the dome light came on. *Good so far.* Sliding the key in, the door chime began as normal. He turned the key, and the engine started immediately. Scott gave a deep sigh of relief. Several of the dash light alerts blinked on and then back off. *Hmmm…*he thought, *maybe not completely fine.* Eventually, the lights settled down. The engine sounded fine, but his temperature and rpm gauge were not working.

He turned his radio on and scanned the dials for FM channels, but heard only noise and static. The AM was about the same, only some weird oscillations sounds at the far end of the dial. Switching over to satellite radio, he had to move the car out of the garage so the antenna could pick up a signal. All of his preset channels were silent. The preview channel was still playing, but just the standard promo ads. Jumping up to the block of channels reserved for news, he began scrolling through each one slowly.

Finally, on the BBC news channel, he heard what amounted to an Emergency Broadcast recording. A very proper British accent pronounced that a significant weather event was taking place that could cause temporary power disruptions but, in essence, it said to "Stay calm and carry on." Ok, not those exact words… but close enough to remind him of the ubiquitous war slogan that had been everywhere a few years back. *Leave it to the Brits,* he thought.

He tried to remember where the satellite company broadcast from.

Scott's mind was trying to imagine the size of the area that had been affected. He was not sure, but he believed they broadcast from New York, or possibly Washington DC. He punched the scan button, and it quickly went through the several hundred stations, stopping only on one other channel that sounded like a Japanese broadcast, possibly of the same information. Whatever the repeating message, it was more frantic in pace than the British one, but also only about fifteen seconds long. Scott sighed and backed the car back into the garage before shutting it off. Grabbing the EDC bag out of the trunk, he headed back inside, beginning to feel like the man in the old Omega Man movie, wondering if he would be one of the last men left alive, wandering the planet in search of other survivors. Glancing up at the two bicycles on the wall, he thought that if he had to wander, it would probably be on two wheels.

SIX

Be prepared. It worked for the scouts. He knew he had no way of knowing the real severity of what had happened today. *Let me work this as a thought experiment then.* Assuming this was a long-term situation, Scott wanted to have a plan. The survival protocols, he knew, were to first get shelter, clean water, and food. Shelter was no problem at the moment as the cottage was solid, off the main road, and somewhat secure. It was on a municipal water line, which was good for the moment but would run out after the county storage tanks ran dry. There was a backup well on the property that had been the primary source of water back in his dad's day. He would need to find some way to provide power to the old pump or come up with another way to get clean water if need be, but at least the well was an option.

Scott checked the small food pantry and cabinets for all the provisions he had on hand, listing perishables in one column and non-perishables on the other. Then he moved to the refrigerator. Opening it up, he snapped a few pictures with his phone and then shut the door quickly. He repeated the process with the freezer before moving on to the refrigerator and the chest freezer out in the garage as well. He already pretty much knew what he had, but felt it was still a good idea to know for sure. Once he was done reviewing the photos and listing all the cold food in the house, he felt he had enough basic supplies to last about two weeks, which he could probably stretch to last three. He had enough meat in the freezer to last several months if need be, but he knew that wouldn't be any good for long if the power remained off.

He pulled out the EDC bag and emptied its contents. His brother had brought the bag for him along with most of the items already in it. Several times while working on the cottage Bobby had made him learn how to use all of it. Having the supplies without the knowledge to use them was worthless, Bobby had said. For countless hours, he had made fires without matches or lighter, purified water, and foraged for food as Bobby guided him. Over time, he had added a few things to it based on suggestions his brother had made. Emptying the various pockets of the Devil Dog pack, it contained: a keychain on which were carabiners, a multi-use can opener, and scissors; a waterproof notepad and pen; a ThorFire tactical flashlight; a mess kit; road maps; a small first-aid guide; a foraging guide; a Leatherman Wave Multitool; a Swedish FireSteel; a small pair of Steiner Binoculars; a Nalgene Water Bottle; a Benchmade folding knife; water purification tablets; a LifeStraw; a Silva Ranger Compass; and a solar phone charger. There was also some freeze-dried food, coffee, and several MREs or Meals Ready to Eat as the military called them.

Scott had a big issue with EDC bags; they needed to be constantly updated. You needed gear appropriate to the season you were in and the area in which you expected to be operating. It was always hard finding the balance of gear to food and clothes. Often he had wondered if it was even worth the effort. Now he was pretty sure it was. He also had what his brother had called a Pocket Survival Kit (PSK). It was a small pocket-sized tin that contained the very bare essentials: an emergency water bag; more purification tablets; fishing hooks and line; another, smaller fire steel; safety pins; a paracord; tinder fire starters; a card of snap out arrowheads; a small knife; a piece of hacksaw blade; and several ranger bands. He hoped he was overreacting with all of this, but felt it was a good exercise just the same. Besides, his big brother would be proud of him.

He gathered all the flashlights, batteries, candles and fuel he had on hand in the cottage, which amounted to not very much. He realized he had no idea how long natural gas would keep flowing to his stove. He probably needed a portable cook stove. That got him thinking about a wish list. What items did he need, or more accurately, what should he have gotten already? The wrong time to prep is after the shit hits the fan.

He started a new page with this list. It started slowly but grew quickly. Emergency and long-term food; bulk bags of rice, beans, and flour; bleach; vinegar; honey; coffee; sugar; and salt—to preserve meat, among other things. He added batteries, bottled water, and ammo for the one pistol he had; some freeze-dried foods and emergency MRE's and some camping supplies in case he did need to bug out. He continued to brainstorm and in about an hour he felt the list was pretty complete. *Now if I had only done this last week!* he thought. He had no idea how to get any of this now, but he could focus on that tomorrow. He turned the twist knob on the lantern, which died down and slowly faded out.

Sitting in the darkness his mind conjured up terrible what-if scenarios. While this was just a precautionary thought experiment, he was not going to be naive. It could be looking at needing to hold out for several weeks until they got the power up again. *Could be even longer.* Frustrated, he crawled into bed.

SEVEN

Day 2

At some point during the night, the power came back on. Scott awoke when one of his mp3 playlists started blaring from the stereo. As the fog of sleep began to lift, he noticed the AC was on, as were some random lights throughout the house—no doubt as a result of flipping switches as he'd entered darkened rooms in search of provisions and supplies.

He lay there for several minutes enjoying the breeze from his ceiling fan and the cool air coming from the AC vents. "Thank God…it wasn't that bad after all." Just in case, he got up and put his cell phone on the charger and did the same with every other rechargeable battery he had found. He closed the windows that he'd opened, punched the power button on his laptop, and switched on the TV in his bedroom. The flat screen lit up with the manufacturer's logo, then showed the message "No Signal". Remembering that his set-top box had also been out, he punched the button on the remote to turn that on as well.

His laptop was not coming on and power lights were dead. He slid it from the desk and reached for the metalized travel case containing his backup computer. Opening it up, he was relieved to see it booting up as normal. He verified that his primary satellite modem was working as he had already realized the secondary hard line modem was showing no connection. Due to his government work he had to maintain multiple systems and redundancy's in all his hardware. His email opened automatically and immediately began searching for mail. Scott opened up a browser window which came up blank white. He set the small computer to the side to focus on later and to allow the countless emails that were probably waiting to download.

Looking back to the TV, he flipped through the channels. Most were black or showed only a logo screen. Flipping over to one of the 24-hour news channels, he finally saw what appeared to be an actual broadcast. Smiling, he thought, *I am not the last man on Earth*. The news report seemed less polished than usual and did not appear against the usual set. *Likely broadcasting from another location*. The anchor described what had been a very catastrophic day. While communication was still out in most areas and reports coming in were mostly unverified, a massive solar event had indeed knocked out power grids and communications networks all over the country and possibly worldwide. While the solar event had been over twelve hours earlier, solid information was just trickling in; reports of numerous fatalities from accidents... thousands of people stranded in elevators in every major city... traffic gridlocked and a large percentage of cars on the road immediately shutting down. What few Emergency Services vehicles still ran were having little success navigating through most urban areas, and with nearly all communications down, 911 services were no help.

Apparently sporadic radio broadcast and amateur HAM radio operators had been the most reliable in providing what information there was. There were reports of looting in the inner-cities. Emergency services like fire protection, public safety and 911 were all unavailable. Without phones and power, all they could react to was what they saw personally. Reports seemed to suggest that the Northeast and Europe were probably the worst affected; most of these areas remained blacked-out as the number of substations and transformers with problems fell within what officials were calling an "Extremely significant" level of damage, whatever that meant.

Questions were already being raised about the new "Smart Grid" system the government had been touting for quite some time: The primary news anchor asked, "Billions spent on this already and wasn't it designed to protect the US from such an event?" Scott listened as one of the talking heads, a so-called energy expert, described the smart grid system as "Essentially a more effective monitoring and distribution tool. In the case of an emergency like this, it took a more strategic role, taking the power from less demanding regions and channeling it to areas that had failed. The updated grid could also redirect electricity as needed to places with a higher priority need, like major urban areas, military bases, or critical infrastructure centers." He went on to say, "None of our improvements to the grid did anything to defend the system against EMP or CME blasts."

"As these more outlying plants that knocked offline restart, they will begin filling in the gaps of the nationwide grid instead of just to the customers in their immediate vicinity."

"So we should expect more blackouts even if we have power right now?" one of the panelists asked.

The expert frowned and said, "Possibly, there could be some rolling blackouts if the demand exceeds the immediate supply, which is not an unlikely possibility. I would strongly suggest that we all be very conservative with power usage at the moment. As bad as today was, we may have dodged a bullet."

They continued to talk, but it quickly became obvious to Scott that they had no real facts. Fully awake now, he turned his attention back to the laptop. His home page was offline, and his Cryptocat messenger was also unable to connect. Outlook also showed zero new mail messages in his work email account. *That's not good.* He checked the connectivity by pulling up a command prompt window. Due to his work, Scott's networking setup was unique. He used a secure Satellite-based Internet provider, or "ISP," with a hardwired backup from a local cable TV provider. Pulling up a command line window he pinged several popular servers, beginning with his service provider's mail server, which came back with a slow but adequate connection. Trying to reach any Google servers returned nothing, nor did Yahoo, Reddit, or Twitter. He then tried many of the same sites using the IP addresses that he had memorized many times. Several of these did return connection pings back, so he knew those, at least, were still online. He was still curious as to the scale of the disaster. Knowing what servers or sites were up would let him figure out who still had power—although some could be running off of emergency generators for the moment.

He went back to the browser window and instead of the URL he entered 173.194.112.178, which he knew to be a Google server. Sure enough, the Google page popped up. He clicked the advanced tools and selected "News" to restrict his search only to news feeds. He added a filter to only show news from the past twelve hours. This action should have returned hundreds or even thousands of stories. Instead, only a handful of search results popped up at all, all with very disturbing headlines:

Passenger Jet Crash
Denver, CO – All Passengers feared dead

Massive Blackout Effects
NYC, LA, and Chicago – Widespread Looting

Solar Storm – CME Event
NOAA offers 8 min warning of impending event

European Research Lab on Lockdown
Infectious Disease Storage Containment Breach reported

Israel Poised for Attack
Palestinian and Arabic world celebrate

Kardashian Reality Channel Announced
The popular show will now have its own network

NASA Loses contact with ISS Space Station
Systems offline. No word on condition of crew

EIGHT

Unfortunately, when he clicked on any of the headlines the browser would go to a blank page. *Shit*, Scott cursed. The news story links were entered as standard URLs, so without knowing the IP number of the server he couldn't view the rest of the story. Obviously, many of the Internet's backbone nameservers that normally matched common URL names to IP addresses were offline. Most IT guys knew this was a real vulnerability of the World Wide Web, but the WWW was just one aspect of the actual Internet. Scott decided to go in a different direction.

Closing all of the open windows he clicked an icon on his desktop and opened up a VPN window. This Virtual Private Network was part of his normal workday. Here he could directly access any other computer that he was authorized to. The VPN essentially acted as a tunnel—through the Internet clutter directly to his company server or, in this case, a server at a division of the DHS where he was currently contracted to provide upgrades and security audits. Thankfully, the connection was quickly made and his log-on window appeared. Entering his credentials, he was then required to provide a biometric scan of his fingerprint on a small reader built into the laptop. The server window opened up slowly but with the familiar files and folders Scott expected.

Scott knew the locations of these computer servers was special; it had its own internal redundant power supplies and was housed adjacent to one of the actual backbone nodes of the original Internet. It even had its own nameservers to speed things up. Once login was complete, he checked messages in his taskbox and found it had not been updated since yesterday morning, so no one had an urgent need for him. He then checked to see what other users were logged in and active at this hour. He had thought he would message whomever he found online, but the results showed zero other actual users. Several higher-level bots (the automated users ever-vigilant to cyber-attack) were active, however, which indicated an increased threat level.

Scott then opened a window that emulated a normal Windows desktop and from there loaded up a modified Web Browser. The homepage for DHS filled the browser window. Initiating a tool to convert website names to a numerical address, he began searching for sites that were still active. Scott knew that most larger sites were "mirrored." In other words, the site would be duplicated in multiple servers, often in different parts of the world. Disaster planning was an active part of modern day web server deployment. Sometimes these were just for what was considered normal load balancing. At other times power outages, earthquakes, and even flooding had knocked complete server farms offline. In those cases, the redundancy protocols would simply route the domain traffic to one of the many other mirrored locations. The chances of all of these being unavailable at the same time would be very unlikely on a normal day. *This*….was not a normal day.

As Scott began entering websites, he first concentrated on major news sites: CNN, Reuters, Bloomsburg, the Washington Post. About half of these did come up, but none were updated. Chances are none of the people that did the updating had electricity, much less a web connection.

He wasn't learning anything helpful here. Scott began to think. He had no idea how long the power or Internet would be working, but he had to assume it might fail again soon. He already knew the basics of what had happened. What he didn't know was how severe the problem was. While he knew it had been deadly to some, was it just an inconvenience to most, or would there be more long-lasting or far ranging effects? A single solar flare would not normally hit all of the earth equally; some of the planet would be faced away from the sun. While the magnetosphere would dissipate energy around the globe, he didn't think it would do so evenly… some areas would likely be much harder hit than others.

He triggered a background program to begin randomly pinging and plotting active servers worldwide. When complete, this would give him a good idea of who still had electricity.

He glanced over at the notebook he had been keeping his supply inventory and wish lists in. "What the hell," he said aloud. "I wasn't very well prepared for today, and it may already be too late, but I've got nothing to lose." Scott still did not expect he would need any of the things on that list even if he could find any to buy. No harm in trying, though, and he was one of the few who would have access. He typed in the IP Address for Amazon and the familiar megastore window popped up nearly immediately. He knew Amazon had some of the best technology in the world and servers and warehouses in nearly every corner of the country. Would they still be taking online orders, he wondered? *Let's find out.*

He logged into his personal account and began sourcing the items on his list, quickly adding them to his shopping cart. As always, he was trying to select the best quality as well as the best value. From his work with DHS, he had access to the kits and supply listing they supplied to field units who worked for them. Scott also had a list of preferred items his brother Bobby had recommended. First, a larger backpack to go with his EDC bag. Then, a multitool, a sleeping mat, glow sticks, an Evermatch, a larger first aid kit, more water purification tablets, cooking gel, a hand crank radio, a pack stove, a Chinese-made portable two-way radio, and considerably more.

What he had so far was a good start, but it was by no means all he might need. Now that he had committed to this path, he felt he should go all in. In the grocery section, he placed orders for all the foodstuffs he had listed earlier. These items that could also be good to trade if needed.

When Scott went to view the cart, he had selected almost $6,000 worth of materials. He decided to put it on his American Express, thinking selfishly to himself *If I need all this stuff, then I likely won't be paying the bill.* Scott made sure he'd selected only items available for immediate shipment and placed the order. He was amazed that the "Order Placed, Thank You" screen appeared. He knew they had a warehouse about 150 miles from Harris Springs. Even so, he'd be shocked if he ever actually received any of this stuff.

He logged back into his store account and found he now had an "Order in Process" status beside the new order number. "I guess we will see," he thought aloud. *Who in the world would have gone into work to pull orders on a day like this?* he wondered. Looking at the corner of the screen, he saw that the time was 5:38 a.m. and he knew he was up for the day.

NINE

The power blinked a few times but stayed on, and Scott spent several hours reviewing what additional information he could find. A few TV channels were coming back on now, but nothing informative just a logo or ticker stating broadcasting would resume later. Before logging off from his worksite, he did review the server map and also ran a diagnostic scan designed by the US government to show a global map with all potentially malicious Internet activity worldwide such as ongoing cyber-attacks. Both maps were nearly empty, but he could also change the settings to show all Internet activity. What normally would have been an indistinguishable web of traffic now showed great empty holes over much of the map. The southern US was active, but far below normal. The Northeast US from Virginia to Boston showed no activity other than a few hotspots around DC. Europe was mostly dark except for Germany, the Netherlands, Spain, and Italy, which seemed about normal. Korea, China, and Japan showed no web activity at all. From what he was seeing, it appeared that over ninety-five percent of the world's web traffic had vanished in the last twenty-four hours. Sighing, Scott realized that his having power was an anomaly. It was going to be a new day—a dark day—for most of the planet.

Once again he tried and failed to reach Bobby on Skype. Finally giving up, he shut down the laptop and decided to have an overdue hot shower.

• • •

Feeling refreshed, he considered what to do next. He felt like doing what he normally did, so he pulled on some shorts, sneakers, and a faded T-shirt and grabbed his slightly grubby Cervelo bike off the wall rack. Locking the house, he easily pedaled the seven miles into the quiet beachside town of Harris Springs. As he crossed the bridge spanning the deep intercoastal waterway before the main street, Scott thought the town looked normal—not like anything earth shattering had happened yesterday. He pulled the bike up to the empty rack in front of the coffee shop just like he did several times a week. Scott loved a good cup of coffee and purposefully avoided making it at home because he knew he would drink too much and, like stress, too much caffeine was not good. He justified that if he put in the exercise to ride the fourteen mile round trip for a large coffee (and maybe an occasional muffin), his body was still getting a good deal.

The coffee smelled wonderful, and the familiar woman behind the bar had it ready by the time he got to the counter. He smiled. "Thanks, Shirley. So glad to see you open. How are things going?"

She smiled and shrugged. He remembered that she was not much for conversation even on the best of days. He added a chocolate croissant, paid cash and sat down at a table near the windows. Taking a tentative sip of the hot, delicious brew, he looked out over the ocean to where the sun was just beginning to kiss the tops of the waves. Other early risers were already out jogging or strolling along the beach for shells, and just behind them a seagull occasionally split from the flock and darted down to snag some small morsel from the surf.

As he sat there enjoying his breakfast and the scenery he began to feel foolish. His prepping, planning and stress last night had been ridiculous. Everything seemed to be normal. He *did* have a tendency to overreact at times, but the apocalypse would be a quick blow, not a lingering event… right? He got a refill on his coffee and returned to his table. Someone had found an actual news broadcast and was turning up the volume on the flat screen TV on the opposite wall. The camera shot of the news studio was replaced by a reporter standing in front of an airport. It looked like Hartsfield-Jackson in Atlanta, which Scott had been through countless times. A crash site lay behind the reporter, and fire trucks surrounded the smoldering ruin of a tail section and other wreckage that was barely recognizable as the fuselage of a passenger jet. As the camera pulled back and panned to the side, more of the surrounding area could be seen. There was another smoking crash site, and then another, each belching dark smoke into the sky. As the camera view pulled back even more, the full scene revealed itself: twenty, thirty, maybe even more planes lay on the tarmac in heaps. The pastry fell from Scott's hand as he stared in horror at the screen. The new ticker crawling at the bottom of the screen declared that least 1,850 flights had been lost yesterday as planes fell from the sky, their electronics failed. Tens of thousands of passengers were presumed dead. All remaining doubts faded from Scott. This was not the end, that was yesterday. Today …today is the in between.

TEN

The sounds in the little shop came to an abrupt silence. Simultaneously the light and picture faded from the TV as the power went off again. Shirley, the shop owner, leaned on the counter looking out in frustration. Sighing in frustration, she announced she was closing up since she wasn't able to ring anything else up on the cash register or brew more coffee. She invited everyone to come up for free refills until it was gone. Scott was the last to leave and as he got the final refill from Shirley, "This is getting to be a pain isn't it? Are you going to be ok?" "Huh…oh yes," She answered. "I'll be fine, just can't make any money with the power off. I hope they get it fixed by lunch. Otherwise, my whole day is ruined." He started to offer his opinion on that, then thought better of it. *Why frighten anyone else with my opinions?*

Since he was unable to take his now full cup of coffee on the bike Scott walked out and sat on the raised sidewalk overlooking the bike stand. Sipping the coffee, he saw a man he vaguely recognized coming in his direction. The man gave a low wave, and Scott nodded in the local custom. The man was probably is in his early thirties and wore jeans and a garishly loud tropical print shirt. He had a big childlike grin as he crossed the empty street and said, "Hi – I'm Jack."

Scott shook his hand and said his name in return.

"Nice day for a ride," looking over at the little Italian racing bike.

Nodding, Scott said, "That it was, until all the shit hit the fan."

Laughing, Jack said, "Amen to that brother," and Scott remembered where he had seen the guy—he was a preacher at the local Pentecostal Church.

"Oh, sorry preacher."

Still laughing Preacher Jack said, "Fear not my brother as the shit indeed, may have certainly hit the fan."

Looking up at the coffee shop with the closed sign on the door, the preacher's smile vanished. "Just my luck, they ran out of coffee giving it to heathens like you," he said looking down in fake judgment at Scott and his nearly full third cup of coffee. Jack's smile beamed large once more.

"Sorry," Scott said with a chuckle, "But yeah, she closed up when the power went back off. Here, have this one if you're okay with black with a tiny bit of sugar."

"No, very kind, but no."

"Seriously, I've had all I can handle. My bladder will thank you."

Preacher Jack thought better of his refusal and accepted the cup of coffee from the outstretched arm. He lifted it to his lips, and Scott could tell he was savoring the smell of it. He also noticed what appeared to be the bottom of a crudely inked tattoo on one bicep, peeking out from under his shirt sleeve. Preacher Jack and Scott chatted for a few minutes, and Scott gave him what information he had. The preacher knew very little about yesterday's events. Scott thought of mentioning the plane crashes but decided against it. The man seemed to have a perpetually cheerful attitude. Why ruin it?

Jack made the obligatory invitation to come to his church and then winked, "Had to y'know, it's in the rulebook." He thanked Scott profusely for the coffee and watched as he remounted the old bike and rode on through the town, scanning to see if anything else was open.

As he rode, Scott continued to process what he knew. The power grid was out or on its last leg. Tens of thousands, likely many more, had died. Phones didn't work. The Internet was down. But life still went on. At least here in Harris Springs, it seemed to be stubbornly refusing to accept anything had changed. Shrimp boats were heading out as normal. People were hauling chairs and umbrellas out to the beach. Scott stopped the bike near the beach boardwalk and tried to get his head around it. Was yesterday the collapse of society as he knew it or just another bump in the road? Was it just the next 9/11 or Katrina or Pearl Harbor...something to be remembered somberly at dinner tables for years to come, or the first day of the post-apocalyptic world? In the end, what made the most sense to Scott was something his dad had often told the boys growing up: Hope for the best but plan for the worst.

Scott pedaled around the small town taking note of the businesses that seemed to be trying to open. Many were putting "Cash Only" signs in windows. That reminded him—he should probably consolidate as much cash as he could. He had adequate savings, as well as a few healthy checking, retirement, and investment accounts. He could probably liquidate about half of that into a single account within the day if the power stayed on and the Internet remained useable, he thought. The remainder would take longer; especially if the stock market crashed or there was a run on the banks. He was pretty sure Wall Street and other trading centers would not have power to even open, much less crash, for several days. Chances were the President would put a freeze on banks, limiting transactions as soon as communication networks were back up.

Due to his varied career working for major banks, investment houses, and various government agencies, Scott knew how vulnerable the US financial system actually was. The housing bubble and the collapse of 2008 had been predicated on the reckless actions of just one small segment of the lending industry. Their short-sighted greed came very close—much closer than most people realized—to collapsing the US economy entirely. Scott had moved most of his banking from a large Chicago bank to a local credit union soon after he moved to the area. Recently he had even consolidated his small inheritance from his parents' estate to a money market account at the same place. He began to wonder how much could he withdraw at one time and what everyone would do if the banks were ordered to close.

Thinking longer term, getting his money out of the bank in cash was fine for now, but if the market crashed or financial systems didn't come back soon, the dollar itself would quickly be worthless. What would be valuable then? Most likely a barter economy would pop up pretty quickly. Gold, silver, fuel, food, guns, ammo, running vehicles… maybe even water could be the currency then. Scott knew he had limited options to convert his cash to anything like that, but he did notice a pawn shop that was open and a jewelry store owner unlocking the doors for business. It also reminded him of some gold and silver exchanges on-line that might still be accepting orders—assuming he could get the net back up again. Then he could use his less liquid assets for them or even max out his credit cards to make up for whatever liquid assets he had to forfeit. He began making plans for the day as he finished his circuit of the town. He turned the bike westward and pedaled over the Intercoastal bridge back toward home.

ELEVEN

Scott Montgomery was not someone to whom most people would give a second thought. He appeared average in nearly every way. Despite that, he had a slightly above average IQ and the helpful ability to focus in on problems and become deeply attuned to probable solutions. Unlike many people he knew, he was intent to never be a victim; Scott had always faced life head-on. He had overcome odds often in his life just like most hard-working people. His failed marriage was his one true regret—not the fact that it had failed—in hindsight that was a relief, but that it had occurred. Despite feeling basically average, at heart he was a competitor. Scott didn't like to fail at anything. The fact that he never seemed to live up to his Dad's expectations or his brothers or especially his ex-wife's had done little for his confidence. Hiding out here, living his life of quiet existence had seemed like enough, but he knew it was not who he was.

Deep down he knew something had fundamentally changed with the Solar blast yesterday, and that the world would never be the same. While such thinking may be premature, he argued to himself, he was quickly becoming committed: he would be responsible for his own survival.

He also knew the clock was ticking if he was to accomplish what he needed to. He needed the power and Internet back on, at least for a short while. He also needed the banks to open and operate as normal. Obviously, he needed a shitload of luck. Martial law could be instituted at any moment, including travel restrictions. Fuel sales could also be limited, and resupplies may not be coming— the whole world had been affected, after all. Food shortages would also be likely. He knew that most stores only kept a very limited supply of food. He already knew that a ground stop was in effect, there would be no flights until all systems were inspected and okayed. And then, who knew about the economy.

Scott felt he had been unforgivably lax before the flare in making any real plan for survival, he was now at a disadvantage. The true preppers and survivalist were probably already hunkered down with their MRE's with AK-47's in hand waiting for the zombie plague. Even now, though, Scott preferred to take steps that could be undone if all of this blew over in a few days. Items he didn't need he could return. Gold could be sold, and cash put back into investment accounts. Food could be eaten, at least in time. He hoped that would be what happened. If so, it would be an inconvenience to return everything, redo his finances, and possibly eat rice and dried beans for the next five years, but if this was as bad as he feared and everything was about to go sideways… he had to start making smart choices and think strategically.

• • •

The power was still out at home, so he filled up the sink, tub and lots of containers with fresh water. He also loaded up the Jeep with every spare fuel container he had in the cottage, then went down to the boathouse and took the two large twenty-gallon fuel tanks off the old flat bottom boat that Bobby kept inside. He looked at the old pump-house and again thought about getting a generator or some solar panels to power it. Scott was beginning to make a list of longer-term items he may need to acquire in case this became a more permanent situation.

Realistically, he wondered how far out he could prepare. All the fuel, batteries, and emergency food he could acquire would only last, how long? Six months, a year, maybe two? He knew that the best resource he had was his intelligence. Information to survive without power had been around for generations. Electricity was a relatively new addition to the human race which had managed up to that point pretty well without it. Not having power did not have to mean life or death. It just meant inconvenience. Jungle tribes didn't need it, crews on sailing ships had managed without it… he just needed to acquire more data to help him learn those life skills that modern living had archived to a dusty closet. He had grown up on a farm; he knew how to hunt and to fish, although, unlike his brother, he was not overly enthusiastic about either. If it came to survival, though, he would do what was needed as long as it didn't harm others. He began to wonder how many others would say the same.

TWELVE

Back inside the small house, the temperature was climbing again, so Scott opened the shuttered windows. Sitting down, he began to make a list of the financial moves he wanted to make once the power came back on....if it came back on. Scott got busy gathering all the logins and passwords so he would be ready when it happened. He was unsure of how much he could withdraw from the local bank at any one time, so he decided to check that as well once he could get online. He cleaned out the cash from his fireproof safe box—about $2,500. He had a few real silver dollars in there which he would save for later, as well as a handful of pure gold Canadian Maple Leaf coins. Each of the coins was about an ounce in weight. They could be very useful if things did get bad. He needed more cash but also wanted to convert as much of it as he could into something he could use or trade when needed. Currency of any kind would be useless if the economy completely collapsed.

There was one more piece of gold in the box: a simple round wedding band. Seeing the ring brought back a flood of memories and pain. Looking back, he had known he was more infatuated with Angela than in love. She was sexy, confident, and, as his co-workers had said, "Way outta your league dude."

He thought about how scared he had been when he finally got the courage to ask her out. Granted, he had done so by text message... Scott had never been sure why she said yes. Yes, to the first date and yes to the awkward proposal the following year. His brother had been his best man and in the anteroom with the preacher on that day he had warned Scott to be careful. Bobby had seen something in Angela that left him unsettled. Scott, on the other hand, was too wrapped up in finally having someone in his life. Having a love of his own.

The marriage had been challenging almost from the very beginning, and four years later, when she left him, Scott was shattered and humiliated. He had moved back down here to get away, to hide out and just be alone. He didn't feel he would ever trust, much less love again. The thought of her did momentarily cause him to wonder how she would be doing in all this, but the fleeting concern quickly faded into nothingness. Pocketing the ring, he knew it would be one of the first things he traded.

He tried his cell phone again. This time, his brother's phone rang but then went almost immediately to voicemail. It was the generic voicemail greeting, not Bobby's normal one, but he left a brief message anyway, "Hey man, it's Scott… look, you told me you were paying the power bill for the beach house but listen… they cut me off," Scott laughed then continued. "Seriously dude, I just wanted to check on you guys—that was some serious shit yesterday, and yes…you were right to be prepared and yes, I am an idiot… I'm okay… power and cell service are erratic but, uh… try and call me when you can. I could use your expertise. Be safe. Love you, man."

Although the brothers had always been close, they were not normally very verbal about their feelings. Today, though, it seemed important. Bobby had been there for him more times than he could remember. Only three years older, he always seemed smarter, tougher and just a cool guy to be around. Bobby had cast a protective shadow over his little brother from day one, daring anyone to ever pick on little Scott.

Looking outside it was a beautiful day, and he wanted to go for a bike ride. Over the years, riding had become a bit of an addiction for him, although one he did not feel guilty about having. On the bike, he knew it would be easy to not think that the world was falling apart. Even on the worst of days, riding the bike cleared his mind and brought clarity. *How often will I be able to ride now?* he wondered. If what he feared was true, he knew much, probably all, of his time would be focused on basic survival. *Maybe ride later,* he told himself. For now, he had more work to do.

• • •

To be honest, he was uncertain of what to do next, but he knew there was not a lot to be accomplished sitting around here while the power was out. Finally, he grabbed his list and laptop bag and headed to the Jeep. He decided to head back to town with what cash he had and try to pick up supplies. If the power was on in town, he wanted to get fuel. That was the top priority, then cash from the bank, some more short-term food, and whatever long-term supplies he could find. He reasoned that the town may have power and he might be able to log onto the Internet from somewhere in town.

Scott had decided to hook up his empty motorcycle trailer to the Jeep, just in case he found stores that were open. Although he had never owned a motorcycle, he had bought the trailer as it was enclosed and a nice size for hauling a lot of things. It was particularly useful for transporting his bike and gear to some of the distant bike races he competed in. Pulling onto the main road to Harris Springs he mentally reviewed his lists, wondering if he could get any of the items on them. As he got closer to town, he was surprised at the number of people walking and the amount of bikes out—both higher than normal—but everything looked mostly like it had several hours earlier…normal.

Either everyone else is nuts, or I am, he joked to himself as he watched the town go about its usual day. *But no turning back now…* he told himself as a flush of doubt rose in his chest. He swallowed it back down as he steered the Jeep onto Main Street. Through the open windows, Scott enjoyed the familiar ocean smells, listened to the sounds of the waves, chatter of gulls, and a distant blast from a ship's horn. It all seemed so normal, his little town just waiting to wake up and start another day. The gas stations on this side of town were dark and had closed signs in the windows. Same for the big Publix grocery store. The big box builders supply store was open, although also dark. As he pulled in, Scott saw the hand-lettered sign: "Cash Only". Walking in he was handed a flashlight and then selected a large rolling cart. There were not many people shopping. *Good*. While he wanted to keep his limited cash in reserve and preferred to use credit or debit, he thought it best to take advantage of this opportunity.

Heading to the sections with the plastic fuel containers, Scott loaded several into the cart. To that he added a stack of clean five gallon pails, several tarps, lighters, lantern fuel, and as many of the camp stove fuel cylinders as they had. He found large bottles of bleach and also picked up several large bottles of granulated chlorine from the pool supplies aisle. He searched for a power generator but saw none. He added several rolls of duct tape, padlocks, some heavy duty chain, batteries, and quite a few smaller items. He also found the handy three-gallon commercial water bottles up front and added six of those.

He noticed two workers standing in the dark with small lights clipped to their work aprons. As he got closer, he realized they were teenagers: a boy, and a cute girl. They were talking in hushed tones, but it was pretty obvious it wasn't work related. The girl had a cell phone in her hand, as if wishing it would come back on might make it so. "He and I are just friends, ya know?" she was saying.

"But you ain't heard shit from him," the boy said. Scott wondered how the younger generation would cope if cell phones or the Internet never worked again. *They'll actually have to talk to one another.* Scott smiled at his private joke. He was pretty sure none of them would be able to develop the communication skills to actually talk to one another. Was it possible that writing notes would even come back in fashion? His mom would have been happy to see that happen, he thought.

"Excuse me," Scott said, "Do you guys have any generators?"

They both looked up, surprised, but the girl smiled and said, "Sorry. Those were gone yesterday."

"That figures," Scott sighed.

She suggested he try the Farmers Supply nearby. "They been closed since the blackout but usually they stock as many as we do this time of year," she offered.

"Hey, thanks," Scott smiled and nodded as he turned and headed back to the front of the store and toward daylight.

Checking out was slow as the cashier had to look up prices while the store manager punched in the price and quantity on an actual calculator. Scott handed them back the flashlight he had been using and thanked them for even being open. The manager smiled, but the cashier didn't.

"It's our pleasure," the man said. "We know our community needs us right now."

Scott suspected that the prices were a good bit higher than they were before the blackout, but he decided to stay silent. He handed over the cash, thanked them, and headed out to load up the trailer. Everything fit inside nicely and he left the fuel containers in the back so he could get to them easily if he found a working gas station.

As he got back on the main street, he was disappointed to see the few traffic lights were off. *Still no power.* On the far side of town, he did notice a few cars and a good number of people at Castro's Place, the local sports bar. His stomach rumbled. He'd eaten there several times before; the food was good, and he figured he might as well get some lunch if they were serving. The Jeep and trailer would not fit on the street side parking, so he pulled into the empty gravel lot next door.

As he got close to the door, he saw another "Cash Only" notice printed on the large sidewalk sign alongside the proclamation "All Seafood Half-Off!" Inside he found that the place was packed, and almost immediately he heard a somewhat familiar voice calling his name.

Preacher Jack was nursing a beer at a high-top table with two other guys. Motioning for Scott to join them, he scooted around to make more room. Scott walked over and made an unenthusiastic effort to decline the invitation. "I can just get something to go—don't need to crash your party."

"Sit your ass down," Jack said.

What kind of preacher was this guy? Scott wondered.

"At the very least I owe you a beer for that lifesaving cup of Shirley's coffee you gave me this morning."

Scott sat down uneasily and studied the three men. The preacher introduced the two other guys as Todd and Bartos. Handshakes followed and within minutes, a cold mug of beer appeared in front of Scott. Todd was a big guy, probably late forties, dark hair and a goatee just on the verge of going gray. He had a gravelly voice, weathered face and a few tattoos on his exposed arm. The other man, Bartos, was slim, bald and looked vaguely Hispanic. His dark eyes scanned the room nervously, and he spoke in a rapid-fire staccato.

"Order some food, Scott," Todd advised. "It's takin' 'em a while."

"I'm just impressed they're even open with no power. I guess cooking and selling it now's a better option than throwing it out tomorrow."

"At least the cerveza's are still cold my friend," smiled Bartos, holding up his nearly empty mug and motioning to a server behind Scott.

Scott ordered the blackened redfish and steamed red potatoes, lamenting the fact that there were no fried dishes available. The servers were bringing out platters of free appetizers to the bar for people to share. Jack went over and filled a basket for the table. The conversation at the table picked up quickly.

Jack continued his introductions; "Todd has a charter fishing business, and Bartos is the town drunk."

Laughing, he continued, "No, this idiot runs the county mechanical shop and is our resident doomsday prepper."

"Shouldn't you be holed up in your bunker then?" Scott joked.

"Don't be a hater," Bartos replied with a semi-serious look on his face.

"What d'you do, Scott?" Todd asked, leaning back in his chair.

Scott gave his standard response. "Computer consultant." Not exactly accurate, but close enough that most people let it go, not wanting to know more.

"I guess most of us're out of work until the power's back up," Todd mused. "Except the preacher here, of course. He can fleece his flock even easier in a darkened church."

Jack gave a distinct, "Fuck you," to Todd, who grinned broadly. Jack asked Scott what he was doing back in town.

"Honestly, I was hoping to get some gas and supplies. I'm concerned this isn't a short-term problem," Scott responded. The three other men looked at each other conspiratorially.

Bartos leaned over and said, "It isn't brother."

Todd looked at Scott and asked, "What do you know about what happened?"

Scott nibbled on a chip and said uncertainly, "Same as everyone else I guess; solar flare took out much of the power grid, what power is left is being rerouted to other areas, giving us these lovely rolling blackouts. Most of the Northeast and many other major cities are in a full blackout. No communications networks are working, at least not with any reliability, and they have no idea how long before any of it's back up. Did I miss anything?"

"Well yes, that's a lot of what's happened, but we think we know a bit more." Todd motioned to his left with a meaty hand, "Bartos here is tied into a network of amateur radio operators, and they've uncovered, well, let's just say some troubling items. You may have seen some of the news footage from Atlanta this morning. It seems only about half of the more modern cars quit due to electronics failure but in the air, that ratio was much worse. The early estimates Bartos heard were that nearly seventy-five percent of all passenger flights in the air worldwide either crashed or suffered hard landings. About 3,800 aircraft," he finished.

"Yea, I think I may have seen one going down out over the Gulf yesterday when I was out on my bike," Scott said.

Todd took a long pull from his beer, so the guy they called Bartos picked up the story. "From what I hear on the ham and what Todd said was coming through on his marine radio, a lot of ships at sea are unaccounted for. With electronic steering, navigation, and autopilots all offline, they are all gonna be in bad shape. At least one out of Port Mobile collided overnight with an abandoned oil platform. Both were listing badly, and the ship's crew didn't even know where they were. Couple other big ships were lost in the shoals off the coast of Louisiana. Just like the aircraft avionic systems, all of the electronics on these vessels was apparently very vulnerable."

"Back on land the situation in much of the country, shit …the entire world is worse," Bartos went on. "Reports are that numerous nuclear plants failed to shut down right, and, at least one in France and three here in the US are looking at potential meltdowns—one in Colorado, one in Illinois and one in central Texas."

"Oh, shit," Scott said, then added, "I really hope you're just fucking with me."

Preacher Jack looked somberly and said, "From what the acting Police Chief told him earlier today, he's right. The unofficial estimates are that in the first hour after the CME, somewhere between 300,000 and half a million people were dead, worldwide. If you add to that the other reports since then of looting, traffic fatalities, all the deaths in hospitals of people with no life support, etcetera… Guys, we could have a million or more dead by week's end." The Preacher crossed himself, offering a small, silent prayer.

"Hang on," Scott said, "something doesn't make sense to me. If it were that bad, wouldn't we know it? I mean, people are heading down to lie on the beach. Most aren't even cutting their vacation short, much less panicking. People are going to work as they do every day. Hell, we're sitting here having lunch at a restaurant. It can't be the apocalypse; we still have beer!"

Todd looked up. "Scott, all those people on the beach are probably looking up at the worst serial killer in history. We all may have thought that when the shit hit the fan, we and everyone else would know it. In actuality, a series of cascading failures was always the worst-case scenario. But people, government, businesses, they don't want to think there's no tomorrow. Many of the leaders in government and industry are out there right now trying to get everything fixed, patched up at least enough to avoid widespread panic. If this is the collapse, they lose everything.

"I'm not an alarmist, and I don't buy into the conspiracy theories that many do. I think if the media knew this, they would be broadcasting it non-stop. I feel sure, on the other hand, that the government would prefer we not know the full extent of the damage and possibly stay calmer."

Scott remembered the BBC recording that seemed to say that same thing. "My Dad used to say the only time to really worry is if someone in authority tells you not to worry."

About then the food came out, looking good and smelling even better. The conversation died down as this unlikely group began to eat. As he looked around the table, Scott realized that he found himself liking each of them. Todd had to be the oldest of the group probably in his late 40's, and Scott figured he was the youngest by a few years. They each seemed like good people, but more than that, they seemed to have common sense. Something he valued greatly. They were also funny—irreverent even—but mainly they genuinely seemed like decent, hardworking guys. He had withdrawn from society so much that sitting here talking with these three was a surreal moment. It wasn't that he hated people, he just generally liked it better when they weren't around. Strangely, he felt these three would add to his life, and quickly decided he wanted to stay on good terms with them.

Without looking up from his food, Todd said, "Scott, you mentioned the Northeast was totally dark. Where did you hear that?" Apparently that had not been in any of the news reports. Most likely there were no working ham radio broadcasts coming out of those areas.

Scott finished his bite and was about to dismiss it as hearsay instead of admitting how he knew, but then decided that since the three of them had been open and honest with him, he should do the same. He told them about getting online early this morning right after the power came on. Each of the guys looked surprised.

"How did you do that?" Bartos asked. "We all tried, but nothing came up for us."

"I have top-secret cyber-ninja skills," Scott said smiling. "Actually, I just realized that it might be possible to see what websites were still running in another less-common way." He glanced up to see every eye at the table on him. Scott went on to tell them the few other pieces of information he had gleaned from being online. None had heard of the Space Station disaster or most of the other news items he'd found, including the reports of celebration in the Middle East and the brief headline of the possible attacks on Israel. The lack of real information was immediate and potentially just as hard to handle as lack of fuel, food or water.

"Do you think you can pull up more websites—get more details—if the power comes back on?" Todd asked.

"Hopefully. But the power and data feeds have to be on where the web servers are as well, and I'll need to have the actual IP address in my files."

"Please try," said Bartos.

"We would all be thankful if you'd share with us whatever you find," Preacher Jack added.

Todd looked at Scott squarely and said, "I know we just met, but you strike me as a pretty smart guy. So let me ask you something, something we've all been asking ourselves. Assuming yesterday was the beginning of our end, our Doomsday. What are the essential skills *you* have to survive?"

Scott suddenly felt like he was in an interview rather than at a casual lunch. He felt the full weight of that question. "That's what I've been struggling with the last twenty-four hours. I guess I'm a fairly smart guy. I have some basic skills… I obviously wasn't smart enough to be better prepared. I was raised on a farm so I've got a good bit of experience outdoors, but those are pretty rusty. I'm just a normal guy, I'm not a soldier, not a tough guy—hell, I ride a bicycle and I support the Sierra Club, for god's sake. I came into town today hoping it wasn't too late to get some food and fuel. When it comes to survival, I waited too late."

THIRTEEN

No one said anything for several minutes. He looked back down at the remainder of his lunch, hoping no one would see the fear in his eyes.

Bartos spoke first, "Hey man, none of us were ready. If yesterday was the end, even I was unprepared. Sure, some preppers said they were ready, even acted like they wanted it to happen. But really man, this is some shit. It's not going to be like camping out for a long weekend; this may be life. Prepping is a fallacy. You can store food and water for a while, but it will run out. Then what? You have to have the knowledge and be able to work together to get the shit working again. Prepping is for the short-term; long-term, we need to survive long enough to adapt to a new world."

"So, assuming the worst—that this is it—what should I do next? What can any of us do that will make a difference?" Scott asked.

Todd smiled, "You should finish your food. I probably caught that fish you're eating, and it's getting cold, and that hurts my feelings.

"I feel sure you've taken some steps to prepare yourself already. You've got shelter, water, seventy-two hours' worth of food, right? That's a step one plan. Looks like you are working on the next step: locating more resources. And although you may not realize it, finding allies. In the Navy, we learned a lot about teamwork. Despite movies loving the lone hero, a group of people working together is much stronger than any individual. You may feel alone, but you don't have to be. We can help, if you'll work with us."

"Why would you guys be willing to help me?" Scott said stunned. "I thought it would be every man for himself in the apocalypse."

Jack said, "You know Scott, I have been through the darkness before.

Not like this but spiritually. I've seen the evil in men, bad shit....and I've also learned to spot the good. You seem to have a lot of good in you. You're smart, resourceful, and a computer programmer slash farmer-in-residence seems like a good acquisition. My friends here trust my opinion, which is that you could be an asset if this mess goes sideways, which seems likely.

"Now, they aren't going to give you the food they have put up for themselves, but they will work with you to get your own or have your back when you need them. That is, assuming you contribute the same—no free rides with us. Now, if the lights come back on for good, hey, you've made a few new friends. If they stay off, then you may have something even more essential—allies."

"Yep," Todd chimed in, "a derelict Preacher, a broken down mechanic, and a fisherman—that's one hell of a survival team." They all laughed.

Scott nodded okay and asked, "What do you think might happen next? I mean.... other than the power and phones being out most people seem to be carrying on as normal."

Todd sighed. "Many are just plain stupid. Others are in denial, which is exactly what Uncle Sam is counting on." He looked around the table before he continued. "Right now everyone in any real form of leadership is in damage control mode. I'm reasonably certain the government, Wall Street, all the corporate head honchos in America, none of 'em want anything close to a panic. If that happens, they all lose. Which means they want desperately to get ahead of it. Make it look like they're in control of the situation, at least until they have a better plan of action in place. They'll likely try to come up with some plausible excuses or try to keep the systems running for the as long as they can. Which'll be difficult. They could even try to influence the news broadcasts, maybe keep them off the air if they feel they're not helping to calm the situation."

"You think they might try and control the media?" asked the preacher.

"More likely they'll misdirect the attention to something more sensational but less meaningful," Bartos said. "Or just cut the power supply off to the offending broadcaster.

"The government'll be in a difficult position trying to minimize media coverage *and* protect the financial markets—oh, and prevent widespread looting and hoarding...

"Gentlemen," he continued, "there's really never been much point in fearing a pandemic, zombies, an alien attack, or even EMPs. What would devastate this country the most is an economic collapse. The US economy is not backed by anything real. We left the gold standard behind years ago. Today our currency is backed only by the presumed value we have in it and our trust in the government. Despite that, the US dollar is still one of, or maybe even the most dominant currency in the world. If the markets fail and the US dollar collapses on the world market, then we're all screwed, nothing will get fixed, and we will be trading seashells for beans for the next hundred years. They'll pull out all the stops to make sure that doesn't happen. That means they'll shift any and all resources and defense to the country's most valuable assets—of which the coastal Mississippi damn sure isn't one. Most of us here remember what it was like after Katrina. We can't depend on anyone else, especially the feds, to protect us. It isn't a question of *could* the government help...in an isolated situation, it can if it wants... but this, it's the overall scope of the disaster. How do you feed, or even provide clean water and sanitation, for millions—for the entire United States? Not just for a few days but for weeks or months. They couldn't even do it for New Orleans. If you're saying the northeast is dark, what'll happen in New York City...much less Harris Springs, Mississippi?"

Todd and Jack were nodding in agreement. Bartos went on, "I think we have to assume that no more food shipments will be coming. The grocery stores only stock about a three-day supply. The gas stations about the same. They rely on multiple resupply shipments every week and being able to place orders for higher usage items when a run starts, like when a hurricane is threatening. What we have now and," he lowered his voice, "what we can get quickly is all we may have for a very long time. As Todd says, right now most people are in the dark— literally and figuratively. They're denying that anything serious is happening. Most will wait for help or official word before assuming the worst."

He paused and took a sip of his beer before continuing, "There may be a small window of time to take care of a few more things. When the power comes back on, assuming it does, more stores will reopen. If we act quickly, we can acquire more food and possibly some supplies. Just as likely, as soon as communications are back up, I wouldn't be surprised to see mandatory rationing instituted. The government won't call it that—they'll put a very positive spin on it—say they are suggesting purchase limits to prevent hoarding and price gouging or something, but we know the truth. So we may have a brief opportunity to top off what we need. We need to be ready if it happens."

The restaurant was beginning to clear out, and the server stopped by the table to ask about refills. Bartos and Scott ordered another drink, and Todd placed a to-go order for someone. Scott wondered if any of the men were married or had a family, but then realized that no one had mentioned any personal information about themselves so far. In truth, other than their names and work, he knew very little about them. *Maybe they're as paranoid and private as I am.* He found his trust in these would-be comrades growing nonetheless.

"Scott, you said you need food and fuel. I'm assuming you mean long-term supplies. What else would be of help?" asked Todd.

He pulled out his crumpled list and passed it to Todd. "I'll need to fix my water supply. I have a well but have to do something to get the pump to work."

Todd was busy reading the list. He took out a pencil, marked through a few items, and wrote in some new lines. He then passed it to Bartos who also inspected it.

"If the gas stations don't open I can help you with the fuel—we have a reserve supply we can tap into," Bartos commented. "As for food, I would recommend you get the essentials, but not so much you couldn't move it if needed. Freeze-dried would work best as it's lightweight and lasts a long time. Go for calorie counts not servings, as you'll likely need the extra calorie intake. You'll be working a lot harder to survive than you used to.

One other thing—think about a bug-out location. Possibly even more than one. I also have some ideas on your water supply that I'll get to you later on."

Scott was familiar with bug-outs as Bobby had mentioned them several times. Contingency plans again. If your primary shelter is unavailable or unsafe, have a backup to fall back or "bug-out" to.

"We haven't done anything to earn your trust yet, so you don't have to answer or be specific, but what general area do you live in?"

Scott told them pretty much exactly.

"That road backs up on the bayou. It's low-lying, but there're some solid homes there. Good fishing and hunting. Not a bad location. Some of those homes around the edge of the swamp are already off the power grid. You are out a good ways, may want to cache some supplies in other areas you can get to in an emergency."

"What about self-defense—weapons, guns, ammo?" asked Bartos.

Scott shrugged, "Not great, unfortunately. My ex didn't like guns, so I only have a single P226 that my dad had left me and a few boxes of ammo. Listen, I'm not opposed to guns, but honestly, I'm not sure I could use one if it came down to it. I'm not a fighter. I wrestled in high school, but I got mugged twice in Chicago… I'm not going to be the next UFC champion."

Surprisingly it was the preacher who looked at Scott and said, "Son, you may want to get ready. Real fucking fast. While I don't think everyone is going to go nuts like they do in the movies, there will be those that feel entitled to take what's not theirs to take. We can all help you with some self-defense training. I have some street skills that might come in handy for you to learn. Also, know that desperate people, *hungry people*, won't think twice about hurting someone to eat or feed their kids. While we might sympathize with their needs and suffering, you need to clear that moral hurdle now so you don't hesitate when the time comes. Being charitable could cost you your life."

Todd looked over at Jack. "Wasn't that one of your sermons, Preacher?"

Jack laughed. "I just think our new friend here could benefit from a bit of KFM."

Scott looked puzzled, unsure of what Jack was talking about but the others grinned and nodded in agreement.

"The Sig Sauer P226 is a solid weapon," Todd said. "Was your dad in the Navy too? How skilled are you with using it?"

"I grew up around guns, but I'm better with rifles than handguns. I've put about a hundred rounds through it shooting nutria and squirrels off the back deck," Scott replied.

"Do you know how to break it down and clean it?" Todd asked.

"Of course," Scott said, a little more defensively than he meant to. His dad *had* been ex-military, and an absolute fanatic at taking care of his tools, especially the guns. The habit had been one Scott could not break.

"You should try and get another pistol—and a rifle or a shotgun, if you can afford it," added Todd.

Bartos cleared his throat. "I know a few people who can do a cash deal."

"Cash is also something I need to get more of," Scott remembered. "I only keep a little on hand and with the banks closed, I'm concerned."

"Don't worry. The banks'll reopen, if only on a limited basis. They won't lose more money than they have to. Just be ready," warned Jack.

Something Scott had read in an old preparedness memo on one of his work servers suggested that, in a national economic disaster, one of the first things the government would do would be to close the banks; declare a bank holiday until markets could reopen and stabilize.

"After listening to you guys, that seems more likely than ever to be what we should expect."

No one disagreed, but they admitted they hadn't thought about it.

"We all use credit cards and online banking for deposits and bill-pay these days—who even carries cash anymore?" Todd said.

Bartos smiled and raised his hand, "I do, but only because my credit sucks and I can't afford to use the cards I carry." They laughed a little.

Scott mentioned that he'd transferred most of his accounts to the local bank already. He was counting on being able to withdraw as much as possible once the doors opened. Each of the other guys at the table said they would do the same.

The conversation was dropping off, and the restaurant staff looked like they were ready to split.

"Thanks for the company," Scott said. "Lunch was great."

Now he wanted to see what supplies he could scrounge up. Jack mentioned a few places that might be open, including a dollar store that carried some food supplies and a sporting goods store just out of town. Scott exchanged numbers with the other three, just in case, but they all agreed to find Preacher Jack if they needed to get a message to anyone else in the meantime.

"By the way guys, thanks for scaring the hell out of me," Scott laughed awkwardly as they shook hands and bumped fists, each dropping some cash on the table as they headed for the door.

FOURTEEN

Hopping back in the driver's seat Scott felt his phone buzz in his pocket. Pulling it out, he was surprised to see that the screen showed a missed call from his brother. The phone hadn't rung; he was sure of that, but maybe that meant the cell network was trying to come back. He swiped the screen to see if there were any voicemails and it showed one new message. He clicked the button to play and heard the distinct voice of his brother Bobby:

"Scott, man I am so glad to hear from you. We're all okay here, but we've been worried sick. Hearing from you helped a lot, but we haven't been able to reach Kaylie over at the University yet, so her mom is freaking out. Power here is going on and off in about four-hour cycles, so looks like rolling blackouts to me. If that holds we should have juice until about 3:00 p.m. Our phones seem to work a little when the power's on but not reliably.

"Listen, I don't know if you'll even get this, but I want to keep it brief anyway. No one knows how bad it's going to get, but I suggest you stock up and hunker down. Keep your EDC bag on you all the time. This could be bad, dude. We love you. Get back in touch when you can and we'll talk more specifics."

Scott hit the dial button on the screen to call Bobby's number, but it went to a fast busy tone, then to silence. He tried again and then called Bobby's wife Jessie's number. Nothing. Well, he felt better knowing they were okay, though he was concerned about Kaylie. She was his niece, Jess and Bobby's only child, and she was in her junior year at Florida State. The college was a few hundred miles away from Harris Springs, but still, he was a lot closer to her than Bobby and Jessie were. Kaylie was a strong-willed teen, now young woman with a stubborn streak that Scott enjoyed but made her parents crazy. Scott felt sure she could hold her own for a while but if things got desperate he wanted her out of Tallahassee as much as his brother did.

Pulling the Jeep out onto the main road, he headed over to the dollar store Jack had mentioned. They were taking credit and debit cards: they had a way to process them manually. "As long as you're local, and you have ID," the cashier said.

He had never been in the dimly lit store before, but its shabbiness was made worse by the battery-operated lanterns placed sporadically around the aisles. He grabbed a cart and immediately began filling it with items from his list. Lots of pasta, sauces, pancake mix, canned ham, stew, soups, and vegetables. When available, he got entire cases of the stuff. He also chose numerous bottles of shampoo, deodorant, soap, razor blades and as many large bottles of bleach as he could find. Marking items off his list, he found energy bars, garbage bags, freezer bags and candles. He cleaned out the disposable lighters, dry beans, rice, and cases of bottled water. He was up to two nearly full shopping carts already. He found the meager section for medicine and took gauze, peroxide, bandages and a lot of over-the-counter cold, pain and allergy medicines, and loaded up on vitamins.

After completely clearing out many of the sections, Scott maneuvered the carts to the checkout line. Most of the others in line only had a few items, and each seemed to be paying with the same kind of debit card; no one was using cash. He was a bit embarrassed as he navigated his loaded shopping carts up to the cashier, but she didn't even blink an eye at it. Once she had totaled it all up, he gave her the credit card and showed his ID. She wrote down the info on the back of an old style credit card imprint receipt. He was quickly out the door and loading up his rapidly filling trailer with loot, very thankful to hang on to his cash a bit longer.

• • •

Several streets over he found the nearly deserted sporting goods store. It was indeed open but apparently no one needed sporting goods today. The parking lot was empty. As he walked in an athletic looking black man with a flashlight met him.

"What can I help you find today sir?"

"Do you carry camping gear?" Scott asked.

"Of course, just follow me." He handed Scott a small flashlight and offered him a shopping cart. Scott quickly found many of the items he needed including a few things that Todd and Bartos had added to his list. He picked up two all-climate sleeping bags, a larger backpack, a good quality multitool, a fire starter, a mini-camp stove, a portable cook set and some extra fuel pellets, a dozen cans of cooking gel, an additional two-burner camp stove and all the green fuel cylinders he could carry.

At this point, he assumed that nothing he had ordered online would show up, but even if it did, it would be smart to have extras. And he could probably trade them if needed.

He picked up several additional water purification straws and chlorine dioxide purification tablets, ten packs of bungee cords, an LED headlamp, and the always-useful paracord. From a nearby display case, he selected a large hunting knife, a wicked looking hatchet, and a good quality pair of tactical binoculars.

The store had a small gun and ammunition selection. Clive said he wasn't allowed to sell any guns without a background check, however; but he did offer to sell him as much ammo as he wanted. Scott chose mostly 9mm bullets but also added several cases of .22 caliber, .45 caliber and 12 gauge shotgun shells, again reasoning that he might be able to pick up at least one more weapon or use them for trade. Scott also picked up a professional looking slingshot, something he had been deadly with growing up on the farm and stocked up on even more bulk packs of batteries in various sizes, as well as several additional solar and fuel operated lanterns.

Scott also was about to clean off the small sections of freeze-dried food when Clive said, "I got some more of that in cases in the back if you want."

Scott said he would probably take all he had.

Clive grabbed another cart and headed to the back while Scott grabbed several smaller items and went in search of fishing supplies. On the way, he noticed racks of men's rugged tactical cargo pants and picked up several in his size, as well as an insulated camo coverall and a separate, heavy jacket. Although the boathouse at the cottage was stocked with fishing gear, he picked up more line, hooks, artificial bait and a couple of compact fishing rod/reel combos.

Clive met him at the front of the store with at least a dozen boxes of freeze-dried camp food. "I just brought it all out so you could pick the ones you wanted."

Scott looked up at Clive, "I'll take all of it."

"Well okay man, you must be heading into the wilderness or dropping off the grid."

Scott smiled. "I think we're all off the grid now. I just want some insurance that I can manage a few weeks if need be."

As Clive rang it all up he said, "They gonna have the power on soon, don't you think?"

Scott saw the total and handed the wad of cash to the man. Shrugging his shoulders, he said, "Hope for the best but plan for the worst."

"Alright, man. Hey, pull your car up front, I'll help you load it."

Not really wanting to let anyone else see the other items he had, Scott said thanks, but he could manage. He needed to do some rearranging of his junk to make room first. Clive said okay, thanked him for the business, and walked back inside the darkened store.

FIFTEEN

Heading back through town Scott decided to check to see what else might be open. The gas stations were still closed, as was the grocery store. The bank had a sign on the door: "Opening at 2:00". Several people were already waiting near the front door. Scott decided to wait the twenty minutes until then as it may be his only chance. He used the time to try his brother's phone again, but still no connection. He pulled the laptop from the bag, which came on instantly when he raised the screen. He looked for an active Wi-Fi connection and was surprised to see one which, judging by the identifier, was coming from the bank.

So the bank had power. Although it was probably running on an emergency generator. He connected to the unlocked service and opened a browser window. No websites came up. He tried his VPN trick, but that failed to connect as well. The browser finally rerouted to an internal bank login screen, so he gave up and decided to walk around downtown until the bank opened.

Harris Springs was a quiet little beach town that had been fighting hard for years for an identity. Most of the architecture was unimpressive, with low flat roofs not daring to rise in the face of frequent hurricanes. The town had been founded as a fishing village in the early 1900's and although not a major tourist destination, its few beaches, intercostal waterway, and nearby wildlife sanctuary were regularly featured on travel shows as a hidden jewel of the Gulf Coast. While the local population numbered less than a thousand, during the summer months that number often swelled to seven or eight times as many. The locals viewed the tourist and seasonal residents with something between disdain and moderate toleration at best. They did appreciate the money the visitors spent, though. The tourists' dollars allowed for low utilities, reasonable taxes, and some of the better schools in the area. The local clinic was more of a hospital because of the steady stream of sunburns and jellyfish stings the visitors stumbled in with during the silly season. Over the years, Scott had become less a visitor and more of a permanent resident and now had no desire to ever leave the idyllic little town.

A hundred yards down from the bank Scott noticed that the local bike store was open. Probably his favorite place to visit, he was glad to see through the window that Hank, the owner, was just inside the door.

"Hank, glad to see you open. How are you doing?"

Never much for conversation, the older man looked up, smiled slightly and nodded, "Oh I'm doing alright Scott. Don't need no power to run a bike shop." He was pumping up the tires on his rental fleet of beach cruisers with a floor pump.

Scott decided to get a few things while he was there. He stocked up on a lot of the better quality tubes and even a few of the expensive but durable Gatorskin road tires that would fit either of his bikes. He had some spares already, but he knew that it wouldn't hurt to have extra. He also got a handful of patch kits, just in case he had to do more patching than replacing from now on. Although he was assuming the worst, he really could not come to grips with the possibility of not being able to ride his bike. *Of all the silly-ass things to focus on*, he thought. Handing over more of his dwindling cash, he headed back to his Jeep and added the bike supplies to the haul. Although still just before 2:00 p.m., he noticed that the gathering of people in front of the bank had thinned considerably, and the few remaining were heading through the unlocked doors. Scott locked the Jeep and followed them in.

• • •

All things considered, everything at the bank went much better than expected. Their account records had been updated in the last twelve hours, and Scott's balances looked correct. He learned they were running on backup power from a solar array on the roof. It had been installed a few years earlier as part of the town's meager "Green Initiative." The manager's plan was to stay open as long as the power lasted and hope the regular power would be back on soon. The teller said that Scott could withdraw any amount he wanted, though anything over $10,000 would have to be approved by the manager and reported to the IRS.

"We have to fill out the forms. Although I'm not sure how they will get them now," she said with a laugh. She did add though that since he had multiple accounts, he could take up to the $10,000 in cash from each one with no forms to complete. He filled out the separate checks and a withdrawal slip, and she began counting out the cash. He requested half of it in smaller denominations, so it took a while.

Once he had the stacks of cash, he asked her the easiest way to liquidate the rest of his accounts for cash. "The simplest way would be to request a large sum cash withdrawal from any one account—move everything to that account and then put in the request. If we have the cash on hand, you should be able to get it within three days. Although—right now it could take just a bit longer."

It seemed the bank had ample reserves right now since none of the expected armor car pickups had arrived to take excess cash back to the main branch in Jackson. She expected there would be no problems receiving his funds. He completed the forms to combine his accounts and signed the required funds withdrawal order. She told him to check back in a few days. Scott walked out of the bank with $30,000. He was feeling much better about his situation—until he remembered it could be worthless paper tomorrow. He only remembered much later that this would be the last he ever saw of the rest of his savings.

• • •

Back on the road, Scott hoped he could get a few more of the essential resources he felt were critical. He felt he also needed to spend the cash while it had value.

One of the gas stations on the way out of town was now open, but limiting fuel to eight gallons per person. There were only a few people in line, so he waited and put the eight gallons in the Jeep, bringing the needle to nearly full. That was fine for now.

He went by the Farmers Supply Store. Like most places now it was dark. Unlike the bank and the gas station, they apparently didn't have a backup power source. Unfortunately, going in, he discovered they had sold out of portable generators as well. He decided to look for other items and found several things he felt would be helpful: more plastic storage bins; an ax; propane tanks for the outdoor barbecue; and some additional cold weather and camouflage gear. As a final purchase, he went to the feed and seed section. Now this is *definitely a long-term strategy*, he thought. Especially considering it was the wrong time of year to plant most things.

He was trying to find the non-GMO seeds, which made the task harder. Genetically modified organisms were products of hybrid seeds. While seeds had been crossbred and hybridized for centuries, the ones today were often genetically modified as well; they would grow fine, but you wouldn't be able to take any of that crop's seeds to replant the following year. Non-GMO seeds were a purer version, the crops of which produce seeds that will propagate year after year. The seeds had been one of the items Bartos had added to Scott's list. Satisfied with his selections, he checked out and tried one more stop before heading home.

Unfortunately, the food stores were still closed, but there were a few trucks with trailers in the parking lot with items to sell. They appeared to be local farmers, probably with late harvest crops to sell. Seeing an opportunity to fill a need and make something from the crops, they were setting up shop here where people would naturally come to buy food. Scott appreciated the mindset of farmers, growing up on one taught you to be pragmatic. Already they were adapting to what was possible instead of dwelling on what was lost. They appeared to be doing a brisk business as well.

Careful not to get items that would spoil quickly, Scott's was not a large haul. One man's wife had set up some jars of preserved vegetables, jellies, pickles, and preserves, though, which all looked great. Scott bought nearly everything she had. He made a couple more great finds including local honey, fresh eggs, and smoked ham. He loaded up everything then had an additional thought. He went back to talk to the farmers. Mainly, he wanted to find out if they planned on coming back, and when. But he also wanted to know where were their farms and if they would be open to him coming directly to them to trade. Being the best customer they'd had all day, they eagerly said yes and gave him the information he needed to find them.

On the way back to the cottage, Scott was feeling really good about things. The power being off was inconvenient, and yes it was incredibly sad that so many lives had been lost, but this was not going to be his doomsday. *We could adapt to this… hell, people already are,*" he thought. As he drove around the next bend in the road, all those thoughts vanished in an instant.

SIXTEEN

The first sign of trouble was the car stopped at an odd angle on the road ahead. The vehicle appeared to be running, but the driver's door was open. Scott slowed to a near-stop as he drew closer, but seeing the body lying partially out of the old model sedan he stomped on the brakes, sending some of his precious supplies crashing toward the front of the cab.

He felt a shiver up his spine again; this could be a trap. Or it could be someone in genuine distress. He could just drive on by. Or he could stop and help. Of course, he had left his pistol at home. But he did have a knife in his EDC bag. Pulling off the road, he positioned the truck as close to the stopped car as was prudent. He scanned the side of the road, hoping to see no one lurking in the shadows.

Scott cautiously approached the person; an older man, he could see now. He reached the man and checked for a pulse, still scanning his surroundings for trouble. No pulse. In fact, the man's lifeless arm was cold and beginning to get stiff. He saw a plastic line running to an oxygen canister. Looking at the small gauge, he noticed it was on red which he guessed meant empty. Several other bottles were in the seat, also reading empty. The dead man wore a medical alert bracelet, as well as what appeared to be a recent hospital bracelet. Putting the facts together, Scott made some deductions.

The man, who apparently had severe respiratory issues, likely ran out of oxygen either waiting for a delivery or, more likely, because he depended on one of those oxygen generators that required electricity to operate. When that failed, Scott guessed, he started using the bottles and, on his last one, must have decided to drive himself to the hospital. Sadly, he didn't make it. His lungs had been starved of oxygen here in his old Buick in the middle of the road. One more victim of this damn blackout.

Worse yet, there was nothing Scott could do. Driving him to the hospital would be futile and a waste of time and gas. He couldn't call anyone to help or pick up the body. Finally, Scott put the man in the back seat and pulled the old car off the road. He turned on the emergency hazard lights, walked back to his Jeep and left. He knew he should do more but in the circumstances, he wondered, what more could—or should—he do?

The rest of the drive home was somber, his thoughts less optimistic. Like most people in America, he had spent most of his life thinking that disasters were what happened to other people. During Katrina, 9/11, the Persian Gulf Wars, and the various local tornado outbreaks and floods, he had suffered from what was called the CNN Effect; he would stay glued to the TV, watching the endless parade of personal tragedy and minute-by-minute updates. It had become a morbid form of entertainment. An anesthetized version of reality where death and loss carried the same detached level of involvement as a football game or a movie. Reality shows, which everyone knew were mostly scripted and manipulated for added drama, had been the top of the TV ratings for years. *Most people are insulated from the real hardships of life.*

The loss of his parents had been as close as he had come to knowing death. Even that, though, had been handled so delicately by the assisted living facility, and later the funeral home, that it was...antiseptic. Real, yes, but less painful than it should have been. Now with planes crashing overhead, ships sinking just off shore, and an unknown man lying dead just down the road, Scott felt this was not just a new day; this was a new and very dark world.

SEVENTEEN

Back home, Scott worked hard to erase the memory of the dead man from his mind. Unfortunately, he kept coming back to the image of the man's lifeless face. He felt helpless and selfish. Did the man have a family? Would he even be missed?

What if that happens to me? he thought.

What had Bartos said? "A million people may be dead by week's end." A million people in the world one week and gone the next. That still seemed too hard to grasp, but the one man in the road was real, very real.

He unloaded the supplies and organized all the items, dividing some of the bulk food into smaller Mylar and plastic bags for longer-term storage. He then added canned goods and other items to create weekly boxes of food. The fresh items went to the kitchen to be eaten first. Some of the boxes of food went into the garage for storage, and some went back in the trailer for bug-out supplies. He did the same thing with the water and the hardware, keeping items he would need sooner in spots that were more accessible, and the longer-term— or as he was beginning to think of them "Desperation Time" items—in storage areas and the trailer. *You little godsend,* Scott thought of his motorcycle trailer.

Finishing up, he decided to fix some dinner while it was still light enough to see. Checking his pictures from the day before, he made his decisions on what he needed before opening the refrigerator. He was impressed at how cool it had stayed. Quickly grabbing everything and putting a few of his newly purchased items in the fridge, he closed the door. He put water on to boil for pasta and began chopping up some of the zucchini, squash, and mushrooms to sauté. He added wine, butter, and grated Pecorino Romano cheese to create a creamy sauce. Dropping the stuffed pasta shells into the now boiling water, he felt that even simple meals like this would probably be a luxury from now on. The fresh pasta only took a few minutes to cook through, and he drained it then dropped the shells into the cream sauce. Giving the pan a few quick flips to bathe the large ravioli in sauce, he plated the mixture and topped it off with the tender veggies and a bit more grated cheese.

Over the years since he'd moved here, to a life of mostly solitude, he had gotten into the habit of making at least one good meal a day for himself. It was too easy to just eat junk food, microwave something, or even just do without. Making a meal like this was second nature to him now and made him dread the possibility of living on rice and dried beans, or worse—freeze-dried food—for any length of time. The food was delicious, and he quickly finished it off, wishing he had a fresh cup of coffee for afterward. Scott frowned, looking to the counter at the expensive coffee machine, which was completely useless right now. He knew he had a French press somewhere in the cabinets and thought Bobby had left an old coffee percolator that could be used on the gas range. Both of those seemed too much effort at the moment, though. Instead of enjoying a good cup of coffee, he cleared his dishes from the table and washed them, as well as the cookware he had used. He then finished off the remaining bit of wine.

• • •

It was beginning to get dark inside the quiet cottage and knew he would need to be lighting the candles and hurricane lanterns soon. He could smell the slightly salty breeze blowing through the shuttered windows. It was not helping to cool the interior of the house very much today, but it was welcome just the same.

Scott wondered just how long he would be able to take refuge or "*Bug-In*" as it was called in this house. So many good memories were here—of his mom and dad, and even more of being here with his brother. Rubbing his hand along the wooden bar top, he remembered how long the sanding and varnishing had taken to get this deep mirror finish. That had been one of his jobs in the remodel, and he still looked at it with pride. The cottage had been a refuge for Scott in other dark times and he hoped he could stay here for the duration.

Finished with his tasks and now well fed, Scott was still unsettled. He knew what was causing it and finally he went to the garage and grabbed a shovel and an old canvas drop cloth. He was soon heading back up the road to the old Buick. He couldn't do much for the man, but he could offer him a decent burial. Getting the now stiff body out of the car wasn't easy, but the man had not been heavy. He looked briefly for ID but found no wallet. To the side of the road was a small open area in the trees. It took only about an hour to dig a moderately deep hole. Wrapping the man in the canvas tarp and laying him as gently into the hole as possible, Scott stood and paid his respects.

"I did not know you in life, but I hope you are at peace." He filled in the hole and walked back to the road. Turning the Buick lights off, he noticed the fuel gauge said half a tank.

Back at the cottage, Scott was tired and ready for sleep. He heard a sound and thought he saw a brief glimmer of light in the darkened rooms. The lights in the kitchen then came on and then back off again. Several long seconds later they came on again, and this time, they stayed on. He checked his watch: 6:00p.m. exactly; one hour until Bobby's power was back on, hopefully. He had a lot to do and no idea how long the power would last. The first thing he did, though, was make himself a small pot of Kona coffee.

EIGHTEEN

Scott found his mood brightening with the lights in the little cottage as the AC and appliances came back on. He closed the open windows to preserve the refreshing cool air coming from the vents. In one way the on and off nature of the power grid was cruel, as it became increasingly clear how dependent he was on it. The more dependent you felt, the less you would be willing to move away from it. He connected his cell phone and some small battery blocks to power adapters to begin charging. He also went to the garage and did the same with an emergency twelve-volt battery backup. Back inside at his work desk he connected his laptop to charge as well, but also opened up the computer and powered it on. The cable modem lights were blinking awake and going through the process of identifying gateways and searching for connections.

Desperate for news, he turned on the television and began scanning channels to find live broadcasts. He was disappointed to find none. He found several channels that contained only crawling news banners, stating that they would resume broadcasting as soon as full power was restored. He then turned his attention back to the laptop.

He had to perform his IP address trick to get any pages to load but found that none had been updated. Appalled at the lack of information, he tried several international websites including Euronews, BBC News, France24, Reuters and Al Jazeera. Thankfully a few of these did have a very basic feed of updated articles. Scott triggered a Clipper program to access and download each of these to separate folders on his laptop so he could review them later. This was much quicker than viewing them all now, and he would have them if the Internet or power went down before he was done.

From what he saw from the headlines, he gathered that things must not be improving. In fact, it looked like things were deteriorating worldwide. His encrypted Cryptocat private chat windows were not connecting, and although his email program connected to the server, it seemed stuck in trying to download new messages. Clicking on his VPN link, Scott was relieved to see that his work servers at DHS came up immediately. Once logged in, his taskbox alert icon was flashing, which meant someone had left him an internal message or some new priority work to do. The taskbox was a way to share information, schedules, and even files or snippets of code with other developers without the material leaving the protected environment of the agencies servers. He clicked the window to open up his message center.

He found new tasking requirements to update and then a request to run continuous audit sweeps looking specifically for intrusion attempts whose patterns tended to originate from North Korea. That was one of his specialties, and he had designed several filters and 'honey traps' specifically to look for that. He deployed those to all active ports on the servers. Additional tasks were not specifically for him but for whatever Level 4 or more developer that was able to log in. Scott was only a relatively new Level 3 analyst. Level 4 was very senior, but when he clicked on the resource links included in the tasking, he was able to view the work folders. Apparently he had been given the equivalence as field promotion. Either that or someone had made a mistake.

In the corner of his screen, his Cryptocat messenger finally connected and immediately a chat bubble popped up. He only had a few contacts on Cryptocat, and he recognized the username on the chat bubble of AlphaCatHCF12. Although he had never personally met the man, he had known him for years. His real name was Tahir, and he lived in Alexandria, VA. He was a young and phenomenally talented former hacker turned white-hat security analyst working for the same government contractor as Scott. Tahir was the person who had first invited Scott to use Cryptocat. It was one of the most secure and private messaging services available.

While most work-related discussions were done in the internal Taskbox app, being able to freely discuss topics the government might frown upon was better done in more anonymous ways like this. Over the years, the working relationship with Tahir, or AlphaCatHCF12, had grown into a pretty close friendship. Scott appreciated the young man's brilliance and the daring nature that showed through at times. The two had also become regular teammates in several multiplayer online combat games where Tahir regularly kicked ass.

The awaiting message was simple and had been sent several hours earlier:

BikerBoy, I saw the logs where you signed on, probably doing the same thing I did to try and pull up any information. Glad you are alive; hope you are doing ok down there in the Bayou. Listen, my friend; I have stumbled onto some fucked up shit. I mean, some serious end of the world level shit going down. Not just the CME blast either, looks like we may all be Pwned. I upgraded your access level and dropped a few things in our shared private folder for you to look at. You will know what it is. Not sure what we can do about it except to be prepared. Dude take precautions, and you know...FFS, be invisible.

Scott was unsure of what Tahir had left him, but it seemed he thought someone might be watching for activity on the server. He sent a quick chat message back to say thanks and that he was doing okay. Hopefully, they could talk live later, but he would use the chat app to leave him messages in the meantime. Pwned was geek speak for someone getting clobbered in a game and FFS was For Fuck's Sake. Now to get back into the work server and see who he was talking about and what else had his friend so rattled.

NINETEEN

Scott quickly navigated to the part of his personal folder that he and Tahir shared. They had set up the encryption protocols on the folder so no one but a full Sysadmin could access it. If that happened, a useful subroutine that the DHS supplied for all top secret work would engage and the data in the folder would self-delete.

He pulled up the only new item, a file called TEOTWAWKI. The name sounded Native American to Scott. He opened up the text document. It was a long file with the title "The End of the World as We Know It". Not wanting to download any files, as that would leave a record, he again clicked his Clipper program to take pictures of the screen and quickly began scrolling to the bottom of the file. In it were several links to other files and folders that just by the address Scott knew were also in Level 4 restricted access areas.

He clicked on the first file folder, named "Catalyst". He was surprised to see that nearly all the files and sub-folders had been updated in the last twenty-four hours. He pulled up several video files included in the top-level briefing folder. The first showed a DHS logo and official "Briefing Only" headline. The screen then showed a green image of the sun with an SDO watermark in the corner. The Solar Dynamics Observatory was responsible for reporting most solar weather events to the government. The timestamp showed that the images were from late morning on the previous day.

Scott watched as several dramatic sunspots came into view and a large arc of plasma looped out from several places, the largest of which appeared to reach the end of its arc and snap away from the sun, blasting into space. A countdown clock started up at the top of the screen: 08:21. The 21 was quickly descending. Not privy to the briefing notes that would have accompanied this video, Scott assumed that the solar flare would reach earth in just over eight minutes from when the flare had broken away. The screen went dark for a moment and was replaced by more video from the European Space Agency. ESA had a solar observing satellite called SOHO—Solar and Heliosphere Observatory. As the video advanced, he saw even more of the looping coronal arcs reach out and break away. Again the clock showed the countdown and the screen of the satellite flared white then went dark as it reached zero.

The next video was recorded apparently from within the International Space Station. It showed the astronauts looking panicked but speaking to someone with a handheld microphone. Scott could not hear the audio due to the limits of the VPN connection. The conversation was animated and very unlike the calm, professional clips usually released to the media outlets by NASA. It appeared to Scott that the crew was beginning to gather belongings, and he saw an open hatch to what he guessed was one of the two lifeboat capsules attached to the ISS. An Asian man was tossing several small bags into one when another astronaut floated over to him and held his arm. Shaking his head, he pointed briefly up past the camera. It appeared to Scott that they both went limp as the camera flared and went dark. The text on the screen said "ISS 10:48 EST All SOB Lost". Scott knew SOB in this case meant "Souls on Board". The initial ultraviolet rays must have been lethal up above Earth's protective atmosphere.

The three other videos were a montage of various clips apparently gathered from around the world in the hours after the CME. One showed a window view of a city skyline he recognized instantly as Chicago. There were no cars moving on the empty streets. Smoke from hundreds of fires streaked the horizon, emanating from several neighboring high-rises. People could be seen attempting to break windows in attempts to get fresh air or maybe just escape. Whoever was filming was apparently using a cell phone as the scene tilted and shook as they ran to the other side of what looked to be a luxury apartment. The awe-inspiring height of the Hancock Building was visible out this window, only its side was darkened, and smoke billowed out of multiple scars down its side. Hanging on the edge of one of the deep gashes in the building was the burnt tail section of a commercial jet. Scott thought briefly about all the times he had flown out of O'Hare and Midway airports and circled up over the beautiful city.

All those flights just raining down on the city he used to call home. That clip ended with a US map covered with hundreds of red dots. The map legend was labeled "Major Known Crash Sites".

Another clip showed celebrations of hundreds of people in a desert region. They had banners, big grins on their face, were firing guns in the air and hugging each other. Scott was unsure of the country but guessed that the loss of electricity was not something that would bother this group if they even noticed. They apparently were just delighted that the Great Satan of the US was finally on its knees. That scene faded and was replaced by what had to be the ruined city of Jerusalem. It appeared the city had suffered terribly, even the always recognizable Dome of the Rock was nothing but scattered debris. Military jets, usually hardened against an EMP blast orbited overhead, but it was unclear if that was Israeli or some other air force.

More video showed looters in various cities around the world. Some of the footage looked professional but most appeared to be taken from security, webcam or cell phone footage. One particular video was of two nurses wheeling an obviously dead naked body on a surgical gurney out of a hospital and into the parking lot. They placed the corpse on a blue tarp, and the shot widened to show hundreds more bodies. The video panned around to the darkened and seemingly abandoned hospital, then up to the windows. Floor after floor of sad faces looked out of nearly every window, taking in the horror around them. Each expression seemed to imply that it too would end up on the overflowing tarp in the parking lot. Apparently unable to go back into that building where they probably could offer no more help, two hospital workers walked out into the dark street.

Other clips showed power transformers arcing blue sparks, some on fire. A plant that Scott thought might be a fuel refinery appeared on screen: a fire raging out of control. Then came a series of grainy CCD videos of what looked to Scott to be nuclear plants belching water and choking smoke from the sides and base of the domes. The faces of the people caught on camera told the story that something had gone horribly wrong.

Some of these videos had not been taken in the US. Others he was less sure about. He finished up the briefing videos and looked at the various other files. He opened and scrolled, capturing everything he could to view them in-depth later. He knew he could probably lose his job for what he was doing, but at this point, that didn't seem to matter. Two other folders caught his eye. The first was named "ASSETS_ACTIVE" and the other "CATALYST-CME". Others such as "CATALYST-PANDEM1", "CATALYST-ECO", "PRAETOR5", "and PRAETOR9" could wait for now.

Opening "ASSETS_ACTIVE" first, Scott viewed two short PowerPoint documents whose slides focused on what were deemed to be trouble spots. One slide deck was labeled "Domestic" and the other "International". It appeared to be the type of boring government data he would sometimes see from the Census Bureau, and indeed some of the slides in the domestic presentation even had the Department of Agriculture seal and copyright. What this was indicating, though, was that the national food supply existed in 15-day increments.

Other slides showed the most vulnerable power sub-stations, power grid-down areas and critical connections, LPT or Large Power Transformer ratings, and specs and resupply information. He was surprised to see that these things were very expensive, custom-built, and mostly over thirty years old. The other thing that caught his attention was that all of the transformers replacements indicated overseas suppliers; virtually nothing was kept in inventory. Apparently these were custom to each site installation and not just a standard item whose inventory could be made in advance and held in reserve. Even worse, the delivery estimates beside each item ranged from eighteen to twenty-four months. That was assuming the manufacturing plants were operating at peak efficiency, and worldwide demand was no more than average. Right now, Scott thought, these plants were probably as dark as everywhere else, and every power grid in the world would likely be needing replacement parts that now would not exist.

Opening more files, he saw timelines and a projected rise of social unrest, looting, limiting media coverage and what appeared to be a minimal domestic FEMA assistance as well as possible troop deployment. Another map indicated certain areas that could remain relatively unscathed, likely those run by private or alternative energy. These areas were so small they barely showed up on the map.

A similar map was dated several years previous and showed a feasibility study for failsafe fallback zones—areas in which power, water, and even food supply routes could be reestablished more easily. Most of these were near a stand-alone power supply: such as a hydroelectric dam, a nuclear plant or a wind farm. The color-coded charts were mostly colorless but showed many areas in the Midwest, California marked in green and blue which apparently meant survivable regions. Scattered around the Southern US were also a few isolated pockets of color. Even here in the Gulf, there was a large section in dark gray. When Scott checked the map legend, it indicated the area was marginal but possibly survivable. *At least we must have some of what is needed*, Scott thought. Much of the country and all of the northern states were a stark, empty white.

Many of the files were of a similar nature. Lastly, he clicked his mouse on the folder "CATALYST-CME and opened up the first file titled "Mission Action Report". The files were coded SAP, or Specialized Access Program, a condition of ultra-high confidential and secret data. It was only used for the most sensitive information. Scott knew damn well he did not have this level of clearance and could only assume Tahir had recovered these files elsewhere and placed them here for Scott to view. He probably should just close the folders and cancel the session. Even inadvertently accessing something like this would be big trouble for him.

He paused, looking down at his laptop screen. *This is decision time.* Did he feel that things were going to recover, or was this the end? If it was the end, this information might help him prepare, even survive. The truth was, up until this minute he had been going down dual paths, preparing for the worst but not believing it was that bad. He thoughtfully considered all the data he had and came to the conclusion he had been avoiding. The shit had indeed hit the fan yesterday. The impact of what this meant was enormous but Scott's analytical brain still could see no other possibility. Yesterday was the end. He would review everything and fuck the consequences.

TWENTY

The first of the highly secure documents detailed multiple national studies that the government, US Navy, and several universities had undertaken in the last decade to predict the likelihood of, and resulting disaster from, a Carrington Level CME event.

Reading down, Scott saw that the event was named after the astronomer that first noticed massive solar flare in 1859. During that time, the world's dependence on electricity had still been in its infancy. Telegraph was the main mode of communication over long distance, and only a small percentage of homes and businesses used electrical lighting. Even so, this storm had caused a lot of problems, including fires and possibly even a few deaths. The solar flare had wreaked havoc on the power and telegraph lines. It was later described as a one in one-hundred-year event.

The odds of having a direct hit from another similar sized or greater CLE Carrington Level Event in our lifetime, he read, was nearly 100 percent. Scott paused and re-read that. *The odds of this happening are 100 percent.* That meant that people…that the government knew that this was going to happen. Scott read on.

It appeared to Scott that the decision had been made to water down the report and put the odds as one in twelve, which was still high but wouldn't alarm the public as much. This didn't surprise him as he had been privy to many things in his government work that had never been released in its raw form. In this case though, the raw facts were spelled out on the summary page for whoever had been briefed: **For the average person there will be absolutely nothing they can do to prepare to the level necessary to survive the event or the resultant crisis. Where and how the CME and its subsequent electromagnetic waves**

impact the Earth more random than predictable or preventable, so, the worst case scenarios or survival rates cannot be calculated with any degree of certainty but will likely be the highest in the more developed countries where the populous is most dependent on electrical power.

These words leaped off the screen and grabbed at Scott. The government never left anything to chance. What was most chilling were the spreadsheets of projected mortality rates. In week one: Up to five million people worldwide would likely die. If that were not bad enough, multiple models concluded that in the first twenty months, over ninety percent of the world population would also die, simply from causes relating either directly or indirectly to loss of electrical power.

Scott was stunned at the magnitude and the callousness of the report but kept scrolling and capturing the data to his laptop. Opening and quickly reading yet another file, he read:

"Project Catalyst is one of the contingent plans available during a National SOE (State of Emergency) which, in our opinion, will offer the best option of Continuation of Government. Despite the massive loss of life, this would not be considered an ELE (Extinction Level Event)."

So, mankind would continue although certainly many countries would fall and the world, in general, would be a very different place. In the weeks after the event, attempts would be made to keep power, communication, and supplies flowing although be on a limited basis. This would allow emergency service to be established, shipments of supplies to be routed, and assets transferred to less affected areas. All of this was to help calm the general public and attempt to maintain a state of equilibrium. The political pressure on the media would suggest that the problems were bad but that it would be temporary. Depending on the scale of the disaster, the focus or primary assets targeted was numerous key people who were to be remanded to state custody for safekeeping during the crises. This list seemed to include Scientist, teachers, doctors, and engineers. Scott would have expected military and political leaders to dominate the list. That very absence made Scott wonder again who created this plan.

The reports went on to describe that even those efforts would not last long. Several of the documents were for coordination with the DOD for the military's role and interaction with the state government and National Guard forces. Many of the items were field guides for the designated regional officials. They were instructed to refer to these contingency plans and instructional guides to carry out their responsibilities.

Scott abandoned more of his training and paranoia and began to download the PDF versions of each of the manuals. Several things occurred to him. First, he couldn't tell who had put the plan together or how Tahir had found them, but none of these documents were originated within the DHS. Secondly, he had no way of knowing if the plans had been activated yet or not; no approval orders were apparent, but that in itself would not have been a surprise. What was odd was that not a single person's name was to be found on the reports anywhere.

He felt numb, but rapidly opened and closed each of the files in the folders, making sure that archived images were being stored on his laptop. He saw the emergency plans that went far beyond even martial law, including emergency food shipments, forced rationing, bank closure instructions, asset forfeitures, and even prison cleansing procedures. It seemed that lethal force was to be the recommended course of action for nearly every criminal offense.

The research suggested that in a power vacuum or under any absence of clear authority, gangs and later warlords would likely establish themselves in many areas, practically inevitable in any area without a functional government. Catalyst protocols indicated they would necessarily intervene. In fact, it recommended a very hands-off approach to establishing order in the short-term. Even more confusing, as Scott scanned more of the page he realized that in some instances, it appeared the leadership in such a scenario might even suggest provoking situations to speed up a collapse. The rationale apparently was that the only way to survive as a nation was to reduce population numbers quickly. Triaging the situation, like a Civil War surgeon deciding it better to cut off the damaged limbs than to lose the entire patient.

More documents and guides were included covering everything from reestablishing communication networks to setting up of trade, reestablishing a workable currency, and eliminating all but the most basic of social programs. Lastly came the simple statement that immediately after the CME the US constitution would have to be suspended, along with rights and privileges that document provided for the country's citizens. There was even the outline proposal of a new provisional form of government for the country to use. It was pretty simple. It kept the basic democratic aspects and incorporated much of the original Bill of Rights and the Constitution but would be structured to eliminate some of the most glaring faults of the current system. More power would be provided to the states under this revised form of government, and personal responsibility was really the key component. If what Scott was seeing was accurate, it would also be designed to be compatible with the proposed governments of all other surviving new world governments. The solar event would be the catalyst to a new and different world and a new America.

He honestly didn't know how to take in everything he was seeing. While the analyst in him wanted to dissect all of the information, he had more immediate problems to deal with. He would try and go through all of it later. But, two things had occurred to him. If this were an actual plan and not just someone else's, "Thought experiment." It would be a conspiracy at the highest level of our government. Second, if it were put into play, it may have been done for the right reasons, the very survival of the United States. It suggests revisions to law enforcement that would seem outrageous by current standards. Justice would be swift and without mercy. Even the revised governmental structure seemed like a pretty good solution to Scott. Taken as a whole the plans were ruthless and simple; it would potentially correct a lot of the problems of the country's leadership. With only a projected ten percent of the population expected to survive, it would likely take something this draconian to be successful.

It didn't seem feasible to Scott that anyone in Washington, DC would have sanctioned its creation, much less, allowed this Catalyst plan to be put into action. He pinged AlphaCat but got no response. Scott was more aware than most of the troubles in the nation's capital. Politicians' main job these days was no longer to help run the country it was to get re-elected and to help raise money for the political party. One unclassified report at DHS he had read suggested that as much as 60% of members of congress time is spent in fundraising. There were reasons politicians had exempted themselves from the "do not call," telemarketing legislation.

Scott had no love for politicians and admitted a shakeup was needed, if not a complete dismantling of the US political system. His head was buzzing as he left Tahir a message to tell him he had the information and thanks. He would review it more and try to be back in touch soon.

TWENTY-ONE

The power was still on in the little cottage, and the scene could have been of any other Thursday night in August, but it had taken on a much more somber feel to Scott Montgomery. He moved away from the laptop, his stomach churning. The more he considered what Tahir had shared, the more scared he got. He was pretty sure his sphincter had tightened considerably. The ass-clinching ramifications of what he had read were staggering. The world's governments, or at least the US, were going to wipe the slate clean.

Survival of the fittest from here on out. What would survival even mean? What would there be to look forward to? In time, he could see the possibility of a brighter future, even the possibility of a better world, but he would be walking in darkness for many years until that day. The lone man in his cottage had an unfamiliar need; he desperately wanted to speak with someone, anyone. Just another human voice. Looking at the time, he took his cell phone from the charging stand and dialed his brother's number. It rang twice before he heard Bobby's familiar voice.

Relieved beyond words, Scott quickly got caught up on news from his brother and his family. They were all okay but still had had no word from their daughter Kaylie. The situation in their town near Little Rock had been mostly fine so far. The stores had taken to rationing quickly, and fuel stations had been ordered closed by the governor. Thankfully Bobby and Jessie had worked his disaster plan, quickly topping off all the fuel, food, and supplies they could gather. Bobby said they were fine for now but ready to head to his bug-out cabin up in the Ozarks if it looked like things were heading sideways. They were desperate to reach Kaylie, though. "Scott," his brother said, "Only Dad's old truck is still running. The CME killed my new Ford pickup and Jessie's car. If I can get the transmission working a little better on the old pickup, we could take it down there. It'll use all the fuel we have just to get down to her. I know it's risky and probably not a smart use of resources, but we're getting pretty desperate to reach her. I wish we had some way of knowing if this is just temporary or that it really is The Big Crunch." His big brother had always called any doomsday scenario by this term.

"Bro, I think this is it. In fact, I think the other day was probably the last easy day any of us will ever have." Scott decided to tell his brother some of what he had learned in the last few hours.

Bobby seemed to take it all in, then said, "That doesn't sound like any government response we would expect. They're just going to leave millions of people to die? That's some seriously fucked up shit. What about the military? All their stuff is supposed to be hardened against EMP blasts. Why wouldn't they be recalled to the mainland to help preserve order? Keep some level of continuity of government? I'm not sure I believe the other branches of government would sanction any of that."

Scott didn't know what to reply, "Look, Bobby, I agree with you, and we may be looking at a possible coup of some sort. I haven't gone through even a fraction of the information yet. Maybe I missed something big. This could be just one contingency plan among many that were on the table. Maybe Catalyst's not the one they're actually going to go with. In either case, I just think it's going to get worse from here on." He went on in a somewhat shaky voice, "Bobby, I can go....I can go to the university and find Kaylie. If the situation looks bad there, I'll just bring her back here to the cottage."

Bobby considered it but said no.

"It's okay man, I love her too; she's family, and the school is only about 200 miles away. Hell, I can get there on my bike if I wanted."

"Yeah, yeah, I here you Le Pirat," Bobby said, referring to one of Scott's favorite bicycling champions.

"Seriously Scott, making a trip like this violates all of my rules for survival, and she's *our* daughter. I can't put you in that position." Then in a low voice, he added, "Not yet anyway. Let me see if I can get any of these other cars road-ready. Jess will keep trying to get through to her or some of her friends down there. We may be worrying over nothing." Bobby took a very long pause before continuing. "In the meantime, if you're willing at least, be thinking about how you might safely get to her if we do need you to try."

"You only have to ask, man."

"Listen, little brother, if it does come to that you can't do it alone, though... do you understand me? I know you're the Lone Ranger and all, but you'll need help, a friend, someone to watch your back. The roads are already getting dangerous and the cities even more so."

Scott told him not to worry; he said he thought he had a few new friends that might be willing to help. Bobby asked, "Who the hell would you make friends with?"

"A few guys from Harris Springs. One of them's nearly as crazy as you are about the survivalist shit," Scott answered.

Laughing, Bobby asked his name.

"Bartos," Scott said.

"Oh fuck," Bobby said. "You hooked up with that crazy bastard? I met him when the county was doing some road work near the cottage. He has some serious issues man, although he is a rock-solid prepper... probably a good friend to have. Tell him I said hi and to please ask him to help you not die."

Not totally surprised that Bobby knew the guy, Scott laughed and said he would. The remainder of the conversation contained a brief hello to Bobby's wife, Jessie. She was trying hard to hold it together, but Scott could tell how worried she was. "Jess, I am sure she is alright; the school is probably the safest place right now." She tried to agree, but her voice cracked. She was a mother, and the "not knowing" was making her crazy.

Jess put Bobby back on, and Scott told him about the supplies and plans he had managed to figure out in the short time since the event. Bobby seemed genuinely impressed and only made a few brotherly comments to the effect of, "That's unnecessary" or 'effing' "ridiculous." He was very concerned about Scott's lack of firepower and ammo, though.

"Scott, you will need it. It will likely be what keeps you alive."

"I know, Bobby; I'm just not sure I could actually shoot someone, though. I carry Pop's pistol with me now but…"

"Scott," his brother said, "Listen, you shoot people in those video games you love so much. You better get it in your head quickly. You have to be ready before the time comes. There are going to be some dangerous fucks running around. There are already rumors that the prison population here in Arkansas is being released. They can't keep them fed. You'll have every gangbanger, methhead, and psychotic out on the roads in the next few days looking for easy prey. Even if most people you deal with are decent, you have to assume otherwise. You remember what Dad always said, "Hope for th—"

Scott cut him off, "I know… I get it, Bro. I won't hesitate."

"Make sure you don't," Bobby said. "Listen. It may also be my daughter's life you're protecting. I'll need to know you can do that."

"I got it," Scott said quietly. "You know you guys can count on me. Besides, she loves me best anyway."

"Yeah right, just 'cause you always give her more expensive gifts than Jess and I can," Bobby scoffed.

The other concern that Bobby mentioned was the fact that Scott had no real plan for a bug-out shelter. Scott agreed to think of one. "More than one," Bobby said. "You'll probably need a back-up or two." Bobby had been making notes as they talked and said, "I'm going to make a list of stuff for you to try and find, buy, or steal. Also, some basic rules that might help keep you alive. Our email isn't working, but I'll leave the file on my desktop screen. Think you can manage to log in to our computer like you do when I get you to do remote work on it?" That was a damn good idea.

He'd not even remembered the virtual remote desktop support program they had loaded so he could log in to Bobby's PC and troubleshoot for them when needed. "I'll also try and drop some of the files I got from work so you guys can see what the Catalyst plan is," Scott responded. "There are some big multi-syllable words in it so Jess will probably have to read it to you," Scott said grinning.

"Hey, fuck you, Brother," Bobby laughed.

"Fuck you too," Said Scott lovingly. "I'll come up with a plan just in case you need me to head over to Tallahassee in the next day or two. Love you guys."

He heard Bobby's voice unusually quiet. He knew the proud man did not like asking anyone for help, especially when it put his own brother's life at risk. "Scott, you are a good man, and you are a much stronger man than you know. We'll find a way to let you know about Kaylie. See ya, Brother – love you."

He thought about his niece and pulled out a map to Tallahassee and one of the FSU campus. No way he had the gas to get there, so that was problem number one. Second was he wasn't sure he could even find Kaylie if he did go. She could have tried to get home on her own or not be at her apartment. The final concern was protection. Scott was realizing more and more that he was not a fighter; he had only the one pistol and was probably not ready to face any real trouble. Just seeing a dead guy had royally fucked up his night.

Deep down he knew he was going to have to go to Tallahassee, but he was definitely apprehensive. He decided he would try to meet up with Jack or one of the other guys tomorrow and talk with them about it. For now, though, he fixed himself another cup of coffee, enjoyed the cool AC, and went to take a hot shower. He dozed off afterward to a rerun of the "Tonight Show" from several months earlier. Shortly after that, up and down the coast, the lights in all the houses went dark. Several hundred miles above, the glowing ribbons of pink and red light danced once again.

TWENTY-TWO

Day 3

The early morning salt air felt good—seemed right—Todd thought. Although he did feel guilty having to leave his wife behind today. The fishermen who had booked the charter hadn't shown, and he had the boat rigged and ready for fishing. His assistant had shown up just long enough to help hand-pump the eighty-six gallons of fuel into the *Donna Marie*. Then the kid left, claiming some excuse about looking for his granddad who had gone missing.

His friend Bartos had easily been talked into joining him and had shown up with two cases of beer. They needed one more person to make it a decent fishing trip. It took Captain Todd a while to find the third member of the crew. Walking from the docks over to Shirley's Coffee Shop and then to the church, he couldn't find Preacher Jack at either of his normal hangouts. *Damn phones*, Todd thought. How easy it would have been to just call the guy to see if he wanted to go out today. The power had been on earlier, and he had assumed that phones were down, but he now realized he wasn't sure. He punched the stored number for his friend, who answered on the first ring. As expected, Jack sounded jubilant. He was over at the government building and would be down at the docks in five minutes.

With the three friends settled in and an ice chest filled with the beer, Todd gathered their smartphones and dropped them into a waterproof gear box. Starting the big twin engines, he pushed the lever to maneuver the beautiful boat away from the docks and into the main channel, which led out past the seawall and into the blue waters of the Gulf. There were sailboats out, as well as a few other small boats, but not nearly as many as normal. Getting through the breakwaters and into the open sea, Todd motored down the coast for about five miles. Seeing families out enjoying an early morning on the beach, it was hard to imagine this was not just another day. He knew it was a terrible waste of fuel, taking the boat out like this, but fuel they had, at least for now. Several of the restaurants in town had told him that if they brought in some fresh fish, they would try and continue serving cheap meals for the town's people, who were running low on food. They were willing to trade beer, ice, and other bulk foods as well. Todd also wanted to put some fish back for him and his friends if he could.

Stopping several hundred yards off shore at a marker buoy, the three men cast their small lines for baitfish. Todd ran a casting net on the other side of the boat to do the same. Within about twenty minutes they had a live-well loaded with Spanish sardines, small mullet, shad, glass minnows and more to use further out to sea in catching the larger gamefish. Bartos stowed the lines and net and Todd steered towards to the first fishing, spot about five miles out. Once stopped, Bartos began rigging the primary fishing rods. "What are we fishing for today Cap?" he asked.

"Whatever's biting. I'd like to get about 200 lbs. Not sure we can trade or use more than that. King mackerel, Spanish mackerel, dorado, maybe even a yellowfin. Rig yours and Jack's for top water fishing first. I'm gonna drop some of these shad deeper in the water column and see if I can snag some snapper or grouper."

"Gotcha," came Bartos' quick response. The three had fished together often, and Bartos had served as a first mate on multiple boats growing up. Jack was less comfortable at sea but was always patient, good company, and rarely lost a fish once hooked.

Quickly the three men settled down in the fishing chairs with multiple lines in the water and a cold beer in the cup holder of each chair. Todd asked Jack if he had heard any more news.

"Best information so far was from that young guy at the bar yesterday."

"Scott?" Todd asked. "Yea, I liked him."

"Nice guy. Smart, but maybe a bit naive."

Todd nodded in agreement, "Are you really going to teach him Keysi?"

Jack nodded, "If he wants to learn, yeah. He's in good shape; lower body strength at least. I think he could pick up the basics pretty fast." Jack was well-schooled in the street fighting techniques of the Keysi Fighting Method, or KFM as it was commonly referred to: a nearly-no-rules, hand-to-hand fighting style almost as damaging as the Krav Maga technique. Jack had picked it up somewhere in his checkered past and become an instructor in recent years. He practiced with a small group of devotees in a gym downtown.

The preacher went on, "I was over at the sheriff's office when you called. They have their hands full—a lot of deaths in the county, mostly from existing medical conditions. People who needed ongoing treatments they couldn't get."

Todd grimaced when he heard this, but his friend didn't seem to notice. Bartos made a noise and nearly spilled his beer as the rod closest to him bent sharply in the holder. The reel began to sing as a fish took the line. Grabbing it, he began reeling it in, grinning broadly.

"What else did the Sheriff say?" Todd asked. Preacher Jack leaned up and looked out to where the taut line from Bartos' rod entered the water.

"Just that he's not expecting things to get better. Power'll be on in irregular rolling blackouts. We should expect more hours of grid-down than grid-up. About half of his force didn't show up for shifts yesterday. Some radioed in that their patrol vehicles wouldn't start, but others were just a no-show. The Police Chief is also AWOL. He was out of town at an active shooter table session when the flare hit. They and the Fire Chief have similar issues. The Sheriff's been in touch by radio with the state capital to request National Guard troops, but they don't feel our area has a lot to protect, so they suggested we muster volunteers to help patrol."

Bartos reeled the fat Spanish mackerel over the side and dropped it into the cooler. "Did you mention what we talked about yesterday to him?" Bartos asked.

Nodding his head, the preacher said, "Yes, I did, and he said he wasn't sure he could do any of that unless martial law was declared.

"Why the fuck not?" Todd asked. "If someone doesn't take stock of whatever supplies are still available then looters and hoarders will likely take them. He needs to go to the stores and collect whatever could be used for the communal good and find a safe place to store it under armed guard. Food, fuel, emergency supplies…"

"Believe me, I know," said Jack. "In fact, he told me someone'd already broken into one of the school lunchrooms and stolen a lot of the stored food. What's worse is they left the walk-in cooler door open, ruining everything else they couldn't take." Another reel began to sing, and Todd reached for it.

"Sheriff Jones says that it's too soon to be thinking that way. Said it sounded to him like something that damn fool Bartos might suggest," Jack continued, winking at Bartos as he said it. "He didn't think people around here, or business owners, would take kindly to having their inventory confiscated for the public good."

Todd reeled in the fish and added it to the box. Taking a pull from his beer before re-baiting the line, he said, "The problem is most people are in denial. There's just enough normalcy that no one is panicking yet. We know that the shit hit the fan, but until some more of that shit hits them personally, it's not going to be real to them. When it does, though, there'll be a panic like this country's never seen."

The three men sat talking, drinking and fishing for several more hours. The fish were biting well but beginning to slow when Todd estimated they had about two-thirds of what he'd hoped to get today. He was thinking about moving back in-shore and netting the rest in mullet. Not a great tasting fish but easy to smoke and they'd stay preserved that way for quite a while. Some of the other fish could be salted and preserved as well.

Bartos had the Steiner Marine optics up to his eyes looking southwest. "What the fuck is that?" he said to no one in particular. Handing the waterproof binoculars to Todd, he pointed to the western horizon. Todd could just make out what looked to be a full naval fleet moving in close formation. Destroyers, cruisers, battleships, escort vessels… even Seahawk helicopters orbiting near the larger ships. The entire battalion was steaming ahead, heading east.

"It would appear…" Todd said slowly, "that the electronics shielding on our military vessels was much better than the hardening done to other ships or our national power grid."

"I wonder where they're heading," Jack said.

"No clue, but once they go by I can slip in behind them and probably get a fix on the heading," replied Todd.

Fifteen minutes later the armada was passing about two miles to the port side of the *Donna Marie*. One of the loud helicopters thundered over for a closer inspection. Looking and sounding like an angry hornet, the three men struggled not to act alarmed. They waved from their fishing chairs and held up a beer to the flying war machine bristling with weapons. Apparently they passed inspection and the crew correctly assumed the small fishing boat was not a threat as it soon resumed to its patrol orbit. Before the last of the ships passed by, the large wake generated by the ships began bobbing the fishing boat like a cork in a bottle. Todd started the engine and drove parallel to the fleet in the opposite direction. The movement of the *Donna Marie* helped stabilize it against the rocking waves, for which they were all thankful.

Once the last vessel was about half a mile behind them, Todd turned into the wake and maneuvered the boat directly in line with the trail of the departing ships. Taking multiple readings from the largest of the ships, a cruiser class vessel, he began plotting a bearing on the charts.

Suddenly he felt something, something definitely wrong. Then he heard a humming coming from everywhere. The sound seemed to be emanating from within the very hull of his boat. He looked aft and saw both of his friends pointing at a huge mound of water moving directly toward the *Donna Marie*. The sight did not register with what he should be seeing; water just didn't behave that way. Stepping out of the bridge deck, he noticed that it was not one bulge but two, several hundred yards apart. Todd had spent over twenty years in the Navy, although not all of that had been at sea. He had seen large whales move the water in this way, but this was too large and too fast to be anything natural.

"Oh shit," he said, "Submarines!" he yelled, "Brace for impact!"

One of the behemoths, pushing a nearly twelve-foot wave in front, passed on the starboard side, and the other passed within fifty yards to the port. The combined crushing force of these waves swept over the rear of the *Donna Marie* and for a brief moment most of the fishing vessel was technically underwater. Todd's mind told him, *This is it, I have killed myself and my friends.*

The wave subsided as the subs pushed quickly past, but the damage was done. The *Donna Marie* was listing at an odd angle. Todd found Bartos wedged up against a rear bulkhead, but there was no sign of Jack. Todd called for him but heard no reply. The noise of the water rushing off the deck and back into the sea drowned out all other sounds. Todd helped Bartos to his feet and began searching the nearby water for their other friend. He saw nothing but flotsam from his boat: cushions, life vests, and empty beer cans. He knew Jack could swim, but he might be injured or unconscious. In a panic, he grabbed the Steiner marine binoculars and glassed the area further out. Nothing.

Moving along the narrow path to the bow of the boat, his deck shoes waded through the small river of sea water running back from the bow to the lower rear side. As he reached the front, he could see the two humps of water receding into the distance several hundred yards ahead.

He only saw the smallest part of a conning tower at the surface, which put the main body of the craft about thirty feet below. He knew they must be traveling at top speed to be creating that much of a wave. Just behind the subs, he thought he saw something. He scanned the area again, adjusting the focus dial on the Steiners to sharpen the image. He saw a flash of color again. It moved quickly to the side, then back again. He could just make out a hand on one edge and behind it the shadow of a person's head. *Must be Jack!* he thought, momentarily relieved. *Fuck.*

Leaping back to the bridge he checked on Bartos as he started the engines. Bartos had a pretty large gash on his forearm, and a goose-egg was forming on his forehead, but he yelled that he was fine. The engines turned over several times and for a moment did not sound like they wanted to start. Todd knew the engine, battery compartment, and fuel tanks were in dry areas and supposedly waterproof, though that had been a ridiculous amount of water to sweep over the boat. He was not sure what problems it may have caused. At the very least some had likely gotten down into other areas as the boat was developing a noticeable list to starboard. Finally, the engines caught, and he aimed the waterlogged craft in the direction of the floating white shape where he hoped his friend was still hanging.

Coming up on Jack on the port side, he slowed to a coast and tried to ease the boat close but not so close as to hit him. He needn't have worried as it turned out. The white top of an ice chest cooler came sailing from the water over the side of the boat. Bartos was hanging over the transom pulling an arm. Hurrying back to help, Todd saw that Jack was indeed okay. With the two men pulling him, Jack came sliding over the sidewalls and flopped onto the fishing deck like a giant tuna.

"What the fuck was that all about?" Bartos asked.

Todd, more concerned with his friend, checked Jack from head to toe, but the resilient man appeared to be fine.

"When I saw the wave coming and heard you yell "Brace" I grabbed for a handhold. Unfortunately, what I grabbed was the beer chest, and it wasn't attached to anything. I went ass over feet right over the boat. Then I got caught in the pull of the subs. I could hear the propellers as they pulled me along underwater. Thought I was going to drown." the preacher recounted as he gasped for air.

"Screws," Todd said.

"Damn right" Jack responded.

"No," Todd said laughing. "On subs, they're called screws, not propellers."

"Who gives a good, holy fuck?" Jack said, his panic residing.

"Sorry, old friend, bad habit after a lifetime in the Navy. Are you sure you're okay?"

They checked each other out, and then the *Donna Marie* itself. The bilge pumps on the starboard side were clearing water quickly, and the boat was slowly leveling. It appeared that all they'd lost was the beer cooler, the beer, and the baitfish. "So do you think they were trying to sink us?" Bartos asked.

"I don't think they even knew we were there," Jack said.

"They knew," Todd answered. "They had to come up to surface depth to create that wave. I know they weren't on the surface when we moved in behind the fleet. They weren't trying to sink us, but they were sending a message."

"What kind of message?" Jack asked.

"Don't get too nosy, forget we were here," Todd replied with a shrug.

Bartos had the go-bag out and was getting a bandage for his arm. He looked at the preacher. "You had one job man, just save the beer ...and what did you do?" Laughing, he patted the big man. "Glad, you're okay, Padre."

They stripped off their wet clothes to let them dry. After checking out the boat thoroughly and finding no serious problems, they decided to continue fishing. Todd suggested they head over to the old #148 oil rig to restock baitfish.

TWENTY-THREE

Ugh morning, the house was already suffocatingly hot. Scott stumbled over to open up the still shuttered windows, but the morning air outside was humid and still. He poured the rest of the coffee from the night before into a mug and tried to drink it cold, but he couldn't do it. Standing on the back deck in nothing but a pair of gym shorts, he debated on taking his bike into town for a cup of good coffee and to maybe catch one of the guys there.

Eventually, the need to ride overrode his need for caffeine. He exchanged gym shorts for his cycling outfit, filled a few water bottles for the trip, and pulled the Trek off the wall. The only new addition was a lighter version of his EDC. This one contained the bare essentials, plus the pistol; he had decided to take his new friend's advice and never go anywhere without it.

Scott planned a bike route that would allow him to pretty safely see many of the main roads coming in and out of Bay County. His trip would also come back through town, so hopefully he could still get in touch with one of the guys. Finally, he had an idea about getting more fuel that he wanted to scope out. Locking the house, he clipped his feet into the pedals and headed out, riding west.

• • •

The ride didn't seem that different from any other day. The temperature was rising and already he could feel the heat radiating from the pavement. He could smell the brackish swamp water as he navigated around its perimeter. There was no traffic again today, but he was purposefully avoiding the busier routes. The way he was going would lead him across these roads at several intersections so he could see if any trouble was ahead. Much of the route would run parallel to the busier scenic highway.

Far up ahead, he saw a car parked on the side of the road and immediately his mind fell back to the previous day and the dead man hanging from the car. He slowed as he passed the little hybrid Toyota. Thankfully, no one was inside, alive or dead. Scott considered himself a bit of an environmentalist like most cyclists he knew were. At one time he had considered purchasing a car just like this one. Seeing how vulnerable it had been to the CME, he was glad he had stuck with his gas-guzzling Jeep. He clicked the gear lever and quickly began to pick up speed. While being out on a bike ride this morning may not have seemed like the best way to plan for a rescue trip, for Scott it was essential and allowed him the time to think in transit without wasting any gas.

He could see the familiar black ribbon of road snaking out for miles ahead. As he rode, he paid special attention to the vacation properties in the area. He doubted that many of the owners would ever be back to enjoy these dream homes. He knew some of them could hold valuable resources. While Scott was not ready to resort to scavenging, he didn't rule it out for the future and made mental notes of the most promising looking homes. There was one item that he wasn't above borrowing, as it was a vital part of his plan to get to Kaylie. He needed fuel for the Jeep.

As he rode, he saw virtually no one outside. Even the homes that he knew were occupied seemed ominously quiet and lifeless. He began to wonder why more people weren't out making preparations but thought again to yesterday: how most people were just going about their days, seemingly oblivious to any problems. Sure, the power was off and on, but while that sucked, most were probably more upset at their cell phones suddenly being useless. *No Facebook posts or status updates to comment on.* Scott was unsure why he had taken things so much more seriously than most, even before reading the DHS files.

He noticed a child playing in the front yard of an aging mobile home. As he rode by she gave a little wave with a dirty hand. What did she have to look forward to, he wondered. *What kind of world will she grow up in?*

Coming up on Highway 50 he saw a Sheriff's car and a makeshift roadblock. The Deputy was leaning against the car with a nearly empty bottle of water. Normally Scott would have kept going, but today he wanted information, and a guy in Lycra shorts riding seemed pretty non-threating to everyone, he reasoned. He pulled over. "Hi!" he called. The Deputy's badge said "Warren", but he did not introduce himself to Scott. "Officer, how goes it?" Scott said.

The Deputy replied, "Hotter than shit out here. Don't know how you ride that thing in this." He waved his bottle in the air to make his point.

"So why the roadblock?"

"Oh, you can go on through. I know you live over near the beach, I've seen you out riding before. I'm just here to steer any refugees on elsewhere."

"What do you mean by refugees?" Scott inquired.

Leaning in conspiratorially, the Deputy said, "Beats the fuck outta me. I was told this was my road and not to let anyone but locals in. The Sheriff came by about an hour ago and said to be on the lookout. He just got word that the prison camp over in the next county released all its "non-violent" offenders. Some judge told them they had to if they couldn't provide AC, food, n' hot water. You believe that shit? Probably five or six hundred convicts total, not sure how many are 'non-violent' but guess what's the closest town? Yep, Harris Springs."

Not unexpected but certainly not good news, Scott thought. Most of those guys would likely head back to their homes, but some of them would indeed probably come this way. "That's insane," Scott said, "The power's only been off a few days. What are they going to do when they get out here in the world and discover they probably had it better in prison?"

"Yeah really," Officer Warren said. "Word is the power's likely going to be off more than on for a while, and some judge or politician felt that was inhumane, I am sure it is hot as hell inside those prisons but shit, let 'em camp outside on the grounds or something. It would be tough to keep order, though. With only a few of the guards even able to make it into work, they're just giving up. Today the non-violent ones but in a few more days, they will likely cut 'em all

CATALYST : DOWNWARD CYCLE | 117

loose."

After a few more minutes of conversation, it became apparent that was about all the deputy knew. "Well, thanks, Officer, I appreciate the information and the job you're doing for us," Scott said. "I guess your radios aren't working since the Sheriff came by to update you."

Nodding, the Deputy said, "Nah, they're bricks."

"Well, do you need anything?" Scott asked.

The Deputy smiled and said, "Not unless you got a sandwich on you, or even better some biscuits and gravy. Nothing was open this mornin' when I headed out, so all I got is water."

Thinking for a moment, Scott said, "Hang on a second." He fished around in the small pack and found a couple of peanut butter energy bars and a small bag of trail mix. Handing them to the deputy, he said, "It's not much, but maybe it'll help."

The officer reluctantly nodded his head no, but eventually took the offering. He asked Scott what his name was again.

"Scott. Scott Montgomery."

Officer Warren shook his hand. "Thank you, Scott. That was a very nice thing to do."

Scott nodded and wished the man luck as he began pedaling away.

• • •

The small road Scott was on continued for about eight more miles before it began to parallel the main road into town. Scott could see more cars stopped on the side of the road. Several groups of people were walking, a few on ATV's, and there were a few more people on bikes than yesterday. Say what you will, but the end of the world was certainly going to be better for the environment, he thought. It was nearly lunchtime when he pulled into Harris Springs. Heading first to Shirley's, which was sadly still closed, he then walked over to the sports bar looking for Jack, Todd, or Bartos. One of the servers recognized him and said she'd heard that Todd and the others had gone out on Todd's boat to fish. If so, they'd likely be out until late afternoon. Nodding, Scott asked what they were serving today.

"Beer," she said. "And that's about it." They could fix a few sandwiches with chips, so he ordered both.

Sitting in the bar in his bike jersey and cycling shorts drinking a lukewarm beer was an unusual way to be spending his time, but right now he would rather be eating other people's food than his own. The people in town may all be convinced that everything was fine, but he was no longer that naive.

He thought about the roadblocks and the prisoner release. *That deputy and the others may never even get paid again and yet they're still putting their asses on the line.* He called the waitress back over and asked for a couple more sandwiches and a couple of bottles of beer to go.

"Sure thing hon," she winked and hurried off. Settling his bill, he took the bag of sandwiches and beer and headed to his bike. He stashed the extra food and drinks in his pack and began to circle lazily around the town checking to see what else might be open. Of main interest were the gas stations, but they were all dark and empty.

• • •

He rode over to the docks and looked at the empty boat slip where a painted charter sign identified the *Donna Marie* and Captain Todd's berth. Seeing the phone number on the sign, he thought about calling the guys. He tried Todd's number. It rang and rang but did not roll over to voicemail.

He then tried Bartos', which failed to connect, and then the preacher's. Jack's number went straight to voicemail. Scott declared himself and said he 'd like to speak with them again when they had a minute. He had some new information to share but also needed some advice. They could try and call or he would be back in town tomorrow morning and would try to catch one of them at the boat docks or maybe the sports bar around eleven. He told them he hoped they were having a relaxing time fishing.

He left town the way he had come in, and about twenty minutes later he came up to the roadblock. Deputy Warren was sitting in the shade of his patrol car. He smiled and gave a little wave when he saw Scott approach. Scott took the bag of sandwiches and beer from his pack and passed them through the open window. "Thanks again for what you're doing," he said before riding off.

The Deputy gave him a bewildered look until he opened the bag. Then he smiled from ear to ear.

• • •

The Offshore Oil Platform #148 FPS rig was technically owned by the South American Conseco Oil company, but it had been abandoned for years— although there was still lots of oil beneath its capped wellhead a half a mile below the surface. Its retrieval rate, the low purity of the crude, and a number of environmental concerns around its proximity to the mainland had sealed its fate. Soon after, the BP Deepwater Horizon disaster had happened, about eighty miles away. The decision had been made to abandon the rig but not to dismantle it, as at some point it would likely be profitable to operate again. In the meantime, the rig had become a natural wonder. It was now an artificial reef with many thousands of small fish seeking shelter beneath the structure. Larger fish would also patrol the perimeter, looking for easy meals. Although farther out than Todd would normally have looked for bait, it was always a good stop. While the two guys caught bait, Todd cast lines out for larger predator fish. Tarpon, jack, redfish, and even large sharks were common to the area.

The *Donna Marie* had been drifting lazily around the platform for several hours. Occasionally the wind would cause a clanking of metal on metal high up on the structure. That and the calls of the seabirds were the only distractions. The fishing had been good; the bait bucket filled quickly and the number of fish in the keeper's chest grew steadily.

Jack was snoozing, Todd was busy looking at the charts he had spread out on one of the benches, still trying to guess the route of the Navy flotilla. Bartos' eyes were focused out to sea. Picking up the Steiner Marine Optics again he made a noise. "Lot of damn Sharks over there."

Todd didn't look up, "It's the ocean man, what do you expect?"

Bartos didn't respond for quite some time. Then he put the binoculars down and said, "Cap'n, you need to see this." Handing them to Todd, he pointed out into the distance. Todd could see some splashes and what he assumed were sharks feeding on some larger prey. It could be a whale carcass or even another shark; they were known to be cannibalistic at times. As he got the binoculars focused in, though, he could tell there were dozens of sharks congregating. He thought he saw the pale underside fin of something larger. *Probably whatever the fish are feeding on.* The sharks cleared momentarily, and the pale object became visible again. The fin, or whatever it seemed to be, was enormous and—

"Oh my God," he said loudly, disturbing the preacher from his nap.

There were numbers and a logo stamped on the "fin" which, in fact, had to be the vertical stabilizer of what he recognized as a small commuter jet. "Oh, jeez...." He now understood what the sharks were feeding on.

The gruesome scene was floating closer to them, drawn by the massive current known as the northern Gulf gyre. Like a macabre sideshow attraction, all three men stared in horror and fascination at a mostly intact Delta Bombardier CRJ-700, formerly bound from Houston to Mobile. Sadly, it would never make it closer than this to its destination. The setting sun shone through its windows, outlining the silhouettes of passengers still strapped in their seats. Occasionally one of the heads would thrash as another fish tore a chunk of flesh away.

Jack said prayers as the plane slowly drifted past them.

"That should not be still floating," Bartos said.

Todd agreed, "The pilot must have made a perfect ditch. Like that guy on the Hudson River a few years back."

The three men forgot about the fishing, the excitement of the morning, and even the problems back on land for a moment. They leaned on the rail and watched the surreal scene float toward the horizon. Without any discussion, Todd pulled the anchor line, cranked the motor, and aimed for Harris Springs.

TWENTY-FOUR

Arriving back at his cottage, Scott was still disappointed at not being able to speak with any of the guys. To be honest, it frustrated him even more that he needed them. He was used to working out problems without any help from others. But he knew Bobby was right; he probably wouldn't be able to do this alone. If he had to go get Kaylie by himself, he would have to try. He thought that Bartos or Todd might at least be able to offer some of the fuel they had on hand. Instead, he decided to go ahead and handle that himself as well.

He disconnected the trailer from the Jeep and loaded four of the larger fuel containers in the back. He added a cut length of garden hose, a long funnel, and a few tools including a pry bar. Finally, transferring his pistol to the larger go-bag that contained seventy-two hours' worth of emergency supplies, he headed out.

He planned to hit as many of the dead vehicles on the highway as it took to finish filling up both the Jeep and the fuel containers he had with him. While not as easy as getting it from a gas station, he knew those cars would never run again. The fuel would be claimed by someone in time and if it were left to sit in the tank it would go bad.

Stopping just in front of one of the cars he had noted on his bike ride earlier, he went to work. His first job was to clip the pistol and holster to his belt. Then he walked up to the Buick and, using a screwdriver, pried the filler door open. He didn't view this as stealing, but he also knew this gas was not actually his to take either. Putting his morals aside, he unscrewed the gas cap and dipped the hose into the tank. Pulling it back out, he was pleased to see the wet line was far up the hose. He went back to the Jeep and grabbed two empty fuel containers to fill.

Siphoning the gas was easy, but gravity did not produce a very fast flow rate. He knew his Dad or probably Bobby could likely have come up with a hand pump or something equally useful for doing this. For now, though, this would work. He placed the first of the filled containers in the Jeep. He figured it would take thirty gallons for the trip to Tallahassee, but he also wanted to start building up his reserves.

The Buick had a big tank, but the siphon hose was soon sucking air. He put everything back in the Jeep and headed for the next car on his list. The next two had less than a half of a tank each, but the last car was a big, new pickup with a nearly full tank of gas. It was sitting just inside the intersection of the road with Highway 50. He filled up the remaining fuel containers and began carrying the heavy load back to Jeep. Scott heard a sound and immediately froze in mid-step.

Looking west, he noticed a group of men walking and jogging in his direction. The front two were waving and yelling. No doubt they were looking for a ride …or more. Scott's heart began to pound. All of them looked like trouble, and he noticed the unmistakable remnants of the orange prison jumpsuits on several. They had obviously tried to camouflage the fact by tearing them into shorts or just keeping the pants, no shirt, but it was a feeble attempt at best. The deputy had been right—they were making a beeline for Harris Springs. Right now, they were making a beeline for him.

Scott began to lose his shit; his thoughts were all over the place. He raced awkwardly toward the Jeep. The weight of the fuel containers made it impossible to do it quickly or to look like anything other than what it was. "Blind fucking panic. The men were closing on him fast. Finally, he just dropped the smaller of the containers and cradled the other one in front so it was more balanced. The final twenty yards to the car seemed to take forever, and he could hear the men laughing and telling him they just wanted to talk. He stuffed the one container in the back and jumped behind the wheel. He got the Jeep moving just as the men were nearly within reach. He quickly turned the Jeep in the other direction and sped away. Shaking, he knew those guys may not have been a real threat but felt thankful that his flight or fight response was still choosing the most intelligent option.

He also knew these men would just be the first. *We'll all have to deal with them, or others like them, in the days and months ahead.* Several miles down the road he came upon another roadblock. A uniformed man and woman waved him to a stop. Their old truck said "State Trooper" on the door in very faded lettering. The department was apparently pulling out the old relics in the garage in an effort to find cars that would still run.

One officer stepped to the back of the Jeep; the other politely asked Scott for his ID. Scott handed over the driver's license, thankful he had not waited any longer to trade in his Illinois license for a Mississippi one after he moved down. The officer explained how they were monitoring to ensure nothing but local traffic passed by, and handed Scott the license back. "I know," said Scott. "I talked to a county deputy earlier today. Deputy Warren mentioned the prison release and that some prisoners may be heading our way from the next county. I just saw a group of them heading this way, about five miles back."

Both officers nodded but didn't look overly concerned. "We've been getting them through here for about the last hour or two. Probably twenty in all. We can't detain them, but we are attempting to steer them in other directions. We're getting their names, taking pictures, trying to find out where they're heading. Not that they're necessarily going to be truthful, but from what we hear from other counties it sounds like all of the prisons will be doing similar releases."

"And mental hospitals as well," the female officer added. "If they don't get the goddamn power back on we're going to be neck deep in this shit in a few more days." The officers suggested Scott get on back home before the group did show up.

He thought maybe he should offer to stay and help, but they seemed to have everything under control, and, seriously, how much help would he be? He noticed they appeared to have working radios unlike the deputy he'd met earlier, and he assumed they could call in backup if needed. Scott drove on back in the direction of home.

TWENTY-FIVE

Arriving back at his beloved cottage, Scott loaded the extra fuel containers in the trailer and thought about his home. He loved it, but he knew it was not very secure. Its isolation was probably the best thing it had going for it. It wasn't very visible from the road as the cypress, crepe myrtle, and scrub trees filled in most of the space between. He began to think of other things he could do to make it even less noticeable.

He walked out to the road, intending to pull up the post with the mailbox. Just as he began twisting on it, a large brown van came down the road. Scott was shocked to see the UPS truck. The driver checked the address on the mailbox in Scott's arms, then pulled into the drive. When Scott got back to the house, the driver had begun making a stack of large delivery boxes by the garage door. He couldn't believe it, but they seemed to be the online order he had placed on the night of the event!

He saw the pistol in the tactical holster hanging from the man's belt. *Pretty sure that's not on the approved standards list for driver attire.* "I can't believe you guys are still running!" Scott said.

The man was dripping sweat and hurrying to get the rest of the delivery out of the truck. "Yeah, not sure how much longer we'll be able to but we're tryin'a keep goin'. Most of our trucks don't use the modern ignition systems. Right now they're tryin'a secure more fuel supplies but without phones or In'ernet, there'll prolly be no real need for us to continue much longer. But it's life or death for lotsa people. It may not be the end o' the world, but it is a national emergency. Hell, the Pony Express kept going and they didn't have power."

Scott nodded, realizing that some kind of delivery service would likely always be needed. Even more so in the absence of normal communications. "Well, damn man, I appreciate it. I'd given up on any of this ever showing up" Scott said grinning.

The driver politely leaned in and said, "Sir, if I could, I suggest you get it out o' sight quickly. I'm pretty sure I've had people followin' me all day. I think I scared the last of 'em off a few miles back when I finally drew the gun on 'em. Just... be careful."

Scott was still thanking the driver as he turned and left. The man seemed to land in the driver's seat, start the engine, and have the truck pulling out all in one fluid motion. *Damn, those guys are good*, Scott thought.

Looking at the boxes, they seemed to contain at least some, maybe even all of the order he had placed online. With considerable effort and time, he moved them into the garage and closed the door. *Why did I order that many cases of water?* he wondered. It had taken him three times as long to move it into the garage as it had the driver to unload it. He looked at the stacks of boxes, more excited than he could have imagined. He was beginning to think he had a chance to get through all this. Then he remembered the prisoners on the road.

He walked back out to the end of his drive and picked up the mailbox and post, tossing them into the woods. Off in the distance, he heard automatic weapons fire. It was the same direction the delivery driver had gone in. Now working with even more urgency, he pulled the steel bar gate free from the vines that encircled it. They had always had a gate on the drive when no one was using the cottage but since moving here, Scott had just left it open. He now latched it closed to the steel post with a chain and padlock. Looking into the woods beside the drive, he selected a couple of downed limbs and accompanying vines and pulled them to block the drive as well. Climbing over the gate and looking at it from the road, it did a pretty good job of looking like just another seldom used two-track road. Most cars going by would never give it a second look. Someone on foot might investigate further, though, so he might need to do more but for now, it was a good start.

The power was still off in the cottage, and he was beginning to wonder if it would keep coming back on or not. Scott lit lanterns and opened the garage door just a crack to get a breeze blowing through. He assessed the shipments and decided to stack the bulk food and water for separation later. The new backpacks, sleeping bags, and camping gear he kept near the door. Once he loaded those packs, they would be going in the Jeep.

The boxes with smaller devices went upstairs so he could unbox them and learn how to use them. Some of the batteries stayed in the garage, but about a third went inside. He unboxed one of the small BaoFeng handheld radios he had ordered, glad to see that despite the low price it was in a protective anti-static bag. He installed the rechargeable batteries and turned it on. The unit was tuned for standard ham radio bands. Scott didn't have a license to operate a ham radio, but he had no immediate plans to be transmitting. His main purpose was to listen in to other operators and hopefully gather more information on what was happening elsewhere. For that he would be fine without a license. The little unit could also listen in on marine bands, Emergency, and NOAA weather, if those were even still a thing. And it could also be used as a normal two-way walkie-talkie.

• • •

Several hours later he had sorted all of the water purification tablets into various day kits and combined them with fire starters, binoculars, MRE's and freeze-dried rations. Both of the large backpacks were filled. The last item he added to his EDC was a small night vision monocular. *Pretty badass*, he congratulated himself as he took in his work. He knew the feeling probably wouldn't last.

It was beginning to get dark in the house, and the power did not appear to be coming back on tonight. On one of his trips out to the trailer, he realized he could see the lights from the house when he looked back at the cottage. The lanterns weren't bright, but someone from the road would be able to notice. He pulled a roll of black plastic, a razor and some duct tape from the supply room in the garage. Back inside, he blacked out all the windows on the front and sides of the house. That was going to fuck up his nice ocean breeze, and the interior of the house would warm considerably. It was better than being attacked by road gangs, though.

Scott was getting hungry though he was now too tired to cook anything elaborate. This disappointed him—a good meal a day was one of the luxuries he looked forward to. He picked up his phone to scroll through the pictures of food in the refrigerator and was again surprised to see a missed call notification on the screen. There was no message, but the number was the one he had entered for Todd the previous day. He tried to redial the number but was met with only silence. Frustrated again, he opened the refrigerator and pulled out the ground beef, cheese, mustard, and ketchup. Quickly cooking up two patty melts with sautéed onions, he sat at the wooden counter and gulped down the food. He turned the new radio on again and spent ten minutes going up and down the dial. He heard several distant broadcasts but most were too weak to hear much detail. On one of the frequencies, though, he heard an older male voice. The man, from Tampa, was reporting that parts of the city were under artillery fire from the sea.

He must be wrong, Scott thought. The man said the shelling seemed to be targeting the area of the MacDill Air Force Base. Distant booms of explosions could be heard before the broadcast abruptly cut out.

Something about the broadcast triggered a vague memory. Shutting off the radio and pulling open his laptop he disabled the Bluetooth and Wi-Fi receivers and decreased the screen brightness to lessen the battery usage. He had several spare batteries charged, *but why waste it?* Opening the folder containing the screen grabs from the Homeland Security servers, he began to review what he had saved. He knew he had seen something concerning MacDill, which Scott knew was home to UNCENTCOM or US Central Command, a strategic joint intelligence operations center. Finding the screen grab of the right document, he read what he had only skimmed earlier.

• • •

Scanning the pages, he found the section he wanted. Ten minutes later he finished the page for the third time and was even more confused. The Catalyst Protocol had several early requirements to protect the domestic US homeland, ensure continuity of government and establish civil control. A primary tool among these plans was an elite unit that comprised multiple divisions of hand-picked Marines, Air Force Special Forces, Delta team and many other specialists on subjects including urban warfare, biological disease, healthcare, agriculture and civil engineers. The lead unit was codenamed "Praetor5" and was based out of MacDill Airforce Base. Among other mission critical tasks, the Area of Responsibility for this group would be to assert political and civilian control in the absence of any other operational structure. If Scott was reading this correctly, the size and budget of this force were enormous especially since this was essentially a contingency force that you hoped was never needed. While there were a lot of other assets based at CentCom in Tampa, he could not shake the feeling that someone, another country? Hell maybe even some part of our own government, wanted to make sure these guys never got deployed. Was the Tampa attack confirmation that Project Catalyst had indeed been put into play? If so, what did that mean, a coup or were we under attack by a foreign power? Too many questions and no real answers.

Scott spent a few more minutes on the laptop feeling increasingly uneasy about having this information. Ultimately he was unsure if his brilliant friend Tahir had helped save his life or if he would be the reason it ended. If the black helicopters started circling, he would know the answer. Throwing caution to the wind and years of paranoia indoctrination he decided to go ahead and copy the file folders over to his tablet as its battery would last longer. He could also review the files from bed easier on the small device. Wondering if there was any ice left, he risked opening the small freezer and found most of the ice was still frozen. Grabbing several large cubes, he dropped them in a glass tumbler with several fingers of Macallan eighteen-year-old single malt Scotch. Cold drink and tablet in hand, he headed off to the too warm bedroom to do more research.

Reviewing and sorting the massive amounts of data into what would be most essential to him took quite a while—several refills, in fact. The more Scott read, the more dismal it all seemed. Most of the decision-makers had known the likelihood of this specific disaster as very high. Few steps had actually been taken to affect the impact of such an event at all.

One of the exchanges he read was a transcript between a professor Carl Budding, Ph.D., and several senators on the former President's Science Advisory Council. The senators had made several requests to find what specific steps could be taken to mitigate widespread problems. Dr. Budding had responded that most likely nothing would prevent systemic and systematic failures of all technological and electrical systems around the planet. Creating large scale Faraday cages would possibly help but would likely be impractical as the Faraday cage had to fully enclose whatever it was designed to protect. It did so by redirecting the electromagnetic energy around the framework of the metal cage and into the ground. If, however, you have whatever is in that cage connected to a power grid, a nuclear station, or a network line then you have also opened the door for the electrical energy wave to breach the protective cage and disable the device. So, yes, you could make shielded and protected devices. But they couldn't actually be in use during the unpredictable event.

The Advisory Council's eventual report to the president stated that any warnings or precautions given to the American people would at best have a placebo effect, similar to the government's advice many years earlier telling Americans to use plastic sheeting and Duct tape to prevent exposure in a possible terrorist attack. As ridiculous as it had been, many people did exactly that, thinking it would make them safe. Scott glanced up at the black plastic over his windows, held in place by silver duct tape. Shaking his head, he went back to reading.

The research had gone on for decades. The one positive thing he could see evidence of from all of the studies, subcommittee hearings, and expert advice was the emergency shutdown procedure for nuclear power plants and key refineries, which had been developed specifically for just such a scenario. In the end, it had been determined that essentially nothing more could be done to prevent or even significantly lessen the impact of such a solar event. Instead of wasting money to make it seem like the government was ahead of the threat, they did nothing. At least, nothing public. Instead, it was decided that depending on the magnitude of the event and subsequent damage caused, the plan was to focus on how to survive, ensure continuity of government, and then rebuild. Priorities lay with preserving resources, eliminating ancillary threats such as nuclear fall-out, or war, and establishing safe zones that would be key to rebuilding.

It was pointed out multiple times in the Project Catalyst overview that many, many lives would be lost—sacrificed knowingly, in fact, by the government. Large cities would not be evacuated. Where would millions of people go, and how would they be fed? Areas without any real likelihood of long-term survival would not be receiving any real aid; if a city depended on electricity or refined heating oil to stave off the cold winter, you were likely going to freeze to death come winter. New York City was one of the best prepared, with a reported four million Meals Ready to Eat or military MRE's warehoused around the city. That sounded great until you realized that number wouldn't even feed half the city for a single day.

The message, again and again, was that the scope of the disaster was too large to prepare for. Martial law would not be enacted to protect troubled areas. In fact, the plan preferred the hastened reduction in population in those zones, which would reduce the drain on limited resources and therefore offered the quickest recovery for both the survivors and the nation at large.

Likewise, areas with high farming yields, critical education centers, leading healthcare or even vital manufacturing areas would be somewhat protected. Living here in the gray zone of the coastal states, Scott surmised, they would likely receive little assistance, though it would also be a desirable area to preserve, primarily because of the resources it could provide, such as oil and food.

Scott was getting sleepy but wanted to review some final projections. The final report noted only 2% of the American population are responsible for feeding 100% of its people. Everything else was imported from other countries. It stated that a grid down situation would require remaining citizens to immediately revert to an agricultural and feedstock-based economy. Even then, it would be impossible to feed the masses of people without working vehicles to transport the food to those who needed it. Massive crops of grain in the Midwest would rot in the field since it could not be harvested by hand; great herds of cattle and hogs would die in the stockyard or holding pens as they would not be processed and delivered; more would die on the farms because there would be no feed for them.

The 'good' news came on the following slides. The projected death rates in the US held that between seventy and ninety percent of the population would die in the wake of such an event, so farmers may eventually have only ten percent of the population left alive to worry about feeding. Within four years almost 300 million people in the US alone would likely be dead as a result of having no electricity. The vast majority of those deaths were predicted to take place in the first eighteen months after the disaster.

He laid the darkened tablet on the nightstand. *I've been focusing on surviving for the next few weeks. I need to be thinking about how to survive the rest of my life*, he thought.

Amazon wasn't going to be restocking or filling any more orders. This was it – The Big Fucking Crunch. Laying in the now darkened room, Scott's mind raced. Nine out of every ten people he knew would likely be dead. What chance did he have to be in that ten percent? Hell, what *right* did he have to be in it? He had not contributed to a better world. He did not have children. Shit, he didn't even have a dog. What made him think he was special enough to live through the end of the world?

With no answers, he drained the last of the Scotch and rolled over. Closing his eyes, he could not block out the images of this new world that his overactive mind kept presenting. *How long before society breaks down completely?* he wondered. The data said it could be as little as three to four days— about as long as the food in most homes would keep. People could be patient, even polite for a few days after that, but at some point, the general rules that bind society would begin to collapse. For those without many rules to begin with, it could happen almost immediately. *They'll see opportunity instead of obstacles.* Scott thought back to the videos of looters in the big cities and the gunshots after the UPS driver had left. He knew the time was up.

TWENTY-SIX

Day 8

Todd looked up from his plate. "No fucking way," he said. Pointing across the table to Bartos. he continued: "Even this idiot and all his damn conspiracy theories never laid one out that crazy."

"True bon ami," said Bartos, "You really expect the government and military to sanction wholesale genocide?"

It had taken Scott several days to catch up with the guys again. Apparently the restaurant was feeding them for free although Scott still wasn't totally sure why. The men had shared with him the series of events that had taken place out on the water the other day. He, in turn, had relayed what he had learned online and from the radio operator in Tampa.

Todd and Bartos both thought Scott was full of shit. Preacher Jack seemed less sure. Looking over he said, "Todd, you remember us wondering where that Naval fleet was heading. Could it have been Tampa?"

"Hell, I don't know. You were the dumbass tryin' a hitch a ride with 'em. Did it seem like fucking Tampa was the next stop?"

They laughed, but Scott noticed Todd's smile wasn't really reaching his eyes. A seed of doubt had taken root. "Listen, guys," Scott said, "I'm not trying to convince you. I'm just relaying what I read and heard. I don't even want to believe it myself."

Todd was shaken with the possibility that the Navy—his Navy—might be firing on an American city. He looked at Scott. "You aren't sure who the good guys are, are you Scott?"

Scott shrugged, "Catalyst is awful, but I'm not sure I disagree with it." Pulling the tablet out of his pack he pulled up the document files and passed it over to Todd. "I'm certain I could lose my job, my security clearance and probably go to jail just for just having this, much less sharing it… but just skim through those first few screens."

As the other three sipped on beer, they watched the color drain from the big man's face. Fifteen minutes later he looked up from the screen. "You weren't fucking with us." Motioning for the server, he ordered a double whiskey.

Jack then took the tablet, with Bartos looking on. Todd and Scott continued talking while the others caught up. "What do we do now?" Bartos asked.

Scott shrugged, "I'm not sure." It appeared to him that their home would be left to fend for itself for the next few years. If they became valuable to the rest of the country, they might get some extra assistance and protection, but they'd almost certainly have to fight to get to that point.

"Our isolation works for us here, but it also means we may have trouble trading or getting what we need. That means we have to protect what we have from looters, pirates, gangs—and right now those damn convicts roaming the highways. We also have to be thinking more long-term. Not just how to survive the next few months. We need to be able to get power back on by ourselves. Become self-sustaining and establish trade partners with other survivor groups. The research in the documents indicates that a self-sustainable group of around thirty individuals has the best odds of surviving. Individuals will be picked off too easily, and larger groups are harder to feed and less mobile."

Todd shook his head, "Scott, this town is over six hundred people. Myself, Jack, Bartos, even you are invested in this place. Do we just build ourselves a commune and let Harris Springs burn? We have to try and survive as a town." His words are almost pleading. Any doubt about the situation being dire had now vanished from the group.

"I'm sorry Todd. I like these people, but I'm not sure that's feasible.

Many will likely die regardless. Some have already. A lot of the others will sit back in denial, waiting for help to come. They'll die waiting for a government to feed and clothe them and to reassure them everything's alright. If the projections are correct then in less than two months Harris Springs will be a very different place, and we'll have around half the population it has today. Will the mayor or town council see this coming? Will the state be able to help? Hell, what could the four of us even do?"

Bartos looked up from reading, apparently listening to the conversation as well. "Don't forget, guys, we'll probably be busy trying to survive. Gathering food, staying warm, maybe fighting off bad guys... That doesn't leave a lot of time or energy for plowing and planting farms, building electrical plants or establishing a more viable community. Might be better to take a 'pee-roy' and go hide out in the bayou." Scott knew he was talking about the small canoes some of the locals used that were actually called Pirogue's.

Preacher Jack set the tablet down on the table, looking up with a similar expression to the one Todd had earlier. "Guys, this is going to get mighty dark and desperate before the good Lord feels we've been tested enough."

Todd pulled the tablet over and asked, "Scott would you be willing to let me hang onto this for a couple of hours? I'd like to take a look at more of your intel and talk with my wife. I could drop it back off to you later today if you care to share where you live?"

Bartos smiled and said "I know where he lives, it came to me last night. I think I met this guy's brother a few years ago. Looked just like him, well...except for being bigger, smarter, and better looking with brown hair. Actually, he looked nothing like you Scott, were you adopted?"

"Funny, asshole," laughed Scott, "Bobby said to tell you hi. He also said you'd be a solid friend to have, especially if I needed help finding an open bar." Laughing, Scott looked over at Todd and told him the address. He did add that he had removed his mailbox last night. "So just look for the address number on the gate—Tell you what, if you want, bring your wife by and I'll cook us some dinner. I have some food that needs to be eaten in the next few days. Bring these clowns too if you want. I do need to discuss something else with you all."

"Yea, you mentioned that in your message. What's up?" asked Todd.

Scott looked around the table. "Look, I know you guys barely know me and...well, this is hard to even bring up, but I may need to do a favor for my brother Bobby and...". *Man, this was harder than he'd thought it would be.*

"Spit it out, dude," the preacher encouraged.

"Well, if I have to do the favor I—I'm going to need some help. He and his wife are stranded up in Little Rock, but his daughter is studying pre-med courses over at FSU. No one has heard from her since this shit went down. I offered to go and check on her, maybe bring her back here. He said no, to give it a few more days, but the more I think about it, the more I think waiting will just be worse. I'm planning on heading over early next week. That is if no one hears from her by then. Honestly—and yes, this sounds as chicken-shit as it is—but I'd rather not go alone."

Todd looked over smiling and said no worries; he would be glad to come. And he and his wife Liz would love to come by later for dinner. They could discuss it more then. The Preacher declined the dinner invite as he had a weeknight service and expected it to be packed. Bartos said dinner parties weren't his thing, but if he was over that way later, he might stop by mainly to see how the cottage had turned out.

"Thanks, guys," Scott said. "My brother also informed me I needed to be better armed. After seeing those released prisoners on the road, I think I better make that a priority." Bartos nodded. Scott continued, "I have some cash if you could spend it wisely for me?"

"Sure man, what do you want? I can get it if I don't already have it."

"Bobby said to get a tactical rifle—a Bushmaster, M4 or similar—a twelve gauge Mossberg Riot Gun, and a smaller concealed carry pistol with a holster and a few cases of ammo for each if possible."

Scratching behind his ear, Bartos said, "That won't be a problem, should be able to have it before you head out to Tallahassee." Scott handed the man several thousand dollars in cash. "Man, you can be my Pa-ran. Carrying that much cash."

That was a new one for Scott. "A what?"

"Pa-ran…a Godfather man," Bartos answered, laying on an artificially heavy Cajun accent.

Todd slipped the tablet in his pack and got up with a wink. "You heading home after this?"

Nodding, Scott said he had planned to. Todd walked behind the bar to the back. He came back out a few minutes later followed by a young Hispanic guy who was carrying two commercial size bags of ice. Todd had what appeared to be a plastic bag with a medium sized frozen fish. Todd got the keys from Scott and had the man put the ice and the fish in his Jeep at the curb.

"What was that for?" Scott asked.

"Well, our little Cajun friend here managed to repair the cooling system on the walk-ins and freezers. Somehow he switched them off of the electrical refrigerants systems to propane, which the town has a good supply of. The three of us also caught all the fish they are serving here today, and they're storing the rest of the catch for me on ice. The meals and ice are how they're repaying us."

"But I had nothing to do with any of that," Scott protested.

Clasping a big hand on Scott's shoulder Todd said, "You're one of us. Probably the most important one of us. If anyone is going to keep us alive, it will likely be you. Believe me, we're going to take really, really, good care of you."

Scott dropped his head. "Thank you," he said quietly. "I'm not the guy you hope I am… but I'm truly glad for friends like you. I'll do my best to help us all."

Todd smiled, "One thing—don't cook the fish for dinner, something else please. That snapper is just for you."

"Deal," said Scott. He had something else in mind anyway.

TWENTY-SEVEN

Scott stopped by the burgeoning farmers' market in the parking lot, and several of the farmers seemed to remember him. A couple even said they'd put a few special things aside for him. Scott didn't need much but bought something from every truck. He was truly pleased to see several more cured and country hams hanging on hooks. He bought them all, knowing they would store for a very long time. He headed over to the jewelry and pawn shops where he made some good cash deals for gold and silver as well as other items that would hold value.

Getting home, he put most of the valuable ice in the freezer, which would help maintain the cold a little longer, and moved several items from the refrigerator to the large freezer. He added some good Belgian beers and a couple of bottles of wine to chill. The remainder of the ice went into the smaller freezer along with the perishables like eggs, mayo, cheese and such. He would have to remember to take them out if the power came back on, but the smaller space was still cooler and would be easier to keep cold with the small container of ice.

He'd flipped the plastic up from the windows earlier in the day, and now he opened the back and front doors, letting in a brisk ocean breeze. It wasn't exactly cool, but it was manageable. Scott prepped the items he was going to cook later and put four nice steaks in a light homemade marinade made with soy, garlic, olive oil, herbs, and a dash of sugar and balsamic.

Much of the afternoon was spent organizing the new gear he had and repacking the go-bags. These were larger versions of the EDC bag with more substantial gear. Ideally, you could live out of one for at least three days. He practiced with one of the water filtration straws, going down to the black river behind the house and using the straw to filter a small container of drinkable water. He spat the first swallow out, thinking it tasted pretty much like how a fart smelled. Assuming the straw had taken out the nasties that could kill him, though, he drank the rest. *Better to know how to use all this stuff now.* He needed to be able to trust the gear; his life might well depend on it. No one said he had to enjoy the stuff.

He was thinking about the steaks as he loaded several more cases of MREs into the trailer. He had that trailer nearly full of gear, water, spare clothes, and food. It was nearly a duplicate of what he had inside the cottage. Scott was not planning on taking it to Tallahassee, so he pulled the trailer further out of sight behind the cottage. He covered it with an old brown tarp and laid several downed tree limbs against it. Once he'd decided on a secure bug-out location, he would take it there to unload.

Late in the afternoon he heard music start playing from inside. It was Joe Bonamassa's "Driving Toward Daylight" album. It was one of Scott's favorites and oddly appropriate. He had queued the album on his turntable earlier. *If the power comes back on, that's what I wanna hear.*

It took a few more minutes to fully assimilate the fact that the power was back on. It had not been on at all for the last few days. He went inside, turned the AC on full and put on a load of clothes, some dirty and some of the new stuff that needed a wash cycle to be comfortable. Scott then moved items from the freezers back to the refrigerator so they wouldn't freeze solid. He had an hour before Todd and Liz arrived. That gave him a little time to check some things out. He already had all of his rechargeable items plugged in. He opened the laptop and powered up. As had become his habit, he flipped the TV on and cycled it quickly, seeing no new broadcast. He muted it, preferring to hear the lively strings of Bonamassa's guitar licks.

Scott had tried Bobby unsuccessfully several times today. At first, he only called when he assumed the power was on, provided it was on the same rotation it had been earlier. He'd also tried several other times just in case. Bartos had told him that the cell towers had backup generators, usually propane powered. They could keep working quite a while in a grid-down situation. Seeing that, according to the rolling blackout schedule in Little Rock, his brother's power should be up now as well, he clicked on the "Remote Support" app and keyed in his brother's computer address. It didn't connect. He triggered it again and switched over to check email. None. Work server: unavailable. He tried several of the news sites he'd bookmarked previously. A couple of them came up, so he triggered his clipper app to harvest and download all data from any new links.

The remote support icon was flashing in his taskbar. Bringing it up, he could see it had finally connected to Bobby's PC and was waiting for a password. He entered it from memory, and his desktop was replaced by a mirror image of Bobby's screen. He checked for keyboard activity and saw no one was using the PC. He then turned on Bobby's webcam and saw his still familiar but empty living room. He assumed none of them were near the computer right now. He had no easy way to get their attention. He was going to play some music or a sound when he saw a pair of headphones on the desk. He realized no one could likely hear anything he did. He finally opened up Microsoft Word and typed in large font "Hi Bro!" Then he clicked print. No errors popped up, so the printer must be on. He had pulled this trick on Bobby and Jess before as they couldn't always tell when he had logged in and fixed something.

He saw a folder on Bobby's desktop labeled "Scott Look Here." He opened it up and saw a letter from Bobby as well as a better map of the FSU campus. He downloaded everything in the folder, including a document called "Survival Rules." He then created a folder on his brother's desktop called "Bobby Look Here." Into this Scott uploaded the most vital pieces of information he had collected. He would have done it all, but it would have taken more time than he thought he would have. *This is a clumsy way to communicate, but better than nothing.*

Just then he saw Jess walk in front of the camera and sit down and turn the on TV. He could see most of the TV screen although the angle was bad. As she flipped channels, it looked like she was getting about the same broadcast as him. She did stop on what appeared to be a local Little Rock station, though, showing various demonstrations and street scenes. From what he could see it looked chaotic, with looters and gangs throwing bottles and storefronts smashed in or on fire. Jess put her face in her hands, and Scott thought she must be crying. He didn't like being a voyeur, but he also felt that nothing he could say would help, even if she could hear him. He knew she was thinking more about Kaylie than herself.

As his upload continued, he jumped back to his screen and read the letter from his brother. It was not long but very straightforward. They had still not heard from Kaylie. If Scott felt he could do so safely, would he please attempt to go and get her?

> Do not let her come home, take her back to the
> beach house, please. It's not safe here, and we
> may be bugging out soon. We'll find a way to let
> you know where we are.

The upload completed and just as soon the Internet cut out. Thankfully the power was still on, at least for now. Scott looked over the other information he had gotten from Bobby's computer. It was very thorough: maps, suggested routes, Kaylie's address and several of her friend's address and phone numbers. It even included a scan of Kaylie's student ID. Also, his big brother had included a general survival guide containing everything from suggested planting times for the coastal zone, seasonal weather data and much more than he could digest right now. He pulled up another document called Survival Rules and started reading.

TWENTY-EIGHT

SURVIVAL RULES

Scott,

You are not a very trusting man, which may serve you well now. You are, however, a very giving man, and unfortunately, this could get you killed. Trust and generosity should be metered out carefully in this new world. Every person you meet could potentially kill you. You won't like it, but to survive you must always have a plan to kill them first. The following is a set of rules I have refined over the years. They may not be enough to help you survive, but they will help. I love you brother. It may not be possible to get Kaylie back to us, so don't even try right now. I know you will do your best to keep her safe and be the parent she will need in the days to come.

Take Care and Thank You.

Love, Bobby and Jess

The Rules:

1. Be Smart—Think First, Act Second—but **Do Act.**

2. You can't be smart for someone else. Expect and accept the stupidity of others even when it's suicidal for them—just move on. Ineptitude, like inaction, will usually be fatal.

3. Always have your weapons and your gear close. You must be able to reach them immediately when needed.

4. Priorities are water, shelter then food.

5. Never show weakness. The weak will be preyed upon by the strong.

6. Always cheat; always win. The only unfair fight is the one you lose.

7. Do not share with others unless they are doing so with you.

8. Solve your own problems.

9. Don't let others know what you have or where you have it kept.

10. Maintain situational awareness: head on a swivel, check your six. Always know what you are walking into and away from.

11. Travel light. Hide your supplies in multiple locations. Assume some will be stolen, probably by people you know and trust.

12. Have a way to get to your primary bug-out location(s) from wherever you may be.

13. Have multiple bug-out locations pre-selected.

14. Your gear is precious, but continually learn new skills so you can live without it.

15. Do not put yourself at risk for others. You getting dead helps no one.

16. Trust no one fully. Those you let close can cause you the most pain.

17. Be ready to defend yourself and your property without mercy. In the absence of justice, the lawless will rule, but brute strength and intelligence can prevail.

18. Don't stick your dick in crazy, no matter how hot they are. If you cannot distinguish crazy from sane (SCOTT - YOU CAN'T) avoid them all.

19. Don't quit. That will be the easy way out. Be strong enough to keep going, keep living.

20. Have a back-up plan, because the first one probably won't work. Know when to run. Always having an exit strategy will better your odds.

21. Don't lose your humanity in the face of all this. Many others will be good, helpful and essential to your survival.

Scott smiled, surprised not to see "Do Cardio" as the number one rule as he thought back to a movie they had loved. He missed his family more than ever. He could not begin to understand the pain they were going through over their daughter, but he was even more determined to get her to safety.

The album had finished, and the next one dropped down. The Foo Fighters "One by One" began to play. Hoping the water had warmed up by now, Scott went to take a much-needed shower.

TWENTY-NINE

Scott exited the shower to Dave Grohl singing "Times Like These." Humming along, he went to the rear deck and lit a starter fire in the large ceramic smoker grill. The lump coal wouldn't put off much smoke or odor, and the steak and vegetables wouldn't be over the heat that long. Strange that he had to be thinking about staying undetectable even just grilling dinner. He took the meat out of the refrigerator and dried off the marinade. *Steak like this has to be cooked on the grill.* Nothing else would do it justice. He halved and parboiled several new potatoes and made a quick dressing for the asparagus that would also go on the grill. Finally, he'd partially shucked and soaked a few ears of the delicious looking fresh corn he had gotten from the farmers earlier today.

He was cleaning the mud off some of the freshly harvested onions he had also bought when he saw a dark blue truck pull up to the gate. Looking at the time, he assumed it was Todd. Walking out to the gate, Scott saw Todd and a very pretty woman sitting close beside him. He opened up, and they pulled into the house and parked. Feeling more secure with Todd here, he left the gate open just in case Bartos showed.

Scott shook Todd's hand before Todd introduced his wife, Liz. Scott's mouth dropped open; she had to be one of the prettiest women he had ever seen. He stared for what felt like several minutes until he finally found his voice. "I apologize for being a Neanderthal," Scott stammered, laughing. "I just hadn't expected this homely guy to have such a lovely bride."

She blushed but quickly recovered, "It's okay, I thought he was rich. What did I know? I was young and dumb." They all laughed, and Scott showed them both around.

Todd checked out the Go-bags sitting by the Jeep, smiling and giving Scott a thumbs up. Liz went straight over to the bikes hanging on the wall. "Scott, this Trek is beautiful—both of the bikes are elite rides. Damn, SRAM Red on both…sweet!"

"Oh my God, she's a cyclist," crooned Scott. "Sorry Todd, I'm in love."

Todd threw up his hands, "Freaking spandex nerds. Where can I find a cold beer?"

Scott opened the fridge, and Todd selected a nice Chimay Blue Belgian Beer. Scott grabbed a bottle of wine as well, and they all headed inside. "Liz, can you open this while I try and get the rest of the food on?" He asked, showing her the corkscrew on the counter. "Unless you would prefer a white?"

Looking at the label, she smiled and said, "Oh no, this will be perfect."

Scott grinned and began transferring the half-cooked potatoes to a bowl with a herb and butter mixture. Todd sat Scott's tablet on the counter and looked at the food. "Damn, those steaks look fantastic! I was afraid you were going to fix us some foo-foo tofu shit."

Scott laughed and said, "I already know you're a carnivore. I just assumed anyone dumb enough to live with you would have to be as well. One thing, though, these are wet-aged Chicago bone-in rib eye. I only cook them medium rare. If you can't live with that, you can cook 'em yourself and if so… please go somewhere out my sight to eat it."

Scott's guests laughed and said, "Medium-rare is perfect," almost in unison.

Scott added the potatoes, cut side down, to a roasting pan and slid it into the oven. He then took the wet corn out to the grill along with several whole onions stuffed with bacon and mushrooms. Liz had poured herself a glass of the Argentinean Malbec and was looking at his albums. She selected a Miles

Davis album and put it on the spindle to drop next. Scott liked the way they both seemed comfortable with him and made themselves at home without being the least bit rude. Most people would have made fun of him for preferring vinyl over CDs or MP3s. Neither of them seemed to even notice. Scott soon grabbed a beer for himself and sat at the bar enjoying the cool air.

"I had the power turned back on just for you guys," he said.

Todd was sitting on the sofa looking at the little Chinese handheld radio, "We appreciate that. You have a great house man, but too far out and totally indefensible."

"Tell me something I don't know," responded Scott.

Todd looked up at the TV. "Any news from the world?"

Shaking his head, Scott said, "Not from the TV, and not much in general. My brother has asked me to try and get Kaylie at FSU. It appears there are serious problems developing up where he is, so he wants me to bring her here for now."

Todd drained the beer and headed for another. "We still heading out, when, Monday morning?" he asked nonchalantly.

Scott looked at him. "Well, that's my plan but God… I really do hate to ask you to go."

"You didn't ask," said Todd. "I'm going, enough said." That did seem to settle one of Scott's worries. "I know you said you got fuel, so let's take your 4x4 if you don't mind. My truck is acting a little squirrelly since it got a sunburn. I probably need to let Bartos take a look at it."

Nodding Scott said, "Sure no problem….and thank you."

"You boys have to go and get that girl. She has to be scared out of her mind. Besides, I could use some new female company," smiled Liz.

Getting up, Scott took the platter of steaks and the asparagus out to the grill. He turned the corn over to get some char on the other side and readjusted the onions before adding the asparagus. Todd opened the door and slid out. Scott could hear the throaty trumpet of Miles Davis drifting through the door with the big man. "Hey, I brought you another platter out," he said, setting it down on the custom made cypress cook table. "Listen," Todd began, "What you're doing for your niece is a nice thing. You and I both know this is probably for the long haul."

Scott's eyes began misting up thinking of the letter from his brother. "She's family… and she is a really good kid. Smart, good work ethic, funny too."

Todd watched as Scott pulled the gorgeous looking veggies off the grill, drizzled them with some olive oil and covered them with foil, before opening up all the vents to let the grill get even hotter. "Scott she sounds like the kind of person this new world is going to need…we can't wait to meet her."

"Thanks, man, and all the shit I said about wanting your wife…totally true," Scott said with a wink. He looked over at Todd and noticed that even though the big guy was laughing his eyes were watering a bit too.

"How hot are you going to let that thing get?" Todd looked at the thermostat on the grill.

"Hot," said Scott, "Real hot. In the restaurant I used to work in back in Chicago, we had a steak broiler that stayed around 1,600 degrees. A few minutes in that and you had a perfect sear on the outside and rosy pink in the center. This little guy won't get that high, but once it goes over 800, I'll drop the steaks."

Todd watched as Scott's practiced hand quickly positioned the rib eyes and had the lid closed again within a few seconds. They both drank their beers and stared out over the edge of the bayou, enjoying the intoxicating aroma of the grilling meat. Liz came up behind them, surprising them both.

She was laughing as she put her arms around Todd, "You guys were in man-heaven."

"Nope," said Todd, "In man-heaven, there'd be porn."

She took her arms away and put them around Scott in much the same way whispering, "He's the Neanderthal."

Scott looked over at Todd, winked and said, "Yea…what she said."

The steaks were ready before the beers were empty and they took all the food back inside. Scott grabbed the potatoes from the oven, peeled back the rest of the corn husks, and topped them with sour cream, lime, Mexican cheese, and chili powder, turning the simple vegetable into delicious Mexican Street Corn.

The first wine bottle was emptied quickly as the food began to disappear. Liz went and picked another out of the wine rack, opening it to let it breathe. The food was delicious, and Liz and Todd were impressed. The evening quickly was getting more relaxed. The drinks were a welcome relief to the world outside.

"You cook like this, and you live alone?" Liz asked.

Scott blushed, "Afraid so," he said sadly. "This would be one of my simpler meals. I'm—I was a bit of a foodie. I love to cook."

"Your ex-wife was an idiot," Liz said, shaking her head before taking another sip of wine. "I'm sorry Scott, that was a really awful thing for me to say."

"No…no, it's true. She was that. She was…more than that," Scott said. "But so was I."

Over the course of dinner, Scott learned that Liz was a school teacher currently on leave trying to get her master's degree. She did indeed once do triathlons but had to stop. She had biked more that Scott, back in the day. "I always tried to get Todd into biking. But any free time he has, he wants to be hunting or back on the water. I come in a distant second to *Donna Marie*," she said, using the name of the boat as if it were another woman. Scott could see in both of their looks that this was not true. It was obvious that they were each other's top priority.

"So why did you stop riding?" Scott asked. As Liz was about to answer a sound came from outside. They saw the reflection of car lights coming through the windows.

Looking out Todd said, "That's Bartos and Solo." Scott was unsure who Solo was but went to greet them.

"Glad you found the place, dude," Scott said as Bartos climbed out of an ancient and somewhat fierce looking Ford Bronco.

Bartos smiled, "Hard to miss it, all lit up like a fucking Christmas Tree and all...oh sorry Liz.."

Scott was about to respond when he saw a gorgeous dog hop out of the truck. Liz rushed over and bent down. "Hi Solo," she purred, then stood and gave Bartos a hug. Scott looked sheepishly behind him at the house where every light was on and visible from the road.

He went to shake Bartos' hand, but Bartos put up a hand. "Wait." The dog was looking at Scott suspiciously. "Solo—friend." The dog relaxed, and Scott knelt down but did not move closer. He instead let the dog come to him and let him get a good smell. He must have approved of him, and the steak smell, as he let out a small huff. Scott gave him an affectionate scratch behind the ears. "You must be a dog person," observed Bartos.

"Love dogs," answered Scott. "Couldn't have one in Chicago and just haven't made the effort to look for one since moving down here. Come on in, I have you a plate of food in the oven."

Bartos was dropping the tailgate, "First tell me where you want your new toys."

Peeking in Scott saw an arsenal of weapons and ammo. "Hot Damn! It's redneck Christmas!" an amused Liz said.

"Truly," agreed Scott. "Inside. I'm going to want to know more about all this stuff. Hell, I'll probably want to sleep with it."

Todd looked over at his wife, "Sorry honey, he has a new love, you'll just have to stick with me." It took them several trips to get all the new gear inside.

Bartos looked at the dog who was looking patiently up at him "Solo—

patrol." Todd and Liz had gone back inside to finish eating. Scott was grabbing a cold beer for Bartos as he had made it clear he was not a wine drinker.

"Beautiful dog," Scott said handing the wiry man the unopened bottle. "I can see some German Shepard in him, but I'm not sure about what else."

"Kuvasz," said Bartos opening and taking a long pull on the beer, "Hungarian breed known as much for their protectiveness as they are their rather anti-social behavior. Not a real friendly creature but unbelievably loyal. Some clown decided that breeding one with a Shepard would make a good K9 dog. They're very smart and easy to train, but Solo never made it into the field. He was declared too aggressive. I talked the guys at the Sheriff's office into letting me have him instead of them...well, instead of him being put down."

Scott watched the dog sniffing the ground and checking out the perimeter of the yard. As they headed back inside, Scott thanked Bartos for the guns. "I wasn't expecting them so fast."

"Well, I thought it best to move quickly. When others figure out this shit storm is permanent the prices are going to go up fast. Also, Todd said you two would be making that road trip in a few days. Hey, I did take a few liberties with your brother's suggestions, though. I think you'll approve of what Santa done brung ya."

"I know I will man, thanks so much," said Scott smiling. "Come on and eat!" Scott realized that Todd had already decided he was going to help get Kaylie before he had even asked.

Bartos looked at the plate of steak and potatoes and declared it "A National Fucking Holiday! Hot-damn Scott, I may just marry you."

Todd and Liz had cleaned their plates. Scott asked Bartos if Solo could have the bones. "Hell yea, he'll love you forever, too."

Liz opened the front door, and Bartos gave a curious whistle. Soundlessly the large dog slipped inside and sat near the table. Liz collected the bones and the few leftovers which Scott put on an old plate in front of Solo. Nothing on the dog moved other than his nostrils, which flared wide. Scott looked on in amazement. "You put a rare steak in front of him, and he doesn't even flinch?"

Bartos clicked his tongue twice, and the dog delicately picked up one of the bones and slid down on the floor to savor the meal.

"Amazing," said Scott, adding, "I want one."

Todd laughed and said, "Ignore him, Bartos. He said the same thing when he met Liz."

THIRTY

Solo went back on patrol after he ate. The human members of the party made drinks and went to the back deck to watch the diminishing but still brilliant Aurora Borealis. The ocean breeze was just strong enough to be cool and kept most of the mosquitos away.

"You know, if I hadn't read the stuff on that tablet, I could imagine that this was just an ordinary night. Just some friends getting together for great food and drinks. Except for that of course," Todd said, pointing up at the sky.

They discussed some of what Scott and Todd had learned in the documents. None of it was good. Todd had found a part that discussed some of the global aspects, which indicated that America would likely be recalling all forces from overseas and withdrawing from all international activities. Just like it was for individuals, it was every country for themselves.

After a while, Liz noticed something new was on the TV inside. "Looks like the President is speaking." They all headed back inside to see what the former Senator had to say. Turning off the stereo, Scott noticed the man was looking significantly more haggard than the last time he had seen him on the news. Flipping a few channels confirmed that the speech was being broadcast on every channel that was still working. The President was a generally well-liked leader as presidents go. He had done an admirable job trying to rein in an almost out-of-control government that wanted to keep growing and spending no matter what was needed.

The man spoke softly and even though he appeared to be in the press room, it was pretty obvious he was very nearly alone in the big room. The words were not particularly eloquent, but they were poignant, if not very informative or helpful. He did confirm the rolling black-outs and made clear that martial law had not been declared, but that he had authorized the unmeasured and unlimited use of force if needed to fight looters, criminals or anyone who opposed restoring order. "This is a worldwide problem, and an International State of Emergency is in effect. If we remain vigilant and remain calm, we will get through this. Everything will be okay."

Oh god, we're fucked, Scott said to himself, thinking back to his Dad's warning about; the only time to really worry is if someone in authority says not to worry. When the speech ended, Bartos asked, "What is an exclusionary rule?"

No one answered for a moment, then Scott said, "If I am not mistaken it is a seldom used section of the Miranda rule. Essentially, it suspends the rights of certain criminals, normally terrorists, typically provided to the accused. You can be held indefinitely. You have no right to an attorney. You can be questioned with any means desired, or just be 'disappeared' if they want. Normally, it would take a judge or someone high up to give that decision on a specific case. The President just gave blanket authority to every law enforcement or government agency to use it as they see fit."

"Holy shit," said Bartos. "He just dropped a fucking bomb like that in a speech and yet...no one will probably even notice."

"Yep," Todd agreed. "He must be up against it to suspend constitutional rights like that."

"But if it's that bad, why not just declare martial law, curfews, rationing, travel restrictions—even shoot on sight authorization?" asked Bartos.

"In my opinion, it's because he's already authorized the Catalyst protocol. Several of his phrases came directly from the program briefing, including the Exclusionary Rules he just invoked. Martial law would indicate he was going to try and preserve order. He is not. If anything, the downward spiral is just about to get a lot worse. The government is abandoning everything except what're now identified as safe zones essential to America's survival. Forced conservation of resources will be next."

On the sofa facing the TV, Liz pulled Todd closer, and Scott could see she was afraid. They all were. Bartos shook his bald head and went to the garage to get another cold beer. Scott glanced at Todd and Liz and wished for the millionth time that he had someone that close. He had loved being married; he just did not love his wife. At least not looking back.

He thought he had made a good husband, though, committing himself to it fully like most things that he did. But Angela had been distant almost from the moment they said, "I do." It took years for Scott to accept the obvious, that her needs were being fulfilled by someone else. Someone whom Scott had often called a friend. As cliché as it was, he had really been his best friend. The anger and humiliation had been intense. The only way Scott could go on had been to move here and sever all ties with her and the city they had called home.

It had been years since he had let anyone else get even remotely close. He had convinced himself he didn't need people, much less friends. He lived alone. He did not have to see his co-workers. He even ordered his groceries to avoid going into real stores. Now, almost overnight, he had this growing circle of people around him. People he was learning to trust, not just as friends but with his life. People who were helping him save his niece. People who were already feeling like some of the closest friends he had ever known.

Scott put on a pot of coffee and watched Bartos and Solo out in the yard. *Even they're a team*, he thought, wondering once again why he was so bad at love.

The power went off shortly after the last cup of coffee. Scott lit some lanterns inside and some Citronella patio torches outside. The group had moved back out under the stars. Bartos had been describing various end-of-the-world scenarios and why most were absurd.

"Even if zombies could exist, they would still be at a disadvantage to man. Their brains are dead, they're just hungry bodies running on instinct. Man is not the fastest or strongest predator on earth, but he is still the top one. The undisputed apex predator—why? Only one reason—we're smarter. We can think and reason better than even the cleverest of animals. A brainless zombie invasion would be a mild inconvenience at best."

Liz looked like she would really rather change the subject. "You've given this way too much thought, Bartos," she said.

Todd, sensing his wife's wavering emotions, leaned over and kissed her cheek. "What puzzles me most is this," he began, "Wouldn't zombies fart? I mean, look at their diet…and they're rotting away. Seems like they would have some massive gas issues. How would they ever sneak up on anyone?"

They all cracked up, Bartos shaking his head. It took a while for the conversation to again turn serious.

"What I don't get about Catalyst is why the projected mortality rate is so high. I mean, we haven't been dependent on electricity for that long. Humans migrated to every corner of the globe and successfully adapted to unbelievably harsh conditions without having electricity. Why does a grid-down situation now have to be so devastating?"

Bartos was scratching Solo's head as the dog lay at his feet. "Many isolated areas probably won't suffer at all. Hell, we have hundreds of residents in this county alone that choose to live off the grid. For the most part, though, we've become completely dependent on electricity. Even today's hermits still need supplies and medicine occasionally. No matter where our ancestors settled, they had to have fuel for fire. Whether it was peat bogs in northern Europe or Whale Oil in Newfoundland, they found a way to produce heat, cook food and survive the cold."

"Come on Professor. Get to the point," growled Todd.

Bartos frowned. "Grown-ups are talking," he said as he flipped Todd the finger. "The point, little ones, is this. To survive, not only do we have to go back 150 years and return to an agricultural or a hunter/gatherer society, but we have to do it without many of the resources they had back then. Less land for farming, less game to hunt, less natural fuel for light and heat.

"And we've lost nearly all of that vital knowledge passed down over the eons. Knowledge and skills they used to survive are lost. Without electricity, most of us are just not well equipped to forage or hunt for our food, or even survive a single winter. The heroes of this new world may be the Amish, the isolated jungle tribes, the hermits, hobos, maybe even the Mormons. Groups that have either prepared well ahead of time or simply shunned the modern life. These could also be the only people who can teach us how to live through this.

"Unfortunately, even us preppers get it wrong. It's just not possible to store up for the long term. All food spoils, even MREs. What you want is to have enough supplies to get you through the immediate crises so you can better prepare for the long-term. Skills and knowledge outweigh stockpiles of supplies every time. These thugs out there starting to loot houses will eventually be killing each other for a can of beans. They're dangerous, but they won't be around long. In six months, all prepared foods will probably be gone—then what?"

Scott noticed Liz looking even paler, and she gave another shudder; it was an uncomfortable topic. It was getting late, and Todd and Liz said their good-byes. Liz gave Scott and Bartos both a kiss on the cheek. "You boys stay safe," she sighed as she walked outside.

Todd turned to Scott in the doorway. "Come by the boat tomorrow afternoon so we can go over the trip."

Bartos went back in and got a tumbler of whiskey. "Let me go over the weapons I brought you before I go." Heading to the stack of ammo boxes and gun cases, he began methodically unpacking each and showing Scott not only how to load, aim, and fire, but how to thoroughly clean and store each one. Scott was still in awe of the impressive weaponry: An M4, a Mossberg shotgun, two handguns, and even a tactical vest.

"You and Bobby have a nice place here. It won't stand up to anyone determined to get in, but it should be a good bug-out for quite a while.

"Anything I can do to make it better?"

"First, you need an outhouse. Some way to get rid of waste so it won't cause you health problems. Most likely the number one way people are going to die will be from dysentery or cholera, not starvation. Both are easily preventable, mainly by keeping your water supply clean. I can help you with that. We have some portable outdoor toilets at the county shop we use for special events. I can bring one out. Since no one will be coming to service them, we'll need to pipe it out and dig a trench pit for the runoff and something else for the solids. I can show you how to use it and bring some sacks of lime to use in treating the spoilage.

"You also need some form of electricity, preferably solar panels, but maybe even a generator. You're far enough out that people might not be able to hear it running. You don't want to be advertising that you have power or fuel."

"I tried to find a generator. None were available."

"Well, most of the small residential generators you used to see for sale probably wouldn't last long-term, but we can keep looking. I have some deep-cycle batteries for storage and a spare inverter that might help if you can find some solar panels. You'll have to be able to get fresh water out of that well I saw out there, and a hand pump would be a slow process." Scott was impressed with how much Bartos had noticed since he'd been here.

"I looked over your food stores in the garage as well. You made good choices; the Mountain House freeze dried and bulk foods are especially good, although not as good as tonight's meal. I assume that's what you've hidden in the trailer as well?"

"Damn man," said Scott, "No keeping secrets from you, is there?"

Bartos grinned at him and handed him the empty whiskey glass. "Goodnight Scott, thanks for dinner."

Scott shook his hand. "Thank you, Bartos. Thanks for everything." Scott watched the dog slip into the Bronco just ahead of Bartos. As they left, Scott locked the gate and watched the taillights fade into the darkness.

THIRTY-ONE

Day 10

Sunday morning, Jack and Deputy Warren were leaning against the boardwalk talking as Scott glided up silently on his older Cervelo bike. Both men smiled when they saw him. "There's my hero," the sheriff's deputy welcomed him. Scott smiled back as he rolled the bike to a stop. "Hey guys," he said.

Jack looked at the newcomer, "Brother, I hear I missed something special the other night."

"We missed you, man. Wish you could've made it," Scott replied. "How are things going, Deputy?"

The officer shook his head, "Getting worse fast. I was just telling the Preacher here, a lot of craziness is startin' up."

"Like what?"

"Well," Warren said, "Let's just say that several of those released prisoners got a very different kind of justice. Apparently, a group slipped through the roadblocks and stole a hog from one of the farmers. The farmer and a few of his friends tracked them to a campsite and opened fire on them. All five of the prisoners were shot dead. The hog was still roasting on the fire when we showed up," said Deputy Warren.

"Did you arrest the farmers?" Scott asked.

"Hell no, we made them acting deputies then helped them eat the pig. It was delicious. I really think one of those convicts knew something about barbecuing pork. We did make 'em bury the bodies, but that seemed like punishment enough," the Deputy added sardonically.

Scott noticed Jack was looking uncomfortable, "You okay Preacher?"

"Yeah I guess, just that I know some of those boys. We have—*had* a prison ministry service over there once a month. Some of 'em just don't know any better, they…well, most aren't bad kids."

Warren looked over at him. "Jack, they are bad, or they wouldn't have been there. And it's a new day—we're not taking any prisoners. Shit, we got nowhere to put 'em. Justice has to be measured out in the field. No excuses accepted. Stealing food is going to be a capital offense, as well as most other things. My list is growing by the hour."

Scott could feel the tension rising and tried to change the topic. "Officer, I need to go up to Tallahassee tomorrow, hopefully to get my niece. Any idea how the roads are?"

The deputy shook his head, "First off call me Buck and, to be honest, I wouldn't recommend it. You'll find official roadblocks at nearly every town, highwaymen and raiding parties, stray prisoners and gang-bangers patrolling most o' the main roads. And everyone you meet'll be desperate enough to do stupid shit. Whatever you do, avoid the Interstate. Every exit off of I-10 is quickly becoming a war zone. People are getting hungry, crazy and desperate."

Scott shook his head, "Not what I wanted to hear. If we run into trouble and resort to using lethal force will we be in any trouble?"

"Couldn't say, probably depends on where you are. Some of the counties have—or had, anyway—some very liberal Sheriffs and judges. They may still be trying to coddle and protect the offenders. We've heard rumors that a lotta officers are trying to collect firearms from any vehicle they stop, even if you have the registration on you."

Scott showed the Deputy the map that Bobby had sent with the route he was planning marked.

"Hmm, that looks pretty good, but…" taking a pen from his pocket, the officer marked several different roads and areas to avoid. Taking the paper back, Scott said thanks.

"Todd told me he was going with you," Jack said. "Listen to him, do what he says and you'll get that girl back home."

"I will," said Scott. Thanking both the men, he pedaled over to the boat dock to see Todd.

The deputy leaned over to Preacher Jack. "He does have a car right? I mean…he ain't going that far on a damn bike is he?"

Jack laughed.

• • •

Bartos was with Todd at the boat, and they went over Scott's plan to get to Tallahassee using the new information he'd gleaned from Deputy Warren. Todd suggested they leave very early, as there should be fewer people on the road. They briefly considered taking his boat down the coast about eighty miles and borrowing a car to go the final fifty miles over to the university, but they had no information on that route. They would have also needed to leave the boat at an unknown location, and they had no real guarantee they could get a working car or fuel once they got there.

Even though Bartos would not be going with them, he helped plan it as if his life would depend on it. He made suggestions about what gear to take, especially which weapons and how to avoid trouble. In his opinion, meeting up with law enforcement was likely as dangerous as running into highwaymen.

His suggestion was to avoid taking the Jeep into the city at all. "Stop short of the campus and ride in on your bike to check it out. Much less likely that they'll stop you or that you'll be searched entering the campus."

That would be good because they were going to be packing serious heat: an M4 and AR-15 Tactical Assault Weapon; three different .45 caliber small arms; a scoped .308 sniper rifle; night vision monocular; more ammo that Scott could imagine; a pair of tasers, flex cuffs, two-way radios, and numerous other goodies. They would also be bringing three seventy-two-hour Go-bags kitted out with full survival gear. On top of this, Scott would have his bike and the necessary gear that went with it. Bartos suggested he take twice as much fuel as he thought they would need.

Bartos left, and Todd took Scott out in his pickup for some evasive driving lessons. Scott would be driving most of the way, with Todd very literally riding shotgun. Todd wanted to make sure Scott knew the basics of a reverse-out when coming up on a threatening road block, how not to get blocked in, and to be vigilant about checking each upcoming cross street to avoid being targeted by a potential crash car rocketing out to T-bone the Jeep and drive it off the road.

Scott felt foolish doing much of this and several times he thought he was going to roll the heavy truck. Eventually, he got more comfortable with the aggressive tactical driving.

"If we do get into trouble and have to stop," Todd said, "Use the engine block for cover. Bullets will go straight through everywhere else on the car. Also, be prepared to come out firing when that happens. Delays will be deadly." Scott was finally beginning to grasp the fact that it was shaping up to like the wild west days out there. "You also need to see Jack. He's willing to teach you some fighting moves that may be very important. I wish we had more time, but as soon as we're back, it's a must." Scott could not understand why a preacher would be the best teacher for that. but said okay.

Daylight was fading when Scott began his ride back to the cottage. He and Todd had made plans to meet up at 5:00 AM. Arriving back home, he went through his security sweep, pistol in hand. He closed the gate on the drive and checked the perimeter ensuring all doors and locks looked solid. He then opened the garage and moved in with the bike. He took a tactical flashlight and went through the house, clearing each darkened room before lighting lanterns and lowering the black sheeting over the front windows.

No music, wine, or good food tonight, he thought. He loaded the packs with the supplies they had agreed on and loaded the weapons, fuel and ammo cans inside the 4x4. Despite the amount of gear, it was not as crowded as he had feared. He made sure he had room for Kaylie and at least some of her stuff. He warmed up a can of beef stew, then cleaned his bike before heading to bed. He was tired but felt good about the plans. Despite everything, he was being proactive and careful. Dad would have been proud.

THIRTY-TWO

Day 11

Tyrell had grown up with no father, a mother who was helplessly hooked on drugs, and a granddad that stole their food stamps and welfare checks under the guise of withholding his daughter's drug money. Tyrell hated both his grandparents. He hated the government. He hated people that had money and nice things. He loved his mother. In his mind, she was that way because of all those other people.

He had been a scrawny kid and as a result, he was beaten up regularly by the other boys—and even men—in the projects. Somehow, though, the beatings never really seemed to phase him. Everyone he had ever known had hit him; that was just life. "It's a tough world," his granddad had often said, usually as he was swinging his belt.

Tyrell wasn't stupid. In fact, he had always made good grades and rarely got in trouble at school. He and his mom had moved back in with her parents after she got sick. She was an addict, yes, but to Tyrell, she was just sick. It wasn't long until his granddad had kicked him out. He had been in his early teens. It was the new low point in a life filled with low points. Tyrell had slept outside or under porches and scrounged for food. Somehow he'd kept himself in school even then.

Just after turning fourteen he found himself faced yet again with another older kid looking to prove himself. Beating up the smaller kids helped establish the pecking order in the neighborhood. This time, though, Tyrell had had enough. Enough of bullying, enough of taking it, enough of pain. He fought back.

He fought back with a savage brutality that had been building his whole life. In doing so, he received the honor of the neighborhood dealer's attention:

The Boss. He had no money or food. The Boss let him run errands for him and paid him a little each week.

Their arrangement built trust and Tyrell was given more responsibility for sales and pickups. Eventually, the drug running finally put some real money in his pocket, and before long he was hiring other kids to do the drops, using these kids as cut-outs or go-between's to keep his hands clean. He had already learned something his boss never had.

After working for the man for two years, Tyrell had indirectly helped set him up in a drug sting and then watched him go down in a shootout with the county's drug task force. Tyrell immediately took over the business, and with a vengeance. He vowed never to depend on anyone else again.

The news of Tyrell's growing clout and influential friends had gotten around the hood pretty quickly, and not everyone was happy with the kid's new-found success. As he knew it would—had hoped it would—he was quickly approached by his grandfather, who promptly swung a stick at him. Tyrell lost his cool and pushed the old man down a set of porch steps. He was done being disrespected by this old fool, he thought. The man's hip had been broken, he was taken to the hospital, and he died soon after.

Tyrell's mother had called him a murderer, and later that same year she had overdosed on drugs. Drugs that people who worked for him had supplied her. Drugs that he would never touch himself, nor allow his people to. To him, it was inventory or product, nothing more. It was just a business; if he didn't provide it, someone else would.

He didn't sell meth—that shit was evil. He also didn't allow any of the really hard shit to be sold to kids. They had to be at least in high school. He was not a bad guy, at least not in his mind. While the cops were not a big concern, his cut-outs did the pickups and deliveries. His customers and rivals scared him, though. That's why he surrounded himself with muscle: people whose loyalty he had bought and paid for.

Truthfully, Tyrell never expected to live long, and wouldn't have cared either way if it weren't for his little brother. DeeCee was his pride—smart, fast, and a good kid. Four years younger than Tyrell, he kept a close eye on him and did what he could to keep him out of the business. He should have known it wouldn't work. DeeCee was sixteen when he started using, then got himself hooked. The shit made him stupid, too. Soon he was arrested for four counts of possession with intent to supply Class A drugs. They also trumped up three other offenses, including resisting arrest and assault. Tyrell knew they were going to play him, try and turn him to give them evidence on Tyrell. The truth was his little brother was a minor, he'd get a slap on the wrist, nothing more. Within days, he was back on the street hustling and using. It had taken almost two years to get the boy mostly clean, but the stupid had stayed permanent.

* * *

Scott picked up Todd at the boat dock before sunrise the next day. Todd took his flashlight and checked all the gear before stowing his own seventy-two-hour Go-bags and weapons.

Driving down the darkened roads and through darkened towns felt surreal. The electricity had not been back on in the last thirty hours, and they both knew it might not ever be on again. Scott had used his French press to make a thermos full of coffee, and he and Todd both fixed a travel mug to sip on. Todd scanned for any radio stations that might be broadcasting, including the satellite radio, but none appeared to be on anymore.

It had been a challenge to come up with a route to the FSU campus that bypassed the Interstate and most of the larger towns. What could have been a three or four-hour trip would likely be twice that today. The GPS system in the Jeep had not worked correctly since the CME. Thankfully Scott had his portable one from his bike clipped to the dash. The printed map and directions hung from the same clip.

Scott looked at Todd, "Thank you again for coming. I have no idea why you are helping me. I'm sure that violates several of your rules of survival," he said with a laugh.

"Enough with the thank-you's, I ain't done nothing yet except drink your coffee," Todd growled.

Scott continued despite the dismissal. "Look, I realize I'm out of my league. I'm very ill-prepared for this trip or anything related to surviving this... this shit. I'm not my brother. I'm not Bartos and to be completely honest...I'm a little scared."

Todd looked over at Scott. "Being scared can be useful, just don't let it control you. Listen, Bartos is a hammer and usually sees everything as nails. Don't get me wrong, when it comes to a fight, and it will, no one I'd rather have beside me, but his longer-term strategy... well, not so great. Believe me, deep down, he's as scared as the rest of us."

Scott thought that a hammer sounded pretty good right now. Todd took a sip of coffee before continuing. "Besides, I'm pretty sure you're playing chess while the rest of us are playing checkers. Speaking of which, I've been wondering, what would you do right now to give all of us the best chance to survive?"

"What do you mean?" Scott asked.

Todd looked over at him, "I know we can't just fight our way through this. No one has enough bullets to survive on that alone. Even Bartos doesn't have enough freeze-dried food and propane tanks to make a real difference; you heard him the other night. What can we do now that will give as many of us as possible the best chance to see the other side? I know it'll come down to making smart decisions. You seem to pick up on things a lot quicker than most. So I want your best opinion on how we can all survive."

Scott looked straight ahead, dreading thinking deeper on the topic, but of course, he had been. Slowly, he said, "Like I said at lunch, all of us can't, most of us, most... probably won't. You read the reports. First, we have to survive the collapse, which is just beginning. Realization of how bad it is may be just now settling in for most people. The worst period for the larger northern cities will probably be from about now to ninety days, it said. Down here most of the data seemed to indicate that the worst initial period would be from six weeks to six months long.

"During the initial phase, several problems are going to rise to the surface, gain momentum and then peak. One will be the need for clean water. Tens of millions of people are probably already getting sick and beginning to die from it. Pre-existing health problems are going to take many more. Availability, quality, and access to medicine and real health care are going to deteriorate from here on.

"Worst of all is some—more likely *many*—of those who are unwilling or less capable of providing for themselves and their families are beginning to get desperate. A few may try to adapt, but many will resort first to scavenging, then to stealing, and eventually to *taking* what they need by force until everything is gone. In a lawless land, brute force will rule as you said. Very shortly, all the preexisting supplies, no matter how well prepared you are, will simply run out, and you will starve.

"The only way to avoid being one of the statistics is to survive this initial period. Consolidate and conserve as many long-term supplies and resources as possible. You also have to have the right mix of knowledge, friends, and collective skills to begin building a working community, including having the strength and resolve to defend it from those that will want to take it away. To me, it's key to have someone in a leadership role who will really take charge of local situations. Otherwise, the people that eventually take charge will probably be thugs."

Todd nodded his head in agreement. "The mayor is missing, and the few members of the city council and county commissioners that have turned up are clueless, they're politicians. The Governor is no better. The only people of power left in most of our counties are the sheriffs." Todd looked at the gray landscape passing by outside. "What would you have these so-called 'leaders' doing?"

Scott thought for a few minutes before answering. "Right now, immediately, they need to begin to consolidate all usable resources before they are stolen, wasted or lost."

"Like what?" Todd asked.

"The towns should begin collecting fuel in large storage tanks. Having fuel to help farmers initially will give us the best chance to work enough land to make a real difference later on. Once the larger supplies are under lock and key, begin sending out collection teams to drain all abandoned cars of fuel, as well as collecting batteries and any other useful finds. Collect all food stocks available for the benefit of the community. Get everything from restaurants and schools, to stalled freight trucks and even abandoned houses. If possible, keep refrigeration running in at least one large cooler so perishable supplies and meds can be preserved longer.

"Winter is coming, so planting crops won't be an issue for a few months, but hunting and fishing are essential so they should step that up now. We prepare for spring planting by finding out what help the farmers need. The ones that come to trade at the market would be a good start. We offer fuel, food, and seed and even labor to help grow the food. Some of the seed crops and manpower will need to go to the dairies and livestock producers. The goal is to have a self-sustaining community as soon as possible. Longer-term, we'll also want to be able to establish trade with other similar survivor communities."

"Who's going to agree to that, though?"

Scott glanced over, "Well people have always banded together to survive… it's just easier, even essential, you might say. Those that don't will likely die. I've read that the average size of hunter-gatherer social groups was probably between twenty and forty members. The average size of primarily agrarian communities was 200 to 300. We're probably going to be somewhere in the middle of that. We don't live in the most fertile regions to grow food. Some crops simply won't grow at all in this soil. We do have good amounts of wildlife and fish, though, so as long as we ration the harvesting and use the meat wisely, we have a chance.

"If Billy Bob goes out and kills the biggest buck in the swamp but he has no way of preserving the meat, he eats venison for a few days but then may waste the rest. How many more deer could that trophy buck be responsible for fathering? Perhaps that wasn't the best one of the herd to take. Maybe it would have been better if more of the community could benefit from each kill."

"Sounds like you're talking socialism or communal living," Todd scoffed.

"In some ways, yes. And that goes against my beliefs, but we are talking survival," Scott answered. "The exception, in this case, is that everyone in the community contributes. There can be absolutely no free lunch for anyone. The proposed government structure detailed in the Catalyst documents is pretty sound for this. We wouldn't stick with them forever but in the first few years, I think it would be essential. For anyone who doesn't provide directly, whether as a sheriff, a doctor or a mayor, we as a community all have to agree to feed that person to do only that job. These essential people are going to need to be essential to all of us to have value. We also have to establish quickly what our level of charity is. None of us may want to turn away a mother and small child who are hungry and desperate. However, if we're as close to the edge of survival as I expect, even that level of charity could be fatal for others, maybe even everyone in the community. We have to be willing to make that decision and stick to it before it even comes up."

Todd was looking up at the glow of the sunrise in the east. Much more quietly, he said, "If what I hear you saying is that somewhere between what... maybe 40 and 200 is all we can save no matter what, that means at least two-thirds of our community is already doomed."

Scott nodded his head slightly in solemn agreement. "Well, there is one advantage. We have a lot more knowledge than was common 150 years ago, and at least some of our tools and technology will survive. If we can store medicine and have fuel to use, I think the percentage of potential survivors could go higher—maybe even double—but that would likely be about all. That also doesn't account for the human factor. Each of us would need to be similarly focused, which is unlikely."

"I'm not sure any leader could get much buy-in on a proposition in which half the people will likely die no matter what."

Scott looked over at him. "I think that's why the Catalyst plan was kept under wraps. It is not a 'best plan'. It's more like the least bad of all the plans considered. Besides, we can't look at it that way. If we do nothing, then ninety percent of us will likely die."

Todd nodded glumly. He knew all of this already, but he liked hearing Scott's interpretation of it. He was less convinced that Catalyst was where his moral compass was pointing.

Scott was silent a few minutes as he looked out over the wetlands they were passing. "There is also a possible upside. Despite the fact that this looks like a very bleak dystopian story, it could be a kind of reset for Earth and mankind. We know we've been ruining the planet—pollution, acid rain, fossil fuel depletion, overfishing, and thousands of other abuses. We haven't been on a truly sustainable path for quite some time.

"As survival got easier, we've just kept growing exponentially, and with a human desire for more and more and more. Mankind couldn't keep taking forever. Eventually, something had to change. While it's likely true that only a small part of our population survives this, they'll have the opportunity to emerge into a much better world.

"Dinosaurs owned this planet for 165 million years. Humans have barely been around 200 thousand. In that relatively short span, we've evolved and then nearly gone extinct several times. According to one theory, there may have been as few as 2000 humans left alive on earth after a super volcanic eruption about 70,000 years ago; the so called 'Age of Death'. My point is this: we may just be the most recent tenants, but we've acted like it's ours to do whatever we want. Do we deserve to survive? Have we earned it? Can humans make it 165 million years? There's really only one thing that's kept us alive this long and it's our intelligence, although it seems in really short supply some days. If we can keep our top scientist alive, I know in time they can present better solutions to our fuel, food, and water needs. We may have gone back to the dark ages, but we don't have to stay there. We can move forward. We can be better stewards of the planet, but we will have to start making smarter choices and not repeat the selfish problems of our past. Our planet has a chance for a new start. With or without us. It's going to have its time to recover from all we've done to it."

THIRTY-THREE

Jack heard the Bronco as it pulled up to the curb. Solo was out and in the shadows before Bartos even opened the door. "Hey Padre, can you give me a hand today?" Jack noticed the trailer with a portable latrine and some pipe.

"Sure, is this the stuff for Scott's cabin?"

"Yea, I thought I would go over and set it up this morning while it's a little cooler. I just can't handle it alone, the damn thing's bulky and I need to dig a few trenches."

Jack smiled, "So you need me as a common ditch-digger now?"

Bartos nodded in agreement, "That's about it," he winked with a semi-smile.

Dropping off the portable toilet and setting it up only took a few hours, but by the end of it, both men were drenched in sweat. Bartos left the preacher by the trailer and disappeared around the front of the cottage. He reappeared several minutes later with two ice-cold beers. Jack wanted to ask him how, as he was certain the house was locked but decided to skip it. They sat on the back deck and savored the beer.

"The kid has a really nice place here," said Jack.

"He does," responded Bartos, "but it's too exposed and isolated. If he runs into trouble out here, no one will be able to help."

Jack nodded in agreement. "I hope he and Todd can get that girl without any trouble."

Bartos looked over at the preacher, "It's not that far, they should be fine. Why…do you know something?"

"I've heard a few things, but I just have a bad feeling about it," Jack answered warily. He downed the rest of the beer and looked out over the swamp. "It's just beginning…people are starting to get crazy. The shit we're just starting to see here is changing us. Out there, in the world, I feel sure it is much worse. A month ago death was an unusual thing, now it's getting more routine. I'm trying to visit with all my church members as often as I can. Nearly every day or two I'm finding another one dead or missing. I don't know what scenario's worse: those who starved or the ones that have taken their own life. As a man of God, I admit that I let a lot of things slide, but that to me is a sin. Why don't I blame them, though?"

Bartos looked at his friend and put his hand on his knee. "Thanks for helping me with this Jack. I need to check on someone myself." The men locked up the gate as Solo leaped into the back of the truck. They headed back toward Harris Springs.

• • •

Scott and Todd had driven for several hours without any incidents and were making good time. They had dodged abandoned cars and all manner of garbage apparently looted and discarded from vehicles. Now, however, the little towns along the way were beginning to wake up, and sounds of a passing car in the quiet morning were already getting to be rare enough for people to take notice. They also began to see an increasing number of people walking the roads. They went through their first roadblock outside a town called Bay Minette on the Northeast side of Mobile Bay. A surly looking officer looked pissed but let them go to the bypass road that went around the town. About forty-five miles later, they turned onto a road a few miles south of I-10, on a parallel course to the Interstate.

A thick canopy of trees covered much of the two-lane road and the early morning sun had yet to reach the ground. The Jeep's headlight caught a shape on the road several hundred yards ahead. As they got closer, they could see that it was a small child, a boy. He was standing, although not very straight. He was wearing an unbuttoned flannel shirt and nothing else but what looked to be filthy underwear. The child appeared to have an injured leg and was weakly holding up an outstretched arm toward the oncoming car. Scott began to slow down to see what was up. Maybe they could help.

Todd's hand quickly grasped the wheel and he shook his head no. Pointing to the high grass, Scott could just make out several people, hiding. As he pressed the accelerator down and swerved around the kid, a large man jumped up and fired a pistol at the car. It didn't sound like the round hit anything but Scott began to weave from side to side erratically as Todd had shown him to the day before.

Once they were out of sight Scott relaxed slightly. "What the hell?"

"Yeah, that's some fucked up shit, using the kid like that," Todd growled. "I guess this is the new normal. Trust no one."

They were only about seventy miles from Tallahassee when Todd interrupted their quiet.

"Okay, here we are, pretty much smack in the middle of East bumfuck-nowhere. Pull over when you get to a clear spot so I can take a leak. This coffee has to go." They hadn't seen another car or person for twenty minutes. Scott came to a clearing with open pasture on both sides and a small stand of trees about a mile ahead. He stopped the Jeep in the lane and the two men opened the door and stepped out. Scott immediately unzipped and let loose a long stream of pee arching into the weeds. "Whew that was a relief." Todd reached behind the seat and slung an M4 over his shoulder before stepping out to relieve himself as well. Scott took notice of that habit and realized he was unarmed and out in the open. *Whoops.* Todd had a waist holster and probably a backup gun somewhere else. Finishing before Todd, Scott reached over to the backseat and grabbed a tactical vest and his Sig Sauer P226, which he put into its drop holster. Todd was finishing when they both heard a scream pierce the humid morning air.

"That sounded like a woman," Scott said.

"I'd say it was coming from those trees up ahead," Todd said, pointing. Both men knew it was decision time. Get involved or just keep going? "It could be another trap," said Todd.

Scott knew he was right but didn't respond. A part of him thought *What if it was Kaylie out there trying to get somewhere?* Their decision was made for them soon after Scott put the Jeep in drive. They saw the jerky motion of headlights coming out of the woods and a car pulling rapidly onto the highway heading in the opposite direction from them, the unmistakable outline of a patrol car's lightbar on the roof.

Scott eased the Jeep down the road in the general direction that the other car had pulled out of. There was no undergrowth, and it was easy to see there were no other cars in the thin stand of pines. Scott could just make out a human shape, lying over a downed tree. They looked at each other.

"I'll check it out. You stay here—with the motor running," Todd added as he opened the car door.

Shaking now, Scott nodded. He watched the ex-Navy man slip into the woods and slowly circle the scene. Todd looked at the thing on the tree and then at Todd's figure, approaching on the far side. He stopped, stumbling slightly, then bent double and vomited. Scott opened the door to check on his friend, but Todd was already heading back, waving him to get back in the car.

As Todd opened the door and got in Scott handed him a bottle of water, which he sipped then spat back out the open window.

"Drive. Don't fucking stop for nothin' in this county." Todd shook his head, maybe in an attempt to escape whatever scene he had just found. Scott was not sure what his friend had seen but had them both shaken.

THIRTY-FOUR

The two friends were finally approaching the outskirts of Tallahassee. It had been a challenging day but, contrary to expectations, they were seeing fewer people the closer they got to the city. This was by far the largest of the towns they had been near and their nerves were on edge. In normal times, this was a city of about two hundred thousand, with the large college accounting for about a quarter of that number. As they got closer, Scott and Todd began to notice large aid camps, and what appeared to be makeshift tent cities. Besides the size of these aid camps, both men were shocked at the number of armed guards posted at every street and corner. This didn't look to them like any FEMA operation.

Todd unfolded a map of the city as well as the single page campus map with Kaylie's address penciled in the margin. Comparing it to the GPS on the dash, Todd did the calculations.

"It looks to be about eight miles ahead on this road."

They'd decided after the incident with the law enforcement van, and what with all the armed guards around, that they would listen to Bartos and not take the main road all the way in. *Better to try and avoid trouble, especially from guys with guns.* Lots of eyes seemed to follow the vehicle as they passed. Some of these people had no doubt been stranded when their car failed or the airlines stopped flying. Now, surely they wanted to get home by any means possible.

While those in the aid camps, at least, might be getting the bare basics, none of them seemed to be doing well. Both men imagined that many of the people watching them pass wouldn't hesitate to kill them for a working car to drive out of there.

Scott saw the railroad crossing that they'd marked on the map up ahead. He slowed, Todd with his M4 at the ready. Pulling off the road, Scott climbed out and quickly unmounted the Cervelo racing bike. He knew he was faster on that than nearly anything other than a car, and it was more maneuverable in city streets. Scott handed Todd the keys to the Jeep and took one of the shortwave radios and an ear piece.

"Be careful Scott. Call me when you find her or if you need help." Todd cranked the Jeep and dropped it into four-wheel drive. He guided it gently over the small embankment and found the nearly hidden two-track road that paralleled the railroad tracks. Scott watched the Jeep fade quickly out of sight. Then he clipped in and pedaled toward the campus ahead.

While on the surface it seemed foolish to leave the presumed safety of the Jeep, they had thought this through. As Scott expected, no one gave much notice to a guy whizzing by on a bike. Apparently, to most he passed, riding a bike was no improvement over walking. The fact was he knew he could ride steadily at around eighteen miles an hour, easily covering over a hundred miles in a day if he wanted. Even the best of these people walking could only do about six miles an hour and would be seriously fatigued after a fifteen-mile day. The click of the bike shifting to faster gears gave Scott some of the confidence he had not been feeling until now.

Most parts of the city seemed relatively calm and had very little car traffic. He turned down one street to take him in the direction of Kaylie's dorm and found he was quickly in a much poorer section of town. Scott saw an area ahead with more people crowded in front of several closed banks, and he had to dodge what appeared to be a broken and battered ATM in the middle of the road.

He noticed young men, even kids looting everything from beer to big screen TVs out of the many darkened and broken storefronts. He could understand why someone might steal to survive, but a flat screen TV? *What a bunch of dumbasses,* he thought. *It has only taken a few days to come to this; Human nature on full display, in all its glory.* He knew the people in these neighborhoods were less prepared for a disaster than anyone. They could be doing something constructive to prepare, but most would not think beyond the moment. One of the dumbasses caught sight of the man on the bicycle coming toward them. Stepping back into the street directly in Scott's path, he raised a pistol.

"Get off the bike, white boy," the young man said loudly. Scott saw the pistol at the same time he heard the command.

In all his years of cycling, he had encountered hundreds of dogs chasing him and numerous close encounters with cars unwilling to give him a lane to ride in.

Only once before had he encountered another person standing in the road wanting to do him harm. *That one didn't have a gun.* But Scott had acted on instinct then and did so again now. Using the speed he had built up on the slight downhill, he tucked down presenting the smallest area possible to the punk. He lined up as straight at the thug as possible. His heart was pounding, and fear was close to overtaking him. He scouted ahead, looking for another street he could possibly take.

Scott could see now that the guy was only a teenager. He was holding his pants about half way up with one hand, the silver pistol in the other. Scott glanced quickly down at the GPS. He had the speed creeping close to forty miles an hour and was in a flat-out sprint heading straight for the kid. Although it felt like minutes, the actual time of the encounter was mere seconds.

The gunman seemed to realize, too late, how fast Scott was coming toward him. He yelled, but it was too late, the bike was on him. He went to move to the side but his untied shoes and loose pants tripped him, and he fell sideways into the street, barely avoiding the crazy man and his bike. As Scott went by he blasted him with the can of bear attack spray he had in his jersey pocket. The stream of pepper spray hit the kid right in the face.

"Arrrghh! Mother Fucker!" the boy wailed in pain, firing blindly. Scott saw people ducking back into doorways as he leaned the bike at an extreme angle to take the next side street. He was out of that neighborhood entirely in just another few seconds.

He heard occasional shots from off in the distance. They came from most directions.

He was getting close to the campus and decided to stop and try to calm his racing heart rate. He pulled the small radio from his jersey pocket and called Todd. The familiar voice came back nearly immediately.

"You okay man? I heard a lot of shooting." Todd's voice was anxious.

"I had a little scare but nothing we hadn't expected. I'm at the edge of the university. This campus looks normal. Just going to spin around the area for a few minutes to see how safe it is."

"Roger that," came the reply.

Scott was within a block of the main campus entrance when he saw roadblocks, security vehicles, and a Humvee parked to the side of several armed troops in digital pattern gray camo. Dismounting the bike slowly, he approached the checkpoint. He made sure to keep both hands visible on the handlebars and was careful not to make any threatening moves.

"Stop!" came a loud command from thirty feet away. "Do not approach any closer, Sir!" came another bark. Not overly anxious to see what the response would be if he kept going, Scott stopped immediately. He was pretty sure he had just slightly wet himself.

"I just need to find my niece," Scott said.

"Sorry sir, I'm under orders that no one is to be admitted into or out of the campus. The campus is on lockdown for security reasons," one of the soldiers said.

"Why?" Scott called.

No response.

"Do you have an active shooter threat? Something else?"

Still no response.

The men kept their rifles at low ready, and several stood, focused only on him. Scott could see people walking around the campus. There seemed to be no signs of anything unusual there, other that the armed presence.

"Sir you will need to leave now," one of the men said. "The campus is closed."

"Listen," Scott pleaded, "I've come a long way to check on my niece. Her parents are worried sick about her. I just want to make sure she's okay."

The man who had been speaking eyed the bicycle suspiciously. Scott knew he wasn't buying the fact he'd come a long way on that.

Scott was genuinely confused. Nothing about this situation felt right. The campus on lockdown was somewhat plausible as shots had been fired recently, but people were calmly walking around inside the supposedly 'secure' area. Seeing how long the troops seemed to have been here and how ready they appeared to use lethal force—on someone as clearly non-threatening as Scott, no less—all seemed odd. Strangely still, none of the men had any insignia that Scott could identify, just a combat patch on their sleeve. The patch was a scorpion and what looked like a sword sticking through the middle. The camouflage pattern of the uniforms did not look familiar either. And no name patches on the chest. Something began to tickle the back of Scott's mind.

An older man in the same gray camo walked forward with a tablet. "Who are you here to see?"

Scott sighed with relief. "Oh, thank you, sir—m- my niece. No one's heard from her since all this began. The—"

"I need a name, sir!" The tone of his voice among the other irregularities kept Scott's paranoia on high-alert.

"First, um, could you tell me what this is about?"

The man with the tablet looked at Scott again. "What is your name, sir?" his demeanor seemed to be growing increasingly agitated.

Scott looked back at the man "Donald. Donald Jacobs," he lied, pulling the name of his high school history teacher from a random closet in his memory.

"And your niece's name?" Scott noticed the guards paying even more attention to him now. Several had taken up positions behind him. *Opening up new firing lanes, huh guys?*

Taking his paranoia to even higher levels, he lied again and said with a slight stutter, "Ch…Cheryl Reynolds. Umm. She's from Hattiesburg."

The man ran his hand down a list on his tablet and then tapped it several times to change pages. He began nodding and looked up smiling. "Ms. Cheryl Reynolds left the campus with a bus pass to Mississippi three days ago," he said, "She should be home anytime now. I hope that's what you needed. Please leave the perimeter now, sir."

Stunned at the blatant lie, Scott considered challenging the man's nonsense but, eyeing the men and their guns, thought better of it and turned to leave. But after a few steps, he turned back.

"Excuse me," he said to the man with the tablet who was also walking away. The man stopped and turned back. "Thank you for the information, just… could I get your name and unit so I can let my brother know exactly who I spoke with?"

The man turned and walked away. Another armed guard moved toward him. "Have a nice day now sir."

Sir my ass, Scott thought. He was furious, but he knew better than to let it show. He duck walked the bike a short way before remounting and pedaling away.

. . .

"Todd, did you get all that?" Scott said into the tiny Bluetooth microphone now clipped on his cycling helmet.

"Fuck yes…Did you not hear me yelling for you to get the hell out of there?"

Scott had linked the wireless microphone to the two-way FRS radio when he'd spoken to his friend earlier. He had taken his helmet off when talking to the soldiers, though, so he'd not heard Todd's warnings; not that he would have listened.

"Do you believe what they said about your niece?" Todd asked.

"Is my name Donald?" Scott responded sarcastically. "They fucking lied. I gave them the name of an old classmate of mine and he responded with bullshit just to get me out of his hair. Are you close yet?"

"This is some shit man. Yeah… I just pulled the Jeep up near the spot we marked on the map. The railroad passed within about a mile of the campus, just like we thought. I found an old logging trail to get it in even closer. I should be about a quarter mile from the dormitory. We need to regroup to decide how best to handle this. Can you get over here to meet me?"

Scott thought about it. The campus was huge but only had a limited number of roads in. Why in the hell did Kaylie even *live* on campus? Didn't she know every college student gets an apartment by the third year?

"I can get to you," Scott said into the radio. "I just want to check out a few more things first. Give me twenty minutes."

"Roger that," came Todd's reply through the headset.

Twenty-eight minutes later Scott popped through some brush about twenty yards from the Jeep. Todd was sitting on the bumper with the M4 aimed at him, but he quickly lowered it when he saw his friend. Scott eased up to the Jeep and remounted the bike on the rack.

"You're eight minutes late; any luck finding a way in?" Todd asked.

"Yeah," Scott answered. "Only the main routes in are heavily guarded, then there are roving patrols all over the campus. We should be able to slip over a small wrought iron fence and some thick hedges to get to her dorm."

Todd nodded mutely. "Kudos on how you handled the guards at the gate, quick thinking there. So, who do you think those guys were? The ones guarding the place? And why are they here?"

Scott shook his head, "I'm not sure, they weren't National Guard, and they didn't look regular army either. They were too relaxed and...professional. They looked menacing to me. If I had to guess, they were elite soldiers or some form of Special Forces. I might even assume they're the paramilitaries for Operation Catalyst—part of that "Praetor5 unit" thing."

"Or maybe they're fighting against them like the naval brigade off the coast of Tampa," Todd suggested.

Scott shrugged. "Not sure the 'who' matters right now, but the *why* does interest me. What makes a college campus more valuable an asset than a hospital, or an airport—or a port? Shit, even a bank? I mean, they may have many of those under guard as well... It just seems odd that they're here in such force..." he trailed off. "—The other thing is, it wasn't just swagger...they weren't bluffing. I fully believe they would shoot with very little provocation."

Scott looked nervously at his friend. "Todd, I can't let you go in there."

"Try and stop me," Todd said with a grin.

Scott put the Cervelo bike on the rack and pulled the cycling jersey off, swapping it for an FSU T-shirt he had brought with him. "Look, I can *maybe* pass for an old grad student." Todd looked hurt for a second, then conceded with a shrug. "You look too much like the guys with guns," Scott said, rigging his EDC pack to look more like a messenger bag and slipping on some non-prescription, skinny framed glasses.

Todd had to admit he had a point; Scott now looked like pretty much every other uber-geek college nerd on campus. Todd unclipped the Bluetooth headset from the bicycle helmet and handed it to Scott. "Wear this and keep it turned on. Keep me posted at least every five minutes. I'll shadow you as close as possible to the dorm but out of sight. If you run into any problems, just whisper, and I'll be there."

Scott put the device on his ear and checked his direction with the GPS from his bike. Giving a nod, he began walking toward the dormitory looking more confident than he felt. Todd quickly packed up the last of his gear. He knew he would need to leave some things along the way; he couldn't cross a street into a college campus with assault weapons hanging around his neck. He slung on his pack and headed down the same path that Scott had taken.

• • •

Scott's heart was hammering as he climbed the small iron fence and hid briefly in the hedges on the edge of the manicured green lawn. Getting his bearings, he saw the Thornton Hall dormitory building just ahead. He looked to the side of the brick building to see Todd slip into the shadows against the far-side wall. Not seeing anyone in the immediate area, he mustered his courage and began walking briskly to the dorm, then up the steps and through the front door, just like he belonged here. The power was out as expected, but he'd memorized Kaylie's room number and its basic location the night before.

He could see what must be the building's commons—durable looking sofas and a large screen TV—but the large space was empty. Taking the stairs up one floor, he quickly found his niece's room. He knocked on the door firmly, looking both ways down the darkened hall as he did so. He heard no sound from inside, so he knocked louder and whispered her name...nothing. The door had an electronic lock like a hotel room, but the number pad and lights were dark. He reached down and twisted the knob. Scott knew that these worked with battery backup for a while but normally stayed locked after that. Since these were student rooms, though, someone may have overridden the default feature. He tried the knob and to his relief he heard a click as the lock cleared and the door eased open. Scott clicked on his tactical light and quickly swept the empty room.

"Anything?" asked Todd's voice in his ear. "

Negative, no one home" Scott responded softly. He saw candy wrappers and empty water bottles littering the floor. He was beginning to wonder if he had the right room until he saw a pink camo EDC bag lying on the desk with his niece's initials monogrammed on it. Bobby had mentioned giving her one last Christmas. It had been kind of a joke gift although, he saw now, the contents were real and top quality. Kaylie had loved it and only made the addition of having it monogrammed. She'd said it may be for The Big Crunch, but a girl can still be stylish.

He searched more of the room and found nothing helpful other than a picture of his niece alongside a tall boy in glasses. The picture was recent and looked like it had been taken on campus. Seeing her beautiful face reminded Scott again of how adorable she was. Scott removed it and slipped in his pocket. Her laptop was open on her desk, but the battery was dead. He pulled open the campus map from his bag and looked for the location of the medical building. Kaylie was not technically pre-med, as that was not an available major at FSU, but her studies were essentially the same. Most medical teaching colleges would accept the certification she was to receive next year. He assumed that, in normal times, she would spend a lot of time in those buildings and the research libraries. Scott heard two quick clicks on his earpiece, which was the signal from Todd that someone was in the area.

He looked out the window to see a kid with spiky green hair leaning on the rails by the front entrance to the building. Scott couldn't remember if the dorm was co-ed or not but decided the kid was not a threat. Leaving the building, Scott smelled the overwhelming fragrance of weed. *Some things about college never change.*

Walking over to the stoner, he saw Todd also slipping in behind the kid. Scott sized up the meager morsel of modern youth and asked him if he knew Kaylie. The kid replied lazily. "I dunno man."

"Okay. What's with all the guards?" Scott tried.

Again the kid answered "I dunno." His hair was distracting. Scott looked at his acne-pocked cheeks instead.

"They got the best pot anywhere, though," Green hair added smirking. The kid stiffened as he finally noticed Todd standing just behind him.

What would the guards or militia be doing handing out dope to the students?

"What better way to keep the student population passive and loyal," Todd said as if reading Scott's mind.

Scott showed the kid the picture of Kaylie and his mostly unfocused eyes finally showed some signs of recognition.

"Oh yeah, the hotty from twenny-eight."

Kaylie was indeed a looker, and he knew the kid remembered her.

"When did you see her last?" Todd asked.

"I, uh, I… don't know dude," the kid said. "Seemed like a week ago, maybe…shit, maybe it was yesterday."

Todd was in no mood for stalling. He reached out and slapped the kid hard. That pissed him off.

"Look, dude," he said as he righted himself, wobbling slightly. "Get the fuck away man, before I call the grayshirts." Scott thought back to the Nazi Sympathizers that had gone by a similar name.

"That would be a very bad idea," Todd said in a menacing voice, as the barrel of the large STI 1911 pistol appeared at the stoner's head.

Despite the haze of drugs, the stoner got much more helpful after that, and after a much more subdued exchange, the kid, whose name was Billy, said that Kaylie was usually either in the gymnasium workout room or the medical building as Scott had expected. They also learned that the building was near where the militia's base was, and where the mess hall was located. "Guns aren't allowed though...they'll get you killed – them grayshirts guys don't fuck around."

Scott gave the kid a hundred-dollar bill, and Todd told him to vanish. Billy was gone in a flash. Scott and Todd ducked into the shadows to consult the campus map again. The gymnasium and the med building were not far and in the general direction of the giant Doak Campbell Football Stadium. They waited for a patrol of three grayshirts to pass before splitting up and easing down the small hill toward the buildings. Neither of them took notice of the person watching them from the shadows of an adjacent building.

THIRTY-FIVE

For what had to be the hundredth time Scott wondered what in the hell he was doing. Sneaking through an armed campus looking for one student in a population of thousands and...*oh yeah the end of the world was just a few days ago.*

Scott looked over and could just see Todd working his way around to the opposite side of the building. Todd had found a leaf rake and had put on a ball cap in an effort to look more like a groundskeeper than an interloper. The nondescript building that housed the biological and medical classrooms was not a large structure. Scott walked in the front doors much more confidently than he felt. He began systematically checking the open classrooms down the main hall. He did see some people in the building, but none appeared to be female.

Most of the doors were locked. He heard the Bluetooth headset click twice, and Todd said, "You might want to take cover. Two armed grayshirts coming in."

Scott scrambled to find a suitable place to hide. None of the doors he was near were open, and it seemed like breaking in might be a bit more suspicious than he needed to be right now. *Think.*

He grabbed a nearby stack of papers and began rifling through them as he walked as calmly as possible down the next corridor. His heart stopped in mid-beat as he saw the two guards at the other end of the hall. Fortunately, they entered one of the rooms at the other end of the corridor. Scott stepped back into the shadows of a door to observe. He heard sounds of protest and raised voices.

The two armed men came out of the room with a man in a lab coat. He obviously had no desire to go with them, but he did not actively resist. Scott moved to follow from a discreet distance. As they walked the man down the front steps, his protests got louder. In the daylight, Scott could now see it was not a man in the lab coat; it was a boy. The same boy he'd seen in the picture with Kaylie.

This kid would probably know where she was. He followed behind the trio. Todd was nowhere to be seen, but he heard the clicks in his ear just as a loud voice came from behind him. "Sir! Can I see your campus ID please?"

Turning around Scott saw the voice belonged to a young soldier whose rifle he held in the now familiar and menacing low-ready position. Scott's fake eyeglasses were halfway down his nose, the disheveled stack of papers still clutched to his chest. He stammered something and managed to free one hand, patting his pockets. Scott knew he only had seconds to produce the card.

"Professor?" another voice asked. Scott glanced to the side and saw a young black student stepping toward them from the corner of the building. "I thought that was you," he continued. "Hadn't seen you outside that building since the lights went out." Scott was confused as the smiling boy continued to walk toward him, speaking to him as if they knew each other well. Scott caught sight of Todd standing off to the side raking leaves. He was still unsure what was going on but finally found his voice.

Addressing the smartly dressed young man, he said, "Ah …Sorry, yes I had some important work to finish." The kid held up his ID for the guard and Scott to see. "It's good to see you DeVonte," Scott added.

DeVonte walked over, helped Scott with his falling papers, and whispered, "Just go with it." DeVonte opened a book he was carrying and said more loudly, "If you have a second, I just don't get this theorem you covered here."

Scott looked at the book with great interest, almost as if his life depended on it… which it probably did. He was aware of the soldier moving off now, apparently having lost interest in the student teacher exchange. DeVonte told Scott to follow him.

"Thank you for doing that."

"It's cool," the kid said, "I could tell it was about to get ugly. Grab your yardman," he added, nodding toward Todd, "And we can go someplace safer to talk." *So the kid had had them pegged from the start.*

• • •

Ten minutes later the three of them were crowded into a small antechamber located in the back of what must have once been a small chapel. The rock walls, dark interior, and Spartan furnishings looked out of place on the modern campus. The building appeared to be used for storage, and a quick glance could cover the entire building.

Feeling more confident, Todd relaxed slightly. He had been ready to do whatever was necessary to get Scott away from the guard. When the nice looking dark-skinned youth had calmly eased up near him and said in a low voice, "Relax man, I got this," Todd had not known what to expect. Watching the kid work the guard had been a welcome relief in the face of the much more vicious and likely doomed solution he had been planning.

DeVonte looked at the two guys and smiled a big toothy grin. "I'm guessing you guys don't belong on this campus. I'm also guessing you're wondering why in the hell I helped you. Am I right?" Scott and Todd looked at each other with uncertainty.

"Yes," Scott said, "I'm looking for my niece, and I know that boy they were taking away would have an idea of where she is and if she's okay."

"Who is your niece?" DeVonte asked. Scott showed him the picture he had in his pocket.

"Kaylie Montgomery. You know her?"

"I seen her round. She's a nice girl, but we aren't really friends or nothing. Think we had a few classes together a while back." He paused before continuing. "I watched you two sneak in the campus and then question that doper outside the dorm. You gonna get caught by these militia guys if you keep it up. They ain't stupid. They give these kids free dope so they'll rat out anyone they see breaking the rules. If that happens and they find you, yo' asses'll be disappeared, you know what I mean?"

DeVonte spent the next several minutes telling them what he knew. The grayshirts had shown up the day after the power went out. While they said they were there for added security, the heavy-handed tactics appeared to suggest otherwise. No one was allowed on campus without an ID, and no one was allowed to leave either. The rumor was that the large stadium had been turned into a stockade for troublemakers. DeVonte said fewer and fewer students were around now. His dorm was nearly empty. No one had any idea what was going on, or where students were going if they weren't allowed to leave, but they were all scared.

"So why did you help us?" Scott asked.

"I watched you guys. You worked as a team, an' your friend here's obviously ex-military. I thought you might have a plan to get us all out. Maybe you could help me get off campus. Most of us're thinkin' these military dudes are terrorist. They cut the power supply to the school, then took over. Like in a movie, you know? But then I saw the lights in the sky like we were in the Arctic or somethin' and the lights off everywhere else too. Are they off everywhere?"

Todd and Scott nodded, "Sorry, but yes they are. A massive solar flare took down the grid," Todd said, speaking for the first time. He continued, "Do you still think the military guys…. the grayshirts are bad guys? Have they hurt any of you?"

"No…no one's been *obviously* hurt, but these guys are rough. No bullshit, you know. Anyone gives them crap, starts trouble or *farts* in the wrong direction— they just come up missin'."

"Like Kaylie's friend?" Scott asked.

"Yeah, probly, but that was a little unusual. Normally they take you when no one can see, like at night. Seemed they had somethin' different in mind for that guy."

Todd looked at Scott. "We still don't know if the grayshirts are a threat. They could be protecting the school. Special ops training isn't big on being polite. In almost any urban combat situation, they would first want to subdue any possible internal troublemakers so they could then focus on external threats." Looking at the kid, he said, "DeVonte, thanks again for all your help out there—and the info. I need to know if you've seen any larger weapons, like tanks or artillery. Do you know how many soldiers there are? And any idea if they're army or Navy?"

The bright-eyed kid smiled again. "Nah I haven't seen nothin' like that, but they keep an entire section of the campus blocked off. The old practice fields, the parking lots for the stadium and all the stuff on that side are all off limits. You can't even get close enough to see over there. They could have a platoon and shit, who knows how much hardware. What I do know though is it seems all the soldiers come to the mess hall to eat. The ones in charge and the ones who walk the patrols. I managed to volunteer myself to help on the serving line.

"Thought maybe I could learn more about what was happenin' and maybe get a little extra food to eat. What I gathered from all that was there are 'round 450 troops now. They work in two shifts, so about 200 or 250 are guarding the campus at any one time. I got no idea who they are…like I said we all was thinkin' they might be some kind of terrorist group. Even in their small talk, they don't let anything like that slip out. I was listenin' close as I cleaned tables and such. These people are always on point. They don't slip up, not ever."

Scott looked at Todd and asked him if he had any idea who they were. Todd shook his head no. "The MultiCam appeared similar to a pattern of arctic assault gear some Navy seals have, but the weapons and vehicles seem to suggest army special ops. The tactics and discipline are definitely special ops, but elite soldiers aren't normally used in a pacification mode like this. It's a big fucking question mark at this point," sighed an obviously frustrated Todd.

Looking out through the tiny dirty window, Scott could see more people moving outside now. "DeVonte, do you have any idea where we should look for Kaylie? Do you think she was one of those…" He could barely say the word,

"One of those—taken?" The idea of her being out of their reach in a military prison camp terrified Scott. They couldn't fight through a full battalion of elite soldiers to find her. How would he tell his brother he couldn't get to her?

"Yeah I know where she is," the kid answered with a grin. Todd and Scott both stared at him.

"I saw her head out just before you guys showed up. She had on tight yoga pants and sneakers. Dat girl be bangin' in that outfit man…Sorry. I mean she's uh, hard to miss. Pretty sure she was heading down to the gym. She works out a lot, 'specially with most of the classes canceled," DeVonte said to both men's great relief.

Scott grinned, "I am really glad we met you, man. By the way, my name's Scott. The big yardman here is Todd." They all shook hands. Scott had instantly liked the young man and certainly owed him even more now.

The gym was just down the hill, in the same direction most of the people outside seemed to be heading. Looking out, DeVonte said, "The mess hall is down there too, and it's about lunch time. Probably be best if I check out the gym to see if I can find her."

"We can't ask you to do that," Scott said, "Any ideas on how we could get in?"

"That's going to be risky man…the big guy here really stands out. You might pass, but that other guard spotted you pretty quick. Let me think…" He seemed to ponder several options then said, "Follow me."

The three men went to the front of the building. A small space held a work desk. "One of the school's food service contractors uses this office sometimes," DeVonte said. Rummaging through the desk drawers, he came up with two campus ID badges. The plastic badges had no picture on them, but the word contractor stamped on it with a number. He handed one to Scott and the other to Todd. "Grab a clipboard and lose those bags. I'll go down first. You two watch where I go and then follow. Don't get lost—you have to look like you go there all the time." They nodded. "When I get to the side door of the gym, I'll give you a signal. Get in, find the girl, and send her out to me. You'll get made if they see you mingling with students. She and I will come back here and wait on you two. Make a check on the vending machines and then slowly swing back this way."

Getting into the gym went as planned. The kid was a natural and seemed to blend into every situation. He chatted with friends, ignored the occasional guard, and always seemed to know where the two guys were behind him. As Scott and Todd slipped inside the side door of the gymnasium they did a discreet perimeter sweep. They didn't see any of the grayshirts, but they also didn't find Kaylie either.

They checked the weight rooms, the main gymnasium and even took a quick peek in the showers. Scott went up to the indoor walking track where he thought he saw a girl about her size. Getting to the carpeted oval mezzanine, though, he saw no sign of anyone. He was about to head back down when he heard a small soft voice.

"Uncle Scott?"

He snapped his head around, still seeing no one. He whispered "Kaylie?" No response. He tried again and was about to look elsewhere when he saw a small hand appear from behind a column. He had not noticed the hidden space behind the support beams, but as he walked in that direction, he first saw long chestnut hair and then his brother's daughter stepping out from behind it. Kaylie gave the briefest hint of a squeal as she ran grinning into her uncle's arms.

"When did you get here? Are Mom and Dad okay? Do you know..." Her questions came in a rapid-fire torrent and Scott put up his hand to quiet her. He pulled her into a tight embrace, tears appearing in both their smiling faces. Kaylie was drenched in sweat from what must have been a vigorous workout and Scott was trembling slightly as he held her.

"They're fine. We can talk about the rest later," Scott said. "Right now, we just need to get somewhere safe." Kaylie nodded, and Scott told her the plan. She knew who DeVonte was and after a quick introduction to a grinning Todd, she grabbed her stuff and walked out the side door to meet up with their new friend.

THIRTY-SIX

Todd gripped Scott's shoulder as Scott tried hard to return his breathing to normal. He was nearly overcome with relief as they watched DeVonte and Kaylie walk, carefree, up the hill and into the old church building. "You found her," Todd said, "And she's okay."

"I know," Scott said quietly, "We still have to get her out of here, though."

Todd smiled, "We can do that. We got this far."

"I couldn't have come this far without you, buddy," Scott said looking at his friend. "I'm not used to needing help, much less having people I can count on. You don't know how hard this has been for me, but thank you so much."

Todd looked at his young friend. "Shit dude; DeVonte is right. Your niece be bangin'," he teased, laughing.

Scott let out an amused sigh. "Yes, she is. But please don't ever say that again."

"Deal," said Todd, "if you stop hitting on my wife."

Todd and Scott waited five minutes before walking back and rejoining Kaylie and DeVonte. Kaylie was still all smiles, and Scott took the next twenty minutes to update her on the basics of what he knew, and the last conversations he had with her dad—most of it, anyway.

Kaylie was on board with going and staying at the beach cottage. Scott knew she wasn't grasping the desperation of the situation outside the campus.

"Bubbles," he said, calling her by his pet name for her, "You do need to listen to this. You could actually be safer staying right here. I can't guarantee much of anything; it's bad out beyond these fences. I'm reasonably certain we'll have trouble just getting back to Harris Springs." He sighed a heavy sigh. "We may not even be able to get you off the campus. Food and water are in short supply, and people are getting desperate. The law is unable to help. The basic social structure is breaking down, and we're not even a week into this crisis. I promised your dad I would try and get to you, make sure you were okay. Now you need to decide if it's best for you to stay or go." Looking to the helpful, handsome young man next to her, Scott said, "DeVonte, where do you live? Anywhere close?"

"Yes sir, I'm from just north of Mobile. If you have room, I'd really appreciate a ride. I know these soldiers is up to no good. Just a matter of time before it gets real ugly here."

Todd smiled, "We'll make room for you, friend. Even if I have to put Scott up on the roof. Getting you all the way home might not be easy, though. The bigger cities are starting to become war zones."

"No sir," said Devonte, "I'm from a real small town. If you can just get me close, I'll be okay. My brother's a Deputy Sheriff—he can probably meet us if we can get in touch with him."

Kaylie was looking at her feet and fidgeting. "What is it?" her uncle asked.

"I want to go with you," she said. "I know that's what Dad would want." She paused and seemed to not want to continue.

"But," Scott prompted.

She looked at the floor, "My boyfriend, DJ," She said. Scott looked over at DeVonte, who gave the slightest shake of his head.

Pulling out the picture, Scott pointed at the boy, "Is this your boyfriend?" Kaylie reached out for the picture and clutched it close, a pained expression on her face. "Honey, I'm afraid we can't help him," Scott said as firmly as he dared. "We saw the grayshirts escorting him out of the medical building earlier."

"They were taking him over to the admin building," DeVonte said. "Not to the Doak," he added, referring to the stadium. Scott took his niece's hand, realizing again just how much she looked like her mom.

"Kaylie, we can't take on the military to free your friend. I'm sorry, but we would probably all get 'disappeared'" using DeVonte's word from earlier.

Todd decided that if anyone was going to be the bad guy in this it should be him. "Kaylie, I have a couple of questions. Where is DJ from? Do you know if he would even leave if he had the choice? And do you have any idea what they would want with him?"

"He's from South Florida," she said. "I'm not sure if he wants to go or not. He hasn't said. In fact, we've barely talked since the lights went out. Something he's working on. He says it's important to the army guys... I don't know what it is, but he said they come to get updates every few days. I'm sure today was just another one of those."

"He didn't seem too anxious to go with them," Scott said. "In fact, he looked pretty pissed off."

"That's just the way he gets when he's working or studying," Kaylie said. "DJ is a wonderful guy, but he's a bit of an academic. He can get wrapped up in whatever project or paper he's working on and forget to eat, forget about me. I'm not even that sure he really knows what's going on out here."

Todd looked over at Scott and shook his head. This didn't sound like someone they would have any luck in getting away from here; away from his work. "Kaylie," Todd continued, "Are you prepared to leave without him?"

She didn't answer. Scott reached up and brushed the hair from her face. "What kind of research does DJ do? I mean isn't he just a student?" he asked.

"DJ is quite gifted and already pretty respected in his field. He's doing graduate studies to become a virologist. He specializes in botanical-based treatments. We did some work together in the med labs—that's where we met," she added, tears beginning form in each eye.

"Why would they be interested in that?" Todd asked to no one in particular. "Seems to me they would be more concerned about getting the power back on."

"If the soldiers are interested in it, seems like it would be either to treat an existing outbreak or they are trying to weaponize a pathogen." DeVonte guessed.

"Biological warfare? Doubt it," Todd said. "If these guys are who we think then they have plenty of research on that shit already. Probably have stockpiles of weaponized everything you can imagine. No need to be starting from scratch, especially not at some random college campus. Most wouldn't even be on US soil due to the laws and potential outbreak threat. An outbreak, though, that makes more sense."

Scott thought for a few seconds. "The only information that is even remotely related to this…" He paused trying to remember, "I saw a single headline just after the CME hit. It mentioned a BioResearch facility's containment failing. It was overseas I think… maybe Turkey or Pakistan. This wouldn't be connected to that would it?"

"Shit." Todd looked grim. "Power grid failure, economic collapse, social collapse…. Yeah. A global fucking pandemic is just what we need right now." Todd strode back and forth a few times. The others watched with dark faces. "Still doesn't figure why here, why *this* guy…DJ. Hell, maybe the grayshirts are actually the good guys, then. They could be the advance battalion for Catalyst."

"I've heard that word several times, what is it?" DeVonte asked. The men looked at each other.

"Catalyst? You heard them use that word?" asked Scott.

"Project Catalyst, yeah, I heard them say it more than once," DeVonte answered, "Never when they thought anyone was around, though. They would be saying something about protocols and not forgetting what the priorities were.

It was Scott's turn to pace as he explained. "Catalyst is a government emergency plan to try to reestablish order in the case of a national or global disaster. We can get into it later, but the main point is that if Catalyst is in effect, it will be every man for them self for the next few years."

"Okay," Todd said, "Let's focus on tactics here. DeVonte, you and Kaylie need to pack your shit. Everything you're taking with you—you will not be coming back. We don't have much room, so stick to essentials. DeVonte, I'm trusting you have an idea of how to get out of this place?" DeVonte smiled and nodded. "Is it a daytime or a nighttime plan? Todd asked.

"It'll have to be dark," the boy answered.

"Okay, so we have a few hours. In that time, you need to get packed up, and we need to get our gear stowed close to whatever exit point the kid here chooses. We have to be ready to move. Scott, go with Kaylie. Does DJ live in the dorms?" he asked her. Kaylie nodded.

"He lives in the building next to mine."

"Okay, good, I'll act as watch on the trail from the admin building, the labs, and the dorms. If DJ comes back before it's time for us to bug out, I'll signal Scott's radio. If it's safe, Kaylie and Scott can approach, learn what they can from the boyfriend and see if he wants to make a run for it with us. DeVonte, when you finish up, come back here and find me. I have a few things we could really use, and you may know how to get 'em." DeVonte nodded, his chest swelling a little. He was clearly pleased to have Todd's approval. Todd leaned over and spoke more quietly to Scott. "Look, man, I don't want to try and separate you from your niece just after you found her, but remember what the boy said. That green haired stoner punk probably ran to rat out the two guys looking for the hot girl. If so, they're likely watching her dorm room. Let her go in alone, stay out of sight, and *don't* be a hero."

Scott nodded, knowing his friend was right.

THIRTY-SEVEN

Bartos's friend had been in terrible pain when he had checked on her earlier this evening. Getting her to this clinic had been her idea. He knew the hospital would have been better, but it was much further away. With Todd and the new guy over in Tallahassee, he hadn't been sure what would be the best thing to do for her. The clinic was close and had doctors and medicine, though.

When they arrived at the darkened building, he did not notice the broken door at first. The soft moans coming from the woman had not subsided since he had picked her up from the floor in her kitchen. He knew she was in terrible pain, and he was one of the few people anywhere who knew of the disease that had been stealing her life away for a long time. He heard Solo attack and the scream of a man at the side of the building.

Solo was in a low crouch at the corner of the building as Bartos pointed the rifle at the man's head. The looters had apparently targeted the building for drugs; they all looked like users. All except the guy his gun was pointing at. This guy looked vaguely familiar but in the darkness, he couldn't be sure.

"Call him off!" the man called.

"Ummm…no." Bartos spoke calmly as the other man's volume increased. While many preppers expected there to be widespread social breakdown once the shit had hit the fan, Bartos had never bought into that. He felt that good people would probably remain good. When they got truly desperate, though, he realized even the best of them may do terrible things. He also knew that criminals would remain criminals, and yes, they would get worse in the absence of police. Drug addicts needed supplies, and once the narcotics pipeline stopped flowing, they would have to look elsewhere. The community clinic was an obvious opportunity for these dopers. Bartos did not like to think of himself as a violent man, but what he had seen in the last couple of days was changing him, making him hard. *It's changing everyone*, he thought.

He had just wanted to get some help for his friend, not fight a damn drug war. It was apparent that no doctors or nurses remained alive in the clinic. He hated to leave it to these thugs. Through the broken door he saw what appeared to be a dead body, female in shape, and at least three more figures alive inside the darkened space. The sounds of breaking glass and slamming doors along with the excited whoops and greedy laughs made him angrier still. Those drugs and supplies meant the difference between life and death for a lot of good people in the months ahead. The pleas of the man at the end of his gun suddenly stopped as Solo brushed his leg to get between Bartos and the man he held at gunpoint. The man looked to be scared shitless but did not say anything.

"Get your guys out of there or we will," Bartos said calmly.

"You're not cops... Fuck you!" the man spat out the words. "We'll fucking kill you, man."

Bartos smiled. "I am sorry, but I don't have time for this tonight," he explained as he pulled the trigger. The body of the man had not even hit the ground before Bartos gave the canine a new order. "Solo. Clear." The dog became a shadowy streak as he ran through the front door.

Screams and a few gunshots erupted from inside, but Bartos could hear the dog working his way through the thugs. One stumbled out with a bloody arm, a cheap handgun still held limply in one hand. Bartos dropped him just outside the door with a single shot to the chest. The sounds of a struggle inside the building quieted considerably as a bloody-faced Solo appeared in the doorway. Bartos could swear the dog was smiling although no way he could see that in the darkness. *Could dogs even smile?* he wondered. He took his tactical light from the truck and inspected the clinic.

"Goddamn, you psychotic dog," he muttered as he saw the bodies of three more guys. "I'm glad we're on the same side." Solo's tail wagged as he sat and watched his master, an eager puppy happy to please. One of the dead was just a kid, couldn't have been more that sixteen or seventeen. Another one, Bartos recognized. He had worked at the shop as a temp the summer before last. Bartos had fired him for stealing copper wire. While some guys would have felt remorse at what had just happened, Bartos was not that kind of man. These guys had made the choice, he reasoned. In his mind, he had just helped the town take out some trash.

Seeing no workers from the clinic alive amongst the carnage, he grabbed the bags of drugs and medical supplies the thugs had conveniently collected and put them in the truck. His friend looked worse. He called Solo, and they headed further down the coast to the hospital.

THIRTY-EIGHT

With Todd acting as watch, Scott shadowed Kaylie closely as she and DeVonte approached the dorms. They had discussed a plan in case she was stopped and questioned. DeVonte had also shown them a good place to stash their bags. Scott stayed hidden outside Thornton Hall as his niece went in to grab her stuff. She was back in fifteen minutes carrying her Pink EDC bag and a large duffle. "Damn that was quick," he said.

"For a girl you mean," she grinned, raising her eyebrows in playful disapproval of her uncle's slip. Scott reached out a little sheepishly and took the larger bag from her, worried that it would draw more attention than they wanted. Sticking to the shade, they managed to stash the bags without garnering any attention. Another bag, presumably DeVonte's, was already in the ivy-covered hiding hole.

Scott's Bluetooth gave a series of clicks. "DorkOne this is Overwatch, copy?" Scott hated the call sign Todd had given him for the day but replied in as unbothered a tone as he could muster.

"Go for DorkOne," he said, looking at Kaylie and shaking his head.

Todd's voice came back, "Our spiky-haired friend is back with a couple of serious looking goons. They're heading into Kaylie's building now. You two need to become invisible."

Scott grabbed his niece's hands and pulled her deeper into the brush that ringed this edge of the campus. "We have to hide," he explained to her in a whisper. "Grayshirts may be looking for us." Scott made sure she was well camouflaged and then did the same for himself. They were not close enough to talk, so he just lay there, breathing in the earthy smells and wondering what was probably crawling up his pants leg. Every few minutes Todd radioed in with an update. He also let him know that DeVonte had been back and was now out doing an errand. "He's a good 'un," Todd added, allowing himself this small voicing of approval.

Scott found himself eventually dozing off. The warm Florida afternoon and the intense activity of the day were catching up with him. Occasionally he heard small sounds of movement from Kaylie's direction. He finally gave in and closed his eyes.

The sunlight was more subdued when Scott opened his eyes. The soft click in his ear let him know that Todd was still on duty. Scott guessed he had slept for less than an hour, but he felt much better. "This is Overwatch; the coast is clear. Looks like they decided Spikey was lying. They slapped him around a bit when they came back out. They did an exit patrol right by your location, but I could hear you snoring so I didn't bother you. All three are gone now."

"Roger that Overwatch, thanks," Scott said. "Any sight of Brainiac?" he asked, referring to DJ.

"Possibly," came the reply. "Watching a subject coming from the right direction now. Looks like it could be him, but he'll need to be closer to confirm. Give me five minutes but go ahead and wake sleeping beauty. I think this is it."

• • •

Todd radioed back in just a few minutes to confirm that it was indeed Kaylie's boyfriend, and he appeared to be heading into the dorms. Scott still couldn't figure out why any student—much less a grad student—would live on campus, but apparently the fellowship DJ had provided free room and board. He probably worked all the time, and home was only a hundred feet from where he worked if he stayed here.

Kaylie and Scott had worked their way over to the building and slipped in through the back door. They arrived at DJ's room about the same time as he did. The tired looking young man looked very happy to see Kaylie, but his face darkened when he saw the anxious looking man with her. She quickly introduced them and Scott ushered all of them inside the tiny living space.

To describe DJ's room as utilitarian would give too much credit to his decorating abilities. The entire room was so plain and generic it seemed as if no one lived there. *I'd feel more at home in a medical examination room*, Scott thought, doing his best to reserve judgment about the guy who was dating his niece. He checked the room for surveillance but found nothing obvious. In a worried tone, Kaylie asked DJ if he was okay. "Did they hurt you?" she asked anxiously. Scott looked the boy over in more detail as the couple talked. Without the glasses, Scott could tell he was a handsome guy. The dark rings under his eyes showed exhaustion and stress, though. What DJ lacked in decorating skills or outward appeal he clearly made up for with an engaging smile and understated personality.

He was obviously very bright, as Kaylie only had to give the basic outline for him to pick up on what was going on. DJ looked up at Scott, "Thank you for coming to get her. I've been so worried that I couldn't keep her safe. They have me and the Doctor I work with under so much pressure that I barely get any time to see her."

"What do they have you working on?" Scott asked.

DJ hesitated and hung his head. "I'm not supposed to discuss it with anyone."

Scott nodded and went on to ask about the grayshirts. "Do you know who they are or what they're here for? Who exactly do you meet with?"

The boy shrugged. "I don't know who they are, I always assumed army. Their mission, from what I've been told, is to "secure vital national infrastructure and resources". Our lab is apparently—or was at least—partially funded by a grant from USAMARIID, the national research lab. I guess that gives them the right to be here. The person I meet with never gives me a name or rank, I just refer to him as 'Sir'."

Scott wanted more information, but he was unsure how far to push the young man. "You work as a virologist right?" he asked. "Should we fear a global pandemic or something? It sounds like your research is a top priority for this militia. That worries me. Seems like they would be trying to get the power back on or restore law and order."

DJ was looking down shaking his head, "I don't know," he admitted. "I know we're just one of many labs that are doing priority research right now. I assume other facilities and research labs are working on the power grid, fuel supplies, crop yield technology, who knows what else. The stuff I'm working on is very compartmentalized, so I only know a small piece of what's going on." The young man pulled Kaylie in for another hug, holding her tightly. "My study is more accurately on parasitic, bacterial infections and most of my work so far has been working on gene mapping something similar to the Mycobacterium tuberculosis bacterium."

"Tuberculosis Didn't we beat that a hundred years ago?"

Kaylie answered. "No, we beat back the epidemic. What some used to call the American Plague. But it's still around."

"In fact, many people still carry the dormant TB bacteria inside their bodies," DJ added. "At its height in the early 1900's TB killed one in every seven. The tubercle bacillus proved to be an exceptionally hardy parasite and could trick the body's antibiotic defenses to ignore it."

The cure—or more accurately, the treatment—was eventually found in 1943 and was a new type of antibiotic called Streptomycin that was discovered occurring naturally in certain soil samples. The discovery of it was quite remarkable… it turned the corner on a very dark chapter in our country. That area of naturally occurring antibiotic cells and compounds. What I'm working on is closely related, but focuses on an even more dangerous bacterium than TB."

Scott was having a hard time getting his head around all this; none of it made sense. He decided as, he often did, to just keep gathering data and try to process it later. "Where did this virus come from?" he asked DJ.

The tired young man said nothing for a long time, finally muttering, "I think someone made it." He and Kaylie looked at each other, and he pulled her close before continuing. "The sample I have is labeled from a biocontainment facility in India. The military guys had it with them when they locked down the campus. My assumption right now is that it's a weaponized pathogen. It shares much of the biological structure of TB but also aspects of a prion similar to mad cow disease that attacks the brain. It seems to have a more robust outer shell that, at least in theory, might allow it to live outside the host body for longer periods of time."

Scott, not really wanting to hear the answer, asked the question: "Why are you working on it if you think it's already been engineered by someone?"

DJ sighed. "Judging by the questions I'm being asked each day; I am assuming this bug has gotten loose on the planet somewhere. I don't have enough biological material to know how deadly it might be or what the symptoms could look like, but I do know it would be bad." He paused for a moment, shaking his head. "It *must* be bad. They're desperate for a way to stop it. I am working with Doctor Colton. She is a renowned researcher and Virologist. She was brought in from California. Used to be with the CDC until big pharma lab picked her up." The look of hero worship was evident on the boy's face.

"Wait," Scott said, "You have something that deadly here, on a campus full of people, in an unsecured lab?"

"No," DJ explained, "What *we* have is inert. The ability to fully replicate was removed. Essentially, what I'm studying is a bomb with no payload. But that also makes it very difficult to be accurate with our data. How the bacterium infects or reproduces and the damage it does are some of the main things we need to study. But like I said it's compartmentalized. We file our reports each day, and the computer backups of our logs and images are taken each night by the guys in gray."

Kaylie turned to DJ now. "Don't be a dick. Come with us." Scott saw her squeeze his hand tight. She already knew the answer.

"I have to stay, honey," he said, kissing her softly. "What I'm doing is critical to our planet's survival. I feel it deep down. While I hate working for these assholes, I think they are fighting the ones trying to infect the world. They really want to save it. If I can be of any help, I have to keep trying, and I can do that easier now knowing you're safe with your family."

Finally, the tears that had been welling in Kaylie's eyes began to fall. She nodded her head, but said quietly, "No, no, no."

Scott shook the man's hand and left the room to give the couple some time to say goodbye.

THIRTY-NINE

Scott leaned against the wall of the dorm and called Todd on the radio. "Overwatch, you copy?" Scott had not been broadcasting the discussion with DJ just in case someone might be monitoring. The response from Todd was nearly instant.

"Hey man, how did it go?"

"Brainiac is staying put, but he had some interesting information. They're saying goodbyes now. Do you have any ideas on how we could try and stay in touch with him?"

Todd thought on this for a few minutes. Nothing easy came to mind. "I suggest you leave him one of your little BaoFang radios and the slackline antennae. You have that on you?"

"I got one. Just not sure the range is enough, even with the extra antenna."

"Leave it, during the winter at night it might reach us on the HF band. Give him our backup frequencies and a schedule that you guys can monitor."

"Roger Overwatch, thanks." Scott pulled the portable handheld unit and antenna from his EDC bag along with some spare batteries in a dry pouch. When a very sad Kaylie came out the door, he handed DJ the radio and gave him the frequency and time they would try to be listening in each week.

DJ's eyes were filled with tears as he reached out and took the unit. Scott also gave him his Cryptocat chat handle on a small slip of paper. "Just in case the Internet is ever back up."

"Thank you. And good luck," DJ mustered a smile.

"Same to you. We'll be looking for you to come and see us as soon as you can."

DJ's smile broadened, and he nodded unconvincingly. Scott walked off and after the couple's final short kiss Kaylie turned and followed her uncle.

Scott heard the single click and knew Todd had eyes on them. "Coast is clear for twelve minutes. Come on in."

"Roger Overwatch," Scott responded.

Back inside the old church building, the four of them planned their exit. DeVonte left soon after to help initiate a small diversion he had come up with. Scott took the short lull to brief Todd on some of what DJ had revealed. Todd nodded, unsure what to make of this new world that seemed to be in an escalating death spiral.

"We should go back by the med building. I want to get a couple of survival bags of med supplies." Against his better judgment, Scott was going to agree—they would likely need that stuff.

"No need," Todd interrupted. He pointed under a tarp at four medium sized rucksacks, each with the medical caudex emblem stenciled on. "Just one of the things I had our new friend grab for us," he said, "That kid is amazing, I really want to adopt him."

Laughing, Scott was pleased—and relieved. "What else did you get...or do I want to know?" Todd just grinned.

As go time approached, they heard loud voices from down near the stadium. They could see more and more people heading down the hill toward the disturbance. Todd checked his watch, "That's the signal, let's move. We need to get to our exfil site."

"He means let's get our bags, time to go," Scott said to Kaylie with a wink. The three hustled out of the darkened building into the even darker night. They grabbed their hidden bags continued to the fence, pushing the supplies through the widely spaced bars. Scott gave Kaylie a leg over and quickly followed. Todd tossed over Kaylie and DeVonte's gear. They had planned all of this and Scott knew Todd was going to go to ground here and wait for DeVonte. No way would the kid be able to find them and the Jeep on his own.

Scott and Kaylie were loaded down but made it through the hedges and across the road into the woods. Scott took the lead. "Stay close Bubbles," he said.

"You aren't losing me Pops," she replied. Scott was not completely sure he was heading in the right direction. He knew the Jeep was due west of Kaylie's dorm, but they'd left the campus several hundred yards further south. When they entered the thick woods, Scott had angled slightly right, hoping it would put him close. He knew at some point they would come across the railroad tracks and could navigate from that, but he didn't want to waste time. Todd would be coming in along his original route to pick up the weapons and gear he'd stashed earlier.

He could hear Kaylie struggling behind him and felt they should be in the clearing by now. He took the GPS unit out of his bag and was debating on checking his location when the woods began to thin. Soon after he saw a familiar brush pile. They had emerged from the forest less than fifty feet from the Jeep. Thankfully, no one seemed to have discovered it. Scott cleared the brush away as Kaylie walked to the rear of the 4x4. "Uncle Scott, you brought your bike, really?"

"Hush," he said, "It was a nice day to get in a ride," Scott smiled as he stowed the gear and checked the now empty fuel cans, making sure Todd had refueled. He was debating starting the engine, just to be ready, but wasn't sure how far the sound might travel. Scott noticed that none of the interior lights came on when he opened the door. The battery was still fully charged, but, using his hand to shield his tactical light, he saw the small pile of interior light bulbs in the console tray. Todd was thinking ahead today.

Kaylie got settled in behind Scott while Scott changed out the weakened batteries in the FRS handheld radio; the headset had been dead for a while. The familiar *click-click* came over the radio as the last battery went in: "DorkOne, DorkOne coming in hot. Be ready to roll, may have pursuit." Todd's voice sounded anxious and out of breath. Scott kept all lights off as he started the engine, pulled the Jeep out of hiding, and faced it down the overgrown two-track drive. Using just the light of the fading northern lights was not very easy. Scott had the large M4 pointed out the window when he saw the faintest glimmer of a flashlight beam blink twice. Then the rear door opened, and someone, DeVonte he assumed, got in.

Scott could just about see Todd getting in the passenger's seat by the illumination of a glow stick Scott had dropped in the floorboard. "Go, go," said a breathless Todd, "But keep the lights off for now," Anticipating this, Scott had found his cheap night vision monocular from another bag. Putting it up to his eye, he saw the world in a dark greenish cast. Unfortunately, it gave no depth perception. "Don't hit your brakes... just go slow if need be. Break lights will show up for miles," Todd advised.

"Are you all okay?" Scott asked.

"Mostly," Todd said. "DeVonte may have a slight concussion. Bastards beaned him in the head with a rifle butt."

Scott told Kaylie to check his head for a wound. "There should be a cold pack in your bag."

"Already on it Pops," came the response from the darkened back seat.

The sounds of movement as Kaylie dug through her bag followed by a muffled cry of pain as she put the compress on the boys wound. For several minutes, while Todd caught his breath, the rising odor of sweaty bodies was the most noticeable thing in the darkened car. Scott was concentrating on the road although the cheap night vision was not helping as much as he hoped. They could all see what had to be several jittery flashlight beams working through the woods in their direction.

"DeVonte's distraction drew a little too much attention and they went after him. The grayshirts caught up with him about half-way up the hill and knocked the shit out of him. Thankfully they didn't notice me until I got close."

"What did you do?" Scott asked. "I tazed one of the fucks and popped the other with a dose of Ketamine."

"Ketamine, the horse tranquilizer? Where the fuck did you get ..." Scott started to ask.

"DeVonte had access to the Veterinary Science Building, so I had him picked us up some party favors. Sorry, though man, it took us a bit longer to get over the fence with the kid nearly passed out. The guard I zapped came up full of piss and vinegar and wondering where his shit went. Thought I was going to have to shoot the fucker. He and another one may have spotted us as just we went over. They didn't see where we went into the woods, though. I think I managed to get most of our gear along the way."

"Damn, that was close," Scott exhaled. "Ok, I have to ask. What was the distraction?"

A groggy voice came from the back seat, "the Black Student Union protesting military brutality – they heard some of the white soldiers beat one of our own before dragging him away today."

"DeVonte, where in the hell would they have heard that?" Kaylie asked with a laugh. Scott could see the boys smile even in the darkness of the rearview mirror. "Black folks will protest shit like that at the drop of a hat. I barely had to say anything at all."

The drive down the side road was taking much longer that it had for Todd to come up it earlier. Driving with the night vision in one eye was also giving Scott a headache. After hitting a nasty rut that threw everyone forward, Todd called out. "Hang on—."

Going through the gear on his lap, he handed something to Scott. Reaching out to take the dark object, Scott realized it was a full night vision headset.

"Holy shit," Scott exclaimed as he flipped the unit on. "These must be military grade." They were, in fact much better than the little handheld he had been using. He could see fine detail, had some depth perception, and relatively good contrast.

Todd smiled, "Yeah I was a bit envious when I saw what great gear the grayshirts had. I relieved both of the guards when I took them down. That set is yours, as well as a tactical vest and what I believe is a sub-compact H&K MK416 Assault Rifle," he chuckled.

"Holy shit." Despite his nerves, Scott was amused. "Merry fucking Christmas again, Santa."

"Yea, the problem is they want them back… we have to move."

Even with the improved optics, it was still a welcome relief to get back out to the main road, flip on the headlights, and head west. Soon Tallahassee and the lights of the campus were fading in the distance. "Wait," Scott thought, slowing the Jeep. He was sure there had been no lights at the campus.

Becoming clearly visible in the night sky, though, were two twin beams of high-power searchlights. Scott nudged Todd, but he was already looking back. "I think we may have gotten someone's attention," he said. "They may also be launching drones with NV cameras."

"Should I kill the lights?" Scott asked, driving nervously now.

"Won't help, those birds can probably see in the dark too. Everything they have seems to be next generation tech," Todd said. "Just drive, drive fast and once out of town get off this main road. You need to get lost down some quiet side road. We should have about ten or fifteen minutes before they move this way. We need to be out of sight by then."

FORTY

Day 12

They parked the Jeep along a desolate stretch of country road canopied with oaks and towering pine trees. They hadn't heard or seen anything since losing sight of the campus twenty miles to the east. Todd had wanted to use one of the captured radios to see if there was any pursuit but didn't dare until he disassembled it to make sure the units couldn't be tracked. They were all hungry, and each devoured a couple of MREs. Kaylie was mostly silent, and DeVonte had a huge bump on his head, but otherwise he was deemed in good shape. As Scott restarted the engine to begin the long trek toward Harris Springs, he couldn't believe that it had not even been twenty-four hours since he and Todd had left home; he felt like he had been up for days.

Todd drove while Scott navigated. Their plan was to travel through the night, avoiding all towns—especially larger ones—though this was not as easy as it sounded. The first town they neared had been burned to ashes. Smoke still curled from its charred remnants.

Outside another small town along the lower panhandle, the stench of decay caused them all to gag. The foul smell stayed with them for many miles; it would not be the last time they endured it. How quickly everything was falling apart, they all thought.

They didn't see many people, but campfires seemed regular occurrences along most roads and towns. Society had begun to break down, and Scott knew it would only get worse.

They had been driving for about four hours but weren't making very good time; they had had to change the route they had used earlier to avoid some of the likely trouble spots. The large Eglin Air Force base now lay between them and the Gulf.

"Uh oh," said Todd as they approached another town. "I see a glow in the sky ahead. Looks like another one's burning."

Scott looked at the map. "Yeah, looks that way. The next town is about eight miles—Crestview. I've been looking, but there's no real way around it… It's a busy area. Lots of servicemen. It's near the Interstate and on a major north-south corridor."

"I know that town," said Todd, "It's—it *was* a nice area… but it'll be too dangerous. How far to Highway 4? Maybe we can bypass the worst of it." Scott found the road Todd named but couldn't see a way to get over to it. It also went off to the Northwest so it would take them well out of their travel line.

"Stop," Scott said, and Todd did so. "The only way to get over to it is to backtrack about five miles and probably go off road." Todd looked at the GPS before agreeing. He turned the Jeep around and headed back the way they had just come. They caught the little dirt road heading north and winded onto less and less well-maintained roads. As they got near the I-10, the vegetation thinned and the road became a single line service path that led down the middle of a high-tension power line run. The now useless electrical towers stood in line like silent sentinels to the group's passage.

Topping a small hill, they could just make out that the road they were on ran under the Interstate about a mile ahead. The darkened slab of pavement was an ominous presence to the men. Underneath the overpass were numerous campfires. The warnings about interstates had been right. Todd had killed the lights well before topping the hill, and both men had switched to the night vision goggles. The campfires showing up as bright greenish white beacons. Very few people seemed to be moving down there, "Should we wake up the other two?" Scott asked.

Scanning ahead Todd said, "No. The road itself looks clear. Hopefully, everyone down there is sleeping too, and maybe they don't want any trouble. I am sure they would all like our ride, most of these people were probably stranded on the Interstate when their car died. We'll ride through as slow and silent as we can until we're within a few hundred yards, then I'm going to floor it. It could get a little bumpy, so buckle up buttercup."

"Now I'm Buttercup?" Scott asked, "I preferred Dork."

Todd lowered the driver's window partially and began slowly creeping the Jeep down the trail. "Weapons hot," said Todd, in a voice barely more than a whisper. He flipped the fire selector switch on the little H&K in his lap. "Watch your ejected shells, they'll be hot and'll hurt like hell if you're in the way. Short three-round burst" Scott spread a blanket over the two sleeping passengers then lowered his window and lay the barrel of the M4 on the frame, keeping the smaller MK416 in his lap as a backup. His palms were sweating, and his stomach was in knots. Every stone dislodged by the car's tires sounded thunderous, and he knew the whole camp would be awake by now. This was a bad plan, it didn't feel right, and he wanted Kaylie especially to be anywhere else right now. This was not the homecoming he had envisioned for her.

They could soon see several people standing and looking for a vehicle as they got closer, though none of them seemed to know which direction the sound was coming from. As Todd floored it, flashlights quickly pointed in their direction, temporarily causing the NV goggles to white out. "I'm going to headlights and spotlights in five seconds," Todd said, "Take the NVG's off so you won't be blinded." Todd hit the lights, and they immediately started taking gunfire.

Simultaneously DeVonte and Kaylie sprung up. "Keep down!" Scott shouted behind him. He unleashed a barrage of shots, mainly firing for effect. Todd was sweeping his weapon along the left side of the road ahead, doing the same. "Scott, you have to get him—at your one o'clock," Todd called above the din.

Scott saw instantly whom he meant. A tall man was pushing a motorcycle into the road ahead, apparently in an attempt to block their path. Scott leveled the M4 at the man's torso and pulled the trigger. The motorcycle fell as the man's chest erupted in multiple dark red blossoms as the bullets impacted; he dropped beside the bike. "Oh god," Scott said.

"Later," Todd shouted, "Keep them off." They were passing under the I-10 now, its bottom looming over a hundred feet above them. A shotgun blast peppered the side of the Jeep on Scott's side and he reluctantly returned fire. Thankfully most of the shots seemed to be quickly dying off. Todd kept up the speed but killed the lights again as he flipped on his night vision for the rest of the decent.

Scott hung his head out the window and vomited. He could not believe he had killed someone.

Todd stayed silent and left his friend alone with his thoughts. Kaylie and DeVonte, unsure of what had just happened, were also silent as they came to terms with the world outside their campus.

Ten minutes later Todd found the paved road that would become Highway 4 just up ahead. Turning west, he could just see the smoking ruin of the once peaceful little town of Crestview. Again, the stench of rotting bodies, this time mixed with the smell of raw sewage, overwhelmed the occupants of the car. Was this what every town was going to be like? Is this what lay ahead for them at Harris Springs? In just twenty-four hours so much had deteriorated. They kept driving. If they encountered no other major obstacles, in a few hours they would see how their own small town had fared.

• • •

As the sun began to rise behind them, they took notice of more people out. To their relief, not much seemed to have changed in many of the small residential communities. More people were up early, rising with the sun as they had gone to sleep around dark. Each person carried a firearm. Things had changed but in isolated, out of the way hamlets, the effect was so far less dramatic.

Despite their meandering route, the group had managed to pick up the pace, and they crossed over into Alabama just after sunrise. DeVonte had said he lived in a little town called Mauvilla, just northwest of Mobile. The problem with getting there was that they would have to cross the upper Mobile Bay basin and the Tensaw and Mobile rivers, along with the dozens of other lakes and tributaries. No real roads crossed directly east to west other than the dreaded Interstate and most other major roads went directly through Mobile. On the way out the day before, the two men had purposefully driven well north to avoid the area entirely.

Scott had taken over driving duties giving Todd some much-needed rest. Kaylie had checked DeVonte's injuries in the daylight and proclaimed him "Good to go." The group had entered Alabama near a little town called Seminole, the cross road led to the beautiful tourist beach further south named Perdido Key. Perdido is Lost in Spanish and getting lost at the beach would be far better than what came next. Getting on the North-South Interstate of I-65 was the simplest way to get across the swampy delta region of the top end of the bay. If they could do that safely, they could be across in half an hour and near DeVonte's home thirty minutes after that.

Unfortunately, that violated everything Scott and Todd had agreed on when planning this mission. But they owed their new friend, and were resolved to get him home. Scott had pulled off to check the GPS and topographical maps. Other than an isolated rail line further south, no roads or bridges existed in this no man's land: hundreds of square miles with only a few isolated, small towns, divided by snaking rivers and marshland which spider-webbed across much of this part of the state.

"DeVonte, we need to try and reach your brother," Scott said. "We should be within range right now. Do you know the channel his department uses?"

DeVonte took a few seconds to respond. The fog in his head refusing to clear completely. "I am not sure of the official frequency but I remember one they used to monitor, it was like an unofficial 911 that truckers and other locals used to use to alert them to stuff. Scott handed him the radio, and the kid started adjusting the dial and calling for anyone with the Mobile County Sherriff's office. He tried for fifteen minutes with no luck and was about to give up when he heard a tired and distant sounding voice say, "You are wasting your time kid. They are all gone, gave up, left."

"Who is this? What do you mean gone?

The voice came back clearer this time, "Names Ron and let's just say I was in a position to know things like this. When the lights went off, the law did the best they could, but it was hopeless."

DeVonte had tears in his eyes as he keyed the mic. "Sir, do you know a deputy by the name of Trammell, Lamar Trammell? He's my brother, and I need to know if he's ok."

"Hmmm…sorry, kid, never heard of him…" DeVonte sadly let his hand with the radio fall to his lap.

Todd had roused from his cat nap and reached back for the radio. He was able to get a bit more information from the man calling himself Ron before the signal faded again. What became clear was that their worst fears were confirmed. Mobile County was home to over four hundred thousand people, with nearly twenty percent of those living below the poverty level. Ron said the city had been dealing with a growing gang presence, the ranks of which had now increased with the thousands of newly released prisoners. In the days after the CME, they appeared to be in a feeding frenzy. The addicts could no longer get drugs from dealers, so they were looting drugstores for prescription meds as well as from houses, hospitals. Food, drugs, fuel, ammo and even sex were the new commodities with any value. Fires raged around the city, and armed gangs patrolled the roads looking for hapless travelers. The law quickly had become irrelevant and now was non-existent. Those officers who were not killed or injured in the early hours of the crises simply had no more ammo or working patrol cars. They also had no place to put anyone arrested. Chaos and anarchy had become the rulers of this once proud southern port city.

The occupants of the Jeep grew quiet, and the mood was distinctly darker after hearing how bad things had gotten. No one speculated on the fate of DeVonte's brother, but the anguish was evident on the boy's face. Kaylie and DeVonte were having to come up to the reality of this new world with no time to process it all. The two kids had been immersed in a relatively sheltered environment at the University. Now like a diver emerging from the depths only to find the entire world had changed. They had to take it all in and adapt just to survive. Scott knew that Mobile was probably like countless other towns and cities around the world. In crises, in ruins, good people fighting to survive and losing that fight. Right now Scott just had to find a way to get them all home, and he was running out of ideas.

Before everything went dark, they could have taken the scenic route and gone south to the beach, drove out to the mouth of Mobile Bay near Fort Morgan. From there they could have taken the ferry to the Dauphin Island in the middle of the Bay. Then they could simply have crossed a few bridges, drive back inland on the west side of the bay and been home in an hour or so. Sadly, the ferry would not be running, and that route now had lots of choke points for desperate people to stage ambushes.

This area they were in was just not as familiar to Scott and he voiced his concerns. They all agreed that going south to the Beach was out—too easy to be trapped on the wrong side of the Bay and the city. Chances were that many of the most desperate people in Mobile had begun targeting those wealthier beach towns already. Going north, it was agreed, would take too long and require more fuel than they had. Eventually, they made the decision to shadow the Interstate for about fifteen miles on a parallel road. That would let them see if there were indeed highwaymen along it, or if it might be a viable option.

This wooded stretch of interstate seemed to be remarkably clear. They were especially watching for roadblocks or people on overpasses waiting to ambush potential travelers below, but they saw nothing. It was likely so rural out here that most people had abandoned their stalled cars and left the interstate hoping to find better luck elsewhere. For thirty minutes they watched the road from the relative safety of the woods and only saw one other vehicle go by, heading north. After some discussion, they cautiously took the exit ramp down to the northbound side, which looked to have less stalled cars jamming the lanes. They headed southwest, crossing over the lower bay's northern estuary safely. They exited near Creola, Alabama.

DeVonte navigated them down a series of backroads to keep them away from the suburban sprawl of Mobile. They noticed numerous makeshift roadblocks and had to make quick detours several times. The next time the stench hit them was as they came up to an isolated old strip mall. They could see the cause this time. Thousands of seabirds, crows and vultures were feasting on what appeared to be a blackened mass. Getting closer, they could now tell it was hundreds of dead bodies. There was no other sign of life. Todd slowed but did not stop. No one spoke. As horrific a scene as it was, it was getting to be less unexpected at this point for all of them.

They made it to Highway 45 about fifteen miles north of Mauvilla. "Ya'll can let me out here and then just head straight on toward Georgetown and then turn south. I can get home on this road okay. I appreciate it."

"Probably be better if we drive you closer. You took a pretty hard lick on the head last night, and we owe you that at the very least," replied Todd.

DeVonte wasn't listening; he was already getting his stuff together. "No Sir…My people are probably not going to be very welcoming right now with all this shit going on, and you guys are my friends. I don't want anything to happen to you because of me… I'll be alright." DeVonte climbed out of the Jeep and threw his small duffle over his shoulder.

The area did not look well off. The people around here might indeed be wary of strangers right now, and for good reason. But they were not bad people; just the opposite most likely. The kid's parents, or, at least, his mother and uncle from what Scott understood, had raised a fine boy. His intelligence and common sense had taken him out of the backwoods to the university and now had brought him back and almost home safely.

"Hang on," said Todd getting out of the car as well. He unzipped the kid's bag and put several things inside. "You may need these. There's a radio in there with our frequencies and schedule if you ever need us." Todd hugged him hard, thanking him for everything. Kaylie climbed out, her eyes moist, and gave him a hug and a kiss on the cheek.

"You little shit, I wish I had known you better…before, I mean," she stammered affectionately. "Be safe and I really hope your family is ok."

He and Scott shook hands and Scott held it as he looked him in the eye. "You saved my niece… and me. I can never repay you for what you've done."

"You got me home. man—that was more than I ever dreamed."

Scott's eyes watered as he looked at the young man. "C'mere." Scott led him to the rear of the Jeep where he undid the safety straps and lifted his Cervelo racing bike onto the ground. "You can ride a bike, can't you? I want you to take this."

DeVonte was shaking his head.

"You can't ride a bike?" Scott asked.

"No—I mean, yes. I can ride, but I can't take your bike. It's expensive and…well, it's yours."

Scott laughed, "Then bring it back to me one day. It'll get you home quickly and quietly. And it's built for going long distances. Maybe when things settle down, you can ride it down to visit us at the beach. Besides, I have another one. This is my backup…just take it."

DeVonte finally gave in, obviously relieved not to be making the long scary walk home on foot. Scott went over a few tips on the gears and told him how to scout ahead on each road before plunging ahead. He showed him where the patch kit and pump were. He hugged the young man and watched as the boy mounted awkwardly and began pedaling toward his home. The three remaining held their hands up in farewell as they watched DeVonte ride speedily away.

Todd had tears in his eyes. Scott knew Todd had wanted to do more for the boy as well. "He'll be fine Todd. He's a survivor."

Nodding, Todd said "I know, I'm just worried that home for him may be unrecognizable. His troubles are probably just getting started."

Scott thought that was probably true for all of them.

FORTY-ONE

Day 13

The next hour in the car was much less stressful, and Todd had again taken the wheel. As they crossed into Mississippi, the area was more familiar. Todd had once had family in the area, and Scott biked many of these roads on a regular basis. Things were different, yes, but the morning sun gave promise of a beautiful day ahead, and they were closing in on home.

Scott's mind continued to return to the man he had killed. He knew it had been the right thing to do. The man would have done it to them in a moment. Many others had been ready to kill them on that road. What he felt was not remorse for the man but sadness for himself, for the thing that had died in himself with that act. He knew he would never again be the same and feared that, in time, taking a life might not affect him at all. Most of what he had read suggested that opportunistic and cruel people would quickly take over in a time like this, and it would be every man for himself. Take what you can and fuck everyone else. The weak will suffer as the strong rise-up. What he had seen so far suggested that some of that was already going on.

But there was another side to this, and it was what Scott wanted to remember. While the bad may be rising to the surface, so was the good. Unknown people had helped them, were willing to pull together to help survive the crisis. Total strangers were willing to risk their lives to help him. For a man like Scott, who had withdrawn from society and people in general, this was a revelation. Perhaps he had been wrong about people… He rested his head on the window and let the whine of the tires on the road lull him to sleep.

The sun was already bringing on an oppressively hot late-summer day.

Scott was dreaming of ice cubes tinkling in a glass. Ice. Would he ever even have that luxury again? The tinkling was getting louder as he slowly rose from the depths of the dream. His eyes half opened, but the tinkling sound came again. Looking out the window, he realized that the Jeep was barely moving. Just ahead, a man led a mule loaded down with what looked like his worldly belongings toward a cluster of men. "Roadblock ahead," Todd said calmly. "Don't worry, it's the Sheriff's office, our Sheriff."

Nearly home then, Scott thought. His eyes focused on the collection of battered cookware strung together and hanging from a pack on the mule's back. The pots were softly clinking together. The sound reminded Scott of an ancient Hindu ceremony he had seen once on TV. The little parade advanced until Todd was face-to-face with the deputy.

"Hey Man," the sweat soaked Deputy said, "I heard you'd made a road trip. Glad to see you back in one piece."

"Thanks," Todd responded, "I had my doubts a few times, it's rough out there."

The Deputy nodded. "Been a rough day and night here too. We had looters, murders over at the clinic…several houses burned. Also had a couple o' state troopers go missin'."

"Shit," said Todd, "No place is immune from this."

Shaking his head, the trooper said, "Not hardly friend, not hardly," he paused as he looked inside the car. "Looks like ya'll could use some rest. Probably ready to get home. You be safe now." He waved them on through.

"Thanks, Doug," Todd said as he pulled the Jeep through the barriers. The bearded man and mule lumbered on up the road, watching as the Jeep went by.

Soon they turned onto Highway 50, and Scott saw the route of one of his more familiar rides. Things had changed, he could see. The familiar entrance down to the lake behind the old dam was now blocked with a steel gate that had a small "Closed" sign hanging from it. Farther down the road, they smelled the familiar tang of salty air coming up from the beach. They passed a small cargo truck that had bullet holes riddling the side, a dark shape slumped over the steering wheel. They saw an open suitcase on the road but no persons or car anywhere around. Tropical looking shirts, or maybe dresses, spilled out onto the roadway, their arms reaching toward nothingness. Dark smoke could also be seen rising from several spots ahead. Scott began to wonder if his cottage would even still be there. The trio said little in the final miles into Harris Springs.

• • •

Mercifully, the town looked much as it had. The trash was piling up, and various smells filled in the air, but not all were bad, and some of them were very normal. Todd drove to his house and parked. He was getting his gear out when Kaylie came around the Jeep and hugged him. Scott stayed off to one side. Todd looked over the shoulder of the girl and smiled at Scott. Many words had occurred to Scott, but none came close to expressing his heartfelt gratitude at what Todd had done for him. In the end, they just smiled, shook hands, and embraced quickly. "Get the girl settled in, then let's meet for lunch tomorrow at the bar," Todd said.

"Will do. Give Liz my best."

Scott and Kaylie headed for home. Unlocking the gate and pulling in, he was relieved that all seemed normal. As he pulled around the side of the cottage, though, there was something different: a blue and white portable toilet with a pipe leading to a freshly dug latrine stood in the back yard. "Bartos," Scott laughed. A note on the front door said: *Since you have no security, I let myself in, hope you don't mind. BTW you are out of Scotch.* He didn't mind, especially because he was fairly sure he wasn't out of Scotch, or hadn't been.

Kaylie was excited to see the house where she had spent so much time in her young life. The electricity was still out but seemed to have come on at some point as the cottage was cooler than outside. Scott began unpacking the Jeep as

Kaylie went back to the room she had always slept in on her visits. Once Scott had finished, he went back to check on her and found his niece sound asleep on the bed. He felt like doing the same; it had been an exhausting trip. He cleaned and oiled all the weapons that had been used and placed each in an appropriate location. His dad's lessons were second nature to him no matter how many years had passed.

It felt good to be back home. *Really good*, Scott thought. Even if it wasn't completely safe and they didn't have everything they would need, it still just felt so good. He sat in the living room wishing he had a way to let Bobby know his daughter was okay. His mind began to drift again, thinking about all they had seen on the trip and to all the other things he needed to do now that he was back. His immediate needs included coming up with some way to draw water from the old well… He needed to check the food storage as more of the items in the refrigerator would need to be eaten… He needed to think of ways to put up a lot of food for the winter… He badly wanted a hot shower, but he knew that may never happen again. Finally, the jumble of thoughts in his head went quiet as he let sleep overtake him once again.

FORTY-TWO

Day 14

Waking early the next morning, Scott and Kaylie made a hearty breakfast of country ham steaks, eggs, and biscuits. Kaylie seemed in a relatively good mood despite all she had been through. Scott knew that it would take time for her to emotionally process leaving DJ behind, seeing the death and chaos of the outside world, and—especially—being cut off from her mom and dad. She was tough though and he could see her already steeling herself for these new challenges. Scott also had to adjust to being responsible for someone else. He would no longer be making decisions just for himself.

His plans for the day were to go out and get more fuel, either from the abandoned cars or even some of the empty vacation homes. He was unsure of how safe it was and if he should take Kaylie with him or leave her here. In the end, he decided it best to take her. He also wanted to see how she could handle a gun, but didn't want them to be firing off shots and drawing attention to the house. She could also help stand guard.

It was mid-morning before they headed out. The first cars they tried had already been emptied, so they ventured further out. He decided to try the beach roads; these were less traveled, and the beautiful ocean view helped brighten their moods. Kaylie was staring out to sea when she asked, "Do you think Mom and Dad are okay?"

Scott did not know and had been wondering the same thing. "I wish I knew Bubbles…I really do. Your dad is a survivor and was well prepared for this—far better than I was. I know he's worried about you, and somehow we will come up with a way of letting them know that you're safe."

She looked out at the glimmering water without comment.

Scott pulled up and cut the engine. Swinging out of the Jeep, he walked to the edge of the road and looked at the beach. He saw the telltale marks in the sand from a sea turtle; most likely a loggerhead turtle. The endangered animal came in at night to lay eggs, then make its way back to the ocean, never knowing the fate of its young. Kaylie was now looking where her uncle was. "In about two months there'll be a flock of baby turtles trying to get to the water. Every bird, crab, and fish in the area will be trying to make sure they stop them. I've heard only one in a thousand reach adulthood," Scott said. They each silently contemplated the irony, knowing what all human creatures now faced.

They only got a few gallons out of the next car and Scott was beginning to feel frustrated. He was keenly aware that he was using more gas than he was collecting. Deciding on a change of tactics, he pulled into the private drive of an empty house he had once spotted on a bike ride. The vacation home was on an isolated road that circled a small cove. Only a few homes were on the drive. Much of its front was glass and faced out over the cove. What Scott had noticed when he scouted the place was the enclosed first floor. Most of the beach homes were on stilts or pilings for flood protection, so the second floor was normally the first occupied floor. The bottom area would be used for storage, garage space or just left open. This one seemed to have multiple garage doors all opening to the backside. The houses on this drive were all difficult to see from the beach road, even from his bike. Scott had ridden by them several times before noticing them. The developer had been particularly clever in hiding this beautiful structure in relative obscurity. The privacy had to be expensive.

He parked the Jeep on the side of the house and stepped out with his new H&K Sub Compact slung on his back. Kaylie stayed in the Jeep while he made sure no one was inside. After checking first through the wall of windows and then around the perimeter, he signaled Kaylie to join him. "What now?" she asked.

"We wait a few minutes and listen. I'd like to know if anyone is in any of these houses."

No doubt the last of the summer guests had long since left. After ten minutes and no signs of life, he went to the back and tried the garage doors. All three were securely locked. All of the entry doors and windows were similarly secure. Kaylie was rapping a knuckle on the thick glass wall. Yes, he could break that, although not without some real effort... that was damage he couldn't allow himself to do to such a beautiful home.

Ultimately it was Kaylie who found the solution. "Uncle Scott....if this is a vacation home, wouldn't they probably leave a spare key somewhere for guests, like we used to do at the cottage? I mean I know you are like...a genius and all but 'ya think maybe?" She was right, of course. You never knew who might be coming down for a quick visit, and getting a key to everyone in time was a bitch. Nodding, they began to search. The small but well-manicured yard had a few noticeable possibilities: the small rock-lined planting bed, birdbaths, the flagstone walkways.

Scott began to scour the drive and yard. Perhaps the key was under one of the rocks, or in the birdhouse. Kaylie scoured the teakwood deck by the main door, first under the door mat, then along the top of the door frame. Finally, she noticed the expensive barbecue grill. Opening the lid, she saw nothing. She knelt down and noticed a magnetic key holder barely visible underneath the grill. Holding up the find she yelled to her uncle, "Girls win!" He smiled up at her as she pumped her fist.

The house was immaculate, although there was a strong smell of rotting food. Scott had Kaylie begin searching for food and supplies while he went down to the lower garages. Entering the large space, he immediately saw two jet skis on trailers. Hopefully, that meant gas was also nearby. Being a vacation home, there was little in the way of tools or many other common items you would find in most garages. The whole space was clean and seemed mostly filled with beach gear: chairs, umbrellas, kids' toys. Scott felt uncomfortable rummaging through someone else's stuff. He kept thinking of possible excuses he could offer should the owners drive up, or if a policeman knocked on the door. He laughed quietly to himself at the absurdity. In an isolated storage room, Scott finally found several marine fuel containers full of gas. Hearing a small shout from upstairs and then a giggle, Scott realized Kaylie must have scored something good.

He carried the fuel out to the Jeep while Kaylie came out carrying boxes and bags of food. He could see cereal and cookies stored in large plastic bags. He went back and scouted the rest of the garage, finding nothing useful other than a large machete and an adult wetsuit, both of which he carried to the Jeep. He made a full final sweep of the house and borrowed several pairs of high-quality boots that were in his size. He wasn't sure how long what he had would last. *Better shop now*, he reasoned.

They locked the house back up and got back in the Jeep. While he was pleased with the plunder, Scott did not feel the trip had been a true success so far; they were supposed to be finding gas. He decided to check the other two homes as well. In the second, there was no fuel or food and few residual signs of life. There was an expensive stereo that, had the power been on, would have been an exorbitant addition to anyone's possessions, but as things were now, it was worthless. Kaylie found some jackets and clothes which she bagged. Scott thought she was getting into this game.

The third house looked to be the least promising. It was a little less opulent compared to the others, and a little more worn. It was up on a small rise and so was not elevated. The door lock was easily bypassed with a now useless credit card. Entering, Scott found the home was sparse but appealing. He noticed that what *was* there was all of top quality: Viking ranges, Sub-Zero appliances, even a very expensive Italian-made espresso machine. Sadly, none of this would do them any good. When he got to the garage, though, that changed. He first found several large and completely full fuel containers. Opening a small door at the rear of the space, Scott nearly fell to his knees.: a large Kohler dual-fuel backup generator sat against the far wall. These were well-built machines and relatively quiet. He got his multi-tool out and began loosening the retaining bracket that secured it.

As he struggled to load the heavy generator, he realized it was much less useful now than he would have thought just a few days earlier. To operate it would require fuel, of which there was very little. What fuel there was now would be precious, and probably more valuable than gold. The find would help keep the freezer going long enough to eat what was left, and would hopefully work for the well pump, assuming they could keep finding more fuel to keep it going.

He went back to the storage room as something else had caught his eye. Scott followed what looked to be an auxiliary fuel feed line from the generator through a conduit to the yard. Outside, he walked to the rear of the house and found that the line led to a large fuel storage tank mounted several yards from the rear wall. Scott tapped on the tank, then took off the cap and dipped his fingers in and smelled it. *Not very scientific but it's not as fresh as the stuff in the stalled cars.* It smelled okay but could probably benefit from some stabilizer. He decided to fill the Jeep with what he had found in the tanks and then refill the containers from the large external tank. Even doing so, Scott figured there were at least thirty-five gallons left in the tank, so he made a mental note of the address so he could return later. Kaylie had found several sealed bags of unground coffee and a manual grinder in the kitchen, so those made it into the Jeep as well. Feeling much better about the morning's finds, they left the tidy little community mostly intact. Back on the main road, they headed into town to meet the guys and hopefully have lunch.

FORTY-THREE

At first glance, Castro's Sports Bar appeared closed as Scott's pulled the overloaded Jeep to the curb. Getting out, though, he smelled food and noticed several people inside, one of which was unmistakably Jack. Walking in, they were greeted by a mixture of odors.

"Preacher," Scott said with a grin.

Jack smiled. "I assume this is Kaylie. It's a true pleasure to meet you, dear," Jack said in his deep, rich voice.

"Have you seen the others?" Scott asked.

Looking away, Jack said, "Let's get you guys a drink and something to eat, then we can talk. They're no longer taking cash, but if you have anything to trade, they'll serve you," Jack said as he leaned over the bar.

"We have goods to trade," Kaylie answered quickly, "We found coffee." The Preacher's eyes lit up.

"Shhh now, keep that information quiet. Coffee is running low for most folks, and that's a highly prized commodity. Just canned goods or a little bit of fuel is plenty for lunch," he said, grabbing another beer for himself from behind the bar.

The owner stepped over. "Are y'eatin' or drinkin'?" he asked gruffly.

"Both," smiled Scott as he and Kaylie shared an amused glance.

The owner nodded. "We can settle up later, I know y'oure good f'rit."

"No menus anymore—he just serves you what he has," Jack chimed in as the man turned back to the kitchen. "Get a couple of drinks and let's sit."

Scott rummaged in the chill box by the bar and found a beer. He sat down and poured water from a pitcher for Kaylie, who promptly took his beer. "Hey, young lady."

"She laughed, "I'm not a child anymore Pop's. I like a good beer after a day of 'lootin and 'stealin just as much as the next guy." Scott was going to have to adjust to this new grown up woman that was his niece. Smiling, he shook his head, went and fetched himself another beer.

"I heard about the trip to Tallahassee. It sounded pretty rough," Jack said. Scott looked around the nearly empty dining area and nodded. Preacher Jack put his hand on Scott's arm, "You did what was needed, you did what was right, now let it go."

Scott's eyes began to water, but he fought the urge back. "Where is…" Scott started, but Jack held up a hand.

"Todd isn't going to make it today. His wife Liz is…" Jack was interrupted by a familiar face bringing steaming plates to the table.

"Bartos! Hey, man!" Bartos smiled and set the plates down.

"I was just showing the guys back there how to grill gator. When I saw it was you, I made these plates myself. Bartos' own grilled gator etouffée," he announced. The food looked great and smelled even better. Scott was curious if Kaylie would turn up her nose, but her fork was already digging into the rice and meat. "

So was it your recipe or your gator?" Scott asked.

"Both," came the quick response. "

By the way, Kaylie this is Bartos."

She smiled, mouth full. "This is delicious, thank you!"

Sitting down, Bartos looked at Jack, "Did you tell them about Liz?"

Shaking his head, Jack said quietly "No, not yet."

Scott put his fork down mid-bite and looked at both men. "What? What's wrong, what happened to Liz?"

"She's sick," the preacher said. "Real sick. She has been for a long time."

"Todd never mentioned that—she seemed fine the other night," Scott blurted, shocked.

"Neither of them ever mention it, Scott. They're private people," Jack said. "The illness has a long name, but the result is chronic kidney failure, she's required regular treatments at the hospital for years. Around six months ago her only remaining kidney started failing and she had to start dialysis."

"So what happened?" Scott asked feeling even worse now. Jack looked over at his Cajun friend.

"Bartos promised Todd he would keep an eye on her while you were gone, so he went by to check on her. She was on the floor unconscious. When she came to, she was in excruciating pain. He loaded her up and took her to the after-hours clinic just outside of town, but he ran into some problems. So he took her on to the hospital. She was suffering badly."

"Oh my god," Scott's mind struggled with this new information. "Why did I not go in when I dropped him off?" he muttered to himself. "Why did I even let Todd go with me?" He was looking to the preacher now.

Jack tried to soothe him. "I was waiting inside for Todd, and Bartos was with Liz the entire time. No way either of you could have known. It's just how things go." Scott thought of the beautiful woman he had met just days earlier. How full of life she was. How full of love she and Todd both were.

"Lord…," he sighed, then pulled himself together. "How long will she be there? Do they have any idea?"

Jack put his hand on Scott's arm. "You don't understand."

Bartos looked up, eyes watering, "She needs dialysis but the hospital can't do that anymore. Her blood is poisoning her, and her systems are shutting down." He took a long pause, "They've told them to prepare for the worst. That's what they're doing now."

Tears flowed freely down Scott's cheeks. He could not believe this, could not register it. Kaylie put her arm around her uncle's shoulder protectively. "I've got fuel," he volunteered. "We could…we could get the backup generators running."

"Scott," the preacher said, "Listen. This is just that damnable disease she has, taking its final toll. Yes, continuing treatments might further delay it, but not by much. They both knew this was coming, even before the lights went out. We all love her; we love them both. But we have to accept it as God's will, and to do so with as much grace as Todd and Liz. Listen, they're choosing how to write their final chapter. That's why we're here and not there. When the good Lord mercifully lets her pass, we will be there for Todd. Not until then. We already said our goodbyes. This is their time."

• • •

Day 16

The funeral was two days later. It was small and sad despite what Liz had wanted. Preacher Jack delivered just enough scripture mixed with comforting words, ribald humor, and stories about Liz and Todd to keep them smiling. Scott had set up a discreet wireless speaker and played the Miles Davis songs from his MP3 player. Solo had laid down beside the open grave in apparent understanding that someone valuable had been lost. Kaylie, who did not know Liz, held onto Todd as though he were her father.

Ultimately Scott had found he couldn't completely stay away from the hospital…not say goodbye. He had made it there late the previous night to see them both. He had taken a freshly made thermos of hot coffee and food. Even though Liz was on morphine she had smiled and grasped weakly for his hand. He and Todd barely spoke but sat for a long time. As Liz seemed to weaken, Scott retreated to the waiting area with Kaylie.

With the service over, Preacher Jack and Kaylie took Todd away while Scott and Bartos filled the grave by hand. They had managed to get a casket, apparently now a luxury, but no one had been available to embalm or process the body. Looking out over the field of graves, Scott took in the many unmarked rectangles of fresh earth.

Despite Jack's words Scott blamed himself for Todd not being there when Liz had most needed him. For Todd not being able to enjoy her last good day. Bartos saw his new friend staring out at the graves on all sides and put his hand on Scott's shoulder. "I would tell you not to blame yourself. But you wouldn't listen. Just know that neither of them would want that." The little man shoveled another spade of dirt into the hole. "They were—they are—a perfect couple," he continued. "High school sweethearts who spent most of their life in love with each other. Their love was legendary. Who else finds a soulmate like that on their first try? I'm not sure they ever even dated anyone else."

Scott nodded, "It was obvious just watching them together."

Bartos looked up. "Point is, dude, life and death still happen. It's a cycle, and I believe…I believe they'll be together again one day. This shit we're in now didn't cause this any more than you did. Her disease and this universe don't give two fucks about you and I, but life, life is a cycle, it has a start, and it has an end. Every day has a night. That's why we treasure it. Those that are lucky enough to find a partner to travel through it with, are doubly blessed. Todd will never be alone. He will always have Liz and their love inside. Deep down, I think he may even be glad Liz doesn't have to suffer what the world will yet become." Burying the spade into the mound of dirt, Bartos met Scott's eyes. "I will miss Liz, she was a very special woman, but she could not have survived this." He sighed. "Let it go, Scott, find a way."

Scott wiped his eyes. He would find a way, but it would not be soon. He looked at the surprisingly poetic man and smiled. "Thank you, Bartos." He took his shovel to the earth. "—By the way, what is your first name? Or last name?"

"It's Bartos," his friend replied smiling, "Thought you knew that." Grinning slightly, the little Cajun went back to digging.

FORTY-FOUR

Scott had been stunned, was stunned, by the coldness, the vitriol in her voice. How had such a perfect day turned out so wrong? They had been working together on their new home, their dream home. He had been pulling up the carpet, and she had been cleaning out closets. They had brought loads of debris to the oversized dumpster just outside the porte-cochere. The other house still had not sold, and it was going to be a stretch for a while, but he knew they would manage. The contractors were coming Monday to get started on the renovations…their renovations.

Exhausted, but seemingly happy, they left for home. They were discussing what items could go to storage and what should be donated or trashed. Two people, one couple, living life. Then it had turned in an instant into this. For the life of him, he could not remember what words had set them on this darker path. Looking back now, he knew it wasn't anything that had been said. His wife of four years just suddenly began talking about how miserable she was. If they had ever fought, maybe he would have been better prepared. Miserable, what in the hell was she talking about? The marriage had seemed idyllic. A lovely couple, people said. They both had good careers. It had been Scott's first real grown-up relationship. He had never been good around girls; his first love ended awkwardly when his best friend Gia married someone else. She had never known how he felt about her.

That event had been far tougher to overcome than anyone knew. It had taken Scott years to even consider dating, much less anything more. Now this woman—his wife!—was saying goodbye. She had always said he was hers, but at that moment, he knew better. In truth, he now understood she only loved herself, and would probably had never been honest with him. Scott had listened to his dad's advice. He had been good to his wife. His parents had been married for almost forty-five years when his mom had suddenly passed away peacefully in her sleep.

Now this beautiful, sweet woman was telling him the hard truth: that she had never loved him. The marriage had been a mistake. He knew even before meeting her. He had wanted someone for his own, but perhaps he should have been more specific. Now his wife was saying she couldn't stand even the touch of his hand or his cold lips on hers. Scott was sure she was playing a joke, some twisted game, to see if she could get the best of him. He could not fight back; he didn't feel those ugly things toward her. No, he very much loved her, despite her coldness. This woman seemed to be a different person altogether; this was not his wife.

As he stopped at an intersection trying hard not to look at the woman spewing such hateful words beside him, she suddenly jumped out of the car. "I can't stand to be around you one more second," she cried, slamming the door. "Here," she said, taking the ring off and throwing it in the window. "I am done pretending; I'm done being your whore."

"What is your problem?" he asked. "How have you ever been my whore?" What in the hell is going on with you tonight?" He was completely dumbfounded or maybe blindsided was a better word. He felt as though he was outside his body looking in the car window as this drama unfolded. While the couple didn't always get along, they never fought. It was beneath them; just not how they handled things.

She walked off into the darkening night without response. He did not understand... could not understand. Scott drove around, unsure of where to go or what to do. Although not a violent person, his rage was building... unfocused, undirected hatred. Anger at himself for being such a failure. Angela was beautiful, well-educated and successful. Both of their careers had been doing well. They had achieved a comfortable upper-middle-class existence. Trading up to a newer house and starting to talk about having children. From the outside; a perfect marriage. Now he was letting the perfect marriage fall apart without even realizing it had problems.

Should he look for her? How would she get home? Why was he worrying about her? Maybe she was sick... was she bipolar or something? She certainly did not remind him of the woman he had married. The rage inside him grew.

Two days later she sat across from him amongst the boxes of her belongings. She was calmer but even colder. "I'm sorry Scott, I love someone else..." She stood up, grabbing a box, and quickly took it out to the already full car. The car he recognized. It belonged to Scott's best friend, his only real friend, Jeff.

The divorce was mercifully swift. Apparently Angela and Jeff had recently discovered they were expecting a child, although he later heard they had lost the baby. The couple's assets were easily split as neither of them wanted either of the two houses or any keepsakes from the marriage. Everything had eventually been sold. Five weeks later he bought the Jeep and a trailer and headed south with a few essentials. As he pulled into the garage of the family's coastal cottage, he vowed never to return to Chicago. Scott had eventually managed to subdue some of the growing anger by turning it inward before it blossomed into full rage. He knew it would come out at some point; he feared for anyone around him when it did. Since that night, he had been unable or unwilling to trust anyone or allow himself to have friends, much less seek love. What was love anyway? The ultimate trust... "See where that's got me," *he thought. Fuck love, fuck trust....fuck me.*

Scott put the tumbler of scotch down by the flickering candle on the end table. Why was he reliving those times from so many years ago? He knew why. He knew it was because of Liz. Because he had accepted friends back into his life, with all the pain and problems that inevitably came with them. He hurt for Todd and felt helpless to do anything except revisit his own emotional loss. He had changed since that night, but he had not moved on. Some events fundamentally change you no matter what you do to try and outmaneuver the pain.

Kaylie was sleeping on the sofa, neither of them wanting to be alone tonight. Scott had found it impossible to sleep. He had spoken to Todd after the service. Todd was not the same man anymore either. The pain was etched across his hard face, but his mind had remained clear. He had pulled Scott away from the others. "You know when I asked you what you would do right now to make things better? For the community I mean." Scott nodded, remembering the conversation they had on the way to Tallahassee. Todd looked quickly around the room, "I need you to start doing it... Harris Springs needs you to do it."

"Tomorrow, go and talk to the others—the people in this room. I've already talked to Jack, Bartos and Deputy Warren. They're ready to work with us...work with *you*. I wanted to try and help the town, not let it become like all those others we saw but... I just can't manage it right now. I can't handle the mission...my compass is gone."

Scott hurt for his friend, but this was way out of his comfort zone. "Todd...I'm the idea man... I'm okay with helping out, but—I'm no leader. Anyway, shouldn't that be up to the mayor or the sheriff or something?"

"You are a leader Scott. And in time, you will know that. The mayor is lying in that field with a bullet lodged in her brain. The sheriff hasn't been seen in days. No one here is going to step up because they have their hands full just surviving. No one is thinking strategically. Everyone assumes the government or somebody will ride in and save them." Todd's voice was rising loud enough that others had begun taking notice. If we don't work together to save ourselves, then we're no better than the millions of others who are paralyzed because they rely on someone else to provide for them. I can't bury anyone else Scott... I'm not strong enough to make those calls. You are."

Scott had looked at Todd and asked, "What are *you* going to do?"

"I'm not sure," he said before walking away. "May just go fishing."

FORTY-FIVE

Day 24

Todd had been gone well over a week. Scott had checked his house and the boat docks the day after the funeral. Some of his gear was missing, but the *Donna Marie* was still in her spot at the marina. His house also looked abandoned and lifeless. Bartos said Todd had probably taken his sailboat as it was missing from its normal spot. While Scott hadn't known that Todd sailed, he realized he shouldn't have been surprised. He was genuinely worried about his friend's condition; he knew Todd was not in a good place, but hopefully, out on the familiar waters, he could begin to heal. Scott also had to admit that he still did not feel up to the task that Todd had assigned him. He felt he was barely able to take care of himself, and now he was responsible for his niece. The idea of taking on the task of trying to organize the entire community in this mess seemed impossible, and frankly he still didn't care too much for many of the other locals.

The preacher had asked Scott to meet him, and now they sat with a shared bottle of Scotch while Jack laid it out for him. "Scott, try and understand that none of this is fair, not to you, not to Todd, and not to this town. You have every right to walk away from what Todd asked of you. No one could blame you. But hear me out first—most of the people around here are good people. Not unlike me, Todd, and Bartos. You just happened to get to know us and not them.

"I know nearly everyone here, and the vast majority are worth saving. Yes, they've been ignoring the obvious, no, they didn't prepare, but they've been conditioned to depend on others and trust their leaders. Most cannot understand that, just as much as the CME, it's been the government that's caused many of these problems. We need you, Scott. We need your wisdom, your anger, and your courage. Harris Springs will not survive without you. You won't be alone either. Between us, we can get these people motivated. They're hard workers—well, most are—but the survivors'll come to the front quickly enough. If we don't give these people hope and a mission, all is lost."

That was where it began: Scott reluctantly agreeing and Jack quickly pulling the team together. Jack, Kaylie, Bartos and Deputy Warren had been helpful with the initial organization. After a short first meeting at the sports bar, they came up with the basic plan. The first mission was pretty simple: muster all available resources before they were stolen or wasted. Then develop a plan to protect both the people who were helping and the resources they found. And finally, try and help feed those that were contributing to the community. Beyond that, they had to give everyone hope. In short, <u>keep us safe, keep us fed and keep us human.</u>

Scott had expected resistance from some of the townspeople as the plan became action, but he found he was being met with more apathy than anger. No one in any previous leadership position in the town had materialized during these initial phases. In fact, no one other than a few store owners came forward when they posted notices that stated plans to consolidate resource, including inventories. It seemed that none of the former politicians wanted to take on the responsibility or lead when it involved real work. That's what this was. Work. Not a popularity contest nor a power trip. In fact, no one in the small group ever mentioned titles or anything remotely resembling political offices. What was essential was that shit got done and got done fast.

Their plan was rough, but step one required protection and a level of presumed legal authority where none existed. Deputy Warren had been sworn in as acting sheriff by an old retired judge who attended Jack's church. He immediately declared martial law, which some supported, but many refused. The taste of anarchy in recent days had already whetted the appetite of some of the darker elements of the town.

From the first time the group met, they became a council to make decisions. Scott generally did not vote unless there was a tie or serious disagreement. He had gone back to the Catalyst documents, and albeit premature, he felt the foundation of a new system of government that it described was essential. Here in Harris Springs, on a very limited basis, it was already being put into practice.

He knew that the worst was still ahead of them. Much of the planning was secretive; made for the eventuality that good people would likely become increasingly desperate and bad people would become a malignancy looking to take over. A paranoia existed in all the planning and Bartos was the key element. His mind was devious, but his goals were never selfish. He was the one who could probably have gone off on his own and survived just fine. He didn't need them as they did him. Somehow in this crisis, he had risen to be more than he once was.

Bartos had assembled and managed two small teams to handle the basic recovery operation. They moved cars off roads, draining fuel into a large tanker truck. This they hid in larger storage tanks buried in various spots. They also collected batteries and other useful items from the cars.

The other team focused on provisions: they would commandeer from hotels, schools, institutions and stores. The two teams soon combined and began working their way from house to house through the empty neighborhoods to see what they could find of value. Scott and Bartos set up many hidden caches. Scott was out every day on his bike looking for new locations for storage.

Sheriff Warren handled security along with his two remaining deputies. He also added to his ranks when he could. One of these recruits was a young ex-marine named Clements, who had been a patrolman for the city. They recruited several others with experience either in the military or as part of law enforcement in their previous life. They decided, based on practicality and their limited resources and manpower, to patrol a small, manageable area. This zone did not extend out as far as the old county limits. Scott's home, in fact, was now just outside of the patrol zone.

As had been the practice since the CME hit or "The Big Crunch" as many more were now calling it there were no police arrests. Many more crimes were deemed capital offenses now, and executions by the patrolman would in time become a sad fact of life. They would need to come up with lesser punishments in time for minor offenses. Public humiliation and chain gangs were possible options, but no one would get a free ride sitting in prison anymore. No one wanted to feed someone who had broken the law. The food was reserved for those who worked for it. The threat of capital punishment did wonders for keeping down the mayhem. After Deputy Clements shot a man who had beaten a shop owner, the message was clear to all.

As the days/weeks passed the group had also come up with a schedule for limiting access to the town of Harris Springs, by raising and lowering the three drawbridges that spanned the wide Intercoastal Waterway. They could essentially cut the town off completely if need be. As the county maintained all the bridges, Bartos had keys to control them. A small portable generator was mounted on a trailer and hooked up to each when they wanted to operate it. They made a schedule and posted it for all the townspeople and farmers out beyond the waterway, so they would know ahead of time what bridge would be traversable at what time. A permanently manned guard was posted any time any of the bridges was lowered. While this seemed reasonable to the group, others viewed it as castle mentality, a guard at the moat. No matter what they did some people grumbled, some louder than others.

Perhaps the hardest assignment had fallen to Preacher Jack. He was the countering force to the brutality and absolute rule that was going into effect. Jack's primary job was to keep everyone human; to be the voice of reason and an advocate for the defenseless. That did not extend as far as helping those unwilling to help themselves. Jack himself, was a staunch believer in allowing no entitlements of any kind. But he was more willing to let men prove themselves, even those judged as criminals in the world before. He had taken in several former prisoners who had slipped into the town one way or another: trustees that he had known from his previous prison ministry. These guys had an assortment of useful skills and several eventually found their way onto Bartos' procurement teams. By the end of the first month, Jack had also fulfilled his promise to Todd by starting to train Scott and Kaylie in the art of KFM combat. Scott had been amazed at how quickly the big guy could move and how every point on his body could become a weapon. Kaylie had taken to the sport like a champion. Glad to be back on a workout schedule.

Scott had personally taken on several key assignments. The first was to work with the farmers, fishermen, and hunters to develop a system of crop and game management and establish the basic system of fair trade. From the municipal warehouses, the hunters would get ammo; the council offered them access to previously protected lands, and the sports bar had cold storage for the meat they produced. Fishermen and farmers could get limited rations of fuel and labor, as well as secure storage. No one profited in the new system, but they might survive. He made the rounds of the farms every few days, checking on them to make sure they had what they needed. Farmers proved to be a self-reliant bunch and slow to accept any benefits from the trade plan. Scott knew how they thought though, and didn't force it. He knew, in time, they would need help.

One other issue they worked on was electricity. Many days were dedicated to expanding the town's solar power to reach more buildings. They were adding to the collector array as they found other panels. In his rides, Scott had spotted solar panels on several rooftops and yards. The teams also found them down railroad tracks where they powered the now useless signal lights for trains. So far they had enough solar units and deep cycle batteries to triple the town's current output. Much of what they had planned were very long term projects. First, they had to survive the next few months.

As September gave way to October, plans began to slip sideways. The realization of winter coming at the same time hoarded supplies began to dwindle drove many people over the edge. On the radio, they heard reports of bands of raiders hitting survivor settlements. Scott had seen numerous instances of cruelty, but even he was shocked the morning he saw part of the old housing projects down on the black river on fire. He hadn't noticed the smoke as it was the same color as the gray overcast sky. Stopping his bike, he saw flames shooting from windows of house after house along the old docks. What he didn't see was the people... not until he rode further down the road. Hanging from trees were body after body. Women, children, elderly, black and white. Already the poorest people in the town; none of them deserved this injustice. What little most of them had probably would not have even gotten them through the winter months, but someone decided their life didn't matter. This was to be just the first of a string of new misfortunes that descended on the little town.

Scott and Kaylie had consumed the last of the 'normal' food a week earlier. Now they were living off the supplies, supplementing it with fresh meat when they could. Kaylie looked up from her empty plate, "Is it ever going to get better, Uncle Scott? Will I see my family or friends again?" Scott had dreaded this question but knew it was always on her mind. He reached over and held her hand.

"It's up to us to make it better. I won't lie to you, Kaylie, I can't tell you definitely that you will see them again. We just have to believe that we will."

She nodded. "Is this why you're helping everyone in town, your friends? I thought all preppers walled themselves up alone to survive."

Scott smiled, he had thought the same. "It has been difficult for me. Your dad helped me realize the truth. We need other people, other like-minded people, to survive. This is what society is, people living together for the common good. Unfortunately, a lot of people will feel otherwise. Many are out for themselves. Many will always feel like society owes them. This point in our history is going to be a major reset for that group, and they are not going to go away quietly." They both had been hearing the reports of looters and gangs wreaking havoc out in the county. So far the town had remained calm, though. How long that would last was anyone's guess. Kaylie knew this was why her uncle had been hiding supplies and food caches, as well as making her learn even more about self-defense and how to use all the different guns they had. She wasn't as scared as she'd imagined she would be. She knew they had contingency plans, supplies and most importantly, her uncle seemed to have a purpose again. She was proud of him and the responsibility he had taken on.

It had taken the townspeople several weeks to start pitching together, but now that it was organized, things seemed better. She, Bartos, and a guy named Clive had been working to clear unoccupied houses in the area. Uncle Scott and the preacher had joined them several times recently as they moved subdivision to subdivision. Occasionally they met resistance; when they did, they simply offered them the deal: work with them and share or stay on their own but don't ever ask for help. She knew they were a kind of a gang, but none of the members of the group were out for personal benefit. Sheriff Buck Warren and Bartos had made sure of that.

One of the guys in town had been giving them a hard time, but no one seemed too concerned about him. "A blowhard" was what her uncle had called him. She did know these next few weeks might be the worst yet, though. Food and fuel had long run out for those that had not prepared, and desperate people were capable of anything. She knew her uncle had been stocking up the alternate locations to use in case of emergency, but she hoped she didn't have to leave the cottage. She loved it here. Now that they had the generator running the old water well, she could even take a shower again, although it was a cold one.

Raiding parties were spotted several times on the roads. Most were small groups that a few shots easily scared off, but some with twenty or more men were spotted and had to be avoided. Scott kept shifting resources to other locations and shoring up defenses at the cottage. He had managed to hook up the large generator, not just to the water pump but also the freezer and refrigerator, so what fresh supplies they had stayed somewhat cold as well. They had also taken time to disguise the drive and camouflage the house to make the quaint cottage look more like a derelict. Beyond the road gangs, other unexpected encounters were also unnerving.

After one particularly difficult day in which, among other things, the bodies of two of the more popular townsfolk had been discovered and later buried. An exhausted Scott had gone to sleep the moment his head hit the pillow. With no power, they had gotten used to the total silence in the dark house. At some point, Scott had awoken to something. It had sounded and even felt like a large object hitting the side of the cottage. He knew it could be a dream but for some reason he didn't think so. Silently he made the rounds looking out across the moonlit yard but saw nothing. He could hear the gentle snores coming from Kaylie's room. Scott lay back down thinking it must have been a bird or something.

His mind was active now, though, and sleep would not return. Reluctantly he decided to get up and read some of the Catalyst information again to see if he could come up with some better solutions for the town and himself.

Just before lighting the lantern, he checked the front yard again. To his shock he saw a large man standing there. The man was shirtless, wearing long pants and appeared to be holding something. He was also standing still as a statue. Scott crept back to his bedside and retrieved the Sig Sauer pistol. He decided to wake Kaylie as well, motioning her to be silent as he pointed the man out to her. She started to whisper something, but he shushed her knowing that whispers can often be noticed easier than normal voices. They both waited, looking out the window for much of the night. Scott didn't want to shoot the man for just standing there, but he also didn't take chances anymore. As the eastern sky began to lighten, they could make out more details on the man who still stood in the same spot. He was bald with what looked like a nasty scar along the top of his head. The skull seemed…wrong, misshapen underneath. Scott could see the vague color of tattoos on the man's arms. They also noticed the man's mouth was moving, he was saying something; it appeared to be the same words over and over. Scott could see now that the man was holding what looked to be a girl's hair ribbon.

Scott looked at Kaylie and quietly said, "I don't think he is a threat, I am going to go out and talk to him."

She placed a hand on his arm, "Look at his wrist."

It was now light enough to see pretty well, and Scott could see what his niece had noticed. A ragged light colored bracelet hung loosely from the man's left wrist. Kaylie leaned in, "He was a patient at a hospital."

Scott looked at the man more closely. His eyes were closed, spittle dripped from the corners of his mouth. He was still uttering the same words. A patient yes, but from what kind of hospital? Scott thought about the patients at the mental hospital that he been turned out. He nodded at Kaylie, "Stay here, but come out firing if I get into trouble." Scott stood and quietly unlatched the door and went out into the cool morning air.

The man took no notice of Scott, even after he had called to him several times, "Sir, Sir! Hey! Can I help you?" Scott could see the tattoos were military, possibly Army. *Man this guy may be a disabled vet. A war hero with a head wound. He deserves better than this.* The man's cheeks were sunken in and his ribs were visible. His bare feet were covered with cracks and oozing sores. His pants were stained with all manner of foulness, and the smell of wood smoke was overwhelming. Scott had run into numerous delirious individuals in the last two months, but this was different. Scott touched the man lightly on the arm and instantly the eyes were open and looking directly at him. The mouth kept repeating those same words over and over.

Scott was shaken by the man's alertness but still not overly afraid. He asked him again if he needed anything. Not getting a response or further reaction, Scott called to his niece to come out. She discreetly gave the man a basic medical check and said what Scott had surmised. Dehydration, malnutrition, untreated and infected wounds, and probably impaired mental state due to injury or illness. Scott knew the humane thing to do was to put the man down, but the likelihood that he had been a soldier prevented him from taking that option. They could take him somewhere and drop him, but that just made it someone else's problem.

"Ideas?" Scott asked.

"He needs to be in a hospital or institutionalized, he is incoherent, probably had no idea who he is or what has happened. He can't make it much longer on his own. He may even be a danger to himself...or others." She was using a small squirt bottle to shoot water into the man's mouth and throat. The man took no notice, and most of it just ran out the side of his mouth and down his sunken chest. They tried moving the man over to a tree stump to sit, but he just stayed frozen in place. Checking the man's wrist Kaylie said it was from the VA hospital up in Meridian. She couldn't make out the patient name. Scott kept looking at the length of ribbon in the man's other hand. It unnerved him in ways he couldn't identify. Scott eventually gave up trying to makes sense of it, deciding the man was no immediate threat. He went inside to make some coffee. Kaylie kept trying to get some response from the stranger but after another hour she came inside too. They decided that they could probably get the man in the Jeep and take him into town to see if the Doctor at the clinic could help. Deep down they both knew there was no place in this new world for someone with this man's problems. Packing up their day bags and weapons, Scott pulled the Jeep out of the garage to see Kaylie standing dumbfounded in an empty yard. The man was gone. They looked quickly in all directions but saw no one. They searched the roads, the adjacent fields and even the bayou out back but found no sign of the stranger. Shocked, but somewhat relieved, the two got back in the car and headed off toward town to start their day.

· · ·

Scott was faced with countless other tasks at home and larger ones in his new role with the council. Some would have to wait until they had more people and time. These were only slightly lower priorities, such as a way to do laundry or recover salt from seawater, which was already in limited supply. Setting up the medical clinic had been a top priority and was done as soon as it was safe. They had medics and a couple of doctors but had to locate everything else. Of desperate need were antibiotics and pain relievers. They had gotten lucky in that the small hospital was pretty well-stocked and had not been looted. Several local pet stores carried animal and fish medicines, many of which, some of the doctors said, could also be used for human use.

The council quickly became inundated with special requests, as well as complaints, mostly from those people not doing a goddamn thing to contribute. The response from Scott and the council to this group was generally "Fuck off or handle it yourself."

The priority was to stay alive today. Everyone was hungry, all wanted protection from the roving gangs of criminals. The complainers and real troublemakers in the town were on a steady increase and at times took on mob-like status. In the absence of power or government assistance, this group were made up of truly desperate individuals and they only needed a little push to set them off. The new ad-hoc council's apparent lack of concern for the complaining groups fanned the flames of discontent. These people of the township felt their needs were just as vital as anyone else's, and since Scott's little group were assuming power, that group felt that they should be the ones helping the less fortunate. It was only a matter of time before the two views clashed.

FORTY-SIX

Day 35

Of increasing irritation to the group was the one former politico, a snake who continually raised his ugly head and attempted to penetrate the little group as the spokesperson for the complainers. Ronald Hansbrough was not happy and was suspicious of what these guys were up to. More clearly, he felt they were the quickest way to get his hands on the supplies he would need to survive without actually doing the work required to get them otherwise.

To him, the new town council was just another gang of thugs, stealing and hoarding supplies. The fact that the weasel Cajun seemed to have assumed a position of influence *really* pissed him off. The guy was a fucking mechanic. He was also sure that Bartos had been using his position at the county to help his friends. And his hatred of him for refusing to pave the road into the development park had never really gone away.

Who did the little fuck think he was? Ronald fumed once again as he walked out of the government building he had just been asked to leave, by Bartos himself. Not only that, but the other guy in there, the quiet one with the bike, pissed him off too. He felt sure it was the same guy that had flipped him off on the road the day the power died. What in the fuck was his angle in all this, anyway?

Ronald looked up at the plaque mounted on the well-manicured lawn. His family name was on that plaque. It also lent itself to one of the main streets, and several other important buildings in the county. This was his town, and he would be damned if any of these other shits was going to take it away from him. This was bigger than politics, he felt. This was survival.

Preacher Jack watched the red-faced Hansbrough muttering under his breath as he walked out of the meeting hall and turned down the block toward the other side of town. That man is trouble," he said to no one in particular. Jack knew more about trouble than most people in this area did. He also knew that one of Hansbrough's associates was a Mr. Tyrell Johnson. Tyrell was a big, rough man. He often stayed down at the community center located in the same direction that Hansbrough was now walking.

Jack knew there were only three reasons for a rich guy to associate with a man like Tyrell. He needed drugs, he needed muscle, or he needed both. Jack had heard the rumors about the esteemed Mr. Hansbrough and his affinity for the narcotic OxyContin. Of course, Tyrell would have used that as an excuse to get close to the influential man. Now the two of them would likely be getting desperate. One craving power and drugs, the other craving money and respect. Neither would likely let the small group of friends trying to do good, stand in their way. Jack resolved to keep an eye on them both.

FORTY-SEVEN

Day 48

The next several weeks were filled with non-stop work, decisions, and difficult choices. Scott was already sick of dealing with people and really just wanted to look after his niece and be left alone. He missed Todd but also hated him for giving him this damnable task.

He awoke from an unpleasant night's rest and climbed out of bed. A very haggard looking Scott roamed the darkened house looking for the manual coffee grinder. He cursed under his breath but quickly reminded himself that if this was his biggest problem so far today, he had no reason to complain. He finally found where Kaylie had stashed the device and filled it with a morning's ration of beans. Kaylie had been up late the night before still trying to make contact with Bobby. Scott knew his brother would be worried sick about his daughter. There had to be a way to get word to him, but now that was just one mission among many.

Scott took his morning cup of bitter brew to the back deck. The morning breeze had a slight chill which made him dread the coming months and all that needed to be done in preparation for winter. His normally logical mind was going in too many directions at once. The thoughts tumbled in on top of each other... he desperately needed clarity. The false dawn was giving way to daylight as he made the decision to take a few hours off to clear his head.

Knowing the only real treatment that worked for him, he pulled the bike off the rack and checked the tire pressure. He geared up with the bag of essentials slung over his jersey, woke Kaylie to let her know he would be out for a bit, and left her one of the radios. He knew from talking to Sheriff Warren's guys what roads were the safest. He felt he would be okay, but he would also be prepared for the worst. More and more people had taken to using bikes, in fact, the grumpy old fart's bicycle shop in town was booming. While it may be a slightly foolhardy and dangerous activity, for Scott Montgomery, it was still essential. He reasoned to himself that he would also be doing recon on the area beyond the patrol borders but, in reality, he knew that he just needed time on the bike. He had made one concession in replacing his now empty pepper spray canister with a tactical holster mount for the Sig-Sauer pistol.

The crisp air felt good and carried with it the increasingly common scent of cooking fires in the area. After about twenty-five miles his head began to clear and his muscles felt like they were just starting to wake up. Scott pulled to the side of the empty road. He took the handheld radio and checked in with his niece.

Kaylie reported back that she was fine, so he dropped it back in his bag and took a long drink of water. Looking over at a mobile home, the unkempt front yard littered with sad-looking old toys and garbage, Scott noticed a familiar tiny face looking at him from beside the concrete block steps. He had seen the child on previous rides down this road. He knew he should probably ride on, but he wanted to know that the girl was okay. Scott saw her looking at him intently. She was clutching a doll that looked more like a dirty rag. He smiled and gave a small wave. "Are you okay?" he asked.

Someone else appeared in the dirty window of the trailer door. The face looking through the grimy window at him was a larger more weathered version of the child's. Taking his bike helmet off, Scott climbed off the bike but did not approach the girl or the house. The cheap door to the home swung open, and the woman stepped out onto the top step with a large gun pointed at Scott.

"What d'ya want?" the mother yelled, cigarette dangling precariously from her mouth.

Scott held his hands up in a placating motion, "I don't want anything, just taking a small break from my ride.

The woman, looking suspicious, nodded slowly as she scowled at him.

"Well… might wanna just get back on that fancy bicycle and get."

Looking up with a smile he said, "I'll do that. Your little girl looks just like you."

The woman took a long drag of her cigarette. "Better that than if she looked like her damn daddy."

Scott went to remount the bike but looked back. "How ya'll making it out here ma'am, any trouble?" he asked. She looked suspiciously at him but lowered the barrel of the gun.

"We got nothin', haven't eaten nothin' but dry cereal for days. Everything in the kitchen spoiled when the power din't come back up."

Scott took a drink of water from his bottle.

"Hell, we ain't even got that," she continued, pointing to the bottle. "Been gettin' water from the stream back up in the woods," she said. "We got our checks, though, soon as the banks open we can get what we need."

Scott shook his head, "What if they don't open?"

She looked puzzled, "They have to open, they're the fucking bank. We got government issued checks they have to take. By law… You know, they can't stay closed. We got rights too." She took a long drag on the cigarette before continuing, "I can't even get to the damn store to use our food stamp card, ain't that some shit? Got money but can't buy nothin'."

Scott sighed. "Do you have anywhere you could go? Anyone else that you and your daughter could stay with until the power comes back and the banks open?" he asked.

"Nah, we not from 'round here… my people are from up north, in Hattiesburg. Don't know anyone around here 'ceptn her daddy and he done run off. Haven't seen him since before all this shit started."

Scott knew Hattiesburg was not that far but looking around he did not see a vehicle of any kind. "I have a few granola bars that you and your daughter are welcome to, that is if you promise not to shoot me."

She laughed, "Damn thing's not loaded anyway. You got anythin' else we can have?" she asked.

Scott looked hard at the girl and then the mother and shook his head no. "I was out looking for food myself," he lied.

"Well, if you find anything, feel free to stop by and drop some off. I could probably make it worth your time," she said, trying unsuccessfully to look enticing.

Scott nodded, "I can try to do that." The mother looked at Scott as if he was speaking another language.

"Yeah sure, go ride your fancy bike and get your exercise while we all starve to fucking death."

In his heart, Scott knew that relying on handouts was the likely reason she was in this position. Anything he did would just delay the inevitable; she would never change her mindset. Still, it wasn't the kid's fault, and if he was honest the mom looked to be no more than a child herself—maybe seventeen or eighteen.

He looked at her and said, "Ma'am, listen, you may not want to hear this but if you want to live…if you want your little girl to live, then you have to do something about it. I know where some aid shelters are being set up, probably less than a day's walk from here. If you have something real to trade or some skills, nearly any town around will give you a basic meal at the very least—maybe even take you both in. I mean, you could even get out and find one of these abandoned cars and some fuel and head back up north to your family."

She threw her cigarette butt on the ground. "Well fuck you, too!" she called as she sulked back inside. The precious looking little girl kept looking at Scott. He dug the last of his protein bars from his jersey pocket and placed them on the path where he stood. The girl's eyes lit up, and the beginnings of a small smile crept through the dirt on her face.

He knew that sweet face along with the faded pink ribbon in her hair would haunt him forever if he didn't try to help her, but her mom…she was a lost cause. Another suffering victim who seemed to blame everyone else for her problems and, worse, fully expected someone else to save her still. Scott shook his head as he remounted the Trek and rode on, refusing to look back. He knew that he was not the same person he had once been. He cared for people, and that number grew every day. He could never again focus only on himself or sit back and do nothing. But he was even more determined to help only those who would help themselves.

FORTY-EIGHT

Day 64

The Gulf of Mexico - Barrier Islands South of Louisiana

The grizzled looking man wandered down the desolate stretch of sandy beach. Todd had never been on this stretch of land before; few people had. The Breton Wilderness was part of a twenty-mile crescent-shaped strip of land well out in the Gulf off the coast of Louisiana. His recent wanderings had brought him to this isolated spot. The fishing pole lay unused at his feet. The *Careless Lady* bobbing just offshore. Growing weary he dropped to his knees. He could not stop thinking about Liz. No matter what, his loss hung from him like a chain. He knew he had to move on from this point; she would not like him being like this. His eating had become erratic, he was losing weight and beginning to make bad decisions. He had gone ashore on the mainland only a few times, mainly to get fresh water. What he saw there each time made him never want to return. Just more death, cruelty and bodies. Everywhere he went he found corpses. The Gulf Coast had been a paradise now it was just the opposite. Tomorrow, he thought. Tomorrow he would be better.

Life in the community of Harris Springs became a routine of hard work and planning. The food that most had put up was gone at this point. What should have been the month of Thanksgiving was instead a time of misery. While many residents had taken to fishing and hunting as well as checking abandoned cars and houses, some foraged closer to home. Dogs in the county had started disappearing. Cattle and hogs had to be kept in hardened paddocks, under armed guards. Even the many squirrels that frolicked in the parks were becoming scarce. Few people retained any illusions of rescue, electricity or any semblance of life as they'd known it ever being restored.

Hope was fading. The thin frames and gaunt faces reminded Scott of daguerreotype's the old photos from the turn of the century. He remembered going through boxes of the pictures at his grandparents' house as a child. Strangers whose hollow cheeks and empty eyes stared out of the leather and velvet frames. He remembered thinking that just having those pictures was wrong; the camera had intruded on a moment of misery that should not have been captured. It surely was misery, but it was also just life; a very hard life. While people in Harris Springs were faring better than most, those in the city were dying in vast numbers. Stories filtered their way back to the community. Stories of dirty water and rancid food taking more and more lives. Even here Bartos' crew had given up on digging individual graves and instead dug a series of trenches for the mass burials that took place every few days.

Preacher Jack looked at the line of bodies in the trench. His heart ached for them all, especially the tiniest bodies and their families. They were wrapped in towels or sheets; no one could bare to see the dead face of a child any longer. "How have we come to this," he wondered. "How can I offer anyone any comfort, much less hope?" He closed the worn Bible and began to walk back in the direction of town. The buzzards circled high overhead, and he knew they would descend as soon as he was out of sight.

Bartos and his crew's scavenging efforts had been impressive, but few people had helped them, and now that the remaining supplies were cached away everyone wanted a handout. The small council was deeply troubled. Turning away hungry families was heart wrenching. None of them were cold-hearted, but still the policy had to be maintained. The one concession was that anyone who came to the aid shelter could get one basic meal in return for a day of work with one of the volunteer work. Fights in the food tents had been constant in the first few days but banishing the offending parties had stemmed most of that. People were hungry and miserable; it was hard to blame them for their behavior.

Scott had done the calculations, and it looked grim. The food that had been recovered looked substantial, but not when you divided it up among 400 people. While the numbers of survivors in the town were actually far less than that, the group supporting the council's effort was growing. This meant more help on recovery projects but more people that needed food and water. The farmers had already brought in the last of the late season crops and other than some fall weather greens and another small culling of pork, there would be nothing until after the winter.

Bartos looked over the table at him, "So, what's the verdict?"

"The verdict is we're screwed. Even with strict rationing, we can only hope that about half will make it to next spring. There's just no way to stretch it any further." Scott responded. They knew this was the likely scenario. A human adult consumes an impressive amount of food in a month. Before the CME, the average adult ate almost six pounds of food a day: a ton of food a year. Since then, they had been getting by on less that two pounds a day and even that was stretching it. Many parents, especially mothers, were giving all their food to their children, starving themselves.

Scott looked at his friend. "For the next five months, to get through the winter, we will need about 250,000 pounds of food to feed everyone. What we have, and can realistically get, including fishing and hunting is closer to 90,000 pounds. Of course pounds of food isn't the only requirement. We also need the right *kind* of food. Our diet is going to be erratic—heavy carbs, a little dairy, fruit, and protein. We need to think of anything possible to get some variety along with just calories to consume."

Scott had considered calling Todd. One idea he had was taking a boat down the coast of Florida to see if they could find any citrus crops to harvest. Unfortunately, none of the boat captains in the town had the fuel or knowledge to accomplish it. One more good idea tabled due to impracticality.

One of the few bright spots had been learning about a group of rice farmers a few counties away. Mississippi was one of only a handful of states in the US that produced a rice crop. Scott had biked the ninety miles to make contact and eventually come up with a trade agreement. They traded fish, venison, and fuel in exchange for bags of the long grain rice. Even better; some of the local farmers were converting their low-lying fields to grow their own next year. Few other attempts at reaching out to outside areas had gone so well, though.

Bartos had lost two members of a recovery crew when venturing out into a neighboring county. The four-man crews had been on the highway going from freight truck to freight truck collecting any items or fuel that remained. The crew had reported by radio that most of the trailers they saw now had already been cleaned out. The next contact, about thirty minutes later, reported they had come under attack. Automatic rifle fire made the men's voices nearly impossible to hear. The broadcast came to an abrupt silence seconds later. No one heard from the crew for several days afterward, until two of the men stumbled across one of the county sheriff's deputies. They had barely escaped. They had lost the supplies and even their truck. They had walked miles through the woods to get back.

The next week Scott accompanied one of the men back to the site. What he saw was a very organized group doing essentially what his crews were doing, only they were apparently willing to defend the cargo with deadly force. This would be something they would need to start considering as well. Up to this point, they had been mostly polite to others they met out scavenging. They had adopted an informal system of "finders-keepers" which, for the most part, everyone had respected. This appeared to no longer be sufficient. If *they* were pushing deeper into other areas, others would be coming this way too.

At the next meeting of the council, they decided to change tactics and issued a shoot-to-kill order in defense of any property deemed essential for the town. The decision was also made for crews to go several miles farther out than they had previously, recovering from homes and trucks further out, then working their way back closer to home. The rationale was that these areas would be the first to be lost to other groups doing the same, and if they made the miles less productive to looters, many would choose to go in other directions—hopefully.

There was no point in sugar coating it; they were another armed gang of looters. They were stealing before someone else could, from others who needed the resources just as much to survive. What made them worth saving? Why should they survive and not the town down the road? No one had the answer, but Jack continued the increasingly challenging tasks of keeping them honest. They did not take lives to recover food and tried to work with others fairly. In the end, they did what they had to survive. The fact that the efforts here benefited an entire group was of solace to Scott. But it was a slippery slope. In time—soon, he hoped—they would turn back toward a more ethical destination.

FORTY-NINE

Ronald Hansbrough generally got his way; he was just one of those guys, disliked and envied at the same time. Thankfully, he had never had a problem with who he was. In fact, he was rather fond of himself: a good looking kid who had become a distinguished professional, an important member of the community. His family lineage was well documented, and that heritage came with a certain air of respect and, of course, superiority. What was going on in his town right now had him in a blind rage. Ronald was hungry. For the first time in his life, he had no way of satisfying that need. His hunger was sadly not just for food.

He had also allowed himself to become familiar with OxyContin in recent years. Sadly, it was one of many things that were no longer available at any price. His current pharmacist had tried to be helpful, but he was a brainless idiot for the most part. Ronald smiled at the thought of Tyrell as a pharmacist. The smile quickly faded as the hunger for food and drugs took over again. His relationship with Tyrell was…well, complicated. The large black man had proven himself most resourceful. He could also, at times, be quite ruthless—a particularly valuable skill-set in the current world order.

Ronald had always considered himself a shrewd businessman, despite the fact that his net worth had decreased with nearly every business he ran. His silver spoon had been the vast estate his father had left him, and which, ten years later, had decreased by more than half in value. Tyrell had seemed intent on rapidly siphoning off the other half with his supply of increasingly costly alternative pain meds. But where others were seeing calamity in the current crises, Ronald saw an opportunity. Land and houses were being abandoned, and he had access to all the deeds and property records at the courthouse. With the little remaining law enforcement out of the way, his guys could take whatever property or goods was needed and, with his former position and clout, he felt satisfied that he could legitimize it. He was also keenly aware that certain commodities would quickly be very scarce, and he wanted to make sure he was the only resource to fulfill those needs. His land and property holdings were already substantial, but soon he knew they would be astronomical.

Despite how people felt about him, Ronald was intelligent… he just occasionally let his emotions overrule his head. His real skill came in getting others to do the jobs he felt were beneath him. He knew politicians, judges and he curried favor with many influential men. Money was the grease that America and the world ran on, he believed. When all this nonsense blew over, he was determined to be in a position of greater power and even more wealth. As one of his father's heroes Sir John Templeton once said: "To buy when others are despondently selling and to sell when others are avidly buying requires the greatest fortitude." One person's misfortune is a wise man's opportunity.

Yes, he knew that millions of people were in a very unfortunate place right now, but a smart person like himself could potentially be set for life if he made the right moves now. Of course, he knew the dollar was dead, as was the stock market—but supply and demand, that was what capitalism was all about. All he had to do was corner the market on the most valuable commodities, and he would be a king. He had seen the list that the council had as priorities and had to admit it was pretty smart. Once they got everything consolidated, he would just step in and take his position as the man in charge. After that, anything a person needed would be available for the right price. In the absence of any real law, he would make the rules, deciding what was right based primarily on how it would benefit him.

The first order of business would be to take out the trash, and by trash, he meant that fucking asshole Bartos. Tyrell's nephew or some other illegitimate relation had been killed by the son-of-a-bitch, so he didn't even have to pay for this one.

Tyrell had already searched the man's house and found it nearly empty.

Even Hansbrough was at a loss as to where he might be until he thought to check the property records at the courthouse. It seemed he'd been paying taxes on a small piece of property out on the edge of the swamp for years. It figured the little maggot would prefer the backwoods to the town. Tyrell's boys had finally spotted him heading that way earlier today. No doubt the Cajun would be dinner for the alligators by nightfall.

Dinner. His stomach rumbled in complaint. Fuck. He had to eat. He knew he could go down to the aid shelter the bike guy and his daughter had set up, but the thought of eating with the unwashed masses was something he preferred not to entertain. The undeniably aromatic fact that he had not washed for several weeks did not occur to the disgruntled man.

Ronald was already pissed that they had set up portable toilets for the town to use. Something about keeping the drinking water clean. Hell, they were surrounded by water. He absolutely would not use those things; they were disgusting. He zipped up his fly having urinated in a semi-private corner of the courthouse.

His empty stomach rumbled again, and he found himself reluctantly walking in the direction of the aid station. One plate of food wouldn't be the end of the world, would it? He decided he could take the stares from people for a few minutes, as long as it meant a free lunch.

Walking into what had been the parking lot to the sports bar, now covered by a giant awning, he felt eyes on him. "Oh, how the mighty have fallen," they all said to him. He knew this was what they were thinking. He pushed out his chest and walked briskly to the serving line, smiling and greeting everyone like he was the one in charge. That stopped when a man held out his arm, blocking him from getting a tray.

"Sorry sir, this is reserved for volunteers only." The young man had a T-shirt on with the local fire department logo printed on the chest.

"What do you mean volunteers? Do you know who I am? What my family has done for this town?" the now red-faced Ronald Hansbrough shouted.

Smiling slightly, the young man replied.

"Yes, we know you, and you're not on the list of volunteers contributing to the survival of our community. Therefore, you get nothing. Who you were or what you did before is irrelevant now."

Ronald got up in the young man's face. "You little shit, you listen to me. You give me a goddamn plate of food right now, or I will have this entire place shut down by nightfall. Everything you have and ever will have doesn't add up to a *fraction* of what I *threw* away last year! You think that just because someone said you have authority you can punish *me?*"

Ronald went to push him out of his way, but a thick arm and a meaty hand came around his neck and pulled him out of the line. Preacher Jack tossed the enraged Hansbrough onto the street.

"Keep your ass out of here, Ronald. If you want to eat, find Bartos and sign up for one of the recovery crews. Do some real work for a change. You need to get it through your head—no one gives a shit who you are. No one is going to share their food with a lazy asshole like you."

Ronald wanted to have an appropriate comeback, but he was speechless. He shuffled backward away from the large man wasn't this guy a preacher or something? He was angry. He was scared. He was pretty sure he had pissed himself. Finally standing up, and at a loss to muster any sign of dignity, he wandered, seething, down the street. He would get his revenge… he would have it all.

FIFTY

Day 78

"Morning Preacher," Scott handed Jack a thermos of coffee as he got into the Jeep.

"Thank you, Brother!"

Coffee was a resource that was disappearing fast. Like cigarettes and other vices, coffee was becoming almost too valuable of a trade commodity to actually drink. Scott was still making a few small pots each week, although even he had taken to rationing and watering it down. "Where are we headed?" Jack asked. Scott's scouting trips on his bike had covered a lot of ground, and he was now venturing farther away and into unknown territory. The missions were two-fold: make contact with more farmers and hunters who may want to trade, and find additional unoccupied houses and neighborhoods for the recovery crews to come and clear for supplies.

"We are venturing into the woods today my friend," Scott answered.

They drove out of the county up Highway 50, then cut over to a smaller road. Finally, Scott turned the Jeep down a two-track dirt trail and dropped it into four-wheel drive. Jack eyed Scott suspiciously. "Are you telling me you came all the way out here on your bike? What is this forty, fifty miles from town?"

"Yeah, I came out earlier this week, the day you and Kaylie were working at the clinic. I went out a bit further and cut over. When I was crossing one of the bridges several miles ahead, I saw something over this way through a firebreak in the trees. I guessed it might be a train, but I wasn't completely sure until now." Scott was struggling to clear some of the deeper ruts with the trailer.

They had been on the trail for about ten minutes when Jack saw what Scott had targeted. On a spur of train track sat what appeared to be an abandoned freight train. "Wow, now there is a target of opportunity," Jack said.

"Yep, several hundred cars, must be nearly two miles long. What's better is it isn't near any houses or major highways... if I hadn't been looking, I would never have spotted it. With luck, no one else knows about it either." The collection crews had already been down all the local tracks collecting batteries and solar panels from the track signals. No one had seen an actual train on any of the railways until now.

"So what's the plan?" asked Jack as they pulled alongside the black, brown and gray railcars.

"I brought bolt cutters and new locks. Many of these cars will contain items we can't use or can't easily get out of here. I do want us to list them, though—particularly any chemicals. Some of them may be dangerous, but all are potentially useful. The cars with grain, fertilizer, or equipment we flag for trade with the farmers, they can come out and recover those. You can use the spray paint we brought to identify those cars. We'll begin checking the enclosed boxcars. When we find something we will list it, flag the number on your pad, and if it's small and valuable enough, we'll take it back with us—at least as much as we can carry."

Jack whistled. "No way we can get this done in one day."

"Nope, we'll be here a few days. Kaylie said she'll be okay, and Bartos is going to check in on her." Scott put the Jeep in park, grabbed the bolt cutters and a clipboard, and began opening the doors on the closest railcar.

The work was dirty, tedious and mostly unsatisfying. He felt sure someone probably knew how to read the codes on the cars or could go up to the engine and find a manifest. Scott had a feeling that everything could potentially be useful, and he wanted to know exactly what was out here before letting anyone else in on the find. He made the first real score with three boxcars full of canned and dry goods, destined for a large wholesale grocery chain. Tomatoes, fruit, crackers, beans and soups. There were tons of food; potentially the difference between life and death for his town, at least for a short while.

Jack found eight box cars loaded with paper products, from toilet paper to diapers. They also found an enormous quantity of TVs, consumer electronics, and computer monitors; what had been one of the most expensive cargos was now the least valuable. Dozens of open rail cars full of new cars and trucks were tempting, although both men doubted any of them would ever work again. They had plenty of abandoned cars around anyway; fuel was what they did not have. Many of the tanker cars had the words "Deadly", "Explosive!" or "Corrosive" on their warning labels. Several of the tanks contained molasses and dextrose. They dutifully recorded all of the specifics on the clipboard.

Scott guessed they had worked through only half of the train cars as night began to fall. Jack had moved the Jeep up closer to one of the open rail cars and began to set up camp for the night. Scott was unsure about a campfire as he knew they could be seen and smelled from a distance, but Jack had devised a clever solution by digging a deep hole, lining the bottom and sides with rocks, and using only very dry wood. The flame couldn't be seen above ground, and it produced very little smoke. It was not cold, and they didn't need the heat, mainly they needed the fire for cooking.

Scott pulled out his go bag and put on a pot of water to boil. Jack was opening several cans of the soup they had found and let them warm directly in the fire, while Scott added some tea bags and honey to the boiling water. Both men had worked up quite an appetite, so Scott also pulled out some of the country cured ham he had packed. As he warmed it on another skillet, the smell was divine.

As both men ate and sipped on the hot tea, the night sounds of the forest began to come alive. "You know, for a computer geek, you seem to have adapted well to all this."

Scott nodded, "It's odd, I loved my work but much of this…suits me. I like the pace and the simplicity of life now. Growing up on a farm gave me the basics, I guess, but the last few years I think some of what I wanted was a simpler life." Both men were looking up at the amazingly clear night sky. Without any man-made light polluting the view, everyone could see the night sky in all its glory again.

"Preacher, a question. Do you think this was God just smacking us around to get our attention?"

Jack didn't answer for several seconds, "I haven't completely come to terms with all this Scott. I don't believe in a vengeful God. Mostly I think he lets us choose our own paths and live with the consequences. Also...like hurricanes or drought, random chance is simply part of nature. The solar flare was simply more of that. The fact it costs so many lives is our fault, not God's. We're the ones who chose to be so dependent on electricity, dependent on the government, dependent on modern medicine. If we had thought things through a little better all of us would have realized something like this was probably inevitable. We should have lived more simply, prepared better, and held on to the wisdom of the past. This isn't evil, Scott. It's simply the hand we have been dealt."

"I like your answer, Jack. What about some of the ugliness we *are* seeing, though? Is this what we have to look forward to? I am worried about the world Kaylie will be growing up in. Are we going to see the worst or the best of mankind come out of this?"

Jack finished off his cup of tea. "Yes."

Scott nodded. Jack expression gradually took on a faraway look. He looked deep into the fire as if he would find answers there. "I haven't spoken of this to anyone yet." He took a long pause before continuing. "The first few days after we started the council, I tried to get in touch with every minister in the area. I only managed to see a handful, but I thought they would be the best to get our message out. In doing so, Buck took me down to a Holiness church over on the south side. I knew the preacher there, a deeply conservative man of God. A good man with a loyal congregation. Buck said all the members of the church had been holed up in the sanctuary praying for a miracle for nearly two weeks. As we got close to the church, we saw birds. Ravens and vultures...they were on the grounds, the roof, the steeple… just sitting up there like gargoyles, watching us approach.

"The smell hit us before we even got near the door. Scott, I will never be able to erase what I saw in that small building. At least a hundred men, women, and children, all dead. They stayed in there, trusting the Lord to deliver, and they starved to death. One father had strangled all of his children. Then I guess he just waited with their bodies until he died too.

"There *is* evil in this world Scott. Lots of it. But it often takes a backseat to stupidity. Those people sat there and died because a man of God convinced them it would make a difference. They could have walked a half a mile and found water. God does not want us to waste our lives or our talents. That's why you are so important to our survival. We need a leader. Someone who can think logically even when the rest of us are falling apart."

Jack cleaned the plates and produced a small bottle of bourbon which they shared. Scott was shaken by the preacher's story. The conversation drifted to their friend Todd, and each wondered how he was doing. Scott asked Jack how long he had known Todd. "He and I went to school together over at Pass Christian. We were friends. He found Liz and…well, I found something much darker. Scott, you never asked me about my past, and I appreciate that, but you surely guessed I came to the church by a less than a righteous path."

"You are a different kind of Preacher but your past; that's none of my business," said Scott, "You're a good man, a good friend, someone I have grown to trust completely. That's all that matters to me."

"I appreciate that," Jack said, his warm smile still visible in the dim light. "The truth is, I simply made bad choices, poor decisions. In high school, I hung out with guys I knew were bad news. We drank too much, smoked too much weed. Over time, we went on to harder stuff. Eventually, I found myself pinned against a wall in the light of an angry cop's flashlight. I served five and a half years for armed robbery. I wasn't armed, but one of the guys was. They had told me they were going in to get something that a guy had been holding for them, but … well, I knew better. I knew they were up to no good. They were takers… I was a taker. I was not a very good person Scott."

Scott looked over at his friend, "What changed you?"

"God changed me. All the other guys that went to jail just got angrier. I just felt ashamed. I knew this was not who I was. I knew I was raised better. Honestly, I was ready to give up. The first day I was allowed to have visitors was my forty-fifth day of incarceration. You know, not a single member of my family came. None of my friends were there either. No one except for Todd. He had joined the Navy by then but got a furlough to come and check on me. Everyone else was ashamed of me. Todd though...he said he was ashamed of himself. He hadn't kept up our friendship when he met Liz. He was blaming himself for where I was. I cried that day... I cried a lot. Todd is a good man— the very best of us. He never stopped seeing the good in me and over the next five years he made sure I saw the good as well. He told me to be tough enough to survive and man enough to learn from it."

Jack continued, "I stumbled several times... one day I beat a man in prison... a man who did very bad things. I would have gotten in some real trouble for it, but the prison chaplain intervened. With his help, I started reading the Bible, like lots of cons do, but I found it calling to me in different ways. After three years I was preaching many of the sermons at the prison chapel each week. I felt renewed! The burden eventually lifted from my shoulders. When I got out, Todd and Liz were waiting. They brought me to Harris Springs, and he set me up with a job and a place to stay. Eventually, they helped me interview with the church I'm in now."

"So what does your church think of an ex-con preacher that drinks and swears like a Navy man?"

"They love me, I'm one of 'em. I don't pretend to be pious or perfect, cause I'm not. I am just a guy; I have the same vices, temptations and temperament as most men. Not all men called by God are meant to be angels."

A quiet moment passed between the two men before a noise coming out of the woods startled them into action. Scott pulled his carbine out, and Jack lifted the shotgun. Scott clicked on the powerful Thorfire flashlight. Just on the edge of the beam of light was a large coyote. Behind him, they could see the eyes of several others. At first, Scott thought it was a wolf as it was so large. The animal growled deeply.

"Don't move, or it will attack," warned Jack. "They're pack hunters. I'm going to swing around slowly and check our six." Scott nodded mutely. He could vaguely see Jack's flashlight sweeping the sides. It stopped on the left side in the direction of the train. "I have two more under the train car."

Coyotes were normally loud… these had snuck up quietly and within twenty yards of them. Scott didn't want to shoot them; the shots might alert other people to their location and the goods the train held. He also knew the land belonged more to the animals than it did him.

Remembering how his dad had dealt with wild dog packs on the farm, he held his focus on the large alpha dog. It looked about twice the size of a German Shepard, though Scott knew they were somewhat similar. Reaching slowly into his Go-bag, he withdrew the slingshot and a pouch of steel balls. He slowly propped the carbine to the side of the Jeep.

"Jack, when I start yelling, you do the same and move toward the ones under the train. Shoot only if you must," he said in a low and even tone.

"Roger that man," Jack said shakily.

Scott mounted a ball in the leather sling and pulled back a shot, aiming for the exposed chest of the beast. He didn't think it would injure the animal, but he could go for his pistol if he needed. He let go the projectile and at the same instant rose up and yelled as loud as he could. He heard Jack doing the same. The animal yelped in pain, and the spell was broken. All of the coyotes fled in a yelping mass.

"Wow," Jack said, "How did you know that would work?"

"Ummm, I didn't," Scott said with a fragile laugh. Both men looked with new respect at the now quiet forest all around them. "I think I will put my sleeping bag in the railcar," Scott said with a laugh.

"Yeah me too," Jack said.

The following day they made even more amazing discoveries. After packing the Jeep and trailer full, they headed back toward Harris Springs. Scott would talk to Bartos and a couple of the farmers about organizing a real salvage mission. They would have to use some of the county's bigger trucks to do the job. He guessed it would probably take a week, maybe even longer to take just the more usable commodities. Both men knew they had scored big with the find, but the real challenge was to get it secured before others located and looted it. They trusted no one at this point except the ones helping do the real work. Scott didn't even want anyone but his most trusted crew knowing the location.

Ultimately he decided he would also speak to Buck about adding an armed guard to the location while it was being cleared. One other thought had occurred to both he and Jack: the locomotive was basically a big diesel engine. Bartos had diesel mechanics on his crew. The CME may have fried the electronics, but Scott felt there was a chance they might move the entire train back down the tracks and nearer to town. With a working train, they would also have the opportunity to use it in future trades, and over much longer distances—assuming they could find enough diesel fuel for the job.

As they crossed back into Bay County and onto more familiar roads, Scott saw the ruined hulk of a burned out mobile home. It took a few moments to realize it was the same place he had stopped and talked to the little girl and her mom only a few weeks earlier. The ruins were still smoldering. Obviously, whatever had happened must have been in the last day or two.

"Oh lord, oh lord…," Scott groaned in anguish. He could see several dark lumps unmoving on the ground in front of the ash pile that had been a home. He pulled the Jeep to a stop and stared.

"Did you know them?" his friend asked.

Shaking his head, Scott mumbled something unintelligible. He tried to get his legs to move; to get out of the car and see if the lumps on the ground were what he feared, but he couldn't. He heard the passenger door open and shut, and saw Jack swiftly walk across the yard. He made a quick circuit, examining everything closely, then went down on one knee. He reached a tentative hand to the darkened mass and Scott could see him lift several strands of blonde hair. Jack put both hands on the ground and said a short prayer. He looked up at the sky and shook his head before getting back in the Jeep.

"Drive on Scott. Nothing here, friend. God has them now."

Scott wept silent tears in an act that was getting to be a habit with him.

• • •

The day the lights went out Tyrell hadn't even noticed. He'd been sitting on the back porch of the community center doing business. One of his rich white junkies had been the first to tell him. Ronald Hansbrough was a complete douchebag, always trying to order people around. Tyrell put up with it only because the dude had more money than God. If the money ever stopped flowing, though… he'd be the first one in line to double-tap the arrogant mother fucker. Right in the middle of that goddamn pasty-white face.

He did have to admit that the greedy man was good at seeing opportunities. All of Tyrell's drug pipelines had dried up overnight when the flare hit. Ronald had been the one to suggest hitting the clinics and pharmacies. It made good business sense to Tyrell. The prices he could charge were going through the roof: the law of supply and demand ruled. Stealing it from the clinics brought the cost for inventory to zero. That is, until his guys hit the clinic outside of Harris Springs. That was the night that bald fucker and his crazy dog had come in and killed everyone. Worst of all his brother DeeCee was working that pickup; he was one of the kids the dog killed.

Whatever humanity he had left died that day along with his brother. His life's purpose now was to get even. He had determined to find that little Cajun guy. It was Hansbrough again who had told him who he probably was and where he lived. His guys had watched the house for a few days then descended on it, but no one was there. Yesterday, though, Ronald had offered another possible location for the guy…the one they called Bartos.

FIFTY-ONE

Bartos spat but still couldn't get the taste out of his mouth. Solo looked at him curiously from the corner of the steps leading up into the old camper. Bartos knew he had eaten nutria before. After fur farmers had introduced the hearty South American rodent to the U.S., they had later released them into the wild back in the forties when it became unprofitable. The giant river rats had nearly taken over New Orleans. Looking more like a beaver than a rat. The little beasts were easy to trap and kill, and they bred like crazy. Bartos had tried roasting them, broiling them, grilling them… he was about ready to give up. "It's that damn Scott and his ribeye steaks…" he remarked to Solo. "I was fine eatin' river crap 'til I tasted that stuff." Solo was apparently uninterested in his master's complaints. He liked the taste himself. Of course, he sometimes liked to lick his own butt too.

The RV was parked on the edge of the swamp and was Bartos' primary bug-out location: more of a base camp. He had a small house up in town but had increasingly shifted more of his supplies out to his backup locations. No one had any idea about this place, and clues left around the house in town let him know people had been snooping around the place. He was also very aware of the enemies that he, Scott, and the Sheriff were making. Someone had burned an entire neighborhood down only a few blocks from his house. He had a pretty good idea who was behind it all.

Apparently one of the guys he and Solo had killed at the clinic was some relative of a local drug dealer, and Preacher Jack had let him know that he needed to watch his back. Bartos felt confident he could handle any problems, but that didn't mean he was itching for a fight. Somehow he had also managed to keep pissing off that Ronald Hansbrough feller again—more than just a few times in the last few weeks alone. The last time they'd interacted, he and Sheriff Warren had physically thrown him out of the now unoccupied mayor's office in which he was trying to set up shop, saying he had been a duly elected leader and that he was in line to fill the vacancy. The Sheriff had reminded him that the town was now under martial law, not civil control, and that the town charter was not even set up that way anyway. Bartos smiled at the memory of the slimy little bastard being flung out into the street.

Getting the town organized had been almost hopelessly chaotic. None of these fools wanted to work together. Most expected someone else—the army or the government—to come to the rescue. Hundreds had sat in a damn church just outside of town and starved to death!

The scene was so fucked up they'd decided to just burn the church down. Bartos didn't really get people. His dad had always said he wasn't fit to be around other people. He'd been a hellion back then, though. His dad hadn't been much better. He hated the government, refused to pay his taxes…They never stayed in one place long and living off the land was an everyday thing for them. Bartos, he knew, was not his real name. He wasn't entirely sure what it was.

In the fading daylight, Bartos got the rest of the gear out of the Bronco and carried it down to the pirogue waiting on the river bank. The little boat was ideal for navigating the shallow, tree-choked channels of the river and the bayous. Tonight he was going out to check his traps and hopefully pick up a gator, or at least some frogs. He wasn't sure how long the rations he had stockpiled would last but he knew eating off the land would be much harder over the winter months. Better to save what he had for those lean times.

He covered the Bronco with a weathered tarp, snuffed out the small campfire, and motioned for Solo to load up. Pushing the canoe back into the water he took a seat and began slowly paddling away from the RV. He had purchased the camper at a seized goods auction for nearly nothing and then proceeded to place it on this piece of land he had bought years earlier. He had spent a great deal of time camouflaging the exterior to blend in with its surroundings. As he looked back, he was pleased to see that it was nearly invisible from less than fifty yards away.

Solo issued a low growl. Bartos ducked lower in the rough little canoe as he heard a twig snap far away. The receding river bank was a confusion of shadows as he tried desperately to see what was happening. Then came a louder sound of glass breaking and he saw the shadows of multiple figures encircling the RV in a firing line. A small flame, obviously attached to a bottle of some kind, was tossed into his small trailer, and immediately a huge fireball erupted, blowing out every window as well as one corner of the roof off. The surprise caused Solo to issue a small bark while the light from the huge fire lit the canoe for everyone to see. While the line of gunmen shifted focus to the bayou, Bartos had his Colt M4A1 Assault Rifle up and firing on full auto. The line of men dropped as the spray of bullets punched neat holes into some and scared the shit out of the rest.

While the pirogue sucked as a shooting platform, Bartos had plenty of cover, and he could see the enemy better than they could see him. He had counted eight men in the original group, three of which were down and never getting back up. Two more were severely wounded. That left at least three others, possibly more. He directed the canoe into deeper shelter.

As he did so, he noticed that Solo was not in the boat. He hadn't heard a sound. Shots began to fly again, and bits of tree trunk and tree limbs rained down around him. Several bullets hit the canoe, and one clipped the side of Bartos' boot, jerking the leg all the way over to the other side of the boat and severely pulling a tendon in the process. Bartos yelled out in pain.

A voice rang out, "You bastards get 'im yet?"

Bartos couldn't hear the response. The voice came again from somewhere closer and off to the right.

"Well shit, whad d'you mean you think you got 'im? Hurry the hell up! We still gotta get dat utter fuck." Bartos saw the shadows of the men separating. Not three, but seven, not counting the one doing the talking, whom he couldn't see. *Too many*, he thought. And if Solo got started he wouldn't stop, then he too would have to engage... Instead of paddling, Bartos slipped out of the canoe, putting the boat between him and the bank, and began retreating deeper into the swamp with the boat in hand. Once out of sight of the still burning RV, he made a short whistle signaling Solo to withdraw. Several minutes passed before he felt the additional weight on the front of the pirogue and smelled wet dog. Climbing into the middle of the boat, exhausted and in pain, Bartos began to paddle deeper into the darkness.

FIFTY-TWO

The Gulf of Mexico 30 Miles South of Biloxi MS

The wind was perfect for the tack that Todd was planning. As he swung the boom, the large mainsail fluttered then caught, billowing out to its fullest. The bow of the thirty-two-foot Catalina cruiser swung westward. The coast of Mississippi was now a distant smudge. He had spent the night moored off of Dog Island, another mostly barren sandbar of land well out into the Gulf of Mexico. The spray of cool morning water as the boat knifed through the waves kept Todd focused on the task at hand. This was what he needed, he thought. He needed to stay busy and not think about his world ending. Not the actual world ending, he didn't give a shit about that now. Liz had been his world, his purpose, and now she was gone.

As the boat heeled Todd looked leeward into the depths, thinking, wishing. It would have been so easy to just let go. He had made a promise to her, though, soon after the diagnosis was confirmed. She knew how much he would hurt, and she knew he would want to give up. She had made him promise her not to. He had to live a life big enough for both of them.

He steadied the course, locked the helm and went to loosen the lines. Losing some of the wind in the sails quickly cut his speed. He was in no hurry, had no destination. The ebb and flow of the northern Gulf currents paled in comparison to his internal turmoil. He felt his compass and his anchor had been stripped away. It had only been a month or so since the funeral, and he had been sailing down the coast toward the Delta region of Louisiana. He had sailed into numerous little coves and bays to fish or just to anchor and let his mind drift.

While he had seen virtually no other boats on the water, he had been cautious about being close to shore. Everywhere he saw the smoke of homes burning. After what he and Scott had witnessed on the drive back from Tallahassee, nothing really surprised him. Early the day before, sailing out near Pass Christian, he had seen the body of a large man floating nearby, several bullet holes clearly visible in his torso and head. He missed his friends and thought again of Scott. Now he felt bad for urging him to try and save the world, but he also knew that the Scott had a depth of character that meant he might succeed.

Reaching up to adjust the jib, he noticed the color of the water beginning to lighten. Where the Mississippi dumped its water into the Gulf, the shoals and water depth changed frequently. Although his boat only had a draw of six feet, it was best to steer carefully in the area. This far from the shipping lanes no one would be around to help if he grounded his vessel. He went and took the helm again, readjusting the course of the *Careless Lady* due south, heading into deeper water. Tonight he would not be in a protected cove; his plan instead was to let her drift in the deep water. Todd looked over at the dark weather radar and grumbled. It would be nice to have at least some of the electronics on the boat working, but he had been at sea long enough to recognize the signs of approaching weather. He knew he would be fine, at least for the next twenty-four hours.

The sun had slipped low on the horizon before the water began to deepen once again. The many fingers of the Mississippi reached far beyond the Delta region out into the sea. A few main channels had been kept clear for heavier vessels to come into port, but Todd knew he was at least a hundred miles from those shipping lanes. He cracked open a warm Red Stripe and watched the beautiful sunset. He and Liz had spent countless evenings watching the sun set over the ocean. *She would love this one*, he thought. He missed her beautiful way of describing what she saw, like an artist describing a painting. He could close his eyes and still visualize many of those happier times just by recalling her words. The sound of a seabird roused him from his solitude. He knew he should eat; in fact, he couldn't recall his last meal. He headed down into the cabin to find food.

While he had packed in a rush, the boat had always been pretty well stocked so he and Liz could take off whenever they both got the urge. Dinner tonight had consisted of freeze-dried lasagna that he had boiled in a pot of water on the little cook stove. He had considered opening one of the bottles of wine that Liz had stocked but knew he wouldn't drink much of it and that the rest would go to waste. He sat in the cabin lit only by a small gas lantern and looked through photo albums that Liz had put together. He knew it was dragging him down to focus on the past, but he was willing to hold onto the pain just so that he would not forget. He had tried several times already to let go, but it didn't work. When his feet were back on dry land, he would have to move on. For now, she was still his. His eyes watered as he listened to the moaning wind blowing through the rigging. The tears crawled down his weathered cheeks like a parade of watery ants. They had been together since adolescence; he had no idea how he could live without her. He didn't have any real desire to do so. Closing the album, he wondered if the world he lived in would even allow him to make new, happy memories. He had lost a piece of himself, probably the best part of who he was. The rocking of the boat was as familiar to him as his bed at home, and he closed his eyes and began to drift with his boat.

He awoke some time later in the night from a fitful dream to a cacophony of bird calls. He walked up to unclamp the hatch and go out on deck. There was no moon, but the starlight helped him distinguish ocean from sky. The boat seemed fine, and the birds were off to starboard side and high up. Odd they would be out this far from land and making sounds at night. He briefly wondered if he had come close to an oil rig, but he knew there were none in this area. Navigating the rigging and around the helm, he stood at the rail trying to get a fix on sounds which seemed to echo in the darkness. He picked up the sound of small waves lapping against something just as he noticed that there were no stars visible on the starboard side at all. The entire sky was dark unless he turned his head to look straight up or far to either side. The sounds of the gulls got louder, drawing his attention back overhead, where he caught glimpses of the white wings in the dark sky.

Wiping his eyes to try and remove the fog of sleep, his mind worked hard to process the clues. When it did, it was almost too late. *Danger* was the first word his sluggish mind dredged up, and he unlocked the helm and turned hard to port. Something big was ahead, and off to the right. Something big enough to block out the sky. And he was about to sail right into it. He dropped the sea anchor and, to his relief, it dug in before it reached the end of its length. The *Careless Lady* heaved over and slowed to a stop just as the smell of something putrid assaulted Todd's senses. The smell made him wretch, and he made it back to the rail just as the meager contents of his stomach emptied over the side.

In the darkened sky, Todd had no way of gauging the size of the thing but began to make out the general shape of what he was next to. Guessing at the top height and length by where the birds were calling from, he was pretty sure the ship rose about two hundred feet. It was maybe five times that long. He could make out what looked like a line of darker anti-fouling paint from a lighter color above. That would normally mean that it probably was not a freighter, as they were usually painted darker. He strained to listen in the darkness but heard nothing but the gulls and the waves. The large vessel did not appear to be moving; grounded, he assumed. Stranded when the CME hit and knocked out its power and navigation, most likely.

The rotting smell was overwhelming, finally driving him below where he found some menthol cream in a drawer that he rubbed under his nose. Unsure of what to do next, he put on some coffee to wait for sunrise before deciding. If it was a freighter, there might only have been a handful of people on board, usually less than twenty. If it were Navy, it could easily have been several hundred. On a cruise ship, the number could be many thousands. The lack of any noise coming from the ship troubled him. Even if most of the occupants were sleeping at this hour, you would expect to hear something. Morning light would reveal all.

FIFTY-THREE

How in the fuck had they found him? Bartos' leg was still throbbing, and he was pretty sure his knee was swelling. Navigating by feel, he had drawn the small boat deeper and deeper into the bayou. The smells of rot came from everywhere. The dog had never liked being on the water and kept shifting his weight, making Bartos' job more difficult. Each time his injured leg bumped the side it sent a jolt of pain throughout his body. He was beginning to think more clearly and in doing so was getting more and more pissed off. "If they burned the Bronco I'm going to go medieval on those bastards…Don't fuck with a man's truck…" he grumbled. Solo didn't bother looking back at his master's ramblings.

Bartos finally came out into a more open channel, part of the original track of the river. The water here flowed more steadily toward the sea, and the smell of decay lessened. Best of all, Bartos now had a good idea of where he was. He did have a kind of emergency shelter in the bayou, but to reach it would take several hours. He reached in his Go-bag and took out a bottle of water. He knew that only left two bottles, but he needed this now. He also opened a small pocket survival kit and extracted two aspirin. Exhausted and in pain, he wasn't sure he could make it to the hide location, but the anger was driving him hard. He silently dug the paddle deeper into the black water and headed back into the bayou.

He still couldn't let go of the fact that somehow they had tracked him to his bat cave. He had never told anyone about the place, not even Jack or Todd. Somehow the preacher had known there was some bad shit coming. No matter who was doing the shooting, it had to be that thug Tyrell—or even Hansbrough— that was behind it. Since it wasn't Ronald's voice he had heard, he assumed it was the drug dealing shitbag Tyrell or one of his goons who'd been stalking around out there. But who was the 'other one' they needed to hit? The sheriff? Probably not. Buck had a small army and a few radios now; it would take more than a small gang of thugs to take him down.

Solo sprung up emitting a low growl. In the dark, Bartos could only make out a shadowy silhouette of the dog but could tell he was looking ahead. His sensitive ears or nose had picked up something moving out in the darkness. Something dangerous.

Bartos had left open water a few hours back, and now he had no view of the sky. The thick canopy of trees kept this area relatively dark, even in full daylight. He had put on the headlamp with the powerful LED beams, but to switch that on now to see the danger would ruin his night vision. He didn't think he had the twenty minutes it would take to regain it and did not want to keep a light on the rest of the journey. Bartos also had a good idea of what Solo was grumbling about. Gators hunted at night, and although not plentiful here, there were a few enormous ones around. He knew he wasn't going to shoot one; the sound would carry, and he had no desire to alert anyone to his whereabouts. His years of hunting them had given him some insight into their curious and territorial natures. He began to make as much noise as possible, banging the paddle on the side of the canoe, and hitting the exposed tree stumps as he cruised by. The last thing he wanted to do was sneak into the gators' domain unannounced.

Solo moved further back in the small boat, looking over the left side. Bartos was now sure it was a gator and not a snake, for which he was very thankful. He heard a plop nearby as something large suddenly dropped below the water's surface. He was tempted again to hit the headlamp but fought back the urge. Bartos had spent the largest part of his life in swamps and bayous and felt as comfortable here as most men felt in their backyard. That did not mean he was immune to the dangers.

Listening, he calculated that a large alligator was hanging about half way below him in the five- to six-foot-deep water. The animal was no doubt trying to determine if the large noisy shape above was a threat or food, using senses honed over millions of years. As Bartos expected, the next thing he felt was a very large bump from underneath his boat. The gator was testing the wooden canoe.

Hopefully, it would now assume it was just another floating log and move on. Solo's growls got louder, however, though, a small finger snap by Bartos quieted the large dog. Bartos gradually resumed his shallow paddle strokes, moving them silently away from the hidden predator.

They finally reached the suspended shelter at about 4:30 in the morning. He had been paddling for over eight hours. He risked using the light now to tie off the pirogue. The shelter was more of a tree house than anything. Suspended about four feet over the water, it was, in essence, a rectangular platform firmly attached to four large trees. The platform had a rudimentary roof and a back wall made of old planking. The entire structure was only twelve feet wide and about eight feet deep. Bartos had felt anything larger would have been noticeable to other hunters and trappers that used the swamp like he did. Most of them would have their own swamp hides to use as a base of operations when they were out here. Mainly just a place to sleep and store gear.

Familiar with the structure, Solo jumped eagerly out of the boat to the platform, nearly swamping the boat when his powerful legs launched his body upward. "Goddammit, dog," Bartos sighed in tired frustration as cold swamp water eased over the side and immediately found the crack of his ass. "You did that on purpose, didn't you?"

Bartos tossed a couple of his gear bags onto the floor of the questionable looking shack, then began the awkward gyrations that would get him out of the pirogue and up to the hide. His injured leg had been stretched out in the bottom of the canoe all night and was swollen and stiff. Finally finding a suitable knot from a broken limb on one of the trees, Bartos pulled his weary body out of the boat and up to the platform. He managed to stay out of the water, but for one leg and boot which dropped from the perch and were soaked.

Solo was already sleeping in one corner when he finally made it up with his gear. "Thanks for all the help," Bartos said sarcastically. He was relieved to see the bags had stayed dry, and pulled out the compact sleeping bag and a cold pack. He was unsettled at the thought of what tomorrow would bring; he knew he should rest a day or two, but he had to check out his hunch and see if he was right. Applying the ice packet to his knee and taking two more pain pills, he turned off the headlamp and was asleep in minutes.

FIFTY-FOUR

As the thick gray morning fog began to lift, the massive vessel revealed itself to be a cruise ship. It did not appear to be grounded; there was some movement, but not much. The enormous anchors were dropped, and it did not appear to be damaged. Todd engaged the small diesel engine and did a pass around the entire vessel. On the port side, all the davits were extended and empty – lines still hung where lifeboats had been deployed. This meant that the ship had probably been full, not empty, when it was moored here.

Some of this was not making sense. He assumed the CME had fried all the computers, radios, and navigation. That shouldn't have rendered all the engines dead, though he supposed it may have. His best guess was that the ship had just begun its voyage, probably out of Houston or New Orleans; the electronics had gone out, and they couldn't signal a distress message without coming back near shore. They'd probably dropped anchor and waited a few days instead of trying to navigate the maze of shoals in this part of the Gulf, and when no help came, loaded onto lifeboats to try to get to land.

If that were the case, though, all the lifeboats should have been gone— not just those on the one side. No way they could have put three or four thousand passengers on that number of boats. Of course, another ship may have come to their aid... The Coast Guard could have pulled off many more had they been notified... But he didn't think the chances of that would have been good: he hadn't seen any Coast Guard vessels since the shit hit the fan.

Midway down on the starboard side of the ship he found a ship tender's access door. He placed the boat fenders on the port side of the sailboat and tied off the *Careless Lady* to several nearby cleats on the outer wall of the huge ship. To his relief, the access hatch had apparently only been dogged shut from the outside as it pushed in and swung to the side when he undid the latch and gave a firm push.

He walked into a darkened cavern, the only light coming in from the door behind him. He reached into his go-bag and pulled out his headlamp and a tactical flashlight. He put the headlamp on his head but left it off for now. Switching on the powerful Surefire Fury Tactical flashlight, he saw he was in a garage of sorts, with jet skis, small watercraft, and all manner of water sports equipment mounted in racks or floating in the small canal of water that went up to a sealed door far down the wall. The area was neat and tidy but unoccupied. Other than the absence of electricity and people, it seemed pretty ordinary.

He began to explore more of the magnificent craft, making his way cautiously up and toward the bridge. He and Liz had taken several cruises and she enjoyed them, but he had always felt trapped. To him, such vessels were just big resort hotel-with attached-shopping mall. The fact that it was on water made little difference when it was ten stories below them for most of the voyage. Liz had enjoyed the food and the massages, and he had enjoyed seeing how happy she was.

The big man paused on his climb up the nearly endless stairs to dry his eyes. At each floor, he opened the door and listened into the long dark corridors, but he heard nothing. Once he had done this five times, he began to smell the strong, foul odor that had called his attention to the ship the night before.

He had an idea of what it was but did not feel particularly anxious to verify his suspicions. He carried on, his shoulders heavy. As he neared the deck level, he began to see the bodies in each passageway he checked. The smell of the bloated corpses thickened as he reached the first deck level, where he pushed through an outside door to catch his breath. Here, the screams of the birds and the stink of rotten flesh hit him like a punch to the gut.

He stepped toward the rail as he took in the surreal scene, stumbling slightly at the horror something snapped beneath his boot. Looking down, he found his foot upon the brittle bones of an arm, pecked clean of flesh and already weakened and bleached by the sun. The days exposed to the hot Gulf sun and carrion birds had made it almost unrecognizable.

Looking over the deck railing his eyes now took in what the earlier fog had obscured, bodies, hundreds of floating bodies in the area around the ship. As far out as he could see in the early morning light, fish and birds fed on the semi-floating bodies, swollen with gasses in the sub-tropical autumn heat. More than once he witnessed one of the bodies erupt, either from the internal pressure or from the puncture of a shark's bite. It spread a vile bloom of viscera and organs like a gruesome volcano. The birds and sharks would vanish momentarily with the mini explosion, then return to begin their ghastly feast once again.

Making his way finally into the bridge, Todd looked for the log book. He needed to understand what had happened here. Opening the book, he read of how the power had cut out just a day out of port from New Orleans. The Captain, a man named Dimitri Gravari, had instructed the deck officers to return to port. Without navigation, though, they could only approximate the location, though they had done so very accurately. The ship's engines had begun to overheat; they were not designed to operate without the computer controlled monitoring system. The ship had dropped anchor, as the water seemed to be shallow in every direction ahead.

Help had not come, and on the fifth day, the captain had instructed all the senior crew to evacuate the ship and go for help. With no electricity, they could not open the tender garage to get the motor launches out and without a power winch, lowering the lifeboats had taken many, many hours. The ship's crew was apparently based out of Europe, so the area was not familiar to them, but they felt confident they could get to shore and summon help. The captain had stayed on board. In fact, Todd was looking over at him as he glanced up from reading the log. The single gunshot wound to the side of his head told him a lot. The passengers and crew had not thought to ration the fresh water as their desalinization systems could make fresh water from sea water. Unfortunately, that took electricity, and by the time that was realized, most of the potable water had been consumed. The next weeks had been one of crazed agony as the passengers slowly went mad from thirst and died of dehydration or threw themselves overboard to get to the vast ocean of cool water below. Todd closed the logbook. He couldn't imagine a more difficult position than the Captains'. Knowing all of the people in your charge were likely doomed to suffer horribly and die. He knew of maritime stories where crews had abandoned ship and left passengers to fend for themselves. Captain Gravari had not done that. He and his men had done their best right up to the end.

• • •

It was midday the following afternoon before the *Careless Lady* released her lines and parted ways with the doomed cruise liner. Todd had filled the sailing ship with as much cargo as he dared take on board. He had also taken the time to plot the ship's location and reseal the doors, just in case he could make it back to her with a larger boat in the next few days.

Despite the gruesome scenes on board, he was in good spirits, as he had been astounded at the supplies that remained untouched. The dry goods alone could keep a town like Harris Springs going for several years. Along with that, the medical supplies and equipment were hospital grade, and he'd also found backup machinery and radios that could be useful now. A lot of the ship could be converted for use on dry land; each part of it was designed to be used in isolation—even the onboard Internet system was Satellite based. Scott and Bartos would have a field day if he could get them out here. He had taken the most valuable and most portable items and secured much of the rest so it would not be easily found if other boarders happened by. Hoisting the mainsails, he found a growing easterly breeze and let the sleek craft pick up speed as it sailed away from the ill-fated cruise ship and its ghastly passengers.

He made excellent time but noticed building clouds during the day. The night brought a fierce squall. He could hear the rolling thunder and see the flashes from miles away. The pitching of the boat was familiar to Todd but rarely had he rode out major storms at sea in a boat this small. He would have never put Liz at risk and generally found safe harbor from storms. When the waves started reaching impressive heights, his confidence began to fade. An experienced seaman, his mind knew they were just rollers, regular and not overly dangerous. The boat was sturdy, and all topside hatches had been dogged tight. Still the violent tossing was unnerving him. Todd calculated that he should be about thirty miles from Mobile Bay. He thought of turning for home as he had passed by twenty miles to the south but decided to keep sailing with the prevailing wind. Now here he was in deep water facing a maelstrom. No way of knowing if it was just a typical summer thunderstorm or something much worse.

He distracted himself over the next several hours below deck hooking up one of the reserve marine radios he had taken from the *Aquatic Goddess*. It had been wrapped in a watertight antistatic foil bag, so he hoped it hadn't been damaged by the CME. The quality was well beyond what he had on either of his boats, and with the right antenna, the range would be hundreds of miles. To his relief, the relatively compact unit came right on when he hooked it into his boat's power system. Todd had switched the antenna from his dead radio over to the new unit and began sweeping through the marine bands.

He caught several very powerful transmissions, but the voices were distorted, probably using a scrambler on each end to keep the conversations private. No one seemed to be broadcasting in the clear. He was reminded of his Dad talking about the original clear channel broadcast that reached the areas of the country that had no local stations. These had originally been for emergency alert broadcasting, but as the cold war went on other forms of broadcast radio, and then TV, took over the responsibility of informing the nation. He wondered if any of these broadcasts would have been re-initialized now. Setting the radio to scan, he poured himself a drink and watched the light show of the storm from the small porthole window.

The radio scanned until it locked on a strong signal, paused for fifteen seconds on the frequency, and finding nothing more, resume scanning. With so many frequencies and bands, it was not a quick process. After about an hour of finding nothing useful, he switched from the marine bands to normal VHF/AM and FM bands. The scanning resumed, and he picked up several AM broadcasts, though most were too faint to hear clearly. He marked several frequencies to come back to then switched to UHF, mainly military channels. The broadcast light went out on this band as it had to have a chip to transmit, but he could monitor. He was amazed at the amount of radio traffic up and down the spectrum. Of course, UHF broadcast traveled great distances and did not need to be anywhere local. Some he felt were aircraft checking in with their base; others seemed to be troops on the ground changing positions. They used lots of jargon and never mentioned specific cities or bases, but he got the sense some of this activity was close by, as they kept identifying water-related targets.

The pitch of the conversations was becoming more animated as he heard the report of another blast of lightning and thunder. He thought he heard a reaction on the radio to the same sound. Todd noticed that the rolling of the boat had subsided. Again came the lighting and thunder. The storm should be subsiding but seemed to be growing in intensity. A curious thought occurred to him. Reaching into his Go-bag he pulled one of the radios he had taken off the grayshirt guard back at the college. Checking each of the preset frequencies that were programmed into the little unit, he entered them on the new radio and listened.

On the third one, he hit pay dirt. He recognized the speech patterns and even some of the lingo of a mission in progress. The voices were calm even when they stated "Incoming fire." The thunder and lightning were nearly continuous now, but the boat remained mostly calm. He turned up the volume on the radio, went to the rear cabin hatch, and opened the watertight door to try and get a stronger signal. The concussion wave knocked him back to the lower deck of the cabin. What he had thought was lighting was artillery firing from a trio of Navy ships about a half mile south. Climbing back up woozily, he looked again. They were firing on what looked to be another group of ships in the direction of Mobile Bay. Behind the naval ships, he could see at least two more large white ships with red crosses painted on the sides: aid ships.

Putting the clues from the radio and what he was seeing together; the smaller ships that were blocking the port from the aid ships were part of the Praetor forces, intending for the port city to fall quickly rather than hang on in a lingering death. The Navy was trying to offer help to the city via the Aid ships. Todd engaged the small motor and for once was thankful the running lights had not worked since the solar storm. He slowly made his way out of the battle, which was growing in intensity. The Praetor naval ships were small and maneuverable and packed some seriously hi-tech firepower. This was the real conflict, he thought. It was not good versus evil, as both groups were trying to save humanity, just in different ways. But he could not agree with the brutal, heartless tactics of Catalyst. At heart, he was a Navy man, and he simply could not stand by and not try to help his military family out, especially knowing they were on a mission of mercy. Unfortunately, there really wasn't much he could do, but …he could pass on the radio frequencies. The Navy could monitor those, maybe even zero in on firing solutions, assuming the ships were using the same channels.

It was all he could do to tear his eyes away from the ongoing sea battle to go below deck and pick up the handset. Since he couldn't transmit on any of the military frequencies, he tuned the radio back to a marine frequency he knew the Navy radiomen here in the Gulf usually monitored.

"Sailing Vessel calling for Naval Flotilla off Mobile Bay." No response. He repeated the call and added. "To assist you please monitor and triangulate enemy broadcast on the following frequencies." He then passed along the specific channels from the Praetor handset. He hated broadcasting this information in the clear but after several minutes, he heard a voice respond, "Acknowledged." He waited, but no other transmission came through. Todd wanted Scott to be aware of this, more proof of what they had guessed. He cycled the dial over the frequency they had agreed on, planning on passing along an update on the Catalyst activity. Just as he was about to hit the transmit key, he heard a familiar voice. It was distant and sounded frightened, but he immediately knew whom it belonged to.

FIFTY-FIVE

Kaylie sat on the side of the bed in the small quiet house. This room was filled with memories, happy memories of family. The trips down with her grandparents had been some of her most special times as a child. She missed everything. She missed her parents. She missed her little dog Ruffles. She missed feeling DJ next to her in the bed.

The tears had been flowing off and on all morning. As much as she loved her Uncle Scott, she did not feel that close to him... not anymore. He had once been happy and funny, but the few times she'd seen him since the divorce, he had not been the same. She had prayed he would find someone to help make him complete, but all he seemed to love anymore was riding his bikes. She had been honestly surprised he even had friends when he showed up to get her, as she'd heard her dad express worry that he had pulled away from everyone.

She was not naïve. She knew how fortunate she was that he and Todd had come to get her. Even though she hadn't seen it, she knew he had killed people to rescue her...as thankful for it as she was, that part bothered her. Selfishly, though, she just really wanted to know what was going on with everyone else; how her friends and family were getting by. She wanted to update her status on Facebook. She wanted to take a hot shower, wash her hair and put on makeup again. She knew her dad was a prepper, and she had mostly thought he was nuts. "How could you make plans for the end of the world?" she had asked him so many times over the years. It was crazy...and yet, he had been right. She had been just a stubborn teenager when she went to college. Everything was apocalyptic to a teenage girl...if she had only known. The tears came again. She did not think she was a survivor. *Why would you even want to survive the end?* Those people out on the road, those bodies, that smell... how could anyone be okay with this? Even the people they had been trying to help seemed so angry and selfish. Or they had already checked out and ended their lives. It was all just so sad, just too much to deal with.

She took her nearly useless smartphone and scrolled through her photos. Mostly images of silly stuff of her friends, ball games, or DJ. She paused when she got to pictures of her mom and dad. "I hope you guys are okay," she whispered. "Please God…let them be okay." Realizing that when the phone battery finally died she would have no pictures of anyone, she reluctantly shut it down. Through the tears, she fought against the waves of despair. She wanted to be strong… she knew it was in her, but she couldn't find it right now. Feeling weak was not something she was used to and knew she had to rid herself of it. The martial arts training was helping but she wanted, no needed to be fierce again. *Do not be a victim.* Her inner voice was struggling to be heard though.

This world, this heat was dragging her down. Everyday life was now a real struggle and it was only going to get worse. She had always put off thinking about joining the real world. Graduating, having to work for a living, responsibilities, bills, all that had scared her before "The Big Crunch" as her dad had called it; now she felt the loss of a life she would never get to live. The potential she would never get to realize—at least in the way she'd imagined.

She pulled out the little ham radio; it was time to listen for DeVonte. She doubted the radio would even reach that far, even with the long antenna. The shortwave radios her dad had were much larger. They took up most of one table in his bombproof room, or whatever the cage thing supposed to withstand an EMP blast was called. Still, she turned it on and listened for thirty minutes before deciding to put it back on the solar charger. Just as she did so, she heard her uncle's voice coming through the speaker, checking in with her. She was relieved to hear he was okay. He had been working non-stop lately, moving supplies and doing what was necessary to try and keep them all alive. Kaylie gave him the 'all is good' report, and they signed off. She put the radio away and lay back down on her pillow. She drifted back to sleep, dreaming again of the life she had lost.

The sound came again, this time much closer. She thought about the night they discovered the man standing in the yard. Was he back? Was this morning going to be like that? She was pretty sure that man had been unstable, serious mental issues. What was he capable of? That damn hair ribbon he kept holding on to. The flood of creepy memories and images flooded her barely awake brain. The chills climbed her skin at the base of her neck. She was frozen—paralyzed with fear. Her ears listened for every noise in the old house. Something faint...it was indistinct but very real. "Shit, shit, shit" *Move your ass girl.* She knew she had to act.

The handgun that Scott and Bartos had been teaching her to fire was on the desk nearby. With what seemed like superhuman effort, she made the soundless crawl over to get it. Putting into a holster she then grabbed the little sub-compact assault rifle

"Hey, little pretty boy..." the poorly enunciated words came from the direction of the road. "I believe you been holding out on us," the voice called again.

Kaylie pulled the weapon from the table, slung the strap over her shoulder and rested the grip in her palm as she'd been taught. She barely knew how to use it but knew a pistol would not be sufficient. *Oh fuck she was scared!*

"Open up motha fucka!" another voice yelled from outside.

Kaylie cradled the rifle firmly as she peeked carefully around the sheet of black plastic covering the window and looked down toward the road. A rough looking group of armed men were lined up across the front yard. Kaylie felt her bladder letting go and the smell of urine a moment later confirmed her terror. Some of the men were moving to the left and right sides of the cottage.

She couldn't take on the nine or ten guys out front, even if she did know how to use this thing. The front door knob began to shake. Make that eleven.

"Bring dat ax, Dean" a voice near the door yelled.

"Hang on," was the distant response.

"Last chance," the singsong voice that had woken her warned.

Kaylie saw the bullet hole appear in the wall above her before she even heard the first shot. Several more shots rang out, most embedded in the solid timbers of the house. Another round found the window, which shattered, covering her with flying glass. Looking down, she saw blood appear where several shards had cut her.

She heard howls of laughter as she crawled to her bedroom and swept up her boots and go-bag in one hand. She quickly looked to make sure none of the men were on the backside of the house yet. As she had done many times as a kid, she pushed out the screen on the rear window, she had taken the precious seconds to throw the radio and a few personal items into her big bug-out bag out, then also grabbed the smaller bright pink camo go-bag and slipped silently out, pulling the window down behind her and stepping off the brick molding and onto the ground.

She heard the front door of the cottage begin to give way under what had been a fierce barrage of blows. Kaylie pasted herself to the back wall of the cottage as she slipped on her boots. She could hear them destroying the house now that they were inside. Her dad had built this place, and these thugs were destroying it. Just the idea of it made her livid, but she was also so terrified. She ducked down and moved deftly over to the back corner of the cottage, the farthest from the noise inside. She caught sight of a dark face looking out of the window she had just slipped through, but it disappeared quickly. *Panic later*, she kept telling herself. Right now she had to think.

She reluctantly decided to head for the road if she could slip past them. As she stealthily eased herself closer to the front yard, something caused her to stop and go rigid. The breath caught in her throat, and her mouth went dry as she saw the part of a sneaker and the tip of a rifle barrel emerging around the next corner. One of the guys was standing less than ten feet away on the front wall of the cottage. She reversed course and quietly slipped back the way she came. *Oh fuck, I'm dead, I'm dead, I'm dead.* Despite all the practice in self-defense with Jack lately, she felt none of the confidence she needed. Nothing had prepared her for a football team of armed men.

There were voices and sounds of destruction seemingly from every room of the small house now. Kaylie knew she had to be smart, but she didn't seem to have a lot of options. *Get under the house* she thought. She knew the house was raised several feet—she'd carried the cement blocks for her dad and uncle when they enclosed it years ago. She looked down the smooth run of blocks. *Shit, no opening.*

She crept back to the rear of the house and looked down. There, about thirty feet away, was a small wooden door that must go under the house. It was painted the same sand color as the blocks, so it was not easy to see. Just above it and a little farther down was the large double French doors leading from the kitchen to the back deck. She knew most of the guys would be there, probably looking for food and stuff to steal. She would be fully exposed if she tried for it; right now the only thing keeping her safe was that they didn't know about her. She had to make sure things stayed that way. Someone yelled from inside, "Tyrone, you and Marcus check the rest of the yard, see what else this shit has we can use."

Fuck. The only thing she could see to do was sprint from the house to the boathouse at the backside of the property. She took off, not daring to look back. She held the pistol and the pink go-bag tight to her chest and pulled the straps of the larger bag on her back tight so nothing would make noise. Her legs felt unusually large and cumbersome as the fear continued to grip her and adrenaline flooded her body. She knew she was slowed with the weight of the large pack on her shoulders, and felt it would serve as a large bullseye to anyone looking her way. She used the few small trees in the yard to shield her from the house. As she reached each tree, she would alter her path to keep the trunk of it between her and the back wall of the house. As she topped the small rise that led down to the boathouse, she felt better. No sounds of alarm had been raised—at least so far.

Kaylie ducked down behind some of the sparse bushes that grew on the riverbanks. The house was now out of sight, but she could just see the top of a head in a hoodie bobbing through the backyard, working its way in her direction. She looked over at the boathouse; it was about seventy-five feet away. She had bad memories of the boathouse and had never liked to go in there. A large black snake had nearly fallen on her from one of the exposed rafters as a child. The panic was still there all these years later. She knew the fishing boat would probably make things a lot easier if she could ease it out, but quickly realized that the ramshackle boathouse would be the first thing to get the attention of the thug coming this way. She began to make her way in the opposite direction.

Her dad and now Scott had kept the river's edge pretty clean cut on their property, but the adjacent lots were mostly owned by the state. They were more overgrown, and as she moved in that direction, the overgrowth forced her further down the hill. Her heart was racing, and her arms felt like lead. Moving as quietly as she could, she forged ahead, driven closer and closer to the black swampy water. The mud sucked at her boots, making progress difficult. She could just see the man walking toward the old boathouse, as she had expected. He never looked in her direction, but she felt sure he would have seen her or the damned pink Go-bag she'd loved so much when she went off to college. Kaylie mentally rolled her eyes at her past self and tucked the bright bag under her dark shirt.

Hearing more shouts, she smelled the distinct odor of burning wood. The thug had not come back out of the boathouse, but she was even more desperate to get away now. Her way forward was blocked by overhanging tree roots dropping down the steep bank. Having no choice, she stepped into the black waters of the bayou. Her first step took her in knee-deep; the next to her waist.

As she moved farther out, the water crept up close to her chest. The water smelled disgusting, and she could feel it rushing into her boots. Even though she knew that no gators were supposed to be up here—at least, none had been seen for years—she still imagined one with every old submerged limb she brushed past.

The man was joined by another as he came out of the boathouse. Through the thicket of vines and cypress trunks, Kaylie could see they were looking her way. Terrified, her dad's familiar words came back to her, telling her "Do what is needed, be scared later." Those men scared her more than the gators or snakes right now. She quietly bent her knees and eased down to neck level in the murky water, backing deeper into the darkness of the swamp.

The blackened fingers of mossy limbs pulled her hair and her clothes with every step. The voices of the men at the cottage were getting louder and more obscene with every outburst. Twice she heard gunshots then howls of laughter. Whatever these men wanted, they were completely unafraid of being discovered. Guessing they had found her uncle's stash of wine and liquor, she wondered what would happen when his bike pulled back in the drive. Her legs were numb, and her teeth began to chatter. Even though the water was not very cold, from her medical training, she knew the initial signs of hypothermia. She looked for anything she could use for protection or shelter. She hoped she could get her body out of the water, and quietly.

Exhausted, her mind did not register the two new men on the bank looking in her direction. She stumbled over a root on the river bottom just as she got to the tree she hoped to climb. Kaylie heard a reaction from the shore; one of them had noticed. She turned and scanned the bank fifty yards away. She could now see them, pointing guns into the dark swamp. If they started spraying bullets, she would surely be hit. Again she froze, panic rising in her, afraid to move, afraid to breathe. Slowly and with tremendous effort she lifted the assault rifle and shakily began to take aim. The front of the barrel was wavering and she had to calm herself. Her sights centered on the one with the hoodie.

She barely noticed as a dark gloved hand reached around her neck from behind and clamped over her mouth. The scream of panic was silenced as her body went completely limp. Too late, she realized she had been found.

FIFTY-SIX

In the weeks since the blast, Scott had taken to riding his bike more and more. Partially because of the limited fuel supply but mostly because he needed time to think and plan, and to see what was going on out in the county. The roads here had stayed relatively safe thanks to Sheriff Warren and his deputies. The few times he had seen real problems were when he ventured too far from home and into adjacent counties. There, he saw highwaymen blocking roads, and the varied and unpleasant remnants of encounters between adversaries. On one trip by a ritzy subdivision, he'd seen bodies hanging from the tree limbs in several of the neatly manicured yards. He knew the isolation of the area around Harris Springs was helping to stave off events like these, but he wondered how long that could last.

For a while, the roads themselves had been clogged with people. Everyone seemed to be hauling crap, walking in various directions, hoping that somewhere, anywhere, had it better than where they'd come from. The council had worried that Harris Springs might become a mecca for the wandering hoards if news of their work or supplies got out. Needless to say, the bridges were staying up more often than not these days. The irregular electricity had flickered on rarely in the last few weeks and all phone service was now gone. No one had illusions anymore of being rescued.

Scott's current problem had been more mundane. Figuring out how to help feed people had led the council to another pressing problem. That food that everyone ate had a habit of coming back out the other end. "How the fuck do we deal with all this shit?" he was wondering as he rode fast down the empty road.

Bartos had told him that even before the CME, nearly twenty million Americans got sick every year from tainted water. The town of Harris Springs essentially sat on a large sandbar surrounded by ocean, canal, and bayou. The only real fresh water supply had been the spring that the town was named for. Long ago it had been capped by the city water treatment facility. The aquifer was known to be close to the surface and very susceptible to pollution. In an effort to address the issue they had dug latrines for the townsfolk to use, but they were woefully insufficient for waste disposal and over time, dysentery, typhoid, cholera, and all manner of other biological nasties could wipe the town just as efficiently as armed gangs or bomb blasts.

Clean water was a more urgent human need than anything other than air to breathe. It was also one of the most fragile. They simply didn't have the chemicals to test the water supply, much less treat it to kill off pathogens. Bartos had proposed using lime to help neutralize the waste, but they didn't have enough to do that either, and it mainly helped reduce the smell and didn't decompose the waste. The farmers had suggested composting the solids like they did with the manure from their cattle and pigs. Unfortunately, Kaylie had quickly pointed out that you cannot do the same with human waste. Not safely at least.

This was a nasty problem, but one they couldn't ignore. They had already instructed people not to use the toilets in their houses and public buildings unless they had their own septic tank. They had also set-up numerous portable toilets around the town that were serviced regularly by being taken inland many miles, away from all water sources, and dumped in what had been a county maintained clay pit. Besides law enforcement, this was one of the highest priority activities for the community volunteers. Scott was worried that it used too much fuel and manpower to service the units. They would also be too cold to use in winter. When that happened, would people take the effort to go to the public toilet, or just go in their yards, or even worse, in their houses somewhere?

Along with everything else they had to deal with had been that damnable asshole Ronald. He wanted to argue against everything the council was doing. He accused them of Gestapo tactics, trampling human rights, racism... anything that could be said to incite a crowd. While the tactic was obvious, Scott admitted the man was good at it. He could use just enough facts amongst the twisted emotional manipulation to make even the ridiculous sound plausible. Lately, he had been refusing to use the public latrines and instead repeatedly using the closed restrooms at city hall.

Preacher Jack had warned Scott about the guy, but Scott had initially found him to be only an inconvenience. That changed when the jerk tried muscling his way onto the council and later that same week they found him in the former mayor's office. Bartos had pulled a gun on the slimy politician, and Scott had been ready to be rid of him right there as well. The guy had become more than just a thorn in their side; he was becoming a real problem, and Scott had no tolerance for problems right now. If he was unwilling to use the public toilets, let him shit in his bathtub at home until he got sick and died. The red-faced, blustering fool was a piss-ant, as Scott's grandmother would have said. They had banished him from the very building that bore his family name. Scott had seen the rage in his face as he walked away. Jack said he would handle him, but Scott wasn't sure it would keep him out of trouble. He pedaled furiously trying to outpace the flood of problems rushing through his head..

Scott was always alert on his rides but certainly had not expected the trio of gunmen blocking the road ahead as he had topped the hill. His initial instinct that they were some of the Sheriff's deputies, but the shot that whizzed a few inches by his head let him know that he was clearly incorrect. As he hastily turned the bike in the opposite direction, he caught sight of a truck up in the woods near the gunmen. A puff of asphalt near his front tire announced a second shot from behind him. He rode back over the crest of the hill and made the descent on the far side in world-class time. His mind was racing, looking for options, solutions. *Maybe they won't come after me*, he thought optimistically. *A guy on a bike doesn't have much to offer in the way of resources… not really worth the effort.* His hopes vanished when he heard the motor of the old truck crank up and begin to accelerate his way. The throaty headers on the V8 motor rumble ominously.

The bike was fast, but he could not outrun a truck. Scott was working on his options as his bike began losing speed up the next hill. He heard another shot and caught a glimpse of the truck only a few hundred yards behind. He looked closely at the crest of the hill, at least fifty yards ahead, and came up with the basics of a plan. He stood up on the pedals and sprinted to the top. His muscles were screaming in agony as he drew in deep gulps of air. Topping the next hill, he built speed for about twenty yards on the down slope before suddenly reversing course again and heading back in the direction of the truck. His foolhardy plan worked as he and the truck crossed paths at the very peak of the hill. The three men in the truck did not have time to react to seeing him, and he slipped by at speed, gaining more on the downhill. Scott heard the brakes lock on the far side of the hill.

As he sped away, the thought that had struck him as they'd passed fully reveal itself. While he had not recognized any of the men in that brief second, the truck he knew—it was Bartos' Bronco. He filed that away for processing later. As of now he wanted to get to a side road before the truck came back over the hill where they could see him again.

Scott made it to the side road near the bottom of the hill and had to take it at an extreme angle due to his speed. His rear wheel slipped slightly on the loose gravel, giving him a momentary fright. He had just leveled back out and hit speed again when he heard the deep-throated Ford top the hill, chasing after him. As soon as the woods grew thicker, he braked hard, jumped off and pulled the bike into the dense cover. He watched from concealment as the truck sped past the little road without slowing down. He listened until it was nearly inaudible.

It was likely only a matter of minutes before they came back, and he felt sure they would check this side road out as well. He could not recall another connecting road for several miles in either direction. He took a moment to down some water. The worst was yet to come. He slid his handgun out of the holster, racked a shell into the chamber, and checked to make sure the safety was off. The sound of the truck returned, engine quieter as it slowly idled back down the road. Scott ducked down deeper into the woods, hoping he had not left any tracks in the dirt they might notice.

He kept the Sig Sauer trained on the truck as it slowly crept to the intersection, then turned onto the side road and continued past where Scott was hidden. A black man drove while a Hispanic guy literally rode shotgun, barrel pointed out the window. The third man was no longer in the truck. The driver held a radio to his mouth, and Scott could just make out the words over the rumbling of the slow moving Bronco. "See anything?"

The response came back loudly. "Nope, lil fuck done vanished."

They took the truck down the road further, and Scott realized they had dropped the third man at the intersection. Scott was trapped, unable to leave in either direction. The man at the intersection watched in all directions, loosely holding an old hunting rifle in the cradle of one arm and a radio with the other hand. The sound of the Bronco diminished as it went around a bend further down.

Scott made his decision, took aim, and shot the single gunman in the chest. He was already moving the bike out of the woods, stopping just long enough to pick up the man's radio and toss the cheap rifle into the woods. He remounted and headed north, mainly because he knew the road was flatter and there were more turnoffs. He barely registered a look at the dead man. His entire chest cavity was a bloody mess. He had shot him in the back and felt no remorse at all.

He heard a voice on the radio. "Did you shoot? Did you get him?"

He ignored it and rode on as fast as his tired legs could manage.

FIFTY-SEVEN

They were working their way to him, he realized with certainty. He was also heading farther and farther away from home. He knew that they would surely kill him if they caught him. The miles slipped by quickly, and although adrenaline flooded his body, fatigue was creeping into his muscles. He had to slow his pace, or he would hit a wall, his muscles would cramp, his energy would be drained, and he would have no choice but to stop.

He'd cut off onto multiple roads and put several miles between him and the guys in the truck, though he was under no illusion that they wouldn't catch up. Several times he heard the powerful engine and even caught glimpses of the truck on other roads in the distance. The lightweight bike was beginning to feel like a sack of lead. The fatigue was crushing, and Scott knew he was nearing the end of his ability. His muscles ached, and the cramps were nearly constant. Worst of all, he'd stopped sweating. From past experience, he knew this was a bad sign. He lifted his head just in time to see a cloud of dust coming from a side road up ahead then he heard the beast of a truck coming his way. Nearing a low point in the road with cow pastures on both sides he knew he could not get away and saw nowhere to hide.

Scott was about to give up any hope of getting away when he caught a glint of water coming up off to the side of the road. Looking closer, he noticed a shallow collection pond on the edge where the cattle pasture met the road. More like a stopped up drainage ditch that the cows had made into a watering hole. Covered with thick green slime, bits of floating manure, and thousands of black flies, it was all Scott could do to crawl under the barbed wire fence, toss his bag up in some dry grass and tuck himself and his bike under the fetid water before the Bronco passed by. The little pond was only about two feet deep and less than a dozen yards wide. He hated the thought of what the water was doing to his bike, not to mention to him. *Yep, clean water was definitely a priority for him now.* He eased up on a shoulder so he could hear better and listened as the truck sounds faded in the distance. Quickly he pulled himself and the Trek out of the vile, muddy mess, recovered his pack, and got back to the pavement, heading in the opposite direction. The putrid smell from the foul water seemed to have permeated his entire body.

The voices on the radio had been pissed upon finding their friend dead. For some odd reason, Scott felt with growing suspicion that the pursuit was personal—almost like they were out looking specifically for him. Why else would they put this much effort into taking down a single guy on a bike? His suspicions were confirmed a half hour later when the recovered radio squawked again.

"Hey this is T, you got that dude yet?"

The reply was mostly inaudible.

"Goddamit, motha-fuckas, what in the hell's you doing? We be drinkin the man's wine, eating his food—we got his girlfriend cornered in the swamp— and you stupid fuckin' idiots can't get one guy on a bicycle?. We took the Cajun out easy 'nough, but we don't get paid 'less bicycle boy tells us where all their shit's stashed. Hansbrough ain't gonna be happy if we don't, and therefore neither will I. Where the *fuck* is he?"

The response sounded scared; the voice was nearly drowned out by the whistling wind and deep rumble of the Bronco's motor. "Sorry Tyrell, we see him up ahead, we'll have him soon."

"Well hurry the fuck up, I got shit to do and places to be. Let me know when it's done."

The expression on Scott's face was grim. These thugs were at his house. They had Kaylie. They'd killed Bartos. More than all that, they were apparently working with that fucking shit-bag, Hansbrough. Scott had expected a play from someone, and Ronald was near the top of his list, but he would never have guessed it would be such an outright and brutal attack. He could hear the truck among the wooded roads behind him. He had been riding for hours to outmaneuver them, but now, he was done running.

He braked hard to stop the bike and dismounted as he watched the Bronco coming quickly up the road behind him. Scott was exhausted, he was angry, he stank and he was not running any further. He left the Sig Sauer in the holster and reached behind for his Go-bag. Already he could see the gunman hanging out the passenger window leveling the shotgun at him. They both knew he was out of range, but not by much. Just a few more seconds and the crazed looking fuck would start sending lead down the pipe toward Scott.

The Bronco was less than fifty yards away now and showing no signs of slowing. Scott had not moved. His legs were so tired, he felt he couldn't move. He needed that truck. He needed it to get back home and help his niece. Scott had his right arm inside his Go-bag, which he now let slip to the ground, revealing the H&K subcompact he gripped in his hand. His finger was already pulling the trigger as he swept the windshield with rounds, stitching a line of shots across the driver's head, which exploded in a bloody pulp, and the chest and head of the passenger. They did get one shot off, but the blast went harmlessly into the floor board of the truck. As the dead driver's foot slipped from the accelerator, the truck stalled and crept slowly to the side of the road.

Scott heard the radio asking, "Well, ya got him?" Neither of these guys would be responding.

Scott dragged the bodies out of the truck and dumped them unceremoniously on the side of the road. He took the several cheap weapons and various ammo and knives off of each, the only worth they had in his mind. On some level, Scott registered the fact that he had killed three more men today, but that simple fact was starting to bother him very little. Right now he had to get back the nearly fifty miles to the cottage. He had to get back to the niece he had promised to protect, now possibly his last surviving family member. He needed to get back in the name of his friend Bartos, who had done so much for him and the town, and he had to end one more person's life today—Ronald Hansbrough would not last the night. He placed the bike in the back of the Bronco and turned the truck in the direction of Harris Springs.

FIFTY-EIGHT

The Bronco was a beast of a truck, although the spider-webbed windshield and the blood and brains all over the place were rather unpleasant additions. Scott Montgomery uncharacteristically had no plan. He knew only that he had to get back and help Kaylie. The rage that had been building in him for far too long was demanding to be released. This feeling that had come over him was not like him. He was no soldier; he could not take on an armed gang alone. But what options did he have?

He was passing back across the county line when to his relief he saw help up ahead: the familiar patrol car of the newly sworn-in Sheriff Buck Warren was partially blocking the road.

Scott saw the figure of the man inside the car, so he slowed down and steered the truck to the side. He knew Buck and his deputies could help even the odds, and probably assist him with Hansbrough as well.

The wind left Scott's lungs as he saw the shattered driver's side window and saw the Sheriff slumped to the side, clearly dead, bullet wounds in his chest and head. The scene shook him. He stopped the truck and climbed out to check on his friend. He knew there was nothing to be done, but he couldn't just drive on by.,

This had been a good man. He'd deserved so much better than this. He had stayed on the job when nearly everyone else had fled. Scott wanted to mourn the man and give thought to his sacrifice, but Kaylie's own desperate situation called him back to the moment. He took Buck's service pistol and the tactical gear and other weapons in the trunk and was on his way again within minutes.

The tears stung his eyes. How had it come to this? A few months ago he had been a computer programmer living a life of peaceful solitude. Today he was fighting a war. He had killed, he had lost friends, and he was probably about to die himself. This newest series of events—men out for the blood of seemingly everyone he cared about—scared him on a very primal level.

But he would put Hansbrough down. And every other one like him he came across. Scott spat out the broken window. *Put them all down*, he vowed, the rage inside him ready to unleash. His hands gripped the steering wheel hard, his eyes unblinking now. He was not a hero, but he was determined he would not go quietly.

He was nearing the turn-off for the road to the cottage when he heard the chirp of one of the radios. The voice coming from the other end sent chills down his spine. He pulled to the side of the road and stopped. Picking up the radio with trembling hands, Scott looked off into the distance as he keyed the microphone. He could see smoke rising from the direction of his house. "Kaylie, is that you?"

It took several long seconds before the whispered reply came, "Yes, Uncle Scott."

She was alive. Relief flooded his body just knowing that fact. Another voice cut in then, a man's voice.

"Scott, where are you?"

"Bartos? Holy shit," he exhaled as relief flooded through him. "You're alive! And you have Kaylie. Jeeze, I—I'm at the turn off above the cottage. I'm in your truck. Are you safe?"

The response came back as Scott heard weapons fire, both on the radio and from out the window. "Safe is a relative term right now," Bartos said. "We need your help though if we're going to get through this."

FIFTY-NINE

Bartos relayed the numbers and positions of their attackers. Scott wanted Kaylie out of the way, but none of them could come up with a safe way of doing that, and Kaylie was having none of it. Bartos had already made that connection to Hansbrough. And apparently Tyrell had been there but just left in a car with someone.

Scott grabbed the bag of weapons that Bartos had asked for from behind the rear seat. He ran them down a side road about a hundred yards, to an old logger's bridge over the swamp's edge. Bartos, Solo, and Kaylie were waiting in the pirogue below. Their relief at seeing each other was tempered by the fact there was no way to reach each other here.

"Bartos, I owe you so much."

The Cajun shrugged it off. "She pretty much saved herself."

They talked quietly, and Scott lowered the heavy bag the fifteen feet down to the boat on a length of paracord. Bartos was sitting oddly in the boat, obviously in pain. He looked up at Scott grinning.

"It's a shame your pretty little cycling suit isn't camo patterned." Scott looked down at his black, white, and blood covered bike jersey and smiled ironically.

"It will do fine," he said. "By the way," he added, smiling, "I shot up your Bronco."

Bartos looked up. "You better be kidding, or you'll be the next one I kill." Laughing he said, "You know what to do?"

Scott nodded and looked down at his niece, relieved to see her muddy Go-bag and her holstered pistol at her waist, "I love you Kaylie. Don't do anything stupid okay?"

"I won't," she promised, a reassuring smile fighting through the concern on her face. "I know the plan. Please be careful Uncle Scott."

"Solo, please take care of her, okay?" Scott called. The beautiful but muddy dog's tail began to wag enthusiastically.

Gruff as ever, Bartos wrapped it up. "Make sure you don't shoot the dog and let's get this done quickly, I'm hungry."

Smiling, Scott went to put the plan in motion.

Kaylie had told her uncle she was pretty sure they had set the cottage on fire—which had made him even angrier, if that were possible. The anger, plus seeing his three loved ones, had re-energized Scott, and although he was still exhausted, he was more than ready for what came next.

If the thugs had set the cottage on fire, they had destroyed their only defensible position, and the smoke would work in Scott's favor. The plan they had come up with was to lure several out into the open using the Bronco as bait. Scott and the H&K would unleash as many rounds into them as possible. Bartos would be using a scoped and suppressed SR-15 sniper rifle to take out anyone else as they came out. Kaylie would watch the perimeter and Solo would then be turned loose to wreak havoc on anyone left. Solo was the most eager looking one of the group for the battle about to start. The plan was not sophisticated, but they were up against thugs, not military strategists. Tyrell's gang mainly counted on numbers and intimidation, not intelligence.

Scott took his bike out of the back and placed it in the overgrowth on the side of the road. Silly, he knew, but he loved that bike. He reached into Buck's tactical bag for several items he would need as the radio squawked twice to signal that Bartos and Kaylie were in position.

He turned the key to start the Bronco. He gassed it, and the throaty headers rattled loudly throughout the wetlands. Drawing so much attention to himself seemed crazy, but he put the truck in gear and began rolling toward his home. The smoke was thick, hugging the ground and he completely missed his now well-hidden driveway. He backed up toward the gate and managed to block in all the various motorcycles and four wheelers the gang had used to get here. Quickly grabbing the gear bag, Scott slipped down and out the far door and stalked into the thick brush lining his drive. He could see movement in the front windows as bodies came out to see who was in the idling truck.

The unmistakable noise of the sound suppressed 7.62x51mm NATO round striking flesh somewhere behind the cloud of smoke was the signal Scott had been waiting on. He carefully flipped the selector on the H&K and used the three shot burst option to unleash hell on each of the four figures now heading toward the truck. Several of them got shots off, but none seemed to register that Scott was firing from their side and not from the direction of the truck. The four of them fell, all mortally wounded. He heard several more of Bartos' rounds followed by more than one agonizing scream. Then a shadow leapt into Scott's peripheral vision and disappeared again into the smoke.

Screams and shots rang out as Solo took care of the remaining combatants inside. Scott had dropped the H&K and unslung the more accurate M4 carbine. He began working his way toward the smoking cottage. Two figures came running out of what had been his garage door. He clipped the one on the right, and another shot took the legs out from under another one wearing a hoodie. Solo's vicious, hungry growls had taken on an otherworldly quality, and Scott felt a moment of fear at what the beast was capable of. He heard more firing from Kaylie's position and watched as another man went down.

The smoke and smell of burning wood was thick in the yard. Scott saw Bartos come into view, limping around the side of the cottage, assault rifle in one hand, pistol the other. The Cajun raised three fingers on the hand clutching the pistol, Scott assumed that meant the numbers of combatants were more balanced now. A movement off to the right caught Scott's eye, and he was firing before it even registered. The figure dropped, but Scott was not positive it had been a good hit. Bartos fired at multiple targets that Scott couldn't even see but heard the screams of the dying men. He and Bartos used what cover there was and approached from different angles. Bartos cautiously approached one of the fallen men and gave two quick headshots just as the man began to reach for his weapon. The sounds of the dog briefly went silent, and Bartos turned gingerly and paced up to the wall of the cottage before dropping flat to the ground and cautiously peeking around the corner. Moments later a man turned that same corner just above Bartos who was already firing straight up. Bullets ripped into the man's groin and exited higher up the body with spectacular gore.

Scott was watching the action ahead and did not notice the figure behind and to his right getting back up to his knees in the smoke-shrouded cover. He saw another enormous black man come charging around the house with Solo right on his tail. Solo trailed blood from a knife wound in his hind leg. The dog leaped toward the man, and his fangs sank deep into the side of his neck, dragging him to the ground. The large man continued to fight until the dog ripped free a large chunk of his throat. The gurgling sounds were accompanied by geyser spurts of blood as the man's body began to die.

Scott was mesmerized by the horrific sight of Solo ripping into his victim. He glanced over to see Bartos looking past him with a curious look on his face, as if he knew something that Scott didn't. As Scott turned to look in the same direction, he felt the sudden impact of the round hitting him in his chest. The lights went out all over again for Scott Montgomery in a thunderous, agonizing blow. Sadly, Scott did not see his assailant die a moment later, or his niece holding the gun that had killed him.

SIXTY

Bartos walked up as Kaylie knelt over Scott's body. A wounded and bloody Solo swept the perimeter, finding no threats. Bartos looked at his friend then felt for a pulse and to his surprise, found one beating strong and steady. Lifting up the ruined and bloodied cycling jersey he began laughing. Scott had a Kevlar vest on underneath, the county sheriff insignia emblazoned on the lapel.

He was out cold and likely badly bruised, possibly a cracked rib or two, but he was alive. Kaylie's tears came in waves as she realized he was alive and well. She leaned in and hugged her uncle, causing him to groan and cough in pain. "Damn, Girl, why do you smell so bad?" No longer realizing his own stench. Bartos stood and, hobbling badly now, went to check on the dog and to turn off the still idling and much beloved truck.

It took Scott half an hour to fully come too and then he really wished he hadn't. He managed to roll to one side before vomiting from the pain. He was looking up at one smoking but still standing wall of the cottage. Kaylie's, chestnut hair framed a muddy face that was still beautiful but no longer innocent. It would be days before she talked about what she had done but Scott could guess just by looking at her.

He turned his head to see Bartos and Solo heading over. "All clear partner," Bartos said with a smile.

"Yeah, I'm fine," Scott said, leaning up woozily. "Thanks for asking."

"Shut up, you pussy. You were wearing a vest. Oh, sorry Kaylie, Didn't mean to curse in front of a lady." Bartos said chivalrously.

Kaylie shrugged.

Scott took them all in. "We all look like shit… the walking wounded," he said.

"To be accurate," Bartos said, "Only <u>we</u> are walking, you've mostly just been lying there napping."

Scott struggled to get to his feet. He was in so much pain and felt like he could only get partial breaths of air, but he was alive, and so were Kaylie, Bartos and Solo. In fact, the dog looked happy as shit, Scott thought.

More seriously, Bartos reported: "We got nine bodies, but I don't think any of them is Tyrell, and by the way, you owe me a windshield." Looking back over at his Bronco he added, "Clean-up too. And a paint job. It was a classic, Scott—you know, a collectible.

Scott grinned, "I guess you didn't notice the shotgun blast on the passenger's side floor, and it shimmies a bit when you're over ninety."

"Oh, you miserable fuck," Bartos toyed, "This is why I don't let people borrow my truck. You just don't fuck with a man's truck."

"Well, you let them burn my house down," Scott said in defense.

"Yeah and saved your niece," responded Bartos.

"Oh yeah, thanks for doing that," Scott said, winking at Kaylie, who was rolling her eyes as she stroked the bloody dog.

"And they didn't burn all of your house, just…most of it. Besides, now you can upgrade to a nice beach condo. Houses are a plentiful man, trucks that run are pretty scarce."

Scott got to his feet, and the three of them gathered up all the weapons and stowed them in the Bronco. Then they used the four wheelers to take their previous owners' bodies to a field further down the road. "Let the scavengers feast for a few days," Bartos had said. They hid the rest of the ATVs and motorcycles in the woods.

While they worked, they discussed Hansbrough and Tyrell. Over one of the captured radios they had heard someone, a frantic Ronald, it sounded like, giving orders to raise all the bridges. They didn't think the news that Bartos and Scott were still alive would have gotten to him yet, nor that Tyrell's men were all dead—no way would they have expected them to have defeated Tyrrell's guys. For now, they had that going for them. They considered riding two motorcycles in as decoys, but they had no helmets to disguise them.

"Well fuck, they are cutting us off from the island." Scott sucked in a painful breath of air. The rage was just as strong, but he was having trouble concentrating. "Bartos, You and Buck went over defense plans for the bridges. Contingency plans on possible breaching maneuvers others might try to cross when the bridges are raised. What did you guys come up with?" Scott asked.

"Boats. The only way—the water in the canal is deep, really deep. It gets dredged every few years for the shipyards over in Pascagoula to use for pulling ship hulls over to the Bay. Alligators are also pretty common, and the tides make for a swift current. The island, the town is on is a really good, defensible location."

The pirogue was pretty badly shot up and couldn't hold them and the gear they needed. Bobby's old boat in the boathouse had become part of the burned wreckage.

"Where's your Jeep?" asked Kaylie, realizing she hadn't seen it.

Scott hesitated several minutes, remembering Bobby's advice on secrecy, "It's...it's at our primary bug-out location. I took it and the trailer full of supplies down this morning before going riding. I was planning to stop back there and retrieve it on my way home. Which reminds me, I have to go back up the road and pick up my bike," Scott said. Kaylie laughed and hugged her Uncle causing him to wince in pain.

"That damn bike. You aren't going to be riding for a while with your chest caved in and all." Bartos said smiling.

"Hey, that bike saved my life and probably helped save yours too." Scott had relayed the story of the pursuit earlier, to Bartos' great amusement.

"It's just like that Spielberg movie. You know, the one with Dennis Weaver trying to get away from the psycho in the big rig truck. Only in your case, it was simply a retard in a girl's swimsuit riding a bicycle trying to get away from two sadistic idiots in a gorgeous classic Ford Bronco."

"Yeah, yeah," Scott said smiling," And, it was three idiots after me to be specific."

Trying to come up with a workable plan Scott continued, "What if we went to the ocean and came about from that way?"

"Won't work. You'd have to either drive to the far side of the wetlands or navigate through them. They extend for forty miles to the west and nearly all the way back to Mobile Bay to the East. Then you have to come back either on the beach or by the sea with the gear you need. That would take several days."

Scott rubbed his aching chest. "Shit, we picked a good spot to operate out of, shame we aren't the ones over there using it."

Bartos agreed.

Kaylie said, "Wait a minute guys, one of the houses we went into near here had a boat in the garage. It's not far, if we can attach it to the Bronco, we might be in business."

Scott smiled, that's my girl, "Is there a place we can launch it on the Intercostal?"

Bartos was nodding his head, "Yeah, yeah, fuck yeah. It wouldn't even have to run...;we could even paddle it across. Let's go!"

The three of them grabbed their bags and loaded into the abused Ford, Solo settling in before they'd even begun. Scott picked up his bike on the way out.

SIXTY-ONE

Tyrell was fully aware that Hansbrough had mostly lost it before this day had even started. He had been giving orders and was so red-faced that Tyrell thought he was going to pop something. Now he too was just as angry; his guys had failed, he'd lost not just his brother but now a cousin last night at the swamp rat's campsite, and today, what should have been an easy grab on the white guy with the bike had apparently turned into a bloody mess. Worst of all was that that son of a bitch Bartos was apparently still fucking alive. He was like a goddamn cockroach, why the fuck wouldn't he die?

When Tyrell had last heard from the boys at the cottage, everything seemed fine. He'd left to go and calm Ron down before the shooting had started. Coming back into town, Hansbrough had him take out the deputies manning the bridges and raise them all himself. As he got into town, he'd seen several bodies lying in the street, building on fire and that idiot Hansbrough running around town with a fucking gun.

The plan today had been to snatch this Scott guy and wipe out any remaining law enforcement. Now that fucking red-faced idiot was just shooting random people in his path. Tyrell knew he should put the stupid bastard down, but he was too busy trying to figure out how to get his own revenge. *He* owned this town, not the fucking former rich boy drug-addict who even now was still trying to give him orders.

· · ·

Bartos unlocked the county service road gate, and Scott backed the Sea Ray Inboard down the cement pad and into the deep green waterway.

"We boosted a really nice boat," Bartos said cheerily.

For real, thought Scott.

They had gotten into the garage and hooked up the boat easily and even found a full fuel tank and a fully charged battery. They hadn't been planning on using the motor to get across but knew they might need it to get away if things went sideways. Bartos checked to make sure the drain plugs were inserted, and Scott dropped the dependable Bronco into reverse and submerged the trailer until the beautiful boat was afloat. Kaylie was already transferring gear bags from one to the other, so Scott pulled the Bronco back up out of sight and came down the bank followed closely by a bloody Solo.

"Time to cross our Rubicon?" Scott said to no one in particular. Once in the water, they had decided to take the boat toward the ocean and slip in, hopefully unnoticed, to the back entrance of the municipal dock. This would give them a virtually undetectable route into downtown, and also save several miles of walking with a shitload of weapons. To do this, they would need the engine, though. Bartos turned the key, and the little Volvo inboard purred quietly to life. Columns of thick smoke could be coming from the direction of town. The war had already come to Harris Springs.

The trip to the marina would only take fifteen minutes. Scott took the time to put on a tactical vest and every armament he could attach to his body. He might feel like shit, but he was going to look like Rambo. Bartos had done pretty much the same, but with a little more planning on what he was taking into battle. The real question was, where to find Hansbrough?

They had heard him talking several times on the radio. The person he was talking with, "T", was presumably Tyrell; he kept cussing about the cheap-ass radios not working worth a fuck. Apparently he couldn't get anyone back at the cottage to respond.

None of the three in the boat were happy that Tyrell was still alive, though his obvious frustration provided some enjoyment. To Scott, though, he was the bigger threat. Tyrell was streetwise and tough, and would soon find out he had lost a lot more of his team today. It was personal to Tyrell, and he would come after them no matter what happened with Hansbrough.

Bartos, on the other hand, felt Ronald was the main target. He was a crazy evil bastard that had to go—first.

The truth was they had no idea how many people they were up against. While they had hurt Tyrell's gang, he undoubtedly had more men. Add to that the fact that Hansbrough probably had as many followers now as haters. He kept promising people free shit and making accusations that the council was hoarding supplies just for its friends.

This was the moment; this was when Harris Springs would cease to exist or find a way to survive. Scott hoped that they would be able to out-think these two idiots and not let it come down to a shoot-out, but it felt inevitable. As he looked at the radios and around the pilot's cabin of the Sea Ray, he had a thought.

"If something happens to us, we really should try and get a message out, let someone know we at least tried." He turned on the marine band radio. "Do you know the frequency Todd normally uses?"

Bartos nodded, reached over, and spun the dial to change the marine channel. He keyed the mic: "Hometown to Careless Lady, do you copy?" He repeated the query four or five more times before a response came through.

"This is Careless Lady, Cajun, that you?"

Bartos' face lit up, as did the others', at the sound of their friend's voice. "Damn glad to hear your voice man." Bartos handed the handset to Scott, who relayed a short version of what was going on.

Todd came back, "Roger that, sounds grim. Could you use a hand?"

"Well sure, if you could cut your vacation short," Scott said smiling broadly.

"I'm about twenty minutes out, already heading that way. I need to make a call, but I'm coming in with a friend, so be ready."

What the fuck did that mean, they all wondered.

"Roger," confirmed Scott, and closed the connection.

Having arrived at the dock, they exited the boat and made their way toward Todd's dock slip. Solo and Bartos took up point positions to watch the strangely quiet town. Scott looked at Kaylie, "You ready for this, Girl?"

"I'm ready, Man." She reached over and kissed his cheek and hugged him hard. Scott was touched by the show of emotion; they had once been very close, but he had let it slip away after the divorce, like so many other things. Today, she had saved his life, this sweet precious creature he had rocked to sleep as a baby. Now she was outfitted in tactical gear and every bit the badass.

"Kaylie, your dad will be very proud of you."

"I know it," she grinned and winked at him. She seemed to be growing up right in front of him. "Here he comes!"

A sleek sailboat running without sails cut into the channel behind them. It was Todd.

On approach, Todd beamed at his friends as he tossed a line to Scott, who wrapped the dock cleat with it. Stepping out, he hugged Kaylie tightly. Following him, they were all shocked to see DeVonte stepping lightly over the gunnels to the dock. "What up, girl?" he asked with his same disarming smile.

"Where the hell did you come from?" Kaylie squealed as she grabbed him in a fierce hug.

"Just hitched a ride. Shit was getting bad down my way, and Captain Todd here just happened to be nearby."

Scott laughed and shook the boy's hand, then hugged him close. "Damn glad to see you, kid. Todd's kind of everyone's guardian angel, isn't he?"

Todd hugged Scott, causing him to wince in pain. "What happened to you?" he asked.

Kaylie, still holding onto DeVonte, replied. "Ignore him, he just wants sympathy. He's being a pussy just 'cause he got shot this morning."

Her uncle flipped her the finger as they laughed. Bartos came down the hill and greeted his close friend as well. Solo nodded his head then licked himself, declining to partake in the emotional reunion.

"Has anyone talked with Jack?" Todd asked after the trio had fully explained the situation.

"No," Scott said, "I don't think anyone has heard from him all day."

Todd looked concerned, "We need to find him. Then we need to get eyes on both targets."

"I think I have an idea how to do that," Scott said, "but since he's here, I could really use DeVonte."

"Yes sir, Mr. Scott. Whatever you need." Scott grinned at the bright young man.

"Please tell me you still know how to speak ghetto."

The young man laughed. "Been a minute since I left da bricks but…fo sho," he said, smiling broadly.

Todd was worried and took Kaylie to find Jack—and see if he could help. They were to also try and find as many of the other volunteers as possible and help keep them safe but also be ready to move. Meanwhile, Scott clued Bartos in on his still-developing plan. Since no one other than Bartos and Scott knew where all the supplies had been stashed, they assumed Hansbrough and Tyrell's guys were not having much success in finding them. They had bypassed stockpiling in the normal locations, assuming anyone might try and steal them eventually. Scott now wanted to use this as a lure to bring all of them all in. Bartos suggested a relatively hidden county building just outside of town near the water pumping station. It would not be on the list of likely storage locations, so had probably not yet been checked by the thugs.

They worked their way over to that side of town as stealthily as possible. As they passed near the sheriff's office, they saw several dead bodies on the steps. Bartos was hard to keep calm at this discovery, and Scott said little, only trying to keep him calm. He remembered Buck in the car. Further down they were shocked to see the fire station on fire. The beautiful ladder truck that had not moved sine the blackout was a charred ruin. Other storefronts were burning, and the fires were spreading. Automatic gunfire was heard somewhere close. They had to take back this town.

DeVonte had been left back on the boat with specific instructions. When Kaylie got back, they were to make contact with Scott, then wait for the signal. Once Scott's team was in place, he would send a double squelch and DeVonte would then broadcast on the other radio—one of Tyrell's. He was to say he had found the supplies in the target building. Scott was counting on mutual greed to bring both men running. Hopefully, Tyrell wouldn't get too nosy about which of his guys was calling in the find.

Twenty minutes later, DeVonte let them know that Kaylie was back and that Todd and Jack would be in place in ten minutes. Bartos and Solo were on the south side of the old brick building; Scott was inside, where he had struggled to get up in the rafters. He was in position now, looking out a ventilation grill. He watched as Todd, Jack and two other men he recognized as Jack's former prison friends each took up concealed positions with good firing lanes. Todd identified all friendly positions while Scott sent the two squelch signals. Soon after, he heard DeVonte send the message. It was freaking perfect, just garbled enough and gangsta enough to sound right. He was exuberant, but the radio kept cutting in and out. But the kid made sure that everyone knew what building it was before switching off the handset. Scott heard several urgent messages asking for more info, but DeVonte had gone dark, just like they planned. Now the trap was set, and the group just had to sit tight and see if the pieces of shit took the bait.

SIXTY-TWO

They didn't wait long. A dark Hummer pulled up on the backside of the building and two men got out. In the front of the building, they also saw Hansbrough walking down from the town square. All of them were armed. Hansbrough carried what looked to be an automatic weapon. The guys in the Hummer had pistols.

The friends waited, they just needed to wait until the players were all together to shut the trap. There was only one entrance to the building, so eventually the two guys at the back would need to come around to the door. Scott wished he knew if one of them was Tyrell. The three men met at the front of the old building.

Hansbrough spoke first. "Didn't ya'll check this one earlier?"

"Not yet, Marcus was going to check it out, but he's still over in the school," the taller of the two said.

"Well, who the fuck called in the find?"

Both guys shrugged, then one added, "Maybe Tyrell knows."

Fuck. No Tyrell. Just as the thought occurred to him, he saw several other men winding their way through the trees and water pipes on the low side of the building lot. Bartos would be exposed. The Cajun was focused completely on Hansbrough and barely noticed Solo go rigid and then quietly disappear behind him.

"Overwatch for Cajun, bogey on your nine o'clock."

Bartos glanced that way but was too focused on his primary target. Scott had Bartos' sound suppressed modified SR-15 sniper rifle, but he only had an angle on one of the men coming from that side. He saw Solo going after one of the gunmen, so he lined up and, as Solo leapt on one, he squeezed the trigger sending the 5.56 frangible round at the other. At this range the deeply satisfying 'cheee-klunk' of the relatively quiet rifle was simultaneous with the impact of the round entered the man's neck; the specialized ammo fragmented on entry and dispersed out multiple exit points. Both men went down immediately.

Bartos' target reacted to the sounds of the impact and the dog attacking; his victim making muffled sounds as Solo's powerful jaws clamped harder on his neck. As he looked in his direction, Bartos fired. The shot should have been a perfect kill shot, but at the last second Hansbrough moved, taking the round in his shoulder. Todd and the others took that as a signal and opened up, and a dramatic amount of firepower was suddenly unleashed into the courtyard of the county building, where the other members of Tyrell's gang were.

Scott dropped the rifle scope on target after target gently squeezing off round after round. He saw one of the men near Jack fall with a massive chest wound. He found the shooter taking cover behind a tree. Like hunting squirrels back in the Ozarks, Scott aimed and clipped the only exposed part of the man. The back of the man's skull evaporated in a blossom of red.

Solo had also found his next target. He went directly for the big man, Tyrell, who stood his ground and began frantically firing at the animal. Solo was too fast, though, he had to alter course slightly, Scott still couldn't get a shot on Tyrell. The angle of the window he was using put that fight just out of sight. He swung the sniper's rifle back around, looking for new targets. He could see Hansbrough had maneuvered behind a large unused cement pipe, dragging a bloodied arm and wailing for help like a baby. Scott knew the appropriate thing to do was to put the man on trial before a town tribunal, make an example out of him, let him have his dramatic say on how, *he had only been trying to do good for the community.* Unfortunately, for Hansbrough, it had already been a long, tiring day. Scott watched as Bartos leveled his rifle and fired the 7.65 NATO round into Ronald's brain; finally ending his miserable existence. Bartos had little time for satisfaction as he was already swinging the barrel toward his next target. Two of Tyrells guys came hurtling out of the brush toward Jack and Todd. Todd was looking and firing in the other direction. With no time to raise a weapon, Jack went into an all-out attack on both men. His speed and training was good but against multiple armed assailants he should have died instantly. Instead the move surprised the men and he bent low and went in for close quarters body shots, reaching back, he wrecked one of the man's arms with a single unbelievably violent jerk then pivoted off of the man with a snapping kick to the throat of the second man. Both were down on the ground immobile in seconds.

Todd looked over at the Preacher with a small smile seeing the carnage. He then noticed movement ahead heading toward Scott. "Overwatch, you copy?"

Todd's voice came over the Bluetooth earpiece. "Go for Overwatch," Scott responded softly.

"Be advised one of the hostiles just entered your location," he said. Lowering the sniper rifle, Scott unsnapped the holster on his dad's Sig Sauer and slung the H&K subcompact into his grip. He scanned the darkened interior for the man. There were more shots outside, and he felt that he should be providing cover for his friends. If he got dead, though, he would be of no use to them.

Scott eased his way through the angle iron trusses as quietly as possible, his aching ribs making each move a pain as he navigated the obstacle course of the dark room. He could barely see. Why hadn't he taken the time to put the night vision goggles in his bag? *Shit.* He had brought everything else. He just hadn't thought he'd need night vision on a bright sunny day. *Amateur.*

He had maneuvered to the center of the room, just above the cavernous space of the old water pumping station. Scott scanned the interior again with eyes and ears without detecting anyone. There was too much piping, too many crates and old pieces of machinery to play 'Where's Waldo' with any chance of success. *This really would be a good place to store supplies*, he thought briefly, and wondered why Bartos hadn't suggested it.

Then he realized why. The floor of the room was alive. No, not alive, but moving. Shadows shifted in the dim light. Rats. Everywhere. *Goddam you, Bartos,*

Scott muttered under his breath. He hung to a beam and nervously eased himself quietly to the floor. Wincing in pain as he did so. He fucking hated the rodents. Apparently the man hiding in here with him did as well, because all of a sudden a distinct, "Aghh, fuck!" came echoing from across the cluttered space.

Trying to zero in on the sound he noticed a flicker of movement off to his right. Scott swept the H&K in its direction, on full auto. The light of the gunfire revealed the large man waving a pistol at a very large rat, standing on its two rear legs from the top of a crate next to him. The bullets from the sub-compact machine gun destroyed the rat but just missed the man they called Tyrell as he dove away.

With his eye's normal night vision ruined by the gunfire, Scott did not see him coming out of the shadows directly at him. The impact into his already bruised ribs as the massive man barreled into him sent him crashing into a pile of old equipment. The pain was gruesome. Scott's vision began to fade, and he struggled to stay in the moment. The sound of scattering rodents made it impossible to know exactly where Tyrell was in the dark room.

Scott's feet finally found purchase on the dirty floor, and he felt the cursed creatures running over his shoes. He scrambled back just before a shot rang out. The round from the pistol hit just behind Scott, but it had also given away Tyrell's location. Scott moved backward, then angled toward the man. As Jack had shown him in the KFM training, he maneuvered for the best line then waited for Tyrell to show himself. Scott felt, more than saw, the hammering fist as it came toward him. Stepping into the blow seemed counter-intuitive, but that was the muscle memory taking over from all of the recent training. The blow slid harmlessly off his shoulder, and Scott brought a knee into Tyrell's groin, driving the wind from his lungs in the process. He heard Tyrell shuffling away into the darkness, but was unsure of the direction. The sounds bounced around the enclosed space and pipes, making it indecipherable.

Scott knew the difference in size was too much for him to overcome, even with his new fighting skills. This was anything but a fair fight. He would have to use the darkness... even the rats... whatever it took. The sounds of gunfire from outside were diminishing. He briefly thought of his friends and Kaylie but again forced his mind back to the present.

He was scared. His chest was on fire, and he was not disciplined enough to be a true fighter. A clipped sound rose above the din of still scurrying rodents. He knew the man was within a few feet. Scott again felt the presence before he saw him. Then caught a glint of light from the gun in Tyrell's outstretched arm. Scott did not move to block the gun but instead, rolled underneath it and grabbed the wrist behind it, pulling it back as he swung behind the big man. He now uncoiled one of his powerful cyclist's legs and shunted it into the side of Tyrell's knee. He felt something give way as the man staggered, then whipped his arm around bringing his gun across Scott's temple in a blow that caused him to see stars. Scott stumbled away and again both men were lost in the darkness.

Think, think Scott, his inner voice was urging him. His mind was cloudy from the pain. *Be smart about this*. He struggled to think clearly, then realized the obvious. Reaching back, he found the H&K still slung around his neck and pulled it quietly into a low-ready position. Slowly reaching into his pocket, he grabbed two glow sticks. He snapped them and threw them across the room. Moving was excruciating, and the effort nearly made him black out again. He was quite sure he had a broken rib now. The sudden, faint light caused Tyrell to freeze mid-step. The gang leader stood stock-still, a pistol in each hand. The room seemed to be spinning, and Scott courted the darkness that threatened to engulf his consciousness. Through the pain, though, Scott reminded himself: *this man is responsible for too much to be allowed to live another day*. Worst of all, he had threatened his family and his friends. Stepping out from behind the pile of rusted pipes, on wobbly legs, he opened fire on full auto. The lead kept coming as Scott pumped more and more rounds into Tyrell's body. What felt like minutes passed in a few seconds, and the dealer was dead before he hit the floor in a heavy cloud of dust and angry rats.

One more rat dead.

Scott secured the weapon, checked the body, and gently slung the sub-compact rifle over his shoulder before walking gingerly out of the creepy, musty old building. Someone else could climb up and get the SR-15 as he was unable to. All was quiet outside as he emerged into the light, and the others began emerging from hiding to meet him.

SIXTY-THREE

DeVonte and Kaylie met up with the group in the middle of town. "Is every day like this here?" DeVonte quipped. "You guys really know how to throw a welcome party. That was a lot of shooting."

"Just for you man," Scott joked.

Todd was nearly carrying Scott as he struggled to stay on his feet. He finally set him down in some shade. "Kaylie, can you check on him, I think he may actually have broken something this time."

Kaylie removed Scott's tactical vest and went to work examining her uncle. Solo also needed patching up, and Bartos tended to him as best he could. One of Jack's new found pilgrims had been shot dead in the gun battle. The man had been a prisoner in the old world, and most would not have welcomed him into the new. Some—maybe many—old ideas and prejudices would need to be revisited, it seemed.

Many, indeed most of the other volunteers, began to come out of hiding. As an emergency plan had been in place since the beginning, they had all gone into hiding at the first sign of trouble. Sadly, Sheriff Warren and his deputies had not survived the day. They would have to be replaced, but for now, they would be mourned.

Scott was not in good shape. Although he wanted to help with checking the town and beginning the recovery efforts, he was given pain meds and a cot in the aid shelter and told to rest. In the aftermath of the skirmish, there were additional unpleasant tasks to take care of and some of Tyrell's men still to round up. Preacher Jack and Bartos put together a makeshift security detail to handle that. They had been reluctant to implement all of the Catalyst rules but seeing the dead enforcement officers had convinced them to adopt even the more stringent clauses. With this, they declared everything owned by Hansbrough and Tyrell to be forfeited to the town, and their houses to be burned. The new world would have no mercy and no tolerance for crimes like these.

Bartos made it clear to all: "Anyone living in those homes gets ten minutes to get out and to leave town." This rule had been discussed and now implemented as a strong deterrent to anyone associating with criminals. As identities of the others in today's activities were discovered, those homes would likely suffer similar indignities.

Over the next several days as things began to settle, it became clear that the uprising had been costlier than they originally thought. In terms of human life and resources, too much had been lost. The population of Harris Springs was estimated to be less than 150 now. A few of the warehouses of food and supplies had been found and looted by Tyrell's gang. While some of the loot was recovered, most seemed to have vanished. An entire tanker of diesel fuel had been torched, presumably because it wouldn't run in any of the cars Tyrell and his thugs drove. The plan to visit the train was put on hold until they had the manpower and the security to again mount such an operation.

SIXTY-FOUR

Todd looked over at Scott. "You up for a little trip?"

Scott was exhausted and filthy from moving supplies all week, but he was mostly recovered from his injuries. "Sure thing."

"Good, we need a computer geek." Todd winked with a devilish look on his face as he took out a small radio—one Scott had not seen him use before. "Charlie One, Charlie One, mission is a go. I say again, mission is a go." Todd put the tiny handheld back in his pocket. Within minutes over the horizon of the Gulf came the thumping sound of a helicopter coming toward them.

The gray Navy chopper settled to rest just outside of town in the old Publix parking lot. "Come on, ride's here," called Todd, already on his way.

Scott hobbled to catch up and Todd helped him clamber in first, immediately coming face to face with a group of dangerous looking men. Todd followed, taking the last remaining seat. The chopper was airborne and heading westward out over the sea within moments. Scott had no idea where they were heading, and the headphones they provided were dead. For the nearly two-hour ride, all he could do was watch Todd's smiling face. Several times he tried to ask him what the fuck was going on. Todd just mouthed the words "You'll see."

The pitch of the rotors changed and the forward momentum translated into an elevator drop straight down. All Scott could see was open water, but while they were still several hundred feet above, the chopper made contact with something solid, and the engine began winding down. All of the men disembarked the chopper, landing onto the stark white landing deck of the still stationary

Aquatic Goddess. Scott was stunned. This enormous, gorgeous boat appeared to be completely empty. His nose detected a faint smell of bleach and a deeper sickly stench of something fouler. But damn, this was a beautiful boat.

Walking down to the bridge, Todd relayed much of what he had found on his previous visit. The ship had enough supplies and equipment to help a small town survive for several years. He wanted Scott to work with the Navy team to get the PLC controls functioning again so they could cool and balance the engines. The Navy was going to help guide the big ship into the Intracostal Waterway behind Harris Springs, where they could use it as needed. A crew had apparently been on deck for several days, removing bodies and restoring power. It was not perfect, but everything seemed functional. The ship had diesel generators as well as a large solar array for electricity, a desalination plant for fresh water, and enormous fuel tanks. The fresh food was gone, but the dry goods lockers were fully stocked. What would have been adequate for 5,000 passengers for the full cruise (plus extra) would indeed go a long way in helping Harris Springs survive the winter.

"Why is the Navy helping?" Scott asked.

"I was in a position to help them out with our friends, the grayshirts," Todd explained. "Afterward, I picked up DeVonte and told him about the ship. This was actually his idea.

Scott had been wondering how Todd had found the boy. Todd filled him in. "Mobile had been overrun, his family…well they had mostly been wiped out when he got home. He hid out until things got even worse. Eventually, thanks to your damn bike he made it down to the bay. He had taken the bridge road out to Dauphin Island, nearly in the middle of Mobile Bay trying to escape the gangs. I finally heard him on the handheld radio and managed to stop nearby and pick him up.

"By the way Scott, the Navy commander would like to speak with you. Actually, he wants to debrief you on what you know about Catalyst once we get this beast back home."

"He knows about Catalyst?" Scott asked.

"He knows some of it, but he needs to know more… we all do," Todd replied.

The following Tuesday afternoon, the *Aquatic Goddess* slowly pushed down the Intercoastal Waterway behind the town, guided in by two smaller Navy tugs. The giant white ship would stand out like a beacon for everyone around to see. While that could be a bad thing at the moment, no one cared right now. It was a refuge. It meant hope. It was a sign of what could be and for many, it would also now be home.

344 | JK FRANKS

SIXTY-FIVE

Out on a rough macadam highway, a lone figure walked awkwardly toward the burned-out structure. Buzzards circled in the afternoon sun, keeping watch on a makeshift dumping ground for decaying bodies. Scott Montgomery stumbled on the steps of the old cottage, which still smoldered slightly. It had been his hiding place, his safe harbor, but now it was gone. Kaylie, Bartos, and DeVonte had removed everything salvageable, which sadly wasn't much. The generator he had hidden under the rear deck had survived, but very little else had. Scott knew it was time to move on. Kaylie had already settled them into one of the beach houses out on the little cove. Scott just had to get his Jeep; he had refused to tell anyone where it was. Kaylie knew but she wasn't telling either.

Over the weeks before the attack, Scott had made the decision to take as many of his supplies as possible to his primary bug-out location. He had become increasingly convinced that trouble was coming, he had just not expected it to come so fast. That day he had taken the Jeep and a full trailer down to his hideout, and with luck, it would all still be there. If Scott had been able to ride his bike he could have been there in thirty minutes. If he had been willing to ask one of his friends for a lift, it would have taken ten. On foot, however, it took several hours. Keeping secrets was something Scott had always been good at.

The roads leading into the bug-out spot were barely visible now, which was good. The Jersey barriers blocked the road completely a few hundred yards in. Scott had found an old maintenance trail through the woods that went around the barrier. He knew this spot very well now, as he had made countless trips to bring supplies out since the CME. He still felt bad for Pete. His forced retirement had not gone well. Scott had found his body in an old RV, parked at a campsite on the reservoirs park land. Scott had taken only the keys from the man's belt. Those keys unlocked every gate and door on the property.

Scott bypassed the road on top and instead walked down the two-track toward the river. Here, he removed the netting and limbs camouflaging the Jeep and its attached trailer. It took a few trips to load supplies from his bug-out inside the dam. He was only taking enough to get by at the new house. He would leave the bulk of the goods here. The old generator room in the dam was huge, isolated, and apparently unknown to everyone. Once he had decided on this location, he had scouted it from every angle and knew it was ideal. While damp and musty, it had been safe harbor several times for them recently. It would have been a great long-term place to ride out the storm of the last few months. If he had done that, though, would he have gotten to Kaylie on campus? Would he have met any of his new friends? Would the town still be standing? The old Scott, the damaged Scott, would have hidden out here until the supplies ran out, likely dying a quiet death like poor Pete the caretaker apparently had.

Now he had a purpose. And he had the will to fight. Scott knew he wanted to live and help as many others as he could to do the same. His refuge here would stand vacant, guarding his emergency supplies, but it would never be home for him. In fact, Scott had been wondering more lately about getting these enormous power generators back online. The old transmission lines still ran in the direction of town. He would have to talk to Bartos and then find an engineer able to help, to see if it was even possible. Electricity would be a wonderful thing to have. Locking up the room, and then the gate on the rust covered security fence, Scott climbed into the Jeep and drove back toward home—a new home.

EPILOGUE

He had felt uneasy revealing what he knew about Catalyst. Scott had been flown over to brief the Navy commander just before the fleet moved out. His internal conflict was obvious to the lifelong Navy man. After revealing most of what he knew, the commander considered Scott for a moment, then said: "You think they are doing the right thing, don't you?"

Scott took a moment, then slowly nodded once. "Yes, sir. I don't like it, but I see the wisdom in it. It's cruel; it's brutal…but we can't save everybody."

The commander smiled and nodded his head. "I agree with you."

"You do?" Scott was surprised. "But you're at war with them—a civil war, or is it a coup?"

"Yes," he said in a tired voice, "Senior staff commanders have known something like Catalyst would be a contingency plan. Marshaling resources, retreating to a more manageable position. It's all coldly logical. We in the Navy have also been aware that, for years, many of our best Seals, Army Delta Team members, and other elite soldiers were being increasingly reassigned into a single black ops project. They are now what you and Captain Todd call the grayshirts.

"You see, Scott, I don't disagree with their goals, I disagree with their tactics. If they were just going to allow cities to fail on their own, we might not have been ordered into battle. As a military man, I—*we* all took an oath to defend the Constitution. That mandate forces me to render aid to our country, no matter the foe. Right now our foe is our brothers in arms, and that sickens me. The fact is, they are actively aiding the country's downfall in many areas, exacerbating the misery. In many cases propping up guys just like the asshole your team took out."

Scott nodded, unable to disagree.

Scott was surprised but probably shouldn't have been; this was not a battle of good versus evil. This was a battle of survival versus humanity.

"Sir, what I haven't been able to grasp is how any of our politicians—our president especially—would have ever allowed a plan like Catalyst to take effect. It robs them of their power, something I just can't see many in DC giving up."

The commander mulled this over for several seconds. "That troubled many of us as well. It seemed...very out of character. Those of us on the senior staff, especially the ones who served in Washington, always felt the rumors of a shadow government were probably true, at least on some level. Too many clues over the years pointed to a select few people that seemed to have the real power. People or organizations just like your DHS, whose reach went well beyond their charter... You have to understand, son, that most politicians are imbeciles, too wrapped up in their own popularity to be able to lead or make decisions for the country. Yet the country keeps functioning just fine. Why is that?

"Consider for a moment that the public face of the government is mostly a farce. Yes, they pass laws and puff their chests, like the issues of the day are of extreme importance, but the real decisions—on things that *really* matter— are almost certainly made elsewhere. In quiet rooms, out of sight of any of the people you would ever have seen on a Sunday morning news show.

"This group obviously saw the inevitability of such a catastrophe and felt that if they didn't help direct the collapse, they and the country would lose everything. You can probably be assured, this group is still alive and functioning just fine."

"Do you have an idea of who these people are?" Scott asked.

The commander gave a faint smile. "Many names have been bandied about. Illuminati, Freemasons, Templars, Trilateral Commissions, New World Order... None of these are true, and most are likely misdirection, put in place by them. We do know they call their battle units, the ones you call grayshirts, The Praetorian Guard—Praetor5 for short. Modeled, apparently, from the Roman

Republic's elite bodyguards.

"Scott, what I am telling you is purely conjecture, though informed conjecture. This group is ancient. Hell, for all we know they've been around since Rome. Certainly before America. They may only be a handful of people. They are intelligent, extremely well-funded, and know what they are doing. They are suspected to have engineered the Civil War, profiting from both sides. Their reach must also be on a global scale—their plans were not just for the U.S. We may likely never learn the identity of any of the people involved."

The commander continued, "These people protect their own. Their power and influence are rumored to be beyond belief. This is probably why elements in the U.S. government have been known to carry out covert operations that seem to make no sense on the surface. Why for years have the CIA and the US government wanted to destabilize a country, throw it into civil unrest, and allow a corrupt dictator to take over? What possible reason could there be for that? The answer is more mundane than you would think, and for that reason more obscene than most would imagine. Several years ago when I began to accept this as fact, our government, which many times in my life and career has seemed insane to me, finally began to make terrible sense.

"One well-documented plan, many years ago, was Operation Northwood. It was a false flag plan to begin a campaign of terror on American soil. American citizens would be shot in front of witnesses; Cuban migrant boats would be sunk on their way to Florida; bombs would go off in every major American city; and an airplane full of American University students would be brought down in a fiery crash. It would have been blamed on Fidel Castro, and would have convinced the American public that it was a good idea to start a war with Cuba.

"President John F. Kennedy was brought in for his approval. Although not a fan of Cuba, he did not agree to it and even considered charging the high-ranking men, but in the end, not a single one was charged—at a minimum a gross miscarriage of justice. The odd thing is that Kennedy was assassinated soon after… supposedly by a man with ties to Cuba. But doesn't it make you wonder what other acts of terror the government has incited? Remember the missing weapons of mass destruction used to justify invading Iraq and toppling Saddam? If you get the media and enough idiots to repeat something enough times, people will believe it and rally behind it as a real issue."

The commander looked squarely at Scott. "Mr. Montgomery, I am not a conspiracy nut, I am a man who has worked within this system for most of my life. I can assure you, the people that run this country have *always* run this country. They are not the ones you might think, and they are definitely not the ones you vote for. Our electoral process was clouded and indirect. For a supposedly true democracy, our process was not all that democratic. The group behind Catalyst desires control. That is all they seek, and they will do anything necessary to retain it."

Scott nodded, having considered this possibility before. Despite his internal conflict at which side to support, he had come to some decisions. "Commander Garett, there is something else you should know… or perhaps you already do," Scott begun nervously. "The pandemic overseas…". He got no further.

The commander leaned forward and made a silencing motion. He went to the door, requested the guard on station to leave, and firmly closed the solid door. He came back to his desk, opened a drawer, and flipped something that looked like an electrical switch.

"Are you telling me that Catalyst is behind the pandemic?"

Scott swirled the tumbler of Scotch in his hand pensively. "Yes, sir. It was part of a larger plan to ensure that other world nations would not be in a significantly better position than the US. I only got fragments of intel from my original research, but we have a contact who has been working with the Catalyst paramilitary doing bioresearch."

The Commander looked stunned, then fell back deeper in his chair, even wearier. "You have someone working with them to concoct that damn doomsday bio-weapon?"

"No, sir, you misunderstand. He's my niece's boyfriend, he's actually just a grad student at FSU. He's not working on the pathogen. They…" Scott paused, "They have him trying to find a cure." Scott let that statement hang in the air, waiting for the obvious question.

The commander instead said, "Go on."

"His best guess has been that it *was* a bio-weapon, an engineered virus that got away from them. It mutated. Whatever cure they previously developed isn't working any longer."

Commander Garett stared in quiet horror out the port window at the darkening sky, the words of the Atom bombs inventor, the late Dr. Robert Oppenheimer's coming to him "What have these fools done? They have become death, destroyer of worlds."

Scott stood up and approached at the rail, looking out over the flat land now surrounding the large ship. Now he truly knew this was only the beginning. Darkness was approaching and with it, much greater trouble.

Made in the USA
Monee, IL
28 September 2023

43599867R00195